A LIADEN UNIVERSE® CONSTELLATION

✧ Volume 1 ✧

BAEN BOOKS
by Sharon Lee & Steve Miller
✦✦

The Liaden Universe ®
Fledgling
Saltation
Mouse & Dragon
Ghost Ship
Dragon Ship
Necessity's Child
Trade Secret (forthcoming)

The Dragon Variation (omnibus)
The Agent Gambit (omnibus)
Korval's Game (omnibus)
The Crystal Variation (omnibus)
A Liaden Universe ® *Constellation: Volume1*
A Liaden Universe ® *Constellation: Volume 2*
(forthcoming)

The Fey Duology
Duainfey
Longeye

by Sharon Lee
Carousel Tides

A LIADEN UNIVERSE®

CONSTELLATION

✧ Volume 1 ✧

SHARON LEE & STEVE MILLER

BAEN

"To Cut an Edge" originally appeared in *Two Tales of Korval*, SRM Publisher, Ltd., November 1995. "A Day at the Races" originally appeared in *Two Tales of Korval*, SRM Publisher, Ltd., November 1995. "Where the Goddess Sends" originally appeared in *Fellow Travelers*, SRM Publisher, Ltd., November 1998. "A Spell for the Lost" originally appeared in *Fellow Travelers*, SRM Publisher, Ltd., November 1998. "Moonphase" originally appeared in *Fellow Travelers,* SRM Publisher, Ltd., November 1998. "Pilot of Korval" originally appeared in *Duty Bound*, SRM Publisher, Ltd., November 1999. "Breath's Duty" originally appeared in *Duty Bound*, SRM Publisher, Ltd., November 1999. "The Wine of Memory" originally appeared in *Certain Symmetry*, SRM Publisher, Ltd., December 2000. "Certain Symmetry" originally appeared in *Certain Symmetry*, SRM Publisher, Ltd., December 2000. "Balance of Trade" originally appeared in *Absolute Magnitude #11*, Summer 1999. "A Choice of Weapons" originally appeared in *Absolute Magnitude #12*, Winter 1999. "Changeling" originally appeared in *Absolute Magnitude #14,* Summer 2000. "A Matter of Dreams" originally appeared in A Distant Soil #27, April 1999. "Phoenix" originally appeared in *Loose Cannon*, SRM Publisher, Ltd., November 2001. "Naratha's Shadow" originally appeared in *Such a Pretty Face*, edited by Lee Martindale, Meisha Merlin Publishing, 2000. "Heirloom" originally appeared in *Shadows and Shades*, SRM Publisher, Ltd., November 2002. "Sweet Waters" originally appeared in *3SF #1*, Spring 2002.

A Baen Books Original

Baen Publishing Enterprises
P.O. Box 1403
Riverdale, NY 10471
www.baen.com

ISBN: 978-1-4516-3923-0

Cover art by Stephen Hickman

First Baen printing, July 2013

Distributed by Simon & Schuster
1230 Avenue of the Americas
New York, NY 10020

Printed in the United States of America

10 9 8 7 6 5 4 3 2 1

✧Table of Contents✧

A LIADEN UNIVERSE®
CONSTELLATION

✧ Volume 1 ✧

⟡ Foreword ⟡

ONE OF THE QUESTIONS that readers often ask writers is, "Where do you get your ideas?"

There are a couple of ways to reply to this, depending on your writer. In general, answers range from Harlan Ellison's now-classic, "I get my ideas from a post office box in Schenectady," to the more factual, and most often disbelieved, "Ideas are easy," to the in-your-face, "Do you mean to say that you *don't* have ideas? For God's sake, tell me how to make them stop!"

Since we've been working in the same fictional universe for quite a number of books now, we're also pretty often asked, "What if you run out of stories?" Or, paraphrasing, "Aren't you afraid that you'll run out of ideas?"

The answer to that is, well. . .we're not going to run out of stories, or ideas for stories. We promise.

And for evidence, there's this book, the one you're holding in your hand, right now.

A brief introduction may be in order before we go any further.

We're Sharon Lee and Steve Miller and, as of the date of this letter to the future, we've written sixteen novels set in a space opera universe called collectively, the Liaden Universe®. By the time you read this introduction, we'll have turned in the seventeenth novel in that universe, and may have contracts to write a couple of more.

Space operas, for those to whom that may be a new term, are

stories of romance and adventure in an imaginary future. Because opera, and romance, and adventure are activities in which people indulge, space opera—at least, space opera as it's practiced in the Liaden Universe®—is about people. Character-driven fiction, that's what we write.

The fact that our fiction is primarily about people who find themselves in strange or exciting circumstances makes us even more certain that we won't run out of either ideas or stories.

Because people, in addition to being endlessly fascinating, are peerless in their ability to surprise.

That's why we write novels about people.

Now, novels . . . novels don't happen in a vacuum. Characters in novels come from someplace, they're going someplace. In simplest terms, they're coming from their past and they're going to their future. That means, among other things, and just like you and me, that they've existed before the story starts, and will continue to exist after the story stops. They'll have done things and known people.

Some of the things they've done are outside the scope of the novel under construction . . .

. . . and some of the people they've known, or know, have stories that are as much worth telling as . . . anyone else's story, really.

And that's what's in this book—the *other* stories, that happened before, or after, or to someone else.

You don't have to have read a Liaden Universe® novel to understand these stories. Several first appeared in venues, such as *Absolute Magnitude, 3SF,* and *A Distant Soil,* where the core audience had never, arguably, heard of our novels. Which reminds us to say that people figure into our writing in another, and very important way, and you've already guessed what we're talking about—readers.

For a number of years—from 1995 to 2011—we wrote and/or collected one long or two (rarely three) mid-length stories into booklets called chapbooks. These chapbooks were titled *Adventures in the Liaden Universe®,* and we produced seventeen of them, under the imprint of SRM Publisher, Ltd. They were a specialty item available from us, and from two or three specialty science fiction bookstores.

Baen Books recently asked if the short stories didn't deserve a wider distribution. We agreed that they did, and so here you are—a constellation of the shorter works from the Liaden Universe®, the first of two and likely more, since we haven't stopped writing short stories, and don't expect to run out of ideas any time soon.

The stories in this volume appeared in *Adventures in the Liaden Universe®* Volumes 1-8, and in the chapbook entitled *Calamity's Child*—seventeen stories in all.

We hope you enjoy them.

Thank you for reading.

—Sharon Lee and Steve Miller
Waterville Maine
April 2012

✧ To Cut an Edge ✧

AS AGREED, he was lost.

He was, in fact, a good deal more lost than he wanted to be. It took him several seconds to realize that the continent overhead was not the one he'd secretly studied for—followed quickly by the realization that it was not even the world he'd expected.

He'd crammed for oceanic Talanar, a planet quite close to the studies he'd been urged to make by his elders. This world was . . . ?

What world was it, after all?

Determining fall-rate overrode curiosity for this present. He located a magnetic pole and arranged to have the ship orient thus, then began a preliminary scan of—well, of wherever it was—as he slowed rotation smoothly and watched the screens.

Air, good. Water, probably drinkable. Gravity, a bit heavier than the training planet: within ten percent of Liaden gravity. Preliminary scan established that this could be any of three or four hundred worlds.

His ship was moving in, as it must. It had been dropped by an orbiting mothership, a carefully timed burst of retros killing its orbital speed. If he worked very hard and was very careful, he could keep the tiny craft in orbit, but that meant immediate expulsion, no appeal, unless he could demonstrate equipment failure . . .

Instead, he nursed the strictly limited fuel supply by using only attitude jets, and hurried the computer a little to give him potential range.

5

Three hours before he hit serious atmosphere. After that, depending on his piloting skills and local weather conditions, he might be in the air for an hour. The world below would turn one and a half times before he landed. He wondered what Daria would have thought—

And quashed the thought immediately. Daria was dead, killed in the drop from the mothership, victim of a freakish solar storm. It had been stupid of them to be so involved, of course. Stupid and beautiful.

Daria was months dead now, and Val Con yos'Phelium would be a Scout. Not partnered, as they'd promised so hastily, protected against all unnamed and unbelieved disasters by the strength of each other's arms. Not partnered. But a Scout, nonetheless.

After he passed the test.

He considered the readouts. There were cities down there, yet not so closely huddled that there weren't plenty of places to land a quick, slender craft. His instructions: achieve planetfall; learn the language, customs, life-forms; survive for six Standard months and sound Recall. This was not the final test, after all, but merely a preliminary. Pass this, then the true Solo and, behold! Scout. Simplicity itself.

He shook his head and began the second scan. Optimism, he chided himself half-seriously, is not a survival trait.

HE SET DOWN in the foothills above an amber valley where fields and possible houses lined a placid river.

Grounded, he initiated the final pre-scan, whistling indifferently. His instrument of choice was the omnichora. A portable—gift from his fostermother on the recent occasion of his seventeenth Name Day—was packed away with the rest of his gear.

It was remarkable the 'chora was there at all. Test tradition was that a cadet carried no tech-gear during prelims, except for that equipment found in a standard kit. However, those who had him under their eyes understood that to deprive Val Con yos'Phelium of the means of making his music for a period of six months, Standard, would be an act of wanton inhumanity. It had been debated hotly within the council of instructors, had he but known it. He knew only the end—that the 'chora was aboard the test ship and that his immediate superior took care to comment that music was communication, too.

Sighing, Val Con studied the results of the scan. Air, a bit light on oxygen, but not enough to present problems. Microbes, nothing to worry him there. Scout inoculations are thorough. Soil samples showed levels of copper, iron, a shade too much sulfur. No harmful radiations. In fact, it was going to be rather dim outside.

Hull temp read orange: too hot for exit.

He stretched in the pilot's chair and released the web of shock straps. Asking the rationboard for a cup of hot tea, he stood sipping, trying to damp the surge of excitement that threatened, now he was really here.

Wherever "here" was.

He grinned suddenly. What did it matter? It was a Scout's task to discover such things, after all! This was what he had been trained for. More fool he, cramming for a world lightyears distant, when he could have been . . . been sleeping.

Resisting the urge to tell the temperature display precisely what he thought of its arbitrary limitations, he bent down, opened the crew locker and brought out two bundles.

The first was his 'chora, wrapped in oiled yellow silk. His fingers caressed it through the fabric as he set it aside.

The second bundle was wrapped in black leather and clanked when he hefted it. He settled back on the floor and twisted the clasps, pulling out a broad belt, also of black leather, hung about with objects.

A Scout must wear a complete belt-kit at all times.

He looked at the heavy thing with deep resentment. Complete? If he came to require local currency, he need only open a hardware concession. Oh, some of them made sense: pellet gun, machete, rope. But a flaregun? Pitons? Surely, if there were mountains to climb, one would know in sufficient time to prepare oneself?

Ah well, regulations are regulations. And if any of the several things he judged useless were not on his belt, should a proctor turn up, he would flunk on the instant.

Sighing, he began the kit-check.

Pellet gun: OK.

Flaregun: OK.

Machete: What can go wrong with a machete? OK.

Stick-knife . . . He smiled and flipped it open to reveal the strong, dainty blade. The stick-knife was pleasing. He found knives in general pleasing, and had studied their construction during his so-called spare time, even attempting to craft a few. The most successful of these was a plain steel throwing blade, which, of course, was not with him at the moment. The stick-knife was not for throwing, but for surprise and efficiency in close, desperate situations. He flicked his wrist, vanishing blade into hilt.

Stick-knife: OK.

A Scout's belt-kit is comprehensive. By the time Val Con finished his check the orange temperature light had gone out.

DAY SEVEN.

He rose and tidied the ship while drinking a mug of tea, checked the monitors, buckled on his kit and went out.

It was dim, like a day threatening downpours on his own bright world, and sultry. A breeze blowing from the south brought a medley of unfamiliar odors with it. He sniffed appreciatively and paused to pick an old reed from the side of the path.

Six days had seen many accomplishments. His eyes had adjusted to the lower light level, even as his body rhythms had reached an acceptable compromise with the overriding song of the world. Sensors had been set out and calibration programs begun. The log was up-to-date.

His failure lay in contacting the people.

Not that there weren't people. On the contrary, there were at least two hundred individuals living in the valley at the end of this path, though the count was necessarily approximate. He found it difficult to differentiate at distance between one large-shelled person and another. Given variation in shell size, person size, decoration and harness, individuality would eventually come through; but it would be a slow process. Worse, he had yet to find one single person who would speak with him—or even acknowledge his presence.

He'd tried all the approaches he'd been taught—and several he'd invented on the spur of the moment—angling for any response at all.

And had been roundly ignored.

Yesterday, he had boldly stepped in front of a group of three, bowed low, as he had seen those small-shelled or shell-less bow when addressing those more magnificent than themselves. The group split and detoured around him, unhurriedly, but with determination.

The path wound around an outcropping of rock and sloped toward the caves and valley floor. Val Con stopped to survey his prospects, idly twirling the reed.

Across the valley, people were about what he now perceived as their daily business. Four individuals were in the fields along the river, working among the growing things with long-handled tools vaguely reminiscent of hoes. Toward the center, a cluster of eight? ten? large persons was engaged in a certain choreographed activity, which could have been dancing, game-playing or military drill. Across the river, large greenish shapes moved among the hulking rounded stones—dwelling places, so he thought: The town itself.

Just downhill from him now, though somewhat distant from the caverns and convenient to a nice flat rock, was a very large individual with sapphire glinting randomly from the tilework of its shell. With it were four small people, shell-less, and bumbling in a way that shouted *children* to him. The largest was scarcely taller than he.

It is dangerous to approach the young of an isolate and perhaps xenophobic people—or, indeed, of any people. But Val Con's observations indicated that he could easily outrun the adult, should it attempt an attack, and children are often curious . . .

So thinking, he walked down into the valley and sat atop the flat rock.

The guardian glanced his way, but turned its back, making no move to herd the smaller ones away. Encouraged, he crossed his legs and settled in to watch.

They were definitely children. They played tag, fell on each other, crowed loudly and shouted shrill, unintelligible taunts. Entertaining, but not particularly productive. The guardian still ignored him, and he nurtured a small flame of optimism as he felt in the belt for the stick-knife.

Best to put waiting to work, he thought, quoting one of his uncle's favorite phrases. Slowly, attention mostly on the schoolroom party, he began to fashion the reed into a flute.

It was the first time he'd attempted such a thing, though he had read how it might be done, and he did not give it primary concentration. This may have accounted for the woefully off-key sound that emerged when he finally brought the flute to his lips and blew.

He winced, and blew again; moving his fingers over the holes to produce a ripple of ragged sound. His fourth attempt yielded something that could charitably have been called a tune, and he glanced up to see how the nursery was taking the diversion.

The guardian stood yet with its back to him, watching as three of the babies enjoyed a rough-and-tumble of wonderful ineptitude.

The fourth was looking at him.

Val Con brought the reed up and blew again, trying for the simple line of a rhyming game from his own childhood. The child took a step forward, away from its quarreling kin, toward the rock. Val Con repeated the rhyming song and began a hopeless rendition of the first ballad he had learned on the 'chora.

Fortunately, the baby was not critical. Val Con abandoned the attempt to wring structured music from his instrument and, instead, created ripples of notes, interlocking them as it occurred to him; playing with the sound.

The baby was right in front of him.

He let the music fade slowly; raised his head and looked into enormous golden eyes, pupils cat-slit black; let his lips curve into the slightest of smiles. And waited.

"D'neschopita," announced the child, extending a three-fingered hand.

"D'neschopita," repeated the Scout, copying inflection and pitch. He extended his own hand, many-fingered as it was.

A hand larger than either swooped out of nowhere, snatching the child from imminent contact, sparing for his abductor one withering glare from eyes the size of dinner plates. It dragged the protesting infant away, holding forth in a loud and extremely displeased voice.

Nurse, Val Con decided, shoulders drooping. *Don't touch that,* he translated freely, giving his imagination rein, *you don't know where it's been! It could be sick! Whatever it is. And look how SOFT it is! Probably slimy, too. Yuck.*

He raised the flute and blew a bleat of raucous wet sound.

The big one spun, moving rather more rapidly than observed in others of her race, dropping the baby's hand and raising her arms.

Val Con grinned at her. "D'neschopita," he said.

She hesitated, lowered her arms slowly, and spun again reclaiming her charge roughly and driving the other three before toward the safety of the center valley.

"TO CONCLUDE," intoned the Speaker for the Trader Clan, "White Marsh feels that the Knife Clan of Middle River owes in the form of information regarding routes of star-trade. This, because the Knife Clan neglected to locate the being known as Silver Mark Sweeney and deliver the knife he commissioned, thereby denying the Trader Clan its fee of information, for sending this business hither."

There was silence as the T'car digested the whole of the Trader Clan's message. Out of the silence, Eldest Speaker's dead-leaf voice: "Will you make answer, T'carais?"

The person so addressed stood away from the bench and inclined his head to the Elders in respect.

"It grieves me," he began, "that the Trader Clan of White Marsh would come before the T'car entire, citing wrongs, before they came to the Knife Clan and requested facts. However, it is done, and answer shall be made.

"It is fact that the Trader Clan brought Silver Mark Sweeney to the Knife Clan, from which he commissioned a blade appropriate to his size. We accepted the task, seeded the cavern and encouraged not one, but many knives of a size and shape that would be fitting to beings of Silver Mark Sweeney's order. In the fullness of time, the blades were ready and the Knife Clan caused a message to be sent as instructed by Silver Mark Sweeney, stating this.

"He did not come to claim his knife."

"It was the responsibility of the Knife Clan to search—" began the Trader Clan's Speaker, with lamentable haste.

The T'carais raised a hand, reminding that it was his time now to speak, and continued in the midst of the new silence.

"The Knife Clan searched. And, when it was found that our manner of search is not efficient among the stars, we employed a skilled tracker of the Clans of Men to perform this task for us." He paused to consider how best to proceed. The Elders, wise beyond saying, were old. They did not always recall that to those yet mobile, change was . . .

"You must remember," he said diplomatically, "how short-lived are the members of the Clans of Men. Where I engaged one to search, his heir reported failure to me, as his father had grown too feeble to travel. It was the belief of these trackers—and also myself—that while we encouraged and refined the blade, Silver Mark Sweeney achieved s'essellata and died.

"Thus, I commanded that the family of Silver Mark Sweeney be found, that the blade might be placed into the hands of his kin. Time passed, and when the first tracker's heir came to me again, he leaned heavily upon his own heir . . ."

The T'carais sighed gustily.

"It seems that Silver Mark Sweeney was both kinless and clanless, as is not uncommon among that family of the Clans of Men named 'Terran'." He paused; signed summation.

"And so the knife is undelivered and the Trader Clan is bereft of its fee. It is to be considered that the Knife Clan had also considerable investment in this venture. There is an entire room filled with blades refined, awaiting only handles and sheathes, all too small for our use."

He inclined his head to the Elders. "Thus does the Knife Clan answer."

There was a large quiet while the Elders conferred silently, after the manner of the very old. In time, Eldest Speaker's voice was heard.

"It is seen that the Trader Clan has come before the full T'car to state its concerns and to give notice of intention to make formal complaint, should there be no balance forthcoming from the Knife Clan.

"It is seen further that the Knife Clan erred in failing to teach the Trader Clan its attempt at solution.

"Thus, it is the decision and will of the T'car that the T'carais of the Knife Clan go to the T'carais of the Trader Clan and speak as egg-kin, seeking to resolve all equitably. If this is not done, then shall the T'car make disposal." She paused, and all awaited her further words.

"It puzzles the T'car that the Knife Clan so hastily encouraged an entire cavern of blades fit only for those of the Clans of Men. However, there has been no complaint made of this, and no judgment is made.

"The matter in this phase is ended. All may go."

HE WOKE SOBBING, the echo of his cry still shuddering the metal walls.

"Daria! Daria, untrue!"

But it was true.

Painfully, he pulled air into laboring lungs, stilled the sobs and straightened from his cramped coil of grief.

Local midnight, by the chronometer on the board. He slid out of bed, dressed deliberately, buckled on the kit, and moved to the door. At the threshold, he bethought himself, turned back to the rationboard and withdrew several bars of concentrated food, which he stuffed into his pouch. His eye fell on the flute he'd made that afternoon and he picked that up, too, thrusting it into his belt as he went out into the night.

There were people abroad in the valley: farming, drilling, and in general about their business under the wan light of the two pinkish moons as if it were full daylight.

Val Con paused to stare out over all this activity and finally proceeded, shrugging.

The path deserted him at the base of the hill and he paused once more, this time because he heard the sound of large persons approaching, talking among themselves.

He hid in the shadow of a sundered boulder and let them go by: a group of three, well-shelled and carrying large objects—containers of some sort, he thought.

They entered the caverns purposefully, the boom of their voices echoing back.

After a moment, Val Con followed.

THE BROODMOTHER STOOD away from the bench in the waiting chamber and inclined her head as he approached.

"T'carais. A word with you?"

Not now, he thought, still rankling from Eldest Speaker's criticism. Hasty, am I? When all with eyes must see that the Clans of Men will give us profit, perspective—

He became aware of the Broodmother still standing, her head bent in respect and put irritation aside.

"Of course. Come within."

He sat upon the bench of office and indicated that she should sit, as well.

But this, in her agitation, she did not do, instead merely stood and gazed mutely up at him.

"What concerns you?" he asked in some puzzlement. Whatever failings she possessed, nervousness was not counted among them. "Are the egglings unwell?"

"They are well, T'carais. At least—" She paused, marshalling words. "It is that—thing, T'carais. The little, black—soft—thing . . ."

He signed understanding. Reports of this one had reached him from other sources, all annoyed.

"It—the T'carais'amp . . ."

This could not continue. "Please tell the tale clearly, Broodmother. Do you say that the T'carais'amp is endangered?"

"I do!" she cried, knotting her fingers together. "It—the soft thing—came out of the hills today and sat upon the stone at the base of the L'apeleka field, a short distance from the egglings and I, and seemed busy with something or another in its—its hands." She paused to collect herself.

"Then, it began to make noises—horrible noises, T'carais,

high-pitched and whining—just as the three youngest began a fight among themselves, which I of course had to attend to . . ."

"Of course," he agreed, since this seemed required.

"When I looked around, the T'carais'amp was—was at the rock, holding out his little hand. And that—thing held out its hand and was going to—going to touch him!" Again she took a time to return to composure.

"I snatched him away, T'carais, and was hurrying back to the others when—it hissed at me, T'carais!"

This was new. "Hissed at you? By all descriptions, this is but a member of the Clans of Men. I do not recall having heard one of this family hiss . . ."

"Well, perhaps it was not itself that hissed. It was—holding a reed, T'carais, and I believe that it somehow caused the reed to hiss at me. When I turned to protect the T'carais'amp, it bared its teeth and said 'D'neschopita'!'"

This was apparently the awful whole, for she unknotted her fingers and stood with head bowed, awaiting his judgment.

It bared its teeth and cried "Pretty"? Odd and odder.

The T'carais had travelled much and judged most of the members of the Clans of Men harmless, if hasty. Their music had a certain charm, their actions a touch of madness bordering on art. Certainly there seemed to be no lasting harm in this one.

"I judge," he said, using the formal intonation, "this individual to be rude and inconsiderate, yet not dangerous. If it frequents the area on the edge of the L'apeleka field, then take the egglings elsewhere for their outings. I will investigate it myself, to ensure it is not of that family called Yxtrang, though its behavior has not been consistent with the nature of that line. If it is not, then we must merely tolerate it for a shell or two. It will soon be gone."

He gentled his voice, "It is not worth troubling yourself over, Broodmother, I promise you," and signed dismissal.

With this she had to be content. She had asked and the T'carais had judged. Better she had slain the soft thing this daylight and endured words of reprisal than this—this empty assurance that something so repulsive was no danger to the children.

Unconvinced, she made obeisance and left the hearing chamber.

HE DID NOT understand how he came to be lost. The cavern was dark; but his ears were as sharp as his sense of direction. Those he followed made no pretense of stealth. There should have been no difficulty.

And yet there had. His guides were a little distance ahead, rounding a corner. Moments later, he rounded the same corner—or, as he thought now, *not* the same corner—and found himself alone in a dark his eyes were unequipped to penetrate.

He stopped, eyes half-closed in the blackness, listening.

Silence, in which his breath rasped.

His nose reported the dry, musky scent characteristic of shelled people, but not with an immediacy that encouraged him to believe any stood near.

Well and good. He pulled the lantern from his belt and thumbed the beam to low, careful of any dark-seeing eyes that might, in spite of his certainty, be watching.

He stood in a pocket of stone, high-roofed and smooth. It was well that he had stopped where he had: another half-dozen of his short strides would have run him nose-first into the endwall.

The wrong corner, indeed. He pivoted on a heel, playing the beam over the floor, but the dustless stone showed no tracks.

Well, there at least was the bend in the corridor. Best turnabout and walk out . . .

HE WALKED FOR twenty minutes by his inner clock, fully twice the time he had walked in behind his guides. Stopping, he played his light around the room in which he stood. It was so vast a place that the mid-beam did not even nibble at the dark along what he imagined must be the walls. The floor was littered with boulders and smitten columns of stone.

He spun slowly in place, running the beam about the room. *This is absurd*, he thought. *I don't get lost.*

Still, he had to admit that he did seem to be lost. It was clear that he would succeed only in becoming more lost if he continued on his guideless way.

It is possible, he told himself kindly, *that you have done something just a bit foolish*.

He sighed and pushed the hair off his forehead.

People did come into the caverns, though it was true that he did not know the schedule of these visitations. Food and water he had—even fresh water, he amended, ears catching a silvering cascade in the dark to his right—and the torch would provide light for months. The wait would no doubt be tedious, but hardly life-threatening, and if he got bored he could use his fishline and markers to map the caverns.

Shrugging philosophically, Val Con sat down and waited to be found.

THE DUTIES OF a T'carais are myriad; the duties of the senior-most Edger many. Happily, several overlapped, so that a visit to the caverns was both present joy and remembered bliss.

He crossed the threshold into First Upper Way, noting that three of his kin—Handler, Selector and Lader—had passed this way but recently.

Around their scents, and as recent, was the odor of something vaguely spicy and somewhat—furry? The T'carais puzzled as he went on. It was like and yet unlike a scent he knew, though not one usually found within the caverns.

An oddity. No doubt all would come clear in time.

Scent told him that his kinsmen had turned down the Second-Full Corridor. They were beginning the harvest of the Lower Ninth Room, then. Good. The T'carais had great plans for that particular crop.

He turned into Third New Way and shortly into Fifth Cavern but One.

The newest crop was good, he noted, well pleased. Only fourteen had been encouraged beyond the strength of the crystal to endure. If only half of those remaining harkened to his own tutelage, it would be a superior harvest, indeed. Seeder had done well. Nurturer had excelled herself. He would commend them.

It was then that he heard the sound.

And what a sound! Thready and fulsome by turns: abrading. Fascinating.

Music, the T'carais understood after a moment. Though of what sort he could not have said, since it bore little resemblance to any he had heard in all his long life.

But whatever kind of music it was, it was absolutely forbidden within the caverns.

With one more glance at the precious, fragile blades, the T'carais went in search of the sound.

ITS SOURCE WAS in the Seventh Old Storeroom, sitting in a glowing pool of energy, many-fingered hands holding something to its mouth.

The T'carais stopped in horror, mentally assessing the damage of so much energy on the infant blades, two levels above. Then he realized that part of what he beheld was merely harmless radiant energy. The force generated by the musician, while more substantial than one would expect from so small a being, was well below the danger level.

He approached the intruder.

Who glanced up, dropped its hands and rolled to its feet with amazing suppleness, whereupon it performed the bow of youngling to elder and straightened, awaiting his pleasure.

An eggling, thought the T'carais, astounded.

Of all who had complained, none had said that the intruder was but an eggling. He remembered, then, the disconcertment this particular eggling had caused members of the Knife Clan, not to mention unleashing harmful energies in the vicinity of growing blades, and stiffened his soul. Withholding any indication of regard for his petitioner, he studied it at his leisure.

It was somewhat smaller than those of the Clans of Men he had previously known, and ridiculously thin. Also, it had no fur on its lower face, though a profusion upon its head, dark brown in color. It was dressed in garments of black leather over another long-sleeved garment of some softer stuff: garb worn by many men, especially those who travelled between stars. Around this one's middle was a wide belt, hung with a confusion of objects.

The T'carais returned his attention to the face, seeing that it was small; looking as if one of his kin had taken a nugget of soft golden ore and used a knife to plane off five quick, angular lines, finishing the work by setting two crystals of the most vivid green possible well back among them, shadowed by long lashes and guarded by straight, dark brows.

The T'carais deigned to speak. "Egglings are not permitted here," he said sternly, and in Terran, so there should be no mistaking his meaning.

One of those straight brows twitched out of line with its brother, as the master of them both looked down at itself, and then back up.

"I am sure that to one of your own magnificence," it said softly, and with a lilt to the words that fell oddly on the ear, "it must appear that I have not yet achieved adulthood. However, I must insist that I am not an—eggling—but a man grown."

An absurd eggling. But not one of those called Terran, by testimony of the way he spoke that family's tongue. The T'carais took thought.

"What is your Clan?" he inquired, this time in the tongue called Trade, which was easier to form.

"Korval," returned the other, obediently following into that language. "And your own?"

And an impudent one. Then the T'carais recollected that, in his consternation, he had presumed to take a member of another Clan to task for misconduct—eggling or adult. And to do this without proper introduction was a far greater impudence than he had now been offered.

"I am called," he said austerely, "in the short form used by the Clans of Men on those things called visas, Eleventh Shell Fifth Hatched Knife Clan of Middle River's Spring Spawn of Farmer Greentrees of the Spearmakers Den: The Edger. Among those of men I have met," he added, "I am known as Edger."

The small one bowed, acknowledging, the T'carais supposed, the greatness of the name.

"I am called, in the longest form thus far available: Val Con yos'Phelium Scout." He glanced up, both brows out of true. "Among those of men I deal with, I am known as Val Con."

The T'carais was charmed. Merely an eggling, after all—he recollected again the damage the creature had done the peace and harmony of the Clan and strengthened his soul once more.

"This," he said sternly, deliberately neglecting the name he had been given, "is the place of the Knife Clan of Middle River. Egglings and adults of other Clans are not permitted here, save by special invitation, and with a member of the Clan. You are trespassing. Further, you have endangered the blades by the energies unleashed in playing your eggling music. You are fortunate, indeed, that you chose to do this in a section of the caverns that is at rest, for you might have ruined an entire crop had you chosen to play in a room that was seeded.

"I am angry that you are here, but because I see you are ignorant, I will raise no complaint to the T'car. Now begone." He folded his arms over his armored chest and glared at the little creature.

Who sighed, and glanced down at the reed in his hand. He seemed markedly uncowed by Edger's avowed anger, and did not smell of fear. When he raised his face he was smiling, as men call it, though very slightly.

"I am sorry," he said slowly, "about the music. It is a new instrument for me and I am afraid I did miscraft it. I did not know the playing was of such poor quality that it would ruin a crop of blades." He paused, vivid eyes intent. The T'carais kept his countenance unyielding, and said nothing.

"Where I am from," continued Val Con yos'Phelium Scout, "knives are made of iron and steel and light. I have made a few of the first two myself, though I am a novice. It would interest me greatly to learn how your knives are formed."

"You might have had the privilege," the T'carais said with deliberate cruelty, "but you chose to cast it away from you and enter without permission."

"And how was I to ask permission," wondered the impudent one, "when there is no person I have found in the valley who will speak to me?"

"Foolish eggling! Do you expect persons of consequence to speak to one to whom they have not been introduced?"

The small one took time to consider this, eyes on a rock at his feet. He looked up.

"You are."

Had he been capable of it, the T'carais would have gaped. As it was, he merely moved his head from side to side, slowly, before speaking with great care. "This is a different matter. Your noise endangered the blades. I am T'carais. Of course I must speak, that I might command you to cease."

"Ah," said the other. "I understand."

Edger thought that perhaps he did and was not comforted. Sternly, he said, "I have ordered you to begone."

"Yes," Val Con agreed readily, "and I would like to comply. But I am lost. It's stupid of me, but my sense of direction seems to have gotten misplaced, and I can't find my way out." He slanted bright eyes upward. "I did try."

Absurd that a being so frail should have so much life in it.

"Very well," said the T'carais stiffly. "I shall escort you to the cavern door."

"Thank you," said the other with a bow. "I am grateful for your kindness." He bent to retrieve the lantern and straightened, face thoughtful.

"I have just considered . . . Will it be dangerous for the blades to encounter light? If so, I must ask if I might hold to your harness as we go. My eyes are too poor to see here . . ."

Edger was touched, both by the eggling's care and the grace with which he accepted his limitation.

"You may keep your light at that level," he said gruffly. "The blades will not suffer from it." He turned, heading back the way he had come. "Follow."

In keeping with his judgment, the T'carais led his charge by a route that avoided the growing rooms and, in due time, they reached the cavern mouth.

Outside, he turned, meaning to leave wordless, as was proper.

"Edger," called the small one, who appeared to have no shame.

Reluctant, the T'carais turned back. "I hear."

He had clipped the lantern onto his belt and stood now, hands out, palms turned up. "You have been very kind and it's true that I am grateful. In spite of this, I feel I must ask for yet another kindness." He took a breath and plunged hastily on. "Would you please introduce me to some of your Clan members? I have come to learn about you—your language and your ways—and it would be much easier if someone would speak with me . . ."

Was he a scholar, then? The T'carais was uncertain of the word "scout."

"What you ask may be possible," he conceded. "I will consider it. However, a decision will not be made this moon's phase, for I leave tomorrow moontime for a visit to another Clan." He paused.

"Perhaps it would be wisest for you to go someplace else. Or, if you must stay here, to avoid the egglings. You frighten them."

Once again that ironic glance down at his soft self, the straight look into Edger's face.

"I think that, beside yourself, the egglings are the only people I have seen here who are *not* frightened of me."

This eggling was out of reason perceptive. Edger turned away, speaking the wellwish.

"K'mentopak, eggling. Be you well."

"K'mentopak, T'carais," came the soft reply. "My thanks to you."

VAL CON STRETCHED taut in the pilot's chair and relaxed, abruptly boneless. The log was once more up-to-date.

He considered the T'carais, grinning as it occurred to him to wonder if that person thought him Terran. There were those of that long, burly race who would not be best pleased by that. Though, to be fair, the general configuration was the same. And perhaps, from a height of nearly nine feet, a seven-foot person and a five-foot one are both merely small.

Knives. Growing knives? They had passed nothing that looked to his untutored eyes to be blades a-growing on their way out of the cavern last night. Of course, Edger had said he might not, as punishment. Possibly, the T'carais had chosen a route that bypassed such wonders.

But growing? And sensitive to—energies—created by music, but not the everyday radiant variety?

What sort of energy, he wondered, nourishes a sense of direction?

A senseless question, certainly: A sense of direction was nothing but itself.

Or was it?

He snapped to his feet; moved to the center of the ship.

Planetary north, he told himself; turned on his heel, pointing.

East. A smaller turn.

South . . .

West . . .

Home. Standing tall, arm raised, finger indicating that area in the Fourth Quadrant where turned the planet Liad.

Sense of direction back on duty, sir.

And where had it been last night? He lowered his arm slowly. Music, but not light. A man lost, who never misses the way. Blades growing out of ancient rock . . .

A sense of direction is a low-level psychic phenomenon.

Music?

Not psychic—a skill anyone might learn, subject to the physics of the universe . . .

Two strides to the storage locker and the 'chora within, still shrouded in yellow silk. He set it on the table and pulled the cloth away, exposing its smooth newness.

This was an expensive portable, far superior to the one he had owned formerly. He had lately had neither heart nor joy to play, but now he flipped the power on; hands flickering over the stops, setting values and intensities.

Lightly, fingers joking, he played the line of the rhyming game that had so charmed the eggling; drifted into the ballad that had defeated him upon the reed.

Gods, what a beautiful instrument.

What sort of energy is music?

He let his fingers slow; flipped off the power. Eyes still on the 'chora, he lifted the kit and belted it around his waist. Hefting the keyboard by its strap, he arranged it across his back—like a shell, he thought, half-smiling.

He left the ship, whistling.

SOUNDLESS, HE SLIPPED out of the vegetation at the path's end—blinked and nearly laughed. To his right, three egglings, running hard from a much larger individual. And walking toward him with infant nonchalance, his acquaintance of the previous afternoon.

"Good morning, youngling," he greeted it in soft Trade. "Will your nurse be angry with me again?"

"D'neschopita," the eggling told him, with emphasis. "T'carais'amp b'lenarkanarak'ab."

He lifted an eyebrow and walked forward. "Say you so?" he murmured, keeping his voice smooth. "Well, she is your kin and I must bow to your judgment in the matter."

At this, the eggling burst into a storm of volubility, emphasized by meaningful blinks of the huge eyes. Val Con shook his head. Too much, too fast, lacking structure . . . Perhaps. He pulled on the 'chora strap, brought the keyboard across his chest; flipped on the power.

The eggling paused for breath, eyes glowing. Val Con moved his fingers over keys, manipulated stops—playing back the rhythm and sound of the child's speaking, wondering what would happen . . .

A much larger sound interrupted the experiment. He looked up to see the nurse approaching, arms upraised for a strike.

The 'chora! Instinctively, he bent forward, shielding the instrument with his body; tensing his shoulders to take the blow . . .

Which did not fall. Instead, she stood over him and loosed an ear-ringing tirade, no doubt listing his faults and probable bad habits, annotated. Cautiously, he turned his head and looked at her out of the corner of an eye.

The abuse cut off in mid-annotation. Thin chest-armor heaving, she grabbed the eggling by the arm and dragged him away.

Val Con straightened slowly, watching them go. Nurse was in no mood for nonsense, it seemed. She jerked hard on the youngster's arm when he tried to hang back, roaring something the man felt must be unsuitable for delicate young ears. The youngling bleated and was borne away.

Bully, Val Con apostrophized her, *just wait until he's grown.*

Then reaction hit and he collapsed cross-legged to the ground, hugging the 'chora and shaking.

"T'CARAIS, I MUST insist—" the Broodmother's words proceeded her, reaching Edger as he walked with his brother Handler. He turned ponderously to face her.

"What is it you must insist, Broodmother?"

"That hideous thing must be slain—or banished—or—or—It is dangerous, T'carais—rabid! I cannot, in my duty as Broodmother—"

Edger lifted a hand and she subsided, though not willingly.

"There is new behavior? Something other than we spoke of past moontime?"

"T'carais, I used your counsel and moved the egglings to the other side of the L'apeleka field for this suntime. All was well, I thought, until I looked about—it was back! And alone with the T'carais'amp! Speaking with him!" She stopped a moment, clearly agitated. "I ran to them, T'carais, and I confess that my hand was raised to strike it . . ."

Strike him? The T'carais recalled the man's absurd frailness. One blow from an outraged Broodmother would shatter him beyond hope of repair. He tasted air.

"Yet you did not."

"I did not," she agreed. "For it looked up at my approach, bowed down and stayed thus, very meekly, while I berated it." She gathered her courage together. "It is evil, T'carais. A danger to the egglings and to the Clan. It must be destroyed."

"No," said the T'carais firmly and his brother, Handler, looked at him consideringly. "This is a sentient being, Broodmother. Ignorant, yes. Young, also. But not malicious. The Knife Clan does not kill wantonly. I go now to speak with him, explaining your preference that he stay apart from the egglings. Though," he added, fixing her with an eye, "it is true that one hungers for children, when one is far from Clan and kin." He gestured brusquely. She bowed and went.

Edger turned to his brother. "Will you come? If you are to judge in my place while I am absent, it is well you know all whom your words enclose."

Handler inclined his head. "I was about to beg the honor, Brother."

THE MUSIC LED them to his seat under the clemktos tree. Halfway across the valley it reached them, full of such force and structure—such power—that the T'carais gave silent thanks the man had not chosen to use this instrument with the caverns.

He had been toying, past moontime, thought Edger. Indeed, what else might one do with music coaxed from a dead stick?

But this—this was in sophisticated earnest. He had not lied when he claimed maturity for himself . . .

The man glanced up as they approached, fingers slowing, stopping on the keys. He set the instrument aside, rolled gracefully to his feet and bowed low.

"T'carais."

Edger inclined his head. "Val Con yos'Phelium Scout. I thank you for the gift of music you freely give our land." He paused. Surely, he was not mistaken? "Why did you not say your whole name to me, when last we spoke?"

The dark brows pulled together. "Forgive me. I meant no insult. It is possible that I do not know my—whole name." He tipped his head. "I would be pleased to learn it from you."

Handler blinked. Did the creature ask the T'carais to name it? Impudence.

But his brother took no offense. He merely raised a hand in the gesture that asked grace and told it, "I will think on this. I also consider that which you asked of me last speaking. These things wait upon my return."

"I understand," said the small one, folding his hands before him.

"I hear," then said the T'carais sternly, "that you have again come near the egglings, thus offending the Broodmother. It was my command that you refrain from these things. What say you?"

Handler blinked again. His brother would judge the thing as if it were a Clan member? It is a thinking being, he told himself, laboriously tracing the thought of a T'carais. It has attached itself to the Clan, whatever its alien reason for doing so. Should it thus be slain? Or heard?

The small one sighed. "I tried to obey you, T'carais. I came here because, in all former days, the egglings and their Broodmother kept to the other side of this field. It was accident that I came into the midst of them. And when the tallest eggling came to me and spoke, I thought it would be—rude—if I refused to answer as well as I might . . ."

The T'carais waited.

Val Con shrugged. "As for irritating the Broodmother—T'carais, I must admit that she has irritated me. Twice she denied this eggling and me the joy of acquaintanceship. If she had his best interest in her heart, she would not teach him fear of what is unknown, but encourage his curiosity and interest!"

An opinionated egg—man. And not a word to say that he had been threatened. Did he not know? Or count it too small a thing to mention?

"I hear your answer, and find it holds some merit. I see how this accidental meeting has occurred. The fault is mine and I will make amends. The Broodmother and the egglings will return to their place near the L'apeleka field. You will not go there."

The small one bowed. "I hear you, T'carais."

"See that you obey me," Edger said, with asperity. "Broodmothers are not lightly angered. This one feels you are a threat and a danger. Annoy her further and she may strike you, thus greatly curtailing the span of your years." He studied the unconcerned green eyes. "Do you understand me, Val Con yos'Phelium Scout?"

"Yes, Edger. I understand you." He tipped his head. "The T'carais has further orders?"

An exhalation like a small tornado. "A question: You named your Clan Korval. I am not familiar with this line of the Clans of Men. I think you are not Yxtrang—"

Val Con tipped his head back, uttering that sound men call laughter. Glancing up, he raised a hand to push dark fur from bright eyes.

"Not Yxtrang," he murmured. "Nor Terran, though—" He paused. Trade did not hold an adequate word, so he settled at last for: "she-who-raised-me is. I am Liaden."

"Ah," said Edger. "I have met Liadens in the past, though not so many as I have Terrans. It is well. Were you Yxtrang, you would not be allowed to remain."

Oh, no? thought Val Con. *A race that thinks it might order mighty Yxtrang and have it regarded more than mere senseless noise? Interesting.*

"Now," continued Edger, "I have said to you that I will be away for a time. This," he gestured; Handler stood forward, inclining his head, "is my brother, the T'caraisiana'ab. He speaks with my voice in all things while I am gone. Though you are not of the Knife Clan, you infringe on our territory, and must be remembered in judgment. Also, your skill in music interests me—I make a study of the music of Men, for the joy of my spirit. You may continue your studies, excepting only that you will refrain from studying the egglings and that you are banned from the caverns. If any offer you insult or harm, you must say to them: 'T'caraisiana'ab e'amokenatek'. This means that you are to be heard and judged by the T'caraisiana'ab. Are you able to say to the words I have told you?"

"T'caraisiana'ab e'amokenatek," murmured the man, the properly-spoken phrase sounding odd in so soft a voice. He turned to Handler and bowed. "T'caraisiana'ab, I am happy to meet you."

Handler blinked for a third time, considered as a T'carais might, and inclined his head.

"I am happy to meet you, Val Con yos'Phelium Scout. Please do nothing to endanger yourself while the eldest of my brothers is away."

Val Con grinned. "I'll do my best."

THE SCHEDULE SPECIFIED six ecological surveys of the area.

He took the last sighting from the hill over the valley, made the notation and stashed paper and stylus in his pouch. Stupid thing. They'd made sure he'd learned the tedious, mechanical ways to insure return to a starting point. This was the first time he'd been grateful for the training. There had been no further abandonments by his directional sense, but once burned, twice shy, as his fostermother would say. He would rather not be cut off from the ship in the middle of a wilderness simply because he couldn't at this present tell his head from his feet.

Stretching, he looked out over the valley—and looked again, more sharply.

A large figure was moving across the open area, using a tall something with which to walk. Val Con leaned against a boulder to watch.

The tall something abruptly became a lance; point gathering the wan light of the moons and dispersing it in glittering ribbons. The figure was Edger, no doubt beginning his journey.

Val Con shifted, took two steps down the path to the valley—and stopped. The T'carais had business to be about, even as he did. Let it be, he told himself sternly.

Yet he stood there, watching until the other reached the edge of the valley and the night hid that large person from feeble eyes.

"Safe journey, Edger," he murmured in Low Liaden, as one might to a friend. Then he turned sharply, snatched up the directionfinder and moved back down the trail toward the Scout ship. Time for rest, if he wanted an early start in the morning.

IT IS A SENTIENT being, one that obeys the words of the T'carais. If it is in need, it has the right to aid.

Thus had Handler reasoned before starting this small expedition. The man had not been seen for days, and though its absence took tension from the Clan, it also added tension.

Handler was nervous. It was difficult to think with the thoughts of a T'carais, enclosing both broodmothers and men. On his way to the hill path, he stopped to speak with the Broodmother.

"I give you good sun," he said politely.

"As I give you good sun, T'caraisiana'ab," she responded, taking the T'carais'amp by the arm and indicating that he should make his bow.

This was done and Handler murmured all things appropriate. Then, "Your pardon, Broodmother, for speaking of a subject that I know is distasteful to you. But—the small, soft being . . . Have you seen i—him recently?"

"No," she snapped, "nor have I any wish to. It is to be hoped the horrible thing has gone away."

"D'neschopita," said the T'carais'amp sorrowfully. "Kanarak'ab."

The Broodmother was not best pleased by these sentiments. Handler left her trying to interest the T'carais'amp in a game of c'smerlaparek with his younger kin.

HANDLER WALKED AROUND the little ship—constructed, after the manner of the Clans of Men, from soft metal, rather than molded of durable rock. After a complete circuit, he tested the air.

The lingering hint of the human's spice-furry scent was days old, direction teased by the winds. He came closer to the ship, but the stink of metal masked any other scent that might have been there.

Finally, he lifted a hand and brought it down—gently—on the hull, making it to ring. He waited a time and repeated this, before circling the ship again.

If Val Con yos'Phelium Scout were inside, he was ignoring Handler's summons.

Well, then, thought Handler, all beings require space apart. Perhaps this is the human's time of quietude and meditation . . .

He backed away, not quite convinced, but unsure of what else, with propriety, might be done.

It must be for my brother to decide whether we will open the ship of another Clan.

An unsatisfactory solution, but he could think of none better. After a time, he left the quiet clearing and the stinking lump of metal and returned to his house.

THE THIRD MOON was risen; the first waning, when a small, swift figure left the safety of the dwelling-places and crossed the L'apeleka field, unerringly striking the hill path.

This was the way his friend came. The path his uncle the T'caraisiana'ab had taken only last suntime.

With the echo of the wonderful sounds the soft one made in his head, the T'carais'amp ran down the path, coming in time to the clearing and the ship.

He barely paused, only sniffing the air to find his friend's scent. The ship he ignored—it was far too small, even if it were possible that someone would live in something that smelled so. His friend's home must be further on.

So he continued—south, with but an occasional wishful hint of his soft friend—and sunrise found him well away from the place of the Knife Clan.

IN SPITE OF the yellow flowers, Val Con made camp in the clearing on the bluff. It was a good place, protected and spacious, with a pool of icy water off to one side, away from the flowers.

He stared at these, hand twitching toward the machete in his belt.

They really are quite beautiful, he offered diffidently; *and it is true that Daria would have loved them. Will you spend your life destroying everything Daria might have loved? If so, best start with yourself and let the innocent universe be.*

He pushed the hair from his eyes with a sigh and turned away, automatically choosing a place to build his fire. Kneeling, he began to cut a shallow pit, carefully thinking of nothing at all.

Tomorrow, he reminded himself some time later, as he went in search of rocks to line the pit, *it's down the hill and into the flatlands.*

Depending on how long it took to find a way around or through the bog, he would be back at the ship tomorrow night or mid-morning the day after.

He spied a flat stone and bent to retrieve it—

"Arraaw!"

Val Con dropped into a crouch, stone forgotten. He stayed utterly still, listening to the echoes of the roar. Nothing he had yet encountered could have produced that noise. Besides Edger's people, the indigenous life was small, skittish and, for the most part, silent. Even the handful of birds were near voiceless—

"ARRAAW!"

Well, he'd been wrong before. And he had the direction of the racket pegged now. He edged toward the bluff, wormed flat among the yellow flowers and peered down.

Dragons?

Closing his eyes, he called up the memory of Clan Korval's sigil: the full-leafed tree, its faithful winged guardian—He opened his eyes and looked again.

Dragons.

Three of them. All noisy. He winced in protest of this excess of sound and peered closer.

Supper was the point of contention. At least, Val Con supposed that the still lump in the center of the group had been intended as someone's dinner.

The smallest of the three suddenly moved on the largest, swinging its paw, leading with its teeth. The largest turned a negligent armored shoulder to the attack, swung his own paw across the attacker's soft throat; used his teeth to thoughtful advantage.

The crunch was quite audible to the man on the bluff, and the littlest dragon slumped and lay still beside its late intended dinner. The largest gathered the disputed item into its jaws and waded off into the bogland, second largest following docilely.

Val Con dropped his chin onto his folded arms. No fire tonight. Perhaps, too, a camp in the rocks instead of the clearing.

Well, at least they don't breathe fire. I think. No wings. And they aren't very fast . . .

But they were right in the middle of his projected route home. Tomorrow was going to be an interesting day.

RAIN WOKE HIM before dawn. Shivering in the warm air, he rose and cleaned up the campsite. He pulled out a bar of concentrate to eat as he walked and left, heading for the flatlands.

Working with his mental map and sense of direction, he plotted a route that would take him in a long loop around the bogs. It would add half to a whole day to his journey, but that was acceptable, if it insured that he did not become a snack for an eighteen-foot dragon.

When he hit open ground, he stretched his short legs, hoping that the detour was safer than the original route. He was acutely aware of the lack of data concerning dragonish habits.

For all he knew, the things hunted right up to the valley of the Knife Clan. Or, into the valley. What did he know? Maybe there were virgin sacrifices. Maybe dragons sat on the Council of Clans. If there was a Council of Clans. Maybe dragons were pets of Edger's people. Maybe Edger's people were—

"AAARRRAAW!"

Oh, damn.

He pivoted slowly on a heel, looking for it. To the east, south, west—clear to the shadowy horizon. Immediately north, his view was cut off by a jumble of rose and gray rock.

"AAAARRRRAAAAWWW!"

Of course. So, then, another detour. He didn't really have to be back at the ship for another five months or so—

"P'elektekaba!" screamed a voice from beyond the rock.

Val Con ran.

He tore around the rockpile and skidded to a halt, spraying gravel. Directly before him, a squalling eggling, frozen mere feet from the safety of a rock-niche. Further—on treacherous sand—Edger, lance couched and ready, facing the dragon.

In dragons, eighteen feet is small.

Val Con dove forward, hitting the eggling with a surprisingly hard shoulder. The squalling cut out abruptly as the baby sprawled half into the niche. He skittered in the rest of the way to avoid his soft friend, who threw a knapsack at him, yelling, "Stay there!" Had he but known.

The rock-niche was comforting, calling up thoughts of home. He made himself as small as possible and stayed very still.

Val Con ran forward, yanking gun from belt; dropped to one knee and fired. The pellet whistled harmlessly off an armorplate side. The dragon did not even turn its head.

It swung at Edger with a long-taloned claw—withdrawn rapidly as the lance leapt to meet it.

Val Con returned the gun to its loop—worse than useless, not even a diversion, for Edger to move into the throat.

He ran, making a wide detour, fishing the machete from his kit. The tail was half as long as the dragon itself, wickedly armed with Val Con-high spikes.

He brought the machete down. Hard.

The dragon screamed. Encouraged, he swung his weapon again. And again.

On the eighth blow, the blade shattered and the dragon screamed—close. He looked up, saw the descending jaws, double-toothed and gaping—

Reflex hurled the useless handle into the descending maw, as he snapped backward into a somersault, away from certain death.

Teeth clicked as he rolled away and Edger cried out, "A'jliata!"— the rest of his words eaten by another dragonish shriek.

Val Con snapped tall, whirling back—

Edger was down.

Dodging the whipping tail, ducking a sweeping paw, Val Con reached the T'carais, set his hands against the place where shell met shoulder—and pushed.

He was not strong enough. Edger tipped, tried to get his feet under him, holding to his lance—and the dragon was turning back, paw raised in a gesture the man had seen from its bogland kin.

It meant death, that gesture. It would sweep Edger over, exposing the softer shell across his chest . . .Val Con stepped back, hands dropping from horny shoulders, staring upward as fingers groped in his belt—

Touched—and had it out without fumble.The safety clicked off as the paw swept down, talons first, toward the struggling Edger.

Val Con fired the flaregun into the towering face, his cry echoing the beast's as the blue-white flash blinded both.

IT IS NOT difficult to dispatch a blinded dragon. One walks up to where it stands clawing at its ruined eyes and cuts the soft throat. It is an act of mercy.

Sentient beings are not allowed this mercy, unless they ask for it, very specifically.

Edger hunkered down before the man called Val Con yos'Phelium

Scout, in the fullest form thus far available. The smallness of him as he rocked back and forth, arms folded across his face, touched the spirit with ice.

"Tell me what I may do to aid you," he begged, feeling ignorant as an eggling.

The small one gave a shuddering sigh. "You are well? It is dead?"

How valiant a being was this! "Yes, Brother," Edger assured him. "A'jliata is dead. I am uninjured, as is this foolish eggling, my heir." He paused, then asked again. "But you—tell me what I may do. You are damaged . . ."

Another sigh, less profound. "Only temporary. I think. The light was so bright . . ."

Truth. Edger had been turned away, shielded by his shell, yet the flash had stabbed his eyes.

Val Con dropped his protecting arms and raised his head. The bright eyes were squinted almost shut, and there was moisture running from them, but it appeared that they functioned.

"I'll be all right," he said slowly. "It may take a little time for me to be able to see—properly." He took a breath, moving his head from side to side. "I am sorry to trouble you, T'carais . . ."

Edger was conscious of a tightening of his spirit, in pride. "There is no trouble, Brother. Ask what you might."

"I was returning to my ship," Val Con explained, "when I happened upon you. If you could guide me . . ." He shook his head, turning his many-fingered hands up, palm out. "I am sorry to trouble you," he said again, "but it may take my eyes some days to—to heal . . ."

"There is no trouble," Edger assured him again. "Are you strong enough to travel immediately? Shall I carry you—I will be careful," he added, conscious of how easily one might crush a being as small as this new brother.

Val Con smiled wanly. "I can walk," he said, "though I may need to hold onto—something—and be guided . . ."

"It shall be done," declared the T'carais, rising to full height. Gingerly, he extended a hand to the small person on the ground.

In a moment, that person also put forth a hand, curling many fingers about Edger's few, and allowed himself to be helped to his feet.

THEY REACHED HIS new brother's vessel in the near dark of the third moon. Edger led, leaning upon his lance; the T'carais'amp and Val Con followed, hand-in-hand. The eggling wore the man's knapsack on his back like a soft leather shell.

Voices carried on the night air: two, raised in disharmony. Edger straightened and lengthened his stride, entering the clearing as a T'carais should.

The Broodmother cut off in mid-lament; bowed as deeply as she was able. His brother inclined his head, reading the weariness in him, but saying nothing, as was his gentle way.

Edger stopped, motioning those behind to come forward.

Hand-in-hand, they did so; stopped before T'caraisiana'ab and Broodmother, waiting.

The Broodmother looked up and resumed her outcry.

"You see what I have told you! It made off with the T'carais'amp, the evil thing!" She turned to Edger, every line of her pleading justice. "Will you not slay it, T'carais? You have seen with your eyes how evil—"

"SILENCE!" bellowed Edger and the Broodmother subsided, blinking rapidly. Handler looked from his brother to the small intruder to the T'carais'amp.

Edger gestured and Handler brought his head up, listening, that he might later recall precisely.

"Let it be known," the T'carais began, regally, and in the tongue known as Trade, "that this man Val Con yos'Phelium Scout has this day saved the lives of both the T'carais of the Knife Clan and the T'carais'amp, placing his life into peril to do so, when he might have run and been safe.

"Armed with a blade of mere metal he came against A'jliata, suffering pain and possible permanent damage in the service of T'carais and Clan.

"Let it further be known," Edger continued, "that this person shall come into the Clan as my brother, which he has earned. His name in present fullness shall be stated at the ceremony of adoption."

He fixed the bewildered Broodmother with his eye, dropping into the only speech she understood. "This person is honored by me, as he will be honored by the Clan, for bravery and service. Know that he alone slew the eldest A'jliata, thereby preserving the line of the T'carais of the Knife Clan. I will hear no further words against him. Do you understand what I have said?"

She lowered her head. "I understand you, T'carais."

"It is good. Now, take the T'carais'amp and attend him. Later you shall tell me how he came to be in danger!"

The Broodmother came forward, hand extended for her charge, who set up a squall and clung to his soft friend.

Val Con shifted away, prying clutching fingers from his arm. "Gently, child," he murmured in Trade, "you'll break me . . ."

The Broodmother added a few quick words of her own on the subject and the T'carais'amp was borne away. Edger looked at his brother Handler.

"Find you our brother, Selector, and choose a worthy blade from the Room of Men."

Handler inclined his head; turned to the man.

"I am proud to have gained so valiant a brother, Val Con yos'Phelium Scout," he said formally. Then he, too, went away.

Val Con turned to Edger, brow up. "I do not understand, T'carais. You slew A'jliata—not I. Why honor me?"

Edger blinked. "I hurried what you had contrived. A blind creature in the wild is already dead. I but showed it the mercy one accords a worthy foe. You gave it death with your light." He slumped, leaning on the lance; it was not necessary to feign tirelessness with this, his brother.

"Will you gather the objects of your name and subsistence, Brother? It is past time that we were home, and I understand men to require some time of sleeping every moontime."

Val Con stood for a long time, as men measure such things, squinting up at the T'carais. Then he smiled and turned toward the ship.

"I will not be long."

"So be it," said Edger, settling to wait. He considered the T'car and sighed gustily.

"Aaii, and they called me hasty anon!"

✧ A Day at the Races ✧

THE SKY WAS nearly Terran blue overhead, shading to a more proper Liaden green toward planetary east. Shadows were beginning their long evening stretch across the lawns, from the topiary maze to the house.

Up the drive came a slender young man in the leather vest and leggings of a spaceworker. Despite the peremptory summons from his sister, he had walked from Solcintra Spaceport, enjoying the taste of natural air.

He paused by the cumbersome landau parked messily across the drive. The crest of his aunt, the Right Noble Lady Kareen yos'Phelium, Patron of the Solcintra Poetry Society, Founder of the League to Preserve the Purity of the Tongue, and Chairperson Emeritus of the Embassy of Form, glittered in the fading light.

Scout Captain Val Con yos'Phelium sighed. Perhaps it was not too late to turn about, catch the evening shuttle to Chonselta City, and thus avoid any contact with his father's sister, a course he had pursued whenever possible throughout his childhood and halfling years.

He sighed again. No, he decided, better to attend to the business at once and have done.

Thus virtuously armed, he continued up the drive and let himself into the house.

Standing in a small sidehall, he listened, marking the sound of two voices. The first was unmistakably Aunt Kareen, the measured tones of the High Tongue ringing in bell-like purity. The answering voice was lower in pitch and inflection: his fostersister, Nova yos'Galan.

Val Con sighed for yet a third time and slipped silently down the hall to the large parlor. He bowed to his aunt and kissed his pale sister lightly on the cheek.

"Summoned, I obey," he murmured in her ear. Then, turning, "Will you drink, Aunt? I see you are unrefreshed."

"Thank you," said that lady austerely, "but no. I am unable to take a crumb of sustenance; nor even a thimbleful of wine."

Val Con blinked and darted a look at his sister, who avoided his eyes. No enlightenment from that quarter. He moved silently to a chair near his aunt. Perching on the carved arm, he shook his head.

"That sounds very bad, I must say. Have you consulted a physician?"

The Right Noble sniffed. "I am quite well—physically. Thank you, my Lord. Your concern warms my heart."

Score one for Aunt Kareen. Val Con hastily schooled his face to that expression of distant interest considered proper when speaking with other members of Society.

"Forgive me, Aunt; I meant no disrespect. The difficulty is that I have only recently returned to Liad. My sister's message met me at Scout Headquarters, and I obeyed her instructions immediately. You will understand that this left me no time to discover the nature of your trouble.

"I am ready to hear," he concluded, most properly, "and feel certain that all may quickly be resolved."

"That is very good, then," said Aunt Kareen, greatly mollified. "It grieves me that the cause of my distress is the First Speaker, your—kinsman—Shan yos'Galan. I am aware of the regard in which you hold him, my Lord; and on a minor matter I would not, of course, approach you. However, this case is such that I am certain it is no less than one's duty to bring it to the attention of yourself, who will lead Korval next as Delm." Her eyes sharpened. "If you will ever bestir yourself to take the Ring, of course."

Val Con resisted the temptation to look at Nova again. With effort, he maintained the proper expression, though one eyebrow did slip upward, just a little.

"Has Shan slighted you, Aunt? It does not seem like him. He is very conscientious in his duty as First-Speaker-in-Trust. It is true that his manner is not quite . . . polished . . . but his heart is good and—"

"He is an outrageous rantipole and a disgrace to the Clan!" snapped his aunt. She took a bosom-lifting breath and dabbed at her temples with an orange silk kerchief.

"Forgive me. It was not my intention to speak thus of a kinsman you hold so dear, though I am certain my feelings on Lord yos'Galan's past . . . adventures . . . have not escaped notice."

"I am," said Val Con dryly, "aware of your antipathy for my brother. You are obviously agitated. I make allowance." He removed his eyes to the Clan sign above the fireplace: Korval's Dragon hovering protectively over the Tree.

He looked back at the Right Noble, both brows up.

"You have not yet informed me what my brother has done to offend you—this—time, Aunt."

She drew herself up. "He is—racing!"

Her nephew achieved a new peak of self-discipline and contrived not to laugh.

"Is he? Racing what, I wonder?"

"Skimmers," said Nova unexpectedly, frowning slightly when he turned to face her. "A new thing off the Terran tracks . . ." She sighed. "They are dangerous, Val Con. Stick and throttle—no electronics, no safeties."

"Ah." He considered it; smiled at her. "But he's not likely to hurt himself, is he? He's quite an excellent pilot."

"Whether or not he does himself some trifling injury is not the essence," announced Lady Kareen. "Consider the scandal, my Lord! The First Speaker of Clan Korval—racing, like a common—" words failed her.

"Pilot? Individual? Rantipole?" He caught Nova's Terran-style headshake and allowed the spurt of anger to subside.

"Aunt Kareen," he began again, more smoothly. "I ask you to

consider what you say. Consider what has made Korval great—" He pointed to the device above the mantle. " *'Flaran Cha'ment'i*: I Dare'. My brother carries on an illustrious tradition—"

"Your *cousin*," she snapped, "does not care a broken cantra for tradition! You speak of his concern for duty. I say it is wonderful we are not already the laughingstock we are doomed to become, unless you, my Lord, very soon take your place at the head of this clan and—"

"Is it so bad a thing," Val Con overrode gently, "to laugh? Better to laugh—even be laughed at—and continue to strive, rather than run away . . ."

"Korval does not run away!'

"No?" He tipped his head. "And yet my father—your brother— abdicated his position, left the clan—ran away. Shan would far rather give over the duties of First Speaker. It would better suit him to return to the *Passage* and the trade route. But in fact he is First Speaker at this present, and thus remains upon Liad, taking what harmless amusement he may to ease his time here." Val Con rested his eyes, bright green and very angry, on his aunt's.

"Shan does not run away," he concluded quietly.

"I see," said the old lady, with brittle calm. "I infer that you will not speak with him. Therefore, since someone must speak to him, I shall dispatch your near-cousin, Pat Rin to—"

Val Con held up a slender hand. "I did not say that I would not speak with Shan, Aunt. Do not trouble my kinsman, your son."

For a long moment they stared, old eyes measuring young. Lady Kareen rose.

"Very well, my Lord. I thank you for your condescension. No— do not trouble yourselves. No one need show me out."

She bent her head briefly to the room at large and swept out. Nova went after, grimly intent upon courtesy.

Returning to the parlor several minutes later, she found Val Con slouched in a hearth chair, legs thrust out, winecup held loosely in his left hand. He appeared to be studying the toes of his boots.

Nova sat on the edge of the chair across from him.

"I apologize for calling you home so summarily, Brother, but the truth is I was at wit's end . . ."

He glanced up, eyes still very bright, and pushed the dark hair from his forehead.

"How long has she been at you?"

Nova sighed. "She's been here every day for the past three months, demanding that 'something be done' about Shan." She shook her head. "Then she began threatening to send Pat Rin to bring him away—and you know that would never do, Val Con . . ."

"Pat Rin would say something pompous and Shan would ignore him," Val Con murmured. "So of course Pat Rin would become more pointed in order to ensure that his thick-headed kinsman had the right of things—"

"And Shan would bloody his nose," finished Nova.

"Imagine me, I implore you," said Val Con, rediscovering his wine and sipping, "fining the First Speaker his quartershare for engaging in fisticuffs with another clan member."

Nova frowned. "But you would not—unless . . . Do you mean to be delm now, Brother?"

He shook his head. "I most certainly would be able—my privilege and duty, as delm-to-be. The reference is *Penlim's Protocol*. Very dusty reading. Best you check it though, Sister, since the trusteeship falls next to you." An eyebrow slid upward. "How long do you think Shan can hold out?"

She set her lips primly. "I will go before the Council of Clans as First-Speaker-in-Trust at the end of the month and Shan will be free to return to the *Passage*."

Val Con nodded. "None too soon, eh? And then skimmer racing may slide away into the past." He tipped his head. "There is more, perhaps? You are still distressed."

"It is a small thing . . ." She looked at him worriedly. "Yesterday she railed at me for nearly two hours—she even missed a session of the Poetry Society!" She sighed. "It is the Terran blood, you see, that makes Shan so wild and threatens to disgrace Korval forever."

"It is fantastic, is it not," said Val Con, "that my aunt holds such opinions? After all, she was offered the Trusteeship when my father abdicated—and refused it, even as she refused to care for his son, leaving all to yos'Galan. At this moment she could be First Speaker."

"Gods forefend," breathed Nova, bringing fingers to lips too late.

Val Con laughed. "So I think, as well." He lifted an eyebrow. "She does well for one unable to take sustenance."

"Ah, you haven't spoken to her cook."

"Nor have I any wish to do so." He was on his feet, moving with Scout silence across the short distance that separated them. Bending, he kissed her cheek.

"I'll speak with Shan, since I have said it. Will you tell me the location of the racing park?"

THE WIND SCREAMED and the skimmer bucked and slithered. Shan fed it more power, leaned right to correct the slide, kicked the throttle to the top and was over the finish line in a burst of breathless speed. He slewed in a half-arc for the joy of it and slashed the power, gliding to a halt by the timer-tower.

"Twelve minutes, forty-two seconds," the mechanical voice informed him.

"Damn," said Shan, heading sedately for the garage. Two minutes to shave at the very least, or he might as well leave *Araceli* home on Trilsday and watch the race from the stands.

Most skimmers carried a crew of two; he'd been foolish to think he could run singleton. He needed another pilot for second—and where was he to come up with one in so short a time? Worse, how to find time for proper training?

"Damn," said Shan again, yanking off the goggled helmet and dropping it to the floor. He locked the board and jumped out.

Perched on the fence directly opposite was a young gallant: fine white shirt and soft dark trousers; a pilot's leather jacket thrown negligently across the fence at his side. He held a glass of wine in his hand.

Shan stretched his long legs, grinning in welcome.

"Well, this is a surprise," he said in Terran. "How long have you been here?"

"I saw your run," Val Con replied in the same tongue. "Wine?"

"Thanks." Shan said and sighed. "I didn't know you were a racing enthusiast."

"I heard there was something new," Val Con said. "A pilot likes to keep abreast . . ."

"Always nice to learn," agreed Shan. "And an education can be had in the oddest places. Staying at the spaceport, are you, Val Con?"

The younger man lifted an eyebrow. "Do I pry into your affairs?"

"Well, now, that's what's odd. Normally you don't. But here I am, where I have taken care not to announce myself, out of respect for our more proper relations; and now here you are—"

"For which I should be thanked," Val Con interrupted. "Aunt Kareen is quite upset. She was on the brink of sending Pat Rin to fetch you home, and was persuaded to allow me to come instead. My aunt," he added earnestly, "thinks you an outrageous rantipole."

Shan snorted. "I'd rather be a rantipole than a pompous ass."

"Yes," soothed Val Con, "I know you would."

"Cultivating an edge, Brother?"

"It is also to be recalled," said Val Con dampingly, "that we are but cousins."

"Dear me!" Shan cried. "I apprehend that Kareen was in the throes of a Mood!"

He sipped, sketched a bow. "Forgive the sermon, *denubia*. Better you than Pat Rin, whatever news." He laughed. "Gods, only imagine the scene! And you would have had to fine me, too! Or I would have had to fine me—and very angry I'd have been at myself." He raised his glass. "Brother, I salute you: you've saved me a rare chewing out!"

"No less than my fraternal duty."

"But you didn't come all this way," pursued Shan, "just to report Kareen's opinion of me? If so, a wasted journey."

"My aunt's health is in decline from worry over the scandal," Val Con said. "Fear of the damage you do Korval's reputation will allow her to neither eat nor drink. One understands the cure for her pitiful condition is for you to come home and behave yourself. She's been at Nova for weeks—with variations upon the theme . . ."

"She's what? At my sister? In my house? By what right? She's not yos'Galan."

"For the good of the clan," Val Con said, lips twitching.

"Bah, what nonsense!" cried Shan, and fell silent, sipping. After a time he looked up, white brows drawn over light eyes. "And what does our sister say? Or you, for that matter? It seems I've heard too much of what Kareen thinks and nothing at all of what Nova and Val Con think."

"Nova has given me a double-cantra to lay upon the race Trilsday-this—Shan yos'Galan to take any of the four highest honors."

"Did she?" Shan grinned like a boy. "We'll make a human being out of her yet, Val Con. And you?"

"I?" He lifted a brow. "I'd like a ride in your skimmer, please, Brother."

WORDS SCROLLED across the screen set into the table. Nova read and sighed, breakfast forgotten before her.

"*Araceli*," the race report continued, "piloted and comanned by Shan yos'Galan and Val Con yos'Phelium, Clan Korval, earned distinction by turning in the slowest finishing time on the day. Neither team member is a professional racer and the time-loss taken when a nerf from first-placing *Tolanda* sent *Araceli* off the course was never regained. It is to the amateur team's credit that *Araceli* remained upright during the mishap and, due to a bit of quick readjustment by the secondman, was able to return to the course . . ."

"It's that stupid braking system," Val Con said over her head. "All very well to have no electronics onship, but why the brakes must be the most primitive of hand-turned vents is a mystery."

His voice was edged with wry irritation. Nova turned her head, but he was at the buffet, clattering covers and pouring tea.

"How's your arm?" she asked.

He glanced over his shoulder, smiling. "Better a bruise than tumbling out of control. And not bad enough to bother with the 'doc." He gathered up cup and plate and sat down across from her. "It's an odd thing, Nova—the craft is so light that my hand on the ground was sufficient pivot-point. If there were a more efficient way of braking . . . As it's arranged now, the pilot may either steer or brake. And he may not brake quickly."

She glanced up at him. "Where is Shan, by the way?"

"At the park, seeing to *Araceli's* packing. He plans to race at the Little Festival."

"He does?" Dismay sounded clearly in her voice.

Val Con lifted a brow. "No faith, *denubia*? It's not a bad little craft—and Shan is very good. If we could only resolve the braking— Ah, no! Before breakfast?"

Nova followed his gaze out the window and stifled a groan as she saw the too-familiar shape of Lady Kareen's landau come to rest across the drive.

"Does my aunt read the racing papers, do you think?" Val Con asked, eyes glinting mischief over the rim of his cup.

"Now, Brother, have pity! Don't make her any worse."

He rounded his eyes, face etched in surprise. "Why, Lady Nova! As if my aunt were ever other than perfectly delightful!"

"Val Con—"

"The Right Noble Lady Kareen yos'Phelium," announced the housebot from the doorway.

"Good morning, Aunt," said Val Con, the Low Tongue all good cheer. "Will you take breakfast with us?'

"Thank you," said the Right Noble, "but no." The bell tones of the High Tongue were gelid. "And you, my Lord, might best wish to speak with me in the study. What I have to say is scarcely fit for a breakfast-table conversation."

"I'm a-tremble," said her nephew. "But I fear you will have a small wait, Aunt, if you must have the study. I am exceedingly hungry and feel I should finish my meal before embarking upon an exhaustive interview." He picked up his tongs to readdress breakfast.

There was a pause, growing painfully longer. A glance from beneath sheltering lashes showed Nova that Lady Kareen's face was rigid with anger. Val Con was proceeding with his meal.

"Very well," said Lady Kareen presently. "If you will have it so." She moved to the nearest chair and stood, eyes on her nephew's bent head.

Horrified, Nova saw Val Con glance up, frown and raise his hand to the hovering robot.

"Jeeves, pray hold my aunt's chair for her."

"Certainly, Captain." The 'bot glided forward and slid the chair smoothly from its place.

"Your Ladyship."

There was a moment's hesitation before she sat. Jeeves retired to a corner.

Val Con smiled. "Now then—ah, but first: are you certain you won't take something, Aunt? Tea? Morning-wine?"

"Nothing, I thank you." She glared at him. "Must you speak in that manner?"

He blinked. "In what—oh, in the Low Tongue! I do beg pardon, ma'am. I was speaking with my sister just now and it quite slipped my mind that I must use the High Tongue at this present, in deference to company."

Nova bit her lip.

"Of yesterday's fiasco," the old lady said after a moment, "there is nothing to say. That you failed to bring your cousin away from the racing-track before he had made a fool of himself and his clan does not surprise. He is as tenacious as he is misguided. It grieves me that his hold over you, the heir and hope of Korval, is such that you were persuaded to lend your countenance to the spectacle. It is to be hoped that you will soon see the unsavory influence Shan yos'Galan exercises over you and will distance yourself from him." She paused to glare at both of them. "On that head, no more."

"Ah." Val Con rose and refilled his cup. When he sat again, both brows were well up.

"You have something to say on another head?"

The Right Noble pressed her lips together. "It is perhaps not a subject you would care to discuss in the presence of your cousin."

"You intrigue me." He glanced at Nova, green eyes dancing.

He turned back to his aunt. "Speak on; we listen eagerly."

"Very well," said the old lady again, eyeing Nova dubiously, and drew herself taut. "It has come to my ears that my nephew, Val Con yos'Phelium, has been seen in a common tavern near the docks in Chonselta City. Has, indeed, been seen walking late and early about town wearing spaceleathers . . ." Lady Kareen faltered under her nephew's steady gaze and had recourse to her kerchief.

Nova sipped tea.

"Spaceleathers," Val Con repeated gently. "And what should one wear, I wonder, when visiting common taverns?"

His aunt bristled. "Spaceleather is very well for working in space. No doubt it serves you admirably in your scouting duties. But when upon Liad, one must dress according to one's station. In the evening, one must always wear a cloak." She took a deep breath. "That the delm-to-be should be so ill-mannered—"

But Val Con wasn't listening.

"Cloak," he murmured. "Of course a cloak . . ." He came to his feet, made his bow and was all but running past Nova's chair, his fingers barely brushing her cheek.

"Aunt, I thank you—your instruction is superlative. Pray forgive my hastiness—Jeeves!" he cried as he passed from the room. "Bring your calculator! I must have a new cloak!"

The robot charged after in a thunder of wheels, orange head-ball flaring. "My calculator is ever at hand, Captain."

Nova sat staring at the empty doorway. "A cloak? Oh, no . . ."

"But why not?" asked Lady Kareen, obviously gratified that her words had at last produced an effect. "What harm can it do him to have a new cloak?" She leaned forward to pat Nova's hand. "Pray tell him to consider it my gift to him, Cousin; he must have the cloakmaker send the receipt to me." She smiled. . . . "After all, an interest in one's appearance is a beginning! I'll deal with the racing later."

SHAN SLAMMED THE skimmer's bonnet, frowning. He'd gotten several offers from mechanics to enhance his engines beyond match regulations. He'd told them all no—a fair race and a fair win, that was what he wanted.

And now here was Val Con, insisting that *Araceli* be brought home for private testing. And if Val Con was willing to tempt fate in such ways . . .

"Practice? Practice how?" he'd demanded when he got the younger man's call. "We need to be on the course to practice, youngling. Practicing on flat grass isn't going to do us any good."

"No, but it will. I think. Please, Brother, bring her home. If it puts you out of pocket, I'll pay the shipping."

So here was Shan, cooling his heels on the stream bank, and Val Con uncharacteristically late—

A flash of bright color caught the corner of his eye. He tracked it—and froze, staring.

"Good evening, Brother!" called Val Con cheerfully.

"What in moon's honor is that?"

"This," announced the younger man, pulling himself stiffly erect and moving his shoulders so the orange micro-silk shimmered, "is the next fashion."

"I'm terrified," Shan said, carefully circling him. "But you're probably right. It just might be ugly enough." He shook his head in repulsed wonder. "You look like a pumpkin."

"Oh, no, do you think so? The cloakmaker will be distressed; he was extremely proud of the work." Val Con grinned. "I have a genius for design."

"What you have a genius for is for driving me mad! Do you mean to say you actually designed this monstrosity? Why? You hate cloaks! You'll never wear it. Unless it's your idea of a joke on Society? Everyone will rush out to have a cloak like Korval's—and you'll have a grand time laughing up your sleeve. Delightful. Except you'll be off-world for most of the time this new fashion of yours is the rage. I'll have to look at the stupid things every time I go out for the next—"

Val Con was laughing.

Shan regarded him sourly. "OK; I bit, did I? Explain. Include," he added after a moment, "why it had to be orange."

"Ah, you see, orange doesn't suit everyone. But with my lovely dark hair and pure golden skin tone . . ."

"Stop." Shan took a breath. "Val Con, you're my brother and I love you. Don't make me kill you."

"Orange is my aunt's favorite color," murmured the other. "I thought, since she so kindly bears the expense . . ."

"I see," Shan said. "Paid good money to hide you, has she? So it's orange and you'll be hidden for everyone to see. Now: Why is it at all?"

"So that we will win the race at the Little Festival."

Shan blinked. "Yes? Could you be more specific, please?"

"Certainly." Val Con linked their arms and gently turned his brother back toward the trees. "If you will only walk with me to the skimmer and have the goodness to give me a ride . . ."

THEIR SISTERS comfortably established in the stands, Shan and Val Con walked leisurely toward the qualifying field. To the left, the jewel-colored pleasure pavilions rippled in the flower-scented breeze. To the right, Te'lesha Lake reflected the colors of the afternoon sky. Already there were people abroad with lovegarlands in their hands.

"Well," said Shan, "at least we've managed to get everyone out of Kareen's way today. Is she checkmated, do you think, Brother? Or will she pull rank on you?"

"She has none to pull."

Shan opened his mouth—closed it, as memory rose:

The boy, Shan, entering the house by a side door and almost falling over his small cousin, Val Con, unexpectedly sitting on the cool stone floor, clutching a martyred orange cat in his arms.

Shan sat on the floor next to the child; extended a hand and ruffled the dark hair.

"Hello, denubia. What're you doing here?"

A long pause during which Val Con studied him out of solemn green eyes. Then, with the terrible succinctness of the very young: "Aunt Kareen doesn't want me."

"Shan." Val Con's voice, here and now.

"Yes?" But even as he asked, he saw them; the Lady leaning on the arm of her elegant escort. "Aaaah, damn. Have they seen us?"

"Hello, kinsmen!" called Pat Rin across the Festival's babble.

"Why must he always remind me of that?"

"Gently, Brother," murmured Val Con. "Only think of the expense; weigh it against satisfaction gained . . ."

"You make it sound so simple . . ." he began. Then Lady Kareen and her son were with them and he chopped it off to make his bow.

Val Con also bowed, graceful and brief. "Aunt. Cousin."

"Nephew," she said icily and paused to draw a deep breath. Into this slight gap—unexpectedly—stepped Pat Rin.

"What an extraordinary cloak, young cousin. And worn at such an odd hour. Unless you wish to establish a—point—of some kind?"

Val Con considered him, eyebrow askance. "I wish to establish a new fashion in cloaks, kinsman. What better place to introduce it than the Little Festival, where hours are for a time banished?"

"Oh, very good!" said Pat Rin admiringly. "You have the touch of a poet, Cousin." He gently disengaged his mother's hand and ignored her glare as he circled Val Con thoughtfully.

After a few circuits, he shrugged. "There is a grain of something there, I allow. It might be possible to adapt it quite successfully. What do you call it?"

"A skimmer," said Val Con gently.

"Indeed? Don't you find that perhaps a bit—vulgar?"

"Ah, but you see, I find myself to be a vulgar person. Which I believe is the topic my aunt wishes to address. Let us allow her room, kinsman." He turned his eyes to the outraged Lady. "Aunt? You have something to say?"

It took her a moment to find her voice. "I will speak with you in private, sir."

Val Con inclined his head. "Lady, I regret. I am here. If you wish to speak—and since you came in search of me—you must perforce speak here."

Pat Rin's eyes sharpened with speculation and he stepped back to his mother's side.

The Right Noble stared at her nephew. A moment stretched to two . . . neared three . . .

She moved her eyes first.

"Very well, sir. If you wish all the world to hear it . . ."

"If your topic causes you shame, madam, pray do not speak, but wait. Call on me at home and we will discuss the matter privately." Val Con's voice was unremittingly gentle. Shan winced and swept a quick glance around the gathering crowd.

Lady Kareen moistened her lips. "That Lord yos'Galan is so lost to propriety as to continue to race skimmers in the face of defeat and ridicule, I can readily believe. That you, of the line and blood of one of the oldest and most respected of the clans, should, after receiving the instruction of the eldest of your line, persist in this scandal is insupportable. Why should you race skimmers, sir? In all the generations since the clans came to Liad no one of Korval has ever raced skimmers!"

"And before Cantra yos'Phelium and Tor An yos'Galan landed the colony ship on this world, no one of Korval had done that, either," Val Con said. Suddenly, his eyes were sharp; his voice ice-edged.

"Your argument, Lady, falls short."

The Right Noble pulled herself up. Pat Rin gasped. Shan bit his tongue.

"As the eldest of Line yos'Phelium," Lady Kareen stated formally, "I forbid you to race—this evening, tomorrow, or at any time in the future. Do I make myself plain, sir?"

A pause, very brief. Then, in the highest possible dialect, that used to address strangers or those barely acknowledged as kin: "You long ago declined the right to so command." And added, in a voice so cold Shan barely recognized it as Val Con's, "Madam, I repeat: Your argument falls short. You are of the line by name and blood, but never by authority."

Incredibly, she opened her mouth to speak further—or perhaps she only gasped with shock. Whatever she intended, it was forestalled as Pat Rin stepped forward, sweeping a bow just this side of too-deep toward them both.

"Indeed," he murmured quickly, "we are grateful for this valuable instruction." He backed gracefully to his mother's side; placed her hand upon his arm.

"A good evening to you both, kinsmen. My kindest regards to your sisters."

Gently, he turned the Right Noble and guided her through the scattering onlookers.

Shan looked at his younger brother, standing stiff and hard-faced in his absurd cloak.

"Are you Balanced now, Val Con?" he asked softly.

Some of the stiffness fled and he turned, mouth wry.

"I think so," he murmured and added, "yes."

THE STANDS WERE packed and Nova stretched her legs carefully.

Next to her, Anthora and her fairlove were engaged in picking out acquaintances in the crowd—against all Festival propriety, of course. Nova sighed and leaned over.

"May I offer either of you wine?"

"Both," said Anthora gaily. She smiled at her companion, who was clearly besotted already. "I'll have red, please."

"And I, canary, Lady. Thanking you . . ."

Anthora gripped Nova's hand. "Two more," she whispered urgently. "Is it red and red? Pat Rin and Lady Kareen are here."

"What?" Nova turned, immediately locating the exquisite Pat Rin, painstakingly conducting his mother across the tiers.

"Damn," Nova muttered and Anthora laughed.

Pat Rin's bow, delivered moments later, was an intriguing concoction of restraint, kinship and tentative coolness.

"Cousins," he said formally. "A good day to you both. My honored mother wishes to view the race and wonders if she might presume to the extent of begging two seats."

What was this? Nova smiled graciously and inclined her head.

"Please do sit, both. There is wine. You prefer red, I think, kinsman? Cousin?"

This was acknowledged with cool thanks; seats were taken. Lady Kareen leaned to Nova.

"Will you have the goodness, Cousin, to point out Korval's craft when it appears? One wishes to keep it in one's eye."

"Yes, certainly." Nova sipped wine to cover her confusion. "You know, of course, Cousin, that there is no possibility of halting the race—or of withdrawing Korval's entry, assuming it has qualified?"

"Of course," said Lady Kareen placidly. "I have seen my nephew and his brother. My error has been shown me," her lips twitched, "with meticulous correctness. One seeks to behave with propriety." She sipped. "What is the name of the craft, please, Cousin?"

"*Araceli*. It should be quite easy to mark. My youngest brother wears his cloak."

"Most proper," said Lady Kareen and turned to say a word to her son.

VAL CON PULLED on gloves as he surveyed the competition. Each craft hovered over its assigned colored oval; from the stands it looked as if eighteen frictionless pucks sat upon eighteen glass disks. The slightest gust of breeze could push a craft off-center, as might the careless lean of a copilot, though once underway the powerful force of the airblasts would nullify all but the strongest wind.

The razzing from the other crews subsided into grumbling and catcalls, though Val Con had had a bad few minutes just as *Araceli* took its place. *Tolanda's* Terran pilot gave vent to an exquisite wolfwhistle while her Liaden partner called out reprovingly.

"Come now, Captain, you needn't give up as easily as that! You've paid the entrance fee; why not try to race?"

Kelti had taken up the assault then: "That orange could blind somebody!"

And so on.

Through it all Shan sat silent in the pilot's slot; and *Araceli* alone of the eighteen craft stayed precisely centered above her disk of color.

The starting cannon boomed, masking the whir and whine of the skimmers' starting blasts. Wind whipped Val Con's face as he leaned back into his niche, clinging to the molded handgrips. At Shan's nod, he shifted left and *Araceli* veered sharply: now they were in the second row and building speed.

Across the course, skimmers were setting up for the first sickle-shaped curve, and *Araceli's* position on the outside was bad. Unexpectedly, speed helped them through the first bunch-up at the base of the turn; they slid away a half-second before the craft to their left lost control and broadsided the skimmer immediately behind.

A short straight and then—the hill.

Most of the field was slowing; pilots gauging the approach, waiting for the exact moment to gun the jets.

Out on the far side, running at a completely absurd angle, *Araceli* charged forward, upward—halfway up, in fact—and began to rotate.

Shan hit the jets; *Araceli* climbed, rotation unchecked. Val Con, ducking to give the pilot a clear view as they proceeded backwards, grinned at the confusion behind.

Several pilots, misreading *Araceli's* rotation as unwanted spin in their own craft, corrected disastrously, slipping sideways—and downward.

Araceli gained ground, rotating gently to face forward again as the hill was crested—four places up in the running; only seven craft ahead.

But on the short straight the superior speed of the newer skimmers showed and *Araceli* dropped to tenth.

"Amateurs!" howled *Scant's* pilot as that craft passed them. "Get off the course if you can't drive!"

Shan waved politely and threw a quick grin at Val Con, motionless in the copilot's seat, cloak tucked carefully around him.

Shan nodded a heartbeat later and Val Con threw his weight to the right as the craft spun sideways to descend the hill, setting up for the second curve. There was a bunch-up at the bottom and several skimmers overshot into a field of grain, releasing a storm of silvery pollen.

Val Con shifted to the left and *Araceli* skidded around, taking the corner raggedly, but in the running as they came into the second longest straight.

"Now!" yelled Shan.

Val Con knocked twice on the thin metal skin and curled himself into a tight ball behind his larger brother; ducking his head inside the silk of the cloak to create a smooth-backed fairing.

They neither gained nor lost on the straight and Val Con stayed hunched over. A gone feeling in his stomach warned him and he was instantly up, sitting far back; trying not to look at the ramp ahead, or at the gap they must jump.

The ramp edge was crossed and he lunged forward, grabbing for the kink at the base of the rollbar—

They went up with a craft slightly to their right and in front; another just behind. Val Con caught a glimpse of that one and winced: they'd entered the ramp wrong and the sharp front of the skimmer was too high. Not only did they lose time as the air flow caught the broad base, but almost flipped as the back sank.

Shan gunned the jets as *Araceli* made the receiving ramp. The shock of it, rather than conscious thought, brought Val Con back into running position.

Araceli was the second of three skimmers approaching together, making a bid to take the next corner sharply and enter the weaving tree-lined "tunnel."

Shan nearly missed the proper moment for reversal of the jets; kicked them and leaned to fight rotation as Val Con jerked hard to the right, sending them into the tunnel between the two challengers.

Out of the trees and into the longest straight, with the start/finish line at its center, and the advantage of the other craft showed again, as three caught *Araceli* before the line and one after, until the frantic braking for the corner broke the flow and reshuffled the field.

By the fifth lap, several skimmers were out of the race. One flipped at the ramp, both crew members still strapped in. Shan had the measure of the course, but *Araceli* was losing precious seconds on each lap. *Tolanda,* in bright blue, was running a conservative third behind the two contenders for the lead.

Araceli was a steady eighth and there was no hope of catching the leaders on speed.

Out of the tunnel, they managed to pass a careless *Kelti* and got a good start on the long straightaway. Shan's voice carried back over the rush of air.

"Now, Val Con!"

PAT RIN WAS annoyed. Worse, he was bored. Races were not among his favorite amusements and to be forced to sit and watch such a race when one might be ribbonfasted or—Well, and here they came again.

He dutifully kept his eyes on the black skimmer with the bright-orange copilot as it rushed past the stands, seventh in the field—gaining perhaps half-a-length on the number six position. Val Con was hunched down in back, using his cloak as a fairing—not too bad a notion, Pat Rin admitted, grudgingly.

Araceli passed number six and was gaining on the leaders, who were starting to bunch up into the braking zone for the curve. Pat Rin tensed. Korval's entry was hurtling on—deeper and deeper into the braking zone! Madness to take the corner at that speed—

He came to his feet, Nova beside him, Anthora hanging on her arm, as a burst of orange exploded from the back of *Araceli*, which could only be Val Con, jumping—

The crowd's groan turned to a cheer, under which Pat Rin heard Anthora's voice, repeating urgently, "He's all right, Sister. They're both all right. Sit down. They're—"

Pat Rin sat slowly, staring at Val Con, who was standing like an orange balloon in the back of the skimmer, his astonishing cloak hauling the craft's speed down from the absurd to the reasonable.

And entering the sickle-curve Korval was fourth, approaching third.

TOLANDA'S PILOT glanced back, disbelief on her face; shouted to her teammate and fishtailed for the nerf—the intentional glancing collision which would push the upstarts off the course.

Val Con snapped half-erect, cloak billowing over one arm, air-braking and tipping *Araceli*—and *Tolanda* was fourth, fighting rotation. Shan was laughing.

The hill loomed. Val Con ducked into his cocoon to preserve speed and snapped out at the crest, catching an over-the-shoulder grin from Shan. They charged downhill neck-and-neck with *Tolanda;* and left it in the dust as the Terran began braking for the corner.

Again Val Con stood, gripping the rollbar tightly; again the cloak went from a bright-orange stream to an inflated airfoil.

Again *Araceli* picked up ground on the leaders.

Cries of "Foul! Foul!" hit them as they whipped past the pits.

Their opponents, faced with a common enemy, charged harder down the long straights, took more risks, tried—with some success—to emulate Korval's airbrake, using shirts and vests. But *Araceli* was a clear second, *Tolanda* third and the former second, fourth.

The lead changed hands several times on the tenth lap.

"Two more laps to win it!" Shan yelled.

Val Con nearly groaned. His arms ached, he was sweaty, his hands within the gloves were raw, his legs throbbed with strain. Two laps—an eternity!

They crossed the start/finish line, lapping several slower racers, and came even with the first place craft just before the braking zone.

Val Con leapt for the bar and blinked: the other skimmer was still even with them, trying to take the coming corner at exactly the proper angle.

Execution fell short. The other craft shivered; started to spin— *Araceli* was past, taking the lead by two skimmer-lengths.

They held that minor lead through the eleventh lap, but the second place craft was showing its speed and inching closer.

Korval threw everything into the turns, dove a little further into the corners, waited a little longer on the straights. Val Con concentrated on the pattern of his movements, grooved in after this hard hour, and ignored the ache in his arms and legs.

They skidded into the tree tunnel nearly two full lengths ahead— Shan yelled, but the words were ripped away by the rushing wind, and Val Con saw the green skimmer charging them from inside the corner, a would-be human airbrake frantically trying to regain control.

Shan choked the jets, trying to throw *Araceli* clear of the charge, fighting spin and time was too short—

Val Con leapt to the bar, arms wide: "Left, Shan! Left!"

Araceli snapped left as Val Con's cloak ballooned and the green skimmer missed them by a hair, the pilot struggling with the stick, trying to avoid the second place craft, just coming into the curve . . .

They were through; out into the straight, and Val Con folded himself into a fairing for the last time. *Araceli* roared as Shan opened the throttle for the long run and Val Con sweated inside the cloak, hearing sounds—sounds of many people, shouting; and, closer, the sound of another skimmer, gaining; a shout from Shan as they slewed sideways and—

"We won! Brother, we won!" Shan was pulling the cloak back from Val Con's head, grinning hugely. "It worked!"

"Of course it worked," said Val Con, somewhat crossly, as they began the victory lap, and sighed. Shan was steering one handed and waving at the crowd as wildly as they waved at *Araceli*. Val Con's arms felt too heavy to wave at anyone.

"Shan?" He called above the roar.

"Yes, my blueblood?"

"We're not going to make a habit of this, are we?"

Shan laughed. "No, *denubia*. Why push the luck?"

THE WINNER'S CIRCLE was crowded. Val Con and Shan managed to squeeze to their sisters' side; each accepting a glass of wine and a kiss.

The Right Noble Lady Kareen yos'Phelium approached and bowed to Shan—the bow of Clanmember to First Speaker.

"Well raced, my Lord," she said, quite audibly. "You and your brother are a credit to the clan."

Shan blinked, inclined his head, murmuring a civil, "Thank you, Lady Kareen."

The old lady was bowing to Val Con now: clanmember to delm.

"You are precipitate, Aunt," he chided softly.

"I think not," she returned. "A ring does not make a delm. You are Korval, whether you judge yourself ready or no. You will do as you deem wise and necessary. For the clan. It is as it should be."

"Ah." He smiled. "Let us have peace between us then, Lady."

"Of course," said the Right Noble. "How else?"

Anthora's fairlove leaned over, whispering in her ear. She laughed softly and linked her arm in his; waving at her eldest brother as they moved off toward the pleasure-tents.

Shan raised his glass in salute; lowered it to drink—and snapped his eyes to Val Con's face as he felt the younger man start.

"If the family will excuse me," Val Con murmured, sketching a bow toward all. "I am reminded of a previous appointment." He was gone, slipping through the crowd like an orange wraith.

Shan, watching from his tall vantage, saw a lady start forward— a blur of dark hair and bright eyes; hand outstretched in welcome. Val Con's arm slid around her waist and he began to turn her toward the pleasure-tents—then his cloak swirled suddenly wide, hiding both from Shan's view.

He glanced down to find Nova's eyes on him.

"The reason Lady Kareen heard of Val Con frequenting a tavern in spaceleathers?" she murmured. "Is he courting a barmaid, Brother?"

He sipped. "She seems a very nice barmaid."

"Shan—"

He sighed and tried to break her gaze, without success.

"All right," he said grumpily. "I'll talk to him." He raised his glass. "Later."

✧ Where the Goddess Sends ✧

TIME AGO ONE went out from Circle, sent by the Mother's Own Word. The one was called Moonhawk, and she knew neither the face nor the name of what she went Seeking.

The course of Seeking wound through the land and through the seasons and brought Moonhawk to a place that stank of Evil.

It is told that she hesitated at the edge of this place and thought she would not go in. This is the first of the things told here which must without fail be said: Moonhawk thought she would not go in.

At the moment of thinking so, she heard the Voice of the Goddess and the Words were: "Enter, thou." Obedient, Moonhawk went forward.

The second thing that must without fail be said is this: Moonhawk was afraid.

"THAT'S MINE."

Lute flashed a grin sideways and upward, chidingly.

"Apologies, Noble Lady. The bag is mine. It contains the necessities of my trade. The repository of magics, you might say. Dangerous in untutored hands." He gripped the disputed item and straightened, smiling with urbane idiocy.

"You will understand my reluctance to place so beauteous a lady as yourself in the slightest peril."

The lady took a breath that brought the principals of her beauty into high display, and thrust out her lower lip.

"It's mine."

"Noble—"

"She said," the walking mountain at her side interrupted, "that the bag's hers, tricksman. Are you calling Lady Drudae a liar?"

Lute sighed inwardly. The intervention of the mountain was as unwelcome as it was inevitable. He made a mental note to curse himself roundly for visiting this Goddess-blasted place at all, and smiled more widely.

"It would give me nothing but joy to surrender my bag into the care of the Noble Lady if I did not know that it contains instruments of dread magic. Even now, I might place it in her hands safely, for I should be here to hold her protected. But think, sir, what if I were to leave the bag with the very Noble Lady and withdraw myself and my protection over the boundary of your delightful village, as we all know I must. What then?" He affected a shudder. "I cannot complete the thought."

It was doubtful that the mountain had ever completed a thought in his life. The lady was more facile.

"You say only you can keep me safe from these dangers?"

"I say it, Noble, and it is veriest truth."

She frowned, then smiled with pretty malice. "Why, then, it is simple! Since the bag is mine—and only you may control it—you must be mine, too!"

She laughed and clapped her hands.

"Take him to the pit, Arto. And leave the bag here."

MOONHAWK CAME INTO the place of darkness and she was afraid. Still, she held her head high and made her step firm, as befits a Witch-in-Circle, and gazed upon those that crept out from between the thatch-bald hovels with calm eyes and compassion.

"Goddess give you good even," she said softly to the one who ventured nearest, though the taste of its emotions sickened her. Terror lanced the creature and it scuttled back to its fellows. The boldest lifted a hand, showing rock.

Moonhawk stopped, anger heating fear. "For shame! Is this how you treat a traveler, most blessed of the Mother? I claim travel-right, and mean you no harm."

"Travel-right?" That was the boldest, rock yet steady. "You claim travel-right in Relzda?"

"If this be Relzda, then I do."

The rock-bearer laughed like another woman's weeping. "If you claim travel-right, you must go to Lady Drudae. I can show the way.'

Moonhawk bowed her head. "It is a kindness, sister. My thanks."

"No kindness. Your cloak is fine." With no further words, she scrabbled between two lean-together huts.

Listening in vain for the Goddess, Moonhawk followed.

Lady Drudae sat upon a wooden throne in the center of a drafty hall. The floor was dirt and the wall-rugs threadbare. Smoky oil-lamps gave uncertain light. There was a musk of rotting wood.

"Come forward." Petulance rather than command. Moonhawk and her guide obeyed.

"Well?"

"This one claims travel-right, Noble Lady," gabbled the bold one, not so bold now. "I brought her. Her cloak, Noble Lady. My bounty, my—"

"Shut your horrid mouth!"

The rock-bearer did so, bending until her unkempt hair brushed the dirt floor. Moonhawk stood forward, sharpening her eyes in the gloom.

The woman on the throne was beautiful: red-gold hair above a face the uninitiated would claim for the Goddess. The robe of doubtful crimson revealed her breasts, in the manner of Circle robes. But this one was not of Circle.

At the woman's side a man—hulking and muscle-gripped—stood stoic. There was a gash below one eye and a purpling bruise along the line of his jaw.

"Well," said the woman again. "Travel-right, is it? You are bold."

"I am in need," Moonhawk replied levelly. "Night comes and I ask the boon of a roof."

"Do you? But this is a hard land from which to scratch a living, traveler. We have little to give. Even the favor of a place to sleep must be balanced by a valuable of your own."

Moonhawk bowed her head. "I will work for the House with gladness. I sing the Teaching Tales, give news, heal . . ."

Lady Drudae was laughing. "Hear her, Arto? She can sing! She does not fear labor!" The laughter stopped. "You misunderstand, traveler. The boon of a roof demands the balance of a—personal— favor." A snap of shapely fingers. "Arto!"

The man's sluggish face lit and his lust was a thrust of jagged ice.

For a second time Moonhawk feared, and stepped back, gathering her mantle close.

"I do not choose to give that gift," she said, flinging the words like stones to stop him.

He laughed then, low and idiotic, and she knew he would heed no words of hers. She retreated, thinking of the door and of the way to the boundary lintels; and the voice of the Mother was thunder within her: "Stay, thou! Do not turn away!"

The man lunged forward, snatching her cloak. Whirling, she left it in his hand and stood 'round to face him, clad in travelers' breech and shirt.

He threw the cloak aside and the creature who had guided her here scrambled forward in the dirt, wadding the cloth against her. The man lunged again.

Moonhawk danced away, but his hand had touched her arm. Thrusting away fear, she stood straight and, staring into his dull, exultant eyes, reached out, as those in Circle may—

His cry was hoarse with terror and he bent double, hands gripping his privates. "It burns! Noble Lady—aid me!"

Moonhawk stepped around him. "Be still and you will have no pain. Seek to harm me and you will burn." She withdrew her attention from the man and laid it upon Lady Drudae.

"I am charged by the Mother's Word to come to this place. I require—"

It was here that the Goddess in Her wisdom withdrew Her hand from about the person of Her daughter and allowed a well-aimed rock to fell her from behind.

✧✧✧

THE EYES WERE open and of indeterminate hue; the face was blank, whether by intent or by nature it was not yet possible to know.

Lute nodded pleasantly and smiled.

"How lovely to see you wake! Allow me to offer congratulations. The mountain has only recently stopped wailing, from which I surmise that your aim is superior to my own. Well-played! I wish I'd been there to see it. Sound is useful, but I sometimes find it a bit confusing when not aided by sight. Don't you?"

The eyes blinked once, slowly.

"Who are you?"

"A thousand apologies, Stranger Lady! I am Lute, Master of prestidigitation, illusion, and sleight-of-hand. No doubt you've heard of me."

The eyes closed. Lute sighed and settled back against the dirt wall.

"Is it a little incongruous," the woman wondered eventually, "for a Master of magics to be sitting at the bottom of a hole with his shirt torn and blood on his chin?"

Lute considered her shuttered face. "A minor reversal of fortunes. Only let me lay my hand upon my bag and neither this nor any other hole may contain me!"

"Oh." The eyes were open again. "Where is it? Your bag."

He pointed upward with a flourish. "Lady Drudae has it in her tender keeping."

"I see." She twisted her angular self gracelessly and sat up. "You're an optimist."

"A pragmatist," he corrected gently. "But enough of me! What of yourself? What are you hight? Whither are you bound? How came you here? How will you go away?"

She raised her hands, feeling in the thick, unraveling knot of her hair. "Moonhawk. Where the Goddess sends me. Upon my two feet. The same." Her hair became a cascade, obscuring gaunt features.

"Moonhawk." He chewed his lip. "This is no good place for a name out of Circle. Call yourself otherwise, if you'll take my advice—unless you've come to convert the heathen?"

She laughed, a pleasing sound in the dankness of the pit.

"Hardly." She ran pale strands through combing fingers. "You are devout?"

"I was raised to the Way and have traveled a good deal—

"Have you been to Huntress City? The lamps—harnessed lightnings, I was told, from the ships that brought our foremothers here." He waved a hand upward, indicating the greasy shadows of oil light. "Far different, this."

"There aren't many places to compare with the glory of Huntress," she said softly. "I would like to visit someday—Goddess willing. The last news I had was that Huntress Circle was collecting everything that might be from the Ships and placing all within a warded treasurehouse."

"So? All the more reason, then, for one of the Circle to visit Lady Drudae. She possesses a most interesting artifact."

He waited, gauging the moment. She was silent, combing her hair.

"You are incurious."

She glanced up. "I am sitting in the mud at the bottom of a hole with a kitchen magician for my companion and a village of depravity above. My head hurts. My cloak is gone. I'm hungry. And cold. I see no way out of the present coil and no reason to be in it at all."

"Ask your Goddess, if you lack reasons." He had not intended his voice to be so sharp. "I'm told She has a plenitude."

"She does not Speak."

Lute shifted and carefully extended his legs.

"If my bag were here, we might dine on cheese and bread and fresh milk," he said musingly. "I would share my cloak and mix you a tincture I learned in the Wilderwood that is efficacious in the soothing of headaches." He sighed. "Rot those lamps—it's getting dark. I hate to talk to someone I can't see."

Moonhawk raised her head, tracing the flicker of Power to the man—and out of him—flowing to the sticky floor.

A small blue flame appeared in the mud between them; faded, flickered, and steadied. The man Lute settled back, sighing as one who has expended much effort.

"Light at least, Lady. I apologize that it does not give heat. If I had my bag . . ." He let the sentence go, peering upward for a moment before settling harder against the fabric of the pit, hope as thin as the wan blue light.

"Please, my name is Moonhawk—and I thank you for the gift. You should conserve your strength."

"My strength will return soon enough. They won't come for me tonight, I think. More likely tomorrow mid-morning—after Lady Drudae is angry."

"OPEN IT!" She augmented the order with a ringing slap across the man's ear.

"Lady, I cannot! It does not—there is no— see nothing—"

"Open it or fry!" This time she aimed her blow at the bag, knuckles sharp, as if she struck the idiot's simpering face.

"Lady, it is not possible!" pled Kat. "Perhaps the trickster told the aye—"

Clink!

They froze; turned as one to stare at the bag sitting, inviolate, on the high wooden table.

Beside it lay a solitary token of the type used to count score in gambling games.

"Where did it come from?" wondered Kat.

"The bag . . ."

"Lady, the bag is not open!"

"Where else would it come from?" she cried. "Do you have such a thing? Do I? It must come from the bag!" She snatched at the clasp, swore; lifted the whole with fury's strength and slammed it upon the table. "Open, damn you!"

The bag sat, shuttered and uncowed.

Lovely shoulders drooping, Lady Drudae turned away.

Plingplinkbinkplunk!

She spun. Rolling unhurriedly down the slope of the table, four bright pottery marbles: red, blue, green, yellow. Lady Drudae stared them to the edge of the table and watched them fall, one by one, to the dirt floor.

"Fetch the magician."

✦✦✦

MOONHAWK SAT AT the bottom of the pit and listened.

Lady Drudae's voice she heard most—strident and scolding, then threatening. Less often came the undistinguished bass rumble of a man's speaking. Least often, she heard Lute's clear, trained voice. He spoke very few words for one who seemed to like them so well. Most of the words he spoke meant 'No'.

"You will open that bag now," Lady Drudae stormed. "If you do not, Kat will break your fingers."

"If he does so, Lady, heed my warning! Run away from here as fast as you may. For the bag becomes its own master if I have no hands to lay upon it. Listen! And believe."

Very nearly did Moonhawk in her pit believe, though straining Witch-sense brought no taste of power, other than the gall of evil.

"So . . ." hissed Lady Drudae. "Kat!"

A moment's incredulous silence was followed by a man's hoarse scream.

They threw him down from the edge.

Moonhawk broke his fall with her body and he rolled away, coiled around his ruined hand, sobbing.

"Lute." She touched him and he shuddered, sob catching on a gasp.

Witch-sense questing, she found a mangled chord of clarity within his terror, caught it and wound it round with calm, feeding comfort in a riverflow until he let her touch the pain and share it.

"Lute. I am Healer." She did not force trust; did not stint on what she gave.

Slowly, the coiled body unwound. He flopped to his back, eyes stabbing hers.

"Good. Now it is my turn to give a gift . . . I must touch it, Lute. I am Healer. Through me flows the love of our Mother. Through me flows Her strength—to you, Her son . . ."

She held the mangled member now; felt and knew utter destruction: the tiny bones ground and shattered and hopeless. Around them, the highly trained muscles mourned.

Moonhawk took breath, drawing in strength, and crossed over into that gray space from which all Healing takes place.

The man beneath her hand screamed; she exerted the Will necessary to quiet him. The Inner Eyes saw bone shards reform, fit together, settle into the cradle of tissue, seal into wholeness—into health.

She let breath escape; removed Will and hand and sat back, face dripping sweat, body shuddering.

"In Her Name it is done."

Lute caught her with two good hands as she toppled sideways, and lay her gently down, head pillowed on his thigh.

MOONHAWK BLINKED IN the gash of sunlight and tried not to breathe through her nose. The one called Kat held her arms twisted behind her back and he stank like last week's slaughter.

Lute's hands hung free. He faced Lady Drudae over a dull blue tube and smiled as if the terror in him was no more real than dreams.

"You know what this is?" The Lady asked him, voice unnaturally calm.

Lute bowed his head. "I do. I beg leave to remind the most gracious and noble Lady that, fried, I am of no use to her."

"How is your hand mended? It was broken beyond praying for—Kat?"

"It was, Noble Lady," his voice boomed over Moonhawk's head. "You know me!"

Lady Drudae nodded, eyes flicking to Moonhawk. "You. How comes the magician's hand to be whole?"

Moonhawk met the mad blue eyes steadily. "I Healed him."

"So." The eyes widened. She lifted the tube. "Do you know what this is?"

"No."

"Then I will show you." Her voice rose. "Arto! Bring the nemrill!"

The Lady backed away, tube lowering. The mountain shadowed the door arch, a bundle of fur swinging from a huge fist.

"Throw it in and stand away!"

The bundle hit the dirt floor, rolled into a puddle of sunlight and came up spitting, fangs showing, tail fat with fury, claws at ready.

This nemrill was none such as they had at Temple, pleased with the world and themselves. The ferocity of this creature startled the Healer; its fear pierced her.

Lady Drudae laughed, pointed the tube and pressed the thumb-stud.

There was a zag of lightning; a stink of ozone. The nemrill was encased in a nimbus of flame, shrieking in mortal agony. Moonhawk reached within; saw Lute start forward while the Lady laughed and—pop!

The nemrill was gone.

The stink of scorched fur and frying flesh reached Moonhawk and she gagged, sagging shamefully in her captor's grip. Lute turned to her; was halted by a shake of the tube.

"Now, magician, listen closely. Open the bag—or *she* fries. You see?"

He lay a hand on the bag; withdrew it. "It is a long process, Noble Lady; and fraught with peril. I have not eaten in some time—a simple oversight, no doubt! My strength is not sufficient to the task. If I err, we may all fry!"

"I marvel you carry so dangerous a thing with you."

"It is wise to keep the danger you know best to hand, Lady."

Hesitation that Moonhawk tasted as her own, even as her powers faded. Food . . . She separated her need, hurled it into the madwoman with the last of her strength.

"Very well. Arto—bring food for the magician. Kat—tie her."

Lute carried the bad bread and doubtful cheese to her, ignoring the tube though his nerves shrieked. He halved the meager portion and raised a cheese bit to her lips. "Eat."

"Look, Kat!" Lady Drudae shrilled. "The magician is kind! He shares his meal with a stranger! Or is she not a stranger? A night in the pit together, with no other entertainment—and she would not have Arto!"

Moonhawk felt the flare of his fury, held his eyes with hers. "My thanks to you, Brother." Shoulders aching with the strain of the rope, she took the cheese and ate.

He fed her the bread and gave her a drink of pure, icy water. Then he ate, taking much longer than he might. She had the sense that he was gauging something, counting . . .

The Lady shifted irritably, fingers tightening on the tube. Lute offered more water; had another sip for himself and turned.

She read no hope in him.

"Now, if the Lady and her bodyguardian will stand well away . . ."

"Stand away! You can't go—" Arto's bellow spun Kat and the Lady around. Lute faded two light steps toward the bag, hope scalding.

Through the arch a ragamuffin crowd jostled, pushing bulky Arto before it like jetsam in a floodtide.

"Noble Lady! See what we bring! Bounty for all!"

"Enough!" The tube pointed unwavering at the center of the crowd. Voices halted and the tangle rearranged itself, becoming four of the village surrounding two who were manifestly not.

The man struggled against the rope that pinned his arms to his sides. The woman stood wary and alert in her bonds, dark eyes flashing.

"He has coins, Noble Lady!" cried one from the village. "And fine clothes! We followed and captured! We demand bounty!"

"You demand?" The tube had one target now and the blue eyes held only madness. The one who had spoken sparked fear and flung himself belly down on the dirt.

"Forgive me, Noble Lady. I spoke hastily."

"Count your wretched life as bounty." The tube averted its stare with reluctance. "And the rest of you! I'll decide your bounty—if any! Go! Now."

They abased themselves and went, Arto following. Kat came and stood behind the captives, grinning.

"Coins?" wondered Lady Drudae, eyeing them. "Fine clothing? And not so bad looking a woman, eh, Kat? We'll give her to Arto, to atone for the one who wouldn't have him."

The man froze, horror pouring out of him. The woman's head went up.

"I am well content with the man I have. We are travelers and sacred. In Her Name you must release us."

Lady Drudae laughed. "Oh, well said! In Her name, release us. Oh, yes! Arto!"

MREEEEEEEEEEEEEEEEEEEEEEEEE!

A noise loud enough to stun the mind burst into the room: all save one were startled.

Now there was a rush of wind filling Moonhawk's head as the room telescoped away, becoming tiny, tinier . . . This was the whole of the Power, as she'd tasted it but twice before: The Mother Herself was looking through Moonhawk's eyes. Before the room was gone entirely from her human sight, she looked for Lute and saw him at the table, one hand on the magic bag, and one hand perhaps in it . . .

THE GODDESS DID pour Herself into the earthly form of Her daughter, idiodic Moonhawk. Rising up, She snapped the puny bonds of hemp.

With a glance, She caused the ropes to fall from the two captives and cried out in a Voice like the Wind That Scattered The Stars:

"Away! Take thy man and go!"

The woman caught the man's hand. For a moment he resisted, thinking he might stay and fight. Then sense prevailed and he turned with his woman and they ran like wise rabbits away from that screeching place.

The murderer Kat started after, hands grabbing. Before his eyes the Mother flung images of past evil and he fell to the ground upon his knees, tears running his cheeks. Lute aided the Mother, striking with a mallet that unguarded head.

Lightning came at Her as the tyrant woman added screams to the din and the Mother laughed, for Lightning is Her Consort and will not harm Her. She raised a hand to the stream and deflected it upward, to and through the rotting roof.

Then the Goddess reached out once more, and put before Lady Drudae's eyes another image, so that she dropped the death-tube.

A hand fell upon Her Person. A voice dinned in Her ears. The Goddess looked about, well pleased with Her work, and returned the body to Her daughter.

❖❖❖

"MOONHAWK! Moonhawk!"

She blinked at Lute, stared at the fallen Kat, at the Lady, back to the far wall, fist jammed into her mouth, eyes fixed with rigid horror on something she alone saw.

"Moonhawk!" A shake that snapped her head on her neck.

"What?"

"The roof's afire! Goddess blast you—run!"

Run. She fumbled at the body's controls and began a shambling trot toward the door, the path she must take through the village to the northern edge unfolding before the Inner Eyes. Lute was right. She must run—

The door was abruptly blocked. Arto. Moonhawk breathed a prayer to the Mother and did not slow.

The mountain fell back and let her by. He was still standing with his hands empty at his sides when Lute passed a moment later, hands and bag ablaze with strange incandescent light.

Running was easier now. More natural. She added speed, weaving between the thatchless hovels, following necessity, oblivious to the shadows, vaguely curious of the light that had kept pace and then was gone . . .

She broke out of the village into a clearing ringed with rock—an ancient corral, perhaps—the carved shapes of boundary markers towered, just beyond.

She raced across the opening, eyes on the markers, necessity urging her on. Her foot struck a hidden rock and she hurtled forward, catching herself on her hands, rolling up—and freezing.

Encircling her, not mere rock, but a crowd of rag-tag creatures. She saw a flash of dark blue—her cloak. And the woman who wore it held a stone.

All of them held stones.

She reached within, but her powers were gone to ash. She reached without and touched nothing but hatred. Necessity burned in her. Fear turned her legs to jelly.

The one who wore her cloak drew back her arm, grinning. Moonhawk braced herself.

"Make way!" cried a voice and the human wall broke as a thin man in a torn shirt burst through, bag in hand. He slammed to a halt and spun in a wide circle, rounds flashing from his hands.

"Gold! Gold for all!"

"Gold!" The crowd fell as one, scrabbling in the knotted grass.

Lute grabbed her arm and pulled her with him, nearly jerking her arm from its socket.

The villagers were still grubbing for the coins when the two of them passed the boundary stones.

"OF ALL THE STUPID—why run this way? The eastern boundary was closer—and easier going beyond. Or am I to believe you came in this way?"

"No," said Moonhawk absently. "I came in by the eastern way. Here."

"Here what?" he demanded, but she was going away from him like a sleep-walker. Cursing under his breath, he followed.

In a moment he heard the voices of the recent prisoners.

"North for a bit, then," the winded traveler was saying. "We'll turn south beyond the hills. There's time for a short detour, isn't there, Maria?"

The woman's doubt was palpable. She hunched in her cloak, dark eyes tired now, not flashing.

Moonhawk stepped around the rock that sheltered them, the magician trailing.

"Go due north," she said, voice deep with Foretelling. "At the end of seven day's walking you will come to a town by a wide river. The name of the town is Caleitha. When your daughter is born, take her to Circle there. They will Know her."

She sagged suddenly and felt Lute's hand beneath her elbow as she smiled. "The Goddess Herself intervened for you, Sister. Be joyful."

LATER THAT EVENING, Moonhawk fed twigs to a fire while Lute grumbled over the state of his property.

"Is your bag really worth so much?"

"So much?" He stared at her in disbelief. "My dear Master, may he rest in the arms of the Goddess forever, taught that a magician's receptacle is his life." He stood, bag in hand. "It's his prop." A sharp shake and legs appeared. Lute set it firmly on the ground.

"His means of living." Bright scarves dazzled in the firelight.

"His safe." Coins glittered and clinked.

"His watchman." A moment of that hideous noise that had started the escape!

"His lightning." A quick flash of pyrotechnic light danced about his hands.

"And his restaurant." A tin arced across the fire and she caught it, laughing.

"Hardly *fresh* milk!"

"Fresher than we had elsewise," he retorted, and came to sit near her, letting the bag stand. "Where do you go now?"

"Where the Goddess sends me."

He nodded and moved his long hands. A wooden top spun in one palm. He played with it, dancing it over his fingers, vanishing it from the right hand to appear in the left. Moonhawk laughed in wonder.

"How are you doing that?"

He glanced up with a grin. "Magic." The grin grew speculative. "Would you like to learn?"

"May I?"

"You seem to have a certain aptitude. And I need an apprentice. Been putting it off far too long. Since we both go where the wind blows us, there's no need for us not to go together, is there?"

"No," said Moonhawk, "there isn't."

"Good," he said and vanished the top. Standing, he went to the bag. "We should, though, head more or less toward Huntress City."

"Why?"

He turned and the firelight glinted off the dull blue barrel.

"I took this from the Noble Lady's hall. It seems to me such a thing belongs with others of its kind, under the careful eyes of those who know their dangers, rather than loose in the poor, half-wild world."

"Will I have learned magic by the time we reach Huntress City?"

Moonhawk wondered and Lute laughed as the weapon disappeared into the depths of his bag.

"It depends on how apt a pupil you are."

THUS DID MOONHAWK *and Lute meet and decide to travel together across the world, this with the blessing of the Goddess, our Mother.*

✧✧✧

The first tale ends here.

✧ A Spell for the Lost ✧

THE WIND WAS out of the southwest, carrying the acrid odor of baking rock. The sun was out of the same quarter, and backlit the magician in the weed-choked square, casting spears of light into the eyes of his audience.

Moonhawk, the magician's traveling companion for this month or so, sat on the cistern wall, face turned aside the sun-spears, and watched each gesture with care.

It was to be a rope trick now. Lute showed the crowd the length of common brown cord, called a lad from the audience to test its strength and, finally, tie it snugly into a loop and hold it high above his head.

Lute held up the circle of steel and waved it under the rope-holder's nose. The lad called out that it was only a saddle-ring.

Moonhawk leaned a little forward where she perched on the wall, opening herself to nuance, as she had been taught in Circle. The ring-and-rope trick always baffled her, though she had seen it fifty times in the past month. Perhaps this time—

"And now," Lute intoned, voice thinned only slightly by the wind, "by the grace of the elements of hemp and iron, by the impermanence of the things we aim to touch and hold, by the wind and by the sun— Ho!" He made a forceful gesture of throwing—and reached forward in nearly the same instant to steady the village lad who had staggered, letting the rope loop sag.

The lad got his feet under him and shouted aloud, holding the rope up so the crowd could see the loop, unbroken, with the saddle-ring threaded neatly as a pendant, spinning lightly in the wind.

There were then as always several from the crowd who must need test rope, knot and ring, all under the magician's tolerant eye.

Moonhawk settled back on her wall, a most un-Witch-like curse on her tongue. Befatched again, Goddess take the man! Well, she would simply ask him the way of it. But it galled her to need to do so.

The crowd had demonstrated to its own satisfaction that rope and ring were inextricable. Lute had the mating back and untied the knot, with a well-worn patter praising the skill of the knot-tier and the efficacy of the knot. He slid the ring free, hung the rope over one shoulder, frowned at the ring and with a gesture vanished it. The audience roared, men stamping their feet and women clapping their palms together, and Lute announced the show was over.

"But if you will, friends, a bit of something for the work expended—a coin, an egg, a loaf, a sup of ale—for, as great as magic is, not even the greatest magician can conjure himself a meal . . ."

It was a giving crowd. By the time its disparate portions had wended home, five eggs, a new loaf, and a quarter-sausage had come to rest on Lute's tattered yellow prop cloth.

"And if a great magician cannot conjure himself a meal, does it follow that he may not conjure a meal for another?" Moonhawk asked, stepping forward and bending to retrieve the three nesting wooden cups.

Lute looked up, mischief glinting in his dark eyes, gaunt face stern.

"The ways of the Craft Magic are not for the student to ridicule," he said austerely. "You will learn these mysteries in the proper order and with the proper respect. Until then, you will keep a civil tongue in your head, madam."

He sounded so like old Laurel, the Witch who had the training of the child Moonhawk, that the adult—woman and Witch in her own right—laughed aloud. Lute grinned, and waved a graceful hand at the accumulated bounty.

"Besides, we've conjured enough for a fine dinner and a bit left aside to break our fast. And—" A flourish, a snatch, and he held out a quarter-moon, brittle with age. "A coin to trade for ale at the inn. I'm told this village boasts an inn."

Moonhawk glanced about her, frowning as much against the ill-kept square as against the sun. "It does?"

"There you go again!" Lute cried, slipping the cups from her hand and placing them carefully in his bag. "I can't recall the last time I spoke to so disrespectful a woman."

"No doubt my early training is to blame," Moonhawk returned. "And the fact that one is used to city comfort!"

"No doubt," Lute agreed, with mortifying sincerity. He finished the various fastenings and straightened, gripping the bag's handle and giving it a sharp shake. The legs retracted with a snap—mechanical magic, this, not sleight-of-hand. He gestured, showing her the dusty square and rag-tag huts.

"Look about you well. For the world is more nearly like this than it is like Dyan City. The lot of common folk is hard work and short lives, relieved—and the Goddess smiles—by love, and by children, and by an occasional diversion such as myself."

He dropped his hand, and in the fading light looked abruptly tired. "For the most part, the Goddess blesses those more, who live nearest the Temples."

Moonhawk kept still. She knew the correct response—knew that every teaching she had ever received told her she put her immortal self at danger, traveling with such a one.

Yet, his voice reverberated with Truth, and Witch-sense showed her his sincerity. She sighed. The man sowed disquiet like gladola seeds. And yet—

"Master Magician!" The woman's voice was breathless with hurry and though she herself was somewhat better dressed than most of the crowd had been, her hair was coming unbraided and dust lay thick upon her. She rushed up to Lute and caught his hand in both of hers; Moonhawk marked how well he controlled the instinct to snatch the precious member away.

"Lady," he said, respectfully, bowing his head, and taking the opportunity to slip his hand free. "How may I serve you?"

"My daughter," she began, and lay her hand against her breast. "Oh, thank the Mother you are here! My daughter said that you would not aid me, but I pray—Indeed, how could you not? It is the responsibility of power to aid the powerless!"

"So I have always been taught," Lute said carefully, while Moonhawk opened herself to the other woman's self and scanned each nuance of emotion.

Distress, she found, but no disorder such as madness might generate. She glanced at Lute and saw he had reached the same conclusion.

"Before aid can be bestowed, we must be aware of the nature of the problem," he told the woman gently.

"Yes, certainly!" she cried, and gave a breathless little laugh, though Moonhawk detected no joy in the sound.

"It is my daughter," she said again. "Three days together she has been gone. Her sister would have it that she is only about some madcap scheme and will return when it occurs to her, but she is not like that! Wild she may be, and heedless of manner, but her heart is good. To worry me so—and she must know that I would worry! No, I cannot believe her so cruel. She must have fallen aside of danger— she may even now be lying in some rock-catch, broken-legged and hoarse from calling . . ." Her voice faltered and Lute stepped expertly into the small silence.

"Lady, I am distressed to hear of your trouble. But surely this is a matter for those of the village who are familiar with the country roundabout and who will know where best to search."

"They have searched," she said, suddenly listless. "They say—they say she must only have gone off with a lover and will return, in a day or six. They say, no one could stay hidden so long, from all the wilder-wise." She bent her head. "They say, unless she is dead."

"Goddess forefend," murmured Lute devoutly. Moonhawk slanted him a slicing look, which he disarmed merely by refusing to meet her eyes. He kept a grave face turned toward the woman. "But this other—that she is gone with a lover to celebrate the Goddess' best joy—is that not possible?"

"With her own betrothed sitting at my hearth, wringing his hands and wondering what is come of her? I say again, Master Magician, she is not a cruel girl."

"Ah." Lute did glance at Moonhawk then, eyes explicitly neutral, then looked back at the grieving mother. "What is it you think I may do for you, Lady?"

"Find her!" she cried, and made as if to clutch his hand again, a move he adroitly avoided. "You have magic . . . power . . . the sight . . . In the name of the Goddess, Master Magician! In the name of she who bore you! My child must be found. My child—" She gasped, bent her head and struck her breast three times, slowly, with a shaking fist.

Lute cleared his throat. "Alas," he said, face and voice betraying nothing but the utmost sincerity, and perhaps a shade of sorrow. "There is magic and there is magic. I have no ability to find what is lost—"

"But I have," Moonhawk said abruptly, and lay her hand briefly upon the woman's head, feeling the warmth of the unraveling hair beneath her palm. "Peace on you, Sister," she said in traditional benediction. She took her hand away and met the woman's incredulous stare with firm coolness.

"You are—Sing thanks to the Goddess! You are of the Circle?" The woman's eyes shone with tears, with transcendent hope. "A priestess?"

"I am Moonhawk," she said austerely. "Witch, Healer, and Seer. I may find that which is lost, by the grace of our Lady." She glanced aside, saw Lute watching her intently; returned her gaze to the woman. "There are certain items I require in order to search most efficiently."

"Certainly!" The woman cried. "Certainly—and you shall have them! You shall come—both of you shall come!—to my house, sup with us, sleep, you may have all I have. Only find her, Lady Moonhawk! Find my child."

"I shall try," said Moonhawk and felt a sudden chill.

THE WOMAN'S NAME was Aster and her house was a large one, set just above the village, with two goats in the front yard and a hen house in back. Taelberry twined up an arbor by the door, the heavy purple blossoms silking the air with fragrance.

"Here we are," said Aster, leading them to the flower-hung porch and working the latch. "Lady Moonhawk, Master Lute—please be welcome in my home."

"Peace on this house," Moonhawk returned in proper ritual.

"Joy to all who live here," Lute said sweetly, bowing his head in respect before stepping over the threshold.

Moonhawk followed, then the host, into a kitchen smelling of new bread and warm spices. By the hearth stood a slim and well-made young man, dejectedly stirring the stew pot. From another portion of the room hurried a girl: brown hair neatly done into a knot at her neck, sturdy hands drying themselves briskly on a clean white apron.

"What's this?" she cried, her eye full of two tall, ragged strangers; then she spied Aster. "Mother? You said nothing of guests—"

"I said I was gone to fetch the magician from the village, if he was still there and looked kindly on my case," said Aster sharply. "As it happens, he did, but could do nothing for me. However, his traveling companion has skill in finding what is lost and she has consented to help."

"Traveling—?" Again, those quick brown eyes counted Lute and Moonhawk, flashed back to the older woman's face. "You bring us a pair of gypsies to guest?"

"Even not, gracious Lady!" cried Lute. "For gypsies have the foresight to bring their houses with them, where I am so dimwitted as to have no house at all!"

"And so we ask travel-grace," added Moonhawk, in her deep, level voice, "from charitable homes along the way."

The boy at the cauldron laughed once, a sharp-edged sound carrying more scorn than merriment. "Bested, Senna," he called out. "Make welcome before they eat you alive."

"Wrong also, young sir," Lute said dulcetly. "For what person of dignity will stay in a house where welcome is not a gift?"

"As it is here," cried Aster, bustling forward, "most sincerely! Senna! Cedar! Your manners want brushing! Bow to Lady

Moonhawk, Witch of Dyan Temple, and to Master Lute the magician! Lady, Master—my eldest daughter, Senna; and—and Cedar, who is betrothed to my youngest—to Tael . . ." She caught her breath hard, then straightened and clapped her hands together.

"Quickly now, children! Senna, show the Lady and Master to the guesting room. Cedar, take hot water to fill the basins. Give them houserobes, Senna, and put their things to wash. I will be along in a moment with wine and a bit of cheese, to help you through till dinner . . ."

So directed, the two young things obeyed with startling will, and it was not too long before Lute was reclining shamelessly among a mountain of pillows, wineglass in hand, dressed in a houserobe of rich vermilion wool.

"Much better than eggs," he announced with satisfaction, and took a deep draught of wine.

Moonhawk looked over from the table at which she was combing her hair and paused, comb arrested. Lute glanced up, eyebrow quirking. "Yes?"

She recovered herself, finished the stroke and began another. "It is only that you look very nearly respectable, dressed so."

His eyes gleamed and he brought his glass up to drink.

"Who is he, Zinna?" demanded a girlish falsetto from across the room. "What do you mean who? That handsome fellow in the red gown, of course! Do you suppose he's a wealthy merchant? Perhaps a noblewoman's son . . ."

Moonhawk laughed, conquering the urge to turn and stare at the girl she knew was not there, put the comb down, picked up her glass and moved over to the pillows. "I didn't say handsome," she protested. "I said respectable."

"My hopes dashed," he sighed, face reflecting unsurpassed sorrow. He assayed the glass, slanted his eyes at her face. "Perhaps I'll have a try for the eldest daughter. This will be hers someday, after all, and with a few manners I'm certain she'd be quite tolerable."

"A mannerly woman is very important," Moonhawk agreed with false gravity and he inclined his head.

"Present company excluded, certainly."

She froze on the edge of hurling the contents of her glass into his gaunt brown face; sighed and shook her head.

"Always one step before me, Master Lute," she said, with equally false softness.

He tasted his wine. "Hardly that. At the most, half-a-step ahead and half-a-step to a side." He leaned forward suddenly; surprisingly extended a hand. "Come, cry friends! I swear I hadn't meant it to sting so sharply!"

Carefully, she put her hand in his, felt his fingers exert brief, warm pressure and then withdraw, leaving something light and cool in her palm. She cupped her hand and turned it over, revealing a tael-blossom.

"Named for the berry that gives the good wine," murmured Lute. "Heedless, but not cruel. And the elder sister's a shrew."

Moonhawk glanced up. "You think she left with forethought—and intent?"

He shrugged. "Perhaps they argued—the shrew and the heedless one—or perhaps love's veil was somehow shredded and she saw that dull young fellow for the boor he is."

"Quick judgments, Master Lute," she chided him. "You were with them for less than a quarter-glass."

"It's my business to make quick judgments," he said, unperturbed. "Magic must be good for something, after all." He waved a hand at the hourglass, now three-quarters done. "We shall soon have the opportunity to make less hurried appraisals. And then you will do your magic."

"Then I will ask the assistance of the Goddess in the pursuit of truth," Moonhawk corrected austerely, and he sighed.

"I WILL REQUIRE a new candle," Moonhawk told Aster, "a length of string or thin rope and something that belongs to Tael—preferably something she often had about her."

"At once," said Aster, face glowing with the half-sick hope that had filled her all through the meal, so that she pushed her food around the bowl and shredded the good, warm bread into untasted crumbs. She turned to her eldest, who was hovering with Cedar by the fire. "Senna. Bring Lady Moonhawk what she requires."

"Yes, Mother," the girl said quickly enough, though her mouth was turned down with ill temper. She bustled out and returned with a new candle in a wooden holder, a cord of fine white wool, a bright blue cloak and a string of pierced beads. She placed them, one by careful one, on the table, saw Moonhawk's eye on the cloak and faltered, a blush warming her cheeks.

"I know some feel it is sacrilege, Lady Moonhawk, for one of the world to wear Circle blue. But Tael loved the color. She spun the thread, wove the cloth, dyed it in taelberry juice, fashioned the cloak—all with her own hands. Being so, I thought it might aid you. This . . ." her fingers caressed the beaded necklace.

"Is my troth gift to her," Cedar finished harshly, and laughed. "Which she hardly wore."

"Still," said Aster, "it must have meant a great deal! Perhaps fear of losing it—"

"Yes, of course!" he said bitterly. "But the truth is that she would rather wear that length of leather and that stupid bit of wood—" He caught himself, folded his lips and made an awkward bow. "Your pardon, Housemother; my concern and grief make me short of temper."

"I see that it does," Aster replied, "but in just a few moments, Lady Moonhawk will find her and—"

"I also require," Moonhawk interrupted, "quiet. You may repair to the parlor. I will call as soon as I have found what there is to find." She looked hard at Aster. "Remember, this lies with the Goddess, not with mere mortal hope."

The older woman bowed her head, hand rising to touch her breast. "We abide by the will of the Goddess," she said devoutly. She beckoned the others with a sweep of her hand. "Come."

Moonhawk bent to arrange the items upon the table: candle to the north, string coiled before her, one end tied securely about the trothing gift. The cloak she considered for a long moment before laying it about her own shoulders and twisting the brooch closed.

"You may leave also," she said, without turning her head to look at Lute, leaning silent against the mantle.

"Ungracious, Lady Moonhawk!" he returned. "You watch my magic, after all. Fair trade is fair trade."

She did look at him then, for the fine voice carried an undercurrent of what—had it not been Lute—she would have identified as worry. "I have done this before," she said, wishing it didn't sound quite so tart. "It's a very simple spell."

"Nothing can go wrong," he agreed pleasantly, then brought a fingertip to his lips. "But here I am babbling when you require silence! Forgive me, Lady." He sank soundlessly to the bench and folded his hands in his lap.

"Silent as the dead, you find me. My master insisted upon the same condition when he was working, so neither of us is novice at our task."

Far more distracting to argue with him than to acquiesce, which she did with a tip of the head. She then ignored him, closing her eyes and offering the prayers that would ready her for the work.

Lute bent forward on his bench, foreboding like a chill handful of stone in his belly.

Moonhawk's breathing deepened; the lines smoothed out of her face, leaving it at once childlike and distantly cruel. She raised her left hand, eyes still closed, pointed a finger and lit the candle. She lowered the hand, lay it on the coil of twine and pulled in the necklace, holding it in her right hand.

She opened her eyes.

"By the grace, with the aid and in the Name of the Mother, I reach out to the one called Tael." With a smooth flip of the wrist, she hurled the necklace far across the kitchen, paying out the twine until the beads hit the stone flooring with a rustling clink.

"With the will of She Who Is, I call Tael to me." Moonhawk intoned, and began, slowly, to pull in the cord.

It came easily at first, sliding over the stones with a half-audible murmur. But midway to the table the cord faltered in its smooth passage through Moonhawk's fingers, picked up—and faltered again.

Lute craned forward, gravel-dread gone to ice in his gut, saw the necklace move jerkily into the circle of light cast by the candle—and stop altogether.

The Witch continued to work the cord, taking up the slack, then tightening the drag, until it stretched taut against the necklace, which moved no more, but lay as if welded to the floor.

He looked back, saw Moonhawk's eyes closed and sweat on her face, the cord taut as a lute-string between her hand and the troth-gift, quivering and giving off a faint, smoky luminescence.

The ice in his belly sent a shaft lancing upward into his chest and he came off the bench in a silent rush, meaning to shake her, to pull away the cord, even to shout—

The beads shifted against the floor with a sound like sobbing and, obedient at last, hurtled through the air to land with a clatter upon the table top, half-an-inch from the Witch's long hand.

Lute froze, staring at her face, willing her to open her eyes, to shake her hair back, extinguish the candle and put aside the blue cloak; to mock him, even, for his terrors—

She sat, still and silent as death. Beside her, the candle flame flickered and went out.

Finally, he moved; relit the candle and set it so the light fell full on her face. It was then he saw that she was crying.

"Moonhawk?" A cracking whisper; much unlike his usual manner. He reached forth a hand and touched her, lightly, on the shoulder. "Moonhawk."

She gasped and hurled back in her chair, lifting a warding hand, eyes wide now, and bright with terror.

"Moonhawk!" He caught the uplifted hand, and nearly gasped himself at the coldness of her flesh.

"Ah!" She cried and bent her head, making no effort to take her hand from his. Her breathing shuddered. "Gone," she mourned. "All gone. Goodbye sun. Goodbye flowers. Goodbye love. Hello dark. Mother? Mother! Where is she? Why is there no rest, no sweet embrace and welcome home?"

"Moonhawk!" He held tight to her, cupped her chin in his free hand—sacrilege, and worth a stoning, to touch the sacred body of a priestess without her aye—and forced her head up. Wide, unseeing eyes stared into his.

"Moonhawk sleeps," she said, still in that young, grief-sodden voice. "Tael was called and Tael is here—and here will remain until right is done." She put her hand up and gripped his wrist in cold, ice-cold, death-cold fingers.

"Avenge me."

THEY WERE GATHERED in a bright-lit parlor two steps down the hall from the kitchen: mother, daughter, and son-to-be, all with a bit of work to hand. The boy was mending a harness—competently, Lute noted with surprise; the shrew was setting tiny, precise stitches into a shirt. Aster sat with her work held lightly in her right hand, needle poised in her left—but she was not stitching. Her eyes dwelled dreamily upon the candle flame and she seemed lost to her surroundings.

Nonetheless, it was she who looked up as Lute paused outside the room, and she who rose to greet him.

"Master Lute. Is there—has Lady Moonhawk found my child?"

He smiled and bowed with professional grace, trying not to think of the mourning wraith he had left in the guesting-chamber, tucked among the pillows.

"The Lady Moonhawk," he intoned, "has wrought a very powerful spell. Your daughter has indeed been located and—Goddess willing—will be home tomorrow morning."

Joy lit Aster's face. She clapped her hands and looked to where her eldest still sat, calmly stitching.

"Senna, have you no ears? Did you not hear Master Lute say that your sister will be home tomorrow?"

She glanced up, brown eyes hard as pebbles. "And did I not say she would be home when she had done with whatever madcap scheme she was chasing?" She bent her gaze once more to her stitching.

"You would believe that some ill had come of her. Ill never comes to the likes of Tael, who laughs at everything." She made a particularly violent jab at the fabric with her needle before concluding, half-whispered, "As she will be laughing at all of us, tomorrow."

"Senna—" her mother began, shock blighting the joy on her face.

"Tomorrow?" That was the boy, rigid as a carving on the stool, harness forgotten in his hands. "If she's close enough to be here tomorrow, why don't we go and fetch her tonight?" He turned wild, glittering eyes on Aster.

"You'd do better not to let your hopes rise, Housemother! What do we know of this Lady Moonhawk, in truth? What word have we, except her own, that she is Circle-trained? Does she come to us properly clad—no! She comes like a ragged gypsy fortune-teller, bearing company with a—"

"Cedar!" Aster commanded. "Hold your tongue!"

"Yes, do," said Senna, bending to put her work into the basket. She stood and glanced from her mother to the boy. "Morning will be here soon enough, and then we can all judge the truth of the foretelling." She yawned, covering her mouth with work-scarred fingers.

"I, for one, believe the Lady, by whatever means she gained her knowledge," she concluded. "And now I am going to bed, the better to speed morning along. Mother?"

"Yes," said Aster distractedly, and turned to lay her mending haphazardly on the chair. "A good notion." She straightened and held out a hand. "Master Lute, thank you for your service to us. I will just step down the hall, Senna, and give thanks to Lady Moonhawk, also, and then—"

"Lady Moonhawk," Lute interposed smoothly, "was exhausted with the working of magic and has since retired. Doubtless there will be a time for speaking together, tomorrow."

"Doubtless," said Senna, sarcastically. She put a surprisingly solicitous hand under Aster's elbow. "Come to bed, Mother. Goodnight, Cedar. Master Lute."

"Dream sweetly," Lute wished, and bowed them out of the room. He turned in time to see Cedar come to his feet, harness falling unnoticed to the floor. He shambled forward, and started badly when Lute touched his arm.

"I see you're as wide awake as I am," the magician said, smiling into the bewildered young eyes. "Do the grace of walking with me. A touch of evening air and a bit of exercise are doubtless just what we both require." The boy simply stared. Lute smiled more widely, took a firmer grip on the arm and pulled him, unresisting, toward the kitchen and the door.

"Come," he said softly. "I'll tell you a story while we walk."

THE MOON WAS high, limning the countryside in silver, and the stars hung pure and unflickering just out of Lute's longest reach. He looked around with genuine pleasure.

"What a delightful scene! What delightful country, certainly, once one climbs out of the village. I thought of settling here this afternoon."

"But your mistress has no mind to rest," Cedar said, with a touch of his former acidity.

"You mistake me, child. I am my own man. And the Lady Moonhawk is indeed a Witch-out-of-Circle, properly attired or not. We happen to travel in the same direction. When either of us chooses a different way, why, then we shall part company."

Cedar unlatched the gate and they stepped through onto the track. Once more Lute looked about him. "Truly delightful! What direction shall we walk?"

Hope flickered in the boy's face, clearly discernible in the moonlight. He turned east, toward the village. "This way," he said eagerly.

Lute extended a hand, caught the boy's arm and turned him firmly west. "I've a fancy for this way, myself. Come, walk with me."

Hope died in that instant; the boy's shoulders sagged and something in his face crumbled—but he stayed stubbornly rooted, resisting the gentle tug of Lute's hand.

"Come," Lute repeated. He gestured with his free hand and plucked a silver bit from the starry air. Taking the boy's resistless fingers, he turned palm up and placed the money there, closing the fingers firmly.

"Here now," he said. "You've agreed to guide me—and taken my coin to seal the bargain. Let us walk this way." He pulled more sharply on the arm, and this time Cedar went with him, walking silently on rock-hard path, with Lute keeping pace beside.

They had gone for some little distance, silent, but for the magician's now-and-again comments on the surrounding country, or the stars, or the breeze, when Cedar glanced over.

"What is the story?"

"Your pardon?"

"The story," the boy repeated impatiently. "You said you would tell me as we walked."

"Ah," said Lute softly. "The story." He went another few steps along the path, glancing upward as if to ask the moon for guidance. "The story," he said again, "is this: Not very long ago—nor very distant—there walked on a path very like this one a young woman and her betrothed. It was a dewy morning, or a brilliant afternoon—though doubtfully evening, for she did not wear her cloak against the chill and it was not the moon's time of fullness—the path would have been too dark.

"So they went, these two, and as they went, they talked. Alas, the talk turned from pleasantries and flirtations to distressful, hurtful subjects. The lover accused the girl of being unfaithful to him, cried out that she refused to wear his troth-gift; that she refused, perhaps, to fix the date of their final vowing. He demanded to know the name of his rival; demanded to know by what right she—a woman grown and mistress of her own life—by what right she continued to wear the necklace she had always worn—the one he had not given her.

"He demanded these things, petulant, and she ignored him—ran a little ahead or to the side or exclaimed over a flower.

"Goaded, he said other things, ugly things, striving to be hateful, to hurt her, as a child will try to wound the adult who has disciplined him." Lute paused, glanced back at the boy, who had stopped on the silvery path and was staring ahead, hands fisted at his sides.

"Cedar?" he said softly. "Is that how it was?"

"She laughed at me!" the boy cried out. "Laughed! But I swear by the Mother—I never meant to kill her!"

"But you did kill her," Lute said, still soft.

"It was an accident!" Cedar half-raised his fists, anguish twisting his face. "She laughed and then she—she said that she was sorry, that of course she wouldn't wear my gift, that she had never—had never considered me a life-partner—" His voice caught, as if on a sob. "She said that she saw she had been wrong, that she had tried to be kind to me, until I outgrew my—my—" He brought his hands down, still fisted, to rest tautly against his thighs.

"I hit her," he said, and bent his head.

"One blow killed her?" Lute wondered, soft as thought. "Or were there more than one?"

"One!" Cedar wailed. "Only one, as the Goddess knows my soul. But she fell—I heard her head hit the rock and then she didn't get up . . . I knelt beside her and tried to—tried to lift her head—" He swallowed hard. "The blood . . ." He looked up and Lute marked the tears that dyed his cheeks silver in the moonlight.

"There is a—a spring-cave not far away. I carried her there; piled rocks around her so that the animals . . ." He swallowed again.

"It was early morning. After—that evening, I went to Mother Aster's farm, asking for Tael. She wasn't there. I waited—and I've been waiting. Soon, they would have given her up! Senna would have decided that Tael simply didn't wish to be found. Aster would have mourned—and taken up more good works in the village—and forgotten. Soon, there would have been—would have been peace. But you had to come and that Mother-blasted woman—how did she know?" he screamed suddenly, lunging forward and swinging a fist, randomly, it seemed to Lute, who merely stepped aside and let the rush go past him.

The boy whipped around, admirably quick, though still a shade uncautious, and braked so strongly he went down on a knee, loose stones clattering across the path.

"Wisdom, boy," Lute said, no longer soft, and plucked a silver sliver from the air. He made a magical pass and showed the kneeling youth a quick succession: sliver, stiletto, dagger, nothing. Sliver, stiletto, dagger . . .

Cedar licked his lips.

"Consider illusion," Lute directed. "Consider reality. You hold the coin I gave you still within your fist. Which of these is real, Master Cedar? Will you gamble your life that I only juggle air?" He ran the sequence again, and again, using the rhythm of the moves to add force to his words.

"The Lady Moonhawk is a Witch. She called Tael and come Tael did, demanding what right remains her—proper burial, benediction—truth. Our duty tonight is to have her home, laid out and decent for her mother to see at dawnlight. Your duty then is to tell the truth—for justice and peace—and your own salvation." He vanished the dagger for the last time and stood staring into the boy's eyes.

"Peace never came from lies, child. And hearts do not forget so quickly." He gestured. "Get up."

Cedar did, as if the gesture lifted him, and Lute nodded. "Show me the place."

"All right," said Cedar and turned westward once more on the path, Lute walking just behind.

IT WAS MANY hours later that Lute went into the laundry; stripped off the fine red robe with all its stains and tears; and washed, scrubbing himself from hair to toenails, rinsing and then scrubbing again. When he was done, he combed his hair and braided it, dug the silver knife from the sleeve of the discarded robe and used it to scrape the stubble from his cheeks.

Lastly, he dressed in his own clothes, damp though they were, and stood, shivering, thinking about the night's work.

Mercifully, the spring-cave had been cool, and the season not yet high summer. Sadly, something had been at one of the hands and there was, after all, the blood and other general nastiness attendant upon days-dead bodies. Her face—her face had been untouched, except for the bruise splashed across the right cheek.

In life, she had been beautiful.

Lute shuddered.

They had laid her in the parlor, across two benches pushed together, draped with an old quilt they had found near the wood box. They had crossed her hands over her breast—whole one over chewed—and combed her hair until it fell in gleaming waves straight back from her face to the floor.

Her eyes had already been closed.

"Blue," Cedar had said distractedly, touching her hair, her face, her folded hands. "Blue as tael-flowers, her eyes. You would have loved her, Master Lute, if you had seen her—as she was."

Lute shuddered again, whether in pity or revulsion he did not know.

The boy had declined to wash or sleep, saying it was not so long until dawn and if he was to see Mother Aster and tell her the whole, he might as well be there when she came down.

"Besides," he said softly, eyes on the dead girl's face. "She's home now. It would be graceless, to let her in the night alone."

Pity locked Lute's tongue. Leaving the reminder of three abandoned nights unspoken, he had gone to wash.

Washed, and in somewhat better control of himself, he quit the laundry and went to the guesting-room, dread 'round his heart like ice.

"MOONHAWK?" In the candle-glow he saw her, reclined among the pillows, wrapped in the blue cloak that she had not allowed him to remove. Her face was smooth, distant, childlike. Her breathing went in and out with regularity. He could not tell if her state was trance or sleep.

Sighing, aching in every joint, he sat on the pillows opposite, set the candle carefully aside and prepared himself to wait.

A scream wakened him.

Aster was the first he saw as he rushed into the parlor. Aster with her fist shoved against her mouth and her face white as her dead daughter's. Then he saw Senna, wide-eyed and staring, but not at Tael—at something, it seemed, upon the floor. At something which, now that he noted it, Aster stared as well.

Foreboding flared, too late, and he stepped into the room, looked over Aster's shoulder—

He had used a leather-hook; it lay by his right hand. The slash it had made across his throat was ragged—and very deep.

His eyes were still open.

"No!" Lute flung forward, went to his knees by the pooled blood, extended a useless hand—and pulled it back, clenched.

"Young fool! There was no need, no need." The tears were hot, they fell into the pooling red.

A hand touched his shoulder; warm fingers gripped him. Behind him he heard Aster shift and clear her throat.

"Cedar was so undone by my—by Tael's death that he killed himself. His love was such—"

"No," whispered Lute, and—

"No," said Moonhawk, as she gently kneaded his shoulder.

"Cedar killed your daughter, housemother—unintended, but he was the instrument of her death. We have the story, if you will hear it. And we will stay and help you bury them, with every proper rite, if you will have our help."

"I STILL DON'T understand why he did it," said Lute, playing a blue counter over his knuckles, disappearing it and reappearing a yellow, a red, the blue again, and, in addition, a green.

Moonhawk fed more twigs to the cook fire and glanced up at the starry sky. "Guilt," she said softly, "and pain—he did love her, I think. In his way. But his way was too sober for her—the heedless one, remember? The one who laughed at everyone." The fire flared and she ducked prudently back, keeping the blue cloak tightly around her.

"It happened so quickly—like a bad dream. To see her again . . . to know her dead . . ." She sighed. "May the Mother pity him."

Lute glanced at her sharply. "And yourself? I find you wholly mistress of your own soul and not sharing it with some heedless, teasing beauty?"

She laughed and tossed her hair back over her shoulders. "My own self and no other," she said softly. "Poor Master Lute. But while we were together, I did—dream." She glanced down, in a sort of maidenly shyness foreign to her usual manner. "I was never a free woman, you know. In the Circle, there is—duty. Some of Tael's memories were—interesting. I shall have think on them more fully, as Sister Laurel would have said."

"More fully," Lute echoed and shook his head, vanishing all four counters. "Well, take some advice and stick to my sort of magic in the future. Less dangerous. More lucrative."

Moonhawk laughed and pulled the pan from the fire. "Eggs, Master Lute?"

❖ ❖ ❖

So ends the second tale of Lute and Moonhawk.

✧ Moonphase ✧

THE WOOD BENCH was cool beneath her bare buttocks, the stone cold under her bare toes. No heat came from the empty fireplace, nor light from the empty oil lamps and candelabra. Despite the season the barred windows high in the walls were open.

She needn't see the walls, canted inward as they rose, to understand the meaning of the word prisoner, though it was a word unsaid by the Sisters and the Mother herself.

"You will be assigned more appropriate duties after you recant, Mendoza," they'd told her, already stripping away the dignity of the name that had come to her unbidden the first time she'd bled.

Mendoza, they called her now. More properly, Priscilla Delacroix y Mendoza. And what of Moonhawk?

She sighed, felt her dry skin shiver, and went to Lessons of Intent to remove her concentration from the discomfort and center it on the reality.

The reality she found was motion and what it meant. The breeze was motion—

Within the light breeze that chilled her bare breasts were odors of the evening: dinner smells from the dining hall for the Maidens-in-Training, the hint of expensive herbs burned by wealthy supplicants down on Mother's Row, the occasional acrid touch of metal and smoke from the foundry on the edge of the bay downriver.

It all meant that the wind was from the west, and the night would

99

be colder than last, and that in the morning they would take her to the Mother's Chamber to say a confession she would not make.

"You will recant," had said the Mother. "You will admit that you never heard Moonhawk calling, that you have always stolen your power from others, and that you were wrong to do so. You will be assigned to more appropriate duties, and given a Name-in-Keeping."

In the meantime they had left her here to meditate, for three days and nights, having left her only the earrings given her by a dead grandmother; Witches knowing better than to trifle with a gift of handwrought silver.

What they had taken! They'd taken amulets of power, bracelets of strength, stones that concentrated will. Then they'd subjected her to spells of unmaking, to other thefts . . .

Priscilla sat stiller now, thinking of the watchers. She'd know from the first moment that they watched, known that they'd taken Moonhawk's bracelets with trepidation, known they'd taken Moonhawk's Amulet only when the Mother and her Three Sisters had stood watching, only when the full Circle had cast spells of restraint and quiet. They'd stripped her then of everything but the earrings. Even her privacy was gone: the only light in the cell suite was the small constant green of an imported glow-ever beside the ancient waterless slot latrine.

To think that they'd feared her so much! If only she had the bracelets, even now—

She shivered. Even now she needed food. She needed drink. She needed Moonhawk as never before and Moonhawk had been forced away from her by the Council.

A tear came, and quickly she regretted it. No water here, no food. They wanted a weak and beaten, near-nameless Maiden, not Moonhawk-in-Training. Every tear was in their favor.

Now the breeze brought something else: the distant hum of voices, and now more, and then the City's temples were all heard, each chanting Tenth Chant.

Priscilla felt her throat seek the words and was surprised by it— she'd sung no chant since she'd been thrown here. She clamped her mouth on the words, but then relented. Tenth Chant Wardsday was Moonhawk's Chant.

She began then, low and quiet, eyes raised in the darkness. But all was not dark: high up was the silver glow of moonlight on the cold stone walls.

Priscilla had held the original of the chant in her own hands in the Library when she'd been permitted the boon of study of her namesake. She covered the trail of history entire: Moonhawk had helped build the world she lived in, had helped create the chants, had designed spells, had defined powers—Moonhawk had been there over and over when the Temple needed help. Priscilla had caressed the pages of those chants, had seen that the words were penned by two hands, not one—and she'd never gotten an answer to that question of why the other hand was a masculine hand. Sister Dwelva denied it, as she denied so much.

Sister Dwelva refused to discuss the notation on the side of the chant, in that second hand:

> *Here's a truth, for the survivor bold,*
> *always take silver, rather than gold,*
> *it's less the weight and more easily sold!*

NONSENSE, even arrogant—

Yet the front of the page was purity itself, words and feeling so perfectly meshed . . .she sang harder.

As the chant came stronger to her throat she saw that page again in the moonspot, felt she caressed the words and paper yet again—

"It was Lute, my dear," came the voice in her head. "It was Lute who made me write that one down. Lute who knew the value of silver and saved me through it. It was Lute you looked for, all unknowing, when they trapped you—aiiieee, girl; they have never let me at Lute again in all these centuries! And what shall we do for you now that they'd make you lie or have you stoned for truth?"

Priscilla never broke chant but she grasped her left wrist frantically, knowing the while that Moonhawk's bracelets had been torn away by magic and force—she'd first heard Moonhawk speak to her when she'd grasped the bracelet at Blood-test and had never been without it again until now—

"Look on the moon, youngster. It carries silver and its path is a bracelet about the planet. You have worked hard for me and it has cost you. Think on me . . ."

Outside, the chanting faded away. But Priscilla's eyes saw the moon gleam and she continued the chant, felt herself growing warmer.

"You'll need energy, tomorrow, too. You'll not be stoned if I have my way of it. If only you could touch the moonlight . . ."

There was a new sound as the city quieted after Tenth Chant. The bars and taverns were closed now, except at the spaceport's foreign zone; the houses were darkening, but there was a new sound—a sound of birds maybe, or rats!

It was not good to dwell on rats. Priscilla knew this. But Moonhawk's voice had told her to think on Moonhawk . . .

The last time she'd been truly filled with Moonhawk's vision and force she'd killed a woman and stunned another senseless. She'd left her post at the Temple and traveled—without permission—to the seedy bar where a Sintian man was about to give stolen Temple secrets over to an outworlder. And when she'd recovered the secrets, she'd let the surviving outworlders, mere spaceship crew—and the thief himself—go.

And she'd given her word—Moonhawk's word—that they would be safe. The single death had been atonement enough, for the dead woman had been the cause of the theft in the first place.

But Circle had wanted more: they'd wanted a show of power. They'd intended to turn the thief or thieves over to the crowds for a proper stoning, to quell the cyclic complaints that the Temple ran far too much of Sintian life.

Show of power? Instead now they would show power by sending her to be stoned for heresy if she refused to recant, or send her to the Temple of Release to be night comfort to the men and women who'd lost their spouses if she did.

"Politics, young one, politics. You did well for one unused to that level of command. Our whole order is based on proper use of intuition and the balance of life: but since the first coven was consecrated, there's always been that other—the greed of power, of personal importance. They'd not believe that I would let the starship people go, but what had they done? Accessories, accidental as they were. And the man? What good stoning him when the true trouble lay dead—aye, so you used a little too much force? It was at my behest, and the woman was dead before she arrived—that was in her eyes. But you hadn't time to see that—they've trained you for ceremonies instead of duty! If only they'd train you properly, let you find your love . . . even if it isn't Lute. I looked for him there, with your eyes, but he is not yet seen. They sing my praises and let me loose with virgins . . . they alter history for convenience and forget the truth—that I was sent on Quest to get me out of Circle because I demand Balance in my dealings and expect the same of others. The whole thing was politics, this time, and I had no time to warn you, that's all."

"But what of the Temple property! Temple secrets! It was important!"

The words sounded hollowly throughout the big room.

"Temple secrets!" mocked the voice in her head. "Samples of what they call the 'catalyst molecule' is what, in exchange for trading rights. They think it can make a Witch out of one without power. Old secrets pulled from the ship records they hide. Ah, they won't learn. Politics! You—*we*—did right to stop the theft, but then we should have fixed *all* of the problem. I swear that's why they haven't given me a smart girl to choose—until you—for three hundred years!"

"Given! Don't *you* choose?"

"I won't discuss it with you now. Later, if there's a way. We must get you strengthened! You must touch the moonlight!"

Priscilla stood then, knowing it was useless. She was slender—scrawny said some, until they saw her standing with Moonhawk's aspect upon her—and fairly tall. But the moonlight was still a half-dozen or more elbow lengths over her head, and the slant of the walls made it impossible for her to climb that high.

She tried standing on the bench that was her bed, and that was too short, as well. And if she leaned the bench against the wall?

She tried it, willing tired muscles to push the heavy wood into place near the wall, and then tried to lean it—no. Logic showed it could not work: the bench would wedge itself in and there was no way she could stand on the end of it then . . .

She pushed the bench over; it fell with a crash, the low backpiece splintering noisily.

She stood in the darkness, naked and exhausted, sweat cooling rapidly on her body. She began to shiver and with it came an inner blackness so total—

"I have failed you, Moonhawk! I am too weak, too—" There was no sound, within or without. Whatever the watchers heard or thought was as hidden from her as Moonhawk.

"They will stone me, then, that's all, and the Circle will continue. Moonhawk can choose a better vessel and all will be well with the world."

She said that and the words came back to her and then struck her full force. She'd seen stonings twice and had been sickened by them; but now, to have the crowd after her?

There was no panic. She would hang herself, that's all. She could use the empty lampholder to tie her hair to, tie it around her neck as well, and then jump from the bench and—

"Will you kill Moonhawk?" came the question.

"Never! Moonhawk lives!"

"Precisely. Moonhawk lives. I may withdraw from time to time, and be subject to meddlings, but I live. Lute lives, too, though they deny it. For that matter, Priscilla Delacroix y Mendoza lives. I swear that if you ever in life attempt an unreasonable suicide again I will abandon you forever! They've pretty well got me walled out, you know, but then they've got a couple dozen full-strength Sisters working on this. Don't fight them with your magic, child; they must believe it's all mine! Now, if you can use your head—"

In the darkness Priscilla moved, tripped on the splintered backrest as she looked at the light on the wall. The moon was nearly to the zenith—the touch of silver light might move down the wall another handspan or two but . . .

"Lady Moonhawk, guide me!" said the girl, but she was already moving. She pushed the bench toward the spot of moonlight on the wall carefully. Then she hurried, bare feet soundless on the cold stone, to the backrest.

It was heavy, but it was long enough. She climbed onto the bench. It swayed slightly, but would surely hold. Then she ruthlessly twisted the ends of her hair into a quick braid, and pulled the braid into the cracked wood at the end of the backrest.

She swayed and missed the spot the first try, and the next—each time wincing as the end of the impromptu pole fell away from its target, straining hair roots unmercifully.

The third time she came close, but her braid fell from the pole. Her arms were cramped and the back of her neck ached. She was sweating and shivering at once as she tugged her hair into the splinters. Somehow it was the other side of that chantpage she saw . . . "less the weight, more easily sold."

"I'm crazy," she said. "They're right. I'm crazy—"

But the fourth time did it. The wide end of the stick landed in the midst of the patch of moonlight and she twisted it in her hands to expose the braid to the silver light.

Nothing happened. She'd expected—

Well, what had she expected, she wondered. Power? Escape? Wings?

She waited. The stick leaned against the wall, taking some of its weight off her arms. She didn't feel as tired as she expected, but—

"Patience. It seems they'll kill you if we're not careful, and you're far too good to be killed over politics. I'm afraid this round's going to be a draw. So call on the Moon for what you really need now, and hurry! But never recant. They can take your power only if you give in!"

Priscilla stood, arms over head, staring at her hair in the silver light. Then she began chanting, the properly measured chant of Moonhawk's own words.

The vision she saw was not of the Moon, nor of freedom, but of a man. Not simply any man, though—a man gaunt of face with fingers so strong they'd crush rock to powder, fingers so gentle they'd caress and tease a breast for hours . . .

Lute! she realized. Lute the Magician. She'd read of him, both good and bad. In the public schools he was a legend and in Temple training he was example. She'd read the tracts explaining away his magic and showing a novitiate how to see through the sleight-of-hands he'd performed . . . the more recent books had him as an amiable charlatan, persuaded of the Goddess through Moonhawk's True Power. They'd been lovers!

The thought burned her: she been taught a Moonhawk strong and pure, celibate. But Moonhawk had had a lover . . .

She'd touched his words, too, then! And could power but go to power? Surely Moonhawk's lover—

"Lute," she called outloud then. "Lute! Lend me your power! Lute, by the Goddess—"

She heard a noise and returned to her chant, her demand still echoing up the walls toward the open windows—

They came quickly: dozens of them, including the entire Inner Circle. They came brandishing open-flamed torches and with silver and stone headdresses. They came with eleven of the fourteen living Names among them, and with spell-proof outworld rope they pulled her from her perch, bruising her breasts and legs. They chanted back, and with two Sisters on each arm and three on each leg they held her face down on the stone floor to stop her voice, and they took the finest of knives and slashed at her hair, cutting and hacking at it till it fell everywhere around her.

"How dare you!" screamed one of the Inner Circle when the hacking was done. "How dare you! To call on a charlatan within the Goddess' own hold? What use can some mere male trickster be to you, fool? Heresy in the Temple itself! In the morning you will recant!"

"No!" shouted the girl, bruising her lips on the floor. "Not while Moonhawk lives! While Moonhawk lives, so does Lute, and he is a Name!"

"You will be stoned for that!" said another of the Circle, tracing stars in the air, and then patterns that glowed bright red. "False Moonhawk! Recant, give up your magic, or it will be taken!"

Within her, the voice, distant, cool. "These fools forget the well they drink from—Never recant! If they take my Name you have yours, Priscilla, never forget! When they take Sintia's blessing you'll be as invisible to them . . . We are angry, Priscilla!"

Within, Priscilla felt heat, and the nearest to her shrank away from the power there.

"I'll not recant!"

Another voice, perhaps the Mother herself, said quietly, "Let it begin then—"

The woman holding her left arm began to twist it, and nearby a sword rattled.

From where she lay she could see her dark hair scattered about the floor and feet, and the glitter of high-level magics on everything. Her cheek hurt.

"I was always concerned of this one—" said someone as she was kicked.

She managed to see the woman who spoke: an older woman, politically secure—

"Will you stone Moonhawk, Ignela Rala y Duedes? You whose names are also Renata Dulavier Francotta and—"

"Stop!" said the woman, using the power of Command, the same command that Moonhawk and Priscilla had killed a woman with. "*Stop!*"

"—Sylvette Anna Ringwald? It isn't required. Moonhawk is walking away from your ken for now, leaving your necessity behind for this generation. Remember that she is in every Temple, and will know how you deal!"

They beat her then, with rods of metal and gems, and each touch was an agony, as if her soul were being drained, and they twisted her arms and spoke Commands and Spells.

When they twisted her arm again she screamed, and when they twisted further, she screamed again, calling out for Moonhawk and Lute. For a moment she felt as if Lute were at the door, drawing sword—

"*No!*" came the word in Priscilla's head. "He can't stand against so many Names yet! He stirs, though, girl—he stirs! I must find him—live your life. You will not be forgot!"

Within Priscilla there was a sigh, and a relaxation of will: Moonhawk could not save her, Lute would not save her. And Moonhawk was elsewhere now.

A jubilant cry sprang from a close-eyed woman in the back of the room: "Gone, Sisters, the false Moonhawk is gone!"

THEY LEFT HER after awhile, in the darkness, having exhausted an amazing amount of magical energy on her. They took with them the wooden bench, and they burnt her hair where it lay, that she'd not have influence over any holder of it, should her false magic return.

She lay naked on the stones, and cried. She was going to die now, or very soon, and badly. The bruises and scrapes ached at her soul. What had she gotten in this life? What right had any of them—all she'd really wanted was to live a good life, in Balance, to honor the Goddess, to live well. What could she do now—

The noises she'd heard before came closer now. Rats? Bats?

There was a clatter. And another. The sound of wings. More clatter. Something fell on her thigh, jerking her sharply awake. She reached—

And found a thing about the size of her thumb, dimpled and light . . . a frenal nut! As she cast around she found more; there was a rain of them now. She'd wanted food, and here was food, of a sort. If she could just have enough strength to face them once more—

There was a louder flutter, and a keening. A large bird swooped past her head, settled in on the stone floor. She could hear it walking, could almost make out its form in the night.

The bird's head bobbed and it dropped an offering—a harvest plum. As it jumped into the air she saw its markings in the distant light: a hawk it was . . .

IN THE MORNING Priscilla Delacroix y Mendoza was declared dead by her mother, in open court. It was a minor thing. Being a civil matter, its transmission to the world was delayed by a more important announcement.

This more important announcement went first to the rest of the Names who Lived, who meditated upon it for some hours before declaring officially to the Temple that Moonhawk was dead. Thence to the underlings went the news by those who would take the message to other Temples in the City, with the true and proper story: young Moonhawk had turned back the theft of all that was Holy and returned to the Temple a key to Balance. In so doing, her mission for the Mother in this life was fulfilled, and she had returned to the fold.

IN THE TEMPLE basement a lone guard stared down at the prisoner a long time before nudging her awake with his foot. He'd considered—but no, not in the Temple, and not with that damn bird staring down at him from the empty lamp holder.

"Get up, you," he said, kicking at her a little harder. "Get out!" He threw her a rough and ragged shift, a castaway from the alms box.

"If you ain't out by next chant, you're up for trespassing in the Temple! Can't trust any of you Nameless."

She was full of pains and aches, but overriding that was an emptiness that was like a drug that dulled her senses. Things weren't as sharp; she could not summon warmth—

Priscilla reached out, unwillingly accepting the new because the past was totally gone; she put the shift on, and stood slowly. She was cold, but here was a little bit of food, and—

The man was staring pointedly at her breasts. She put her head high, felt the ache in the back of her neck, suddenly feeling the weight of his words.

Nameless. Dead. A nothing—No longer Moonhawk. No right to be bare-breasted in public. No right to call the Goddess Mother . . .

Awkwardly, unnaturally, she buttoned the shift across her bruised and chaffed breasts, felt its hem rub on the raw bruises on her thighs.

There was an explosion of wings behind her, and the bird that had been poised there flew out the door and to the left.

"Out, damn you!" snapped the guard. "Look at this mess we gotta clean up! By the Goddess' good foot, get out!"

Numbly, she gathered together a few more of the nuts. Food. A little bit of food.

The man pushed at her roughly.

"Get out! You're not wanted. You're *dead*!"

She ran then, ran out the door and to the left, ignoring the open door to the right that led upramp into the beggars courtyard.

"I'm not," she said to the wall as she climbed the stairs. "I'm not dead."

She stopped at the door to MaidenHall, waiting for the tingle of acceptance at the crossboard in the stone floor—

There was none.

There was nothing. No quiet gong sounding the advent of a maiden, no warning brangle of alarm bells, no roar of tarfire from the pot over the door

Nothing.

She stepped through then and touched the naming stone with a bare foot.

Nothing again. Moonhawk's name was not intoned by the four guard coyotes, long-frozen by spell, nor did they raise hackles and charge. She was there, Nameless.

Moonhawk's words came back to her: too much training had gone before for her to continue without some ceremony.

"Priscilla," she said meekly.

Again nothing happened. No repetition, no echo, no—

She realized then she was a thief in Temple!

She ran with trepidation, furtively, until she found the locker that had been hers briefly but that had always been Moonhawk's.

To stop a thief one uses locks. So had the wise women of Sintia done, and the sight of that silver-bright lock sent shivers of fear and indignation through Priscilla. What could she do now? She'd certainly starve, unable to get at what should be hers. And how dare they assume she stoop to stealing—

Incongruously, she laughed, and it was a true laugh despite everything, one that took in all the ironies—

She felt the sound of added laughter, distantly heard within her a voice new and thrilling—a male voice!

"You've a chance to survive then, haven't you? It isn't always easy, but girl, *look*! It's only a silver lock, all curled about with magic signs that'd burn the hands off any believer still shackled to their cow-eyed vision—"

Priscilla recoiled at that description—felt the distant voice pause—

"—Can't argue with you now, dammit. She needs help for this trick of hers and I—Priscilla, get a pin or a nail."

The voice felt different, even more distant—but Priscilla took one of Delana-who-was-Oatflower's favorite stainless steel pins from her unkempt locker top and found herself in front of Moonhawk's locker, lock held precisely thus—

Her hands pulled on the lock expertly as the pin searched within; she felt her muscles respond to minute ridges the pin struck, felt her wrist twist this way while the other hand pulled that way and the pin slammed home and—

Twang—

"Done. Luck be with you girl, 'cause we can't go beyond the door with you. Never give in!"

Priscilla pulled the lock off the clasp and hurriedly began stuffing the locker contents into a cloth sack: shoes, a belt, work trousers, a few old copper and aluminum coins—

She left to the Temple and its minions the costly clothes, the makeups, the gold armbands and necklets, signs of power, while happily grabbing up the tight-wrapped soya bar she'd left negligently behind the week before. She covered her newly-shorn head with an old blue kerchief that had been a dusting rag for Moonhawk's ceremonies. What else?

Her gaze fell again to the bright-wrought things, eyes full of the greed of necessity. Dare she?

An odd song tickled at the back of her head, though she couldn't catch the words. Still—When she moved on she held her right hand tight to seven silver bracelets.

She turned toward the door, found she still held the silver lock in her left hand, under the twisted top of the cloth bag. Her impulse was to toss it away—

Silver! She looked at the magic symbols, shrugged her shoulders, and dropped the lock into the bag.

"Good girl!" came distant approval. "Silver travels well! Go as far as you can!"

She hobbled out as best she could then, the grief chants of the Temple covering the sound of her ungainly escape.

Across Sintia' the Priestesses waited for the proper hour, and then covered the carved Temple figures of Moonhawk in green cloth, signifying her return to the Goddess, this time.

No one dares mention that the eyes in the statues continued to glow, despite the funereal announcement.

No one dares mention to the Inmost Circle that Moonhawk still lives.

✧✧✧✧✧✧

So ends the 55th tale of Lute and Moonhawk.

✧ Pilot of Korval ✧

Dutiful Passage en route to Venture
Standard Year 1339

MASTER PILOT VEN'DUCCI sighed and folded his hands on the practice board. By these signs, Er Thom knew himself to be in desperate straits.

"I had heard from Captain yos'Galan," the Master said quietly, "that you had achieved a level of skill equal to that of a second class pilot. Perhaps I misunderstood?"

Er Thom inclined his head respectfully. "In fact, sir, I have achieved my second class license."

The Master's eyebrows rose, as if in astonishment. "Have you, indeed? Show it, of your kindness."

Now he was in for it in truth. A short series of keystrokes from the board at which they sat, and Master ven'Ducci could transform the treasured second class license into a mere third class—or into no license at all. Such was the power of a master pilot.

Still, it would reflect poorly on his *melant'i*—and on the *melant'i* of the captain, his mother—if he were seen to either flinch or hesitate in the face of this order. Er Thom neither flinched nor hesitated, but pulled the card from its slot in the practice board and held it out to his instructor in fingers that were, amazingly, steady.

Master ven'Ducci received the license gravely and subjected it to a leisurely, frowning study, as if he had never seen such a thing before.

Er Thom folded his hands forcibly in his lap and set his tongue between his teeth, lest he be tempted to blurt out any of the defenses of his own skill that were rising in his throat.

Halflings defended before they were attacked, and he, Er Thom yos'Galan, was not a halfling. He was a pilot of Korval. Specifically, he was a *second class* pilot of Korval, the license fairly earned on the same day that Daav his foster-brother, boon comrade and fiercest competitor, received his *provisional* second class.

Master ven'Ducci finished his inspection and laid the license on the edge of the board.

"How came you by this?"

Er Thom took a careful breath, and met the man's eyes with what he hoped was grave calm.

"I came by it at Solcintra Pilot's Hall, on Banim-Seconday in the first relumma of the current year." He had more than one cause to remember the day well, though very nearly a full Standard Year had passed. Er Thom licked his lips, hands stringently folded upon his knee.

"Testing that day established me as a second class pilot. Master Hopanik signed the license herself."

"'Testing that day'," Master ven'Ducci repeated. "Yes, I see."

Er Thom felt his face heat, his fingers tightening convulsively. He *would* be calm, he told himself sternly. He would.

Master ven'Ducci picked up Er Thom's license and held it in his palm as if weighing it for merit.

"It is sometimes the case," he said, in the mode of instructor to student, "that the exhilaration of the test itself will call forth heightened response from a candidate. The results of such testings are not invalid so much as misleading. It may well be, young sir, that your proper rating at this time is second class provisional. It is certainly true that your results at these boards, over the time we have been working together, fall significantly short of the results one is accustomed to receive from solid second class pilots."

Er Thom bit his tongue, refusing to beg. If he was a failure, if he lost his license this moment and spent the rest of his life balancing cargo holds, he was yet the son of Chi yos'Phelium—of Petrella yos'Galan. He would not shame his Line.

"So." Master ven'Ducci glanced at the license and slid it into the pocket of his vest. Er Thom's stomach twisted, but he sat still, and, gods willing, showed no distress.

"I will consider the proper course to chart from this circumstance," the master pilot said. "Attend me here tomorrow at the usual hour."

"Yes, Master." Somehow, Er Thom managed to stand, to make his bow and walk, calmly, from the inner bridge.

He was scheduled for dinner this hour and his mother, the captain, had made it plain during his first few days' service that she rated moody, self-indulgent boys who skipped meals just slightly lower than Port panhandlers too lazy to apply themselves to a job.

Er Thom swallowed and deliberately turned his back on the hall that would eventually lead him to the cafeteria. He could not possibly eat. He swallowed again, blinking back tears.

His license. He *was* a second class pilot! The tests had not been in error! If only—if only he could speak to Daav! If only his foster mother, Daav's true-mother and twin sister to Er Thom's mother the Captain—if only Chi yos'Phelium were here. But, of course, she wasn't. He had neither seen nor spoken with her since the day he had won the license.

He had always known that his true-mother would one day claim him to serve on *Dutiful Passage* and learn his life-roles of captain and trader, just as he had always known that Daav would someday leave home to attend Scout Academy. He had simply been caught . . . unprepared . . . when "one day" became "this day," and he was suddenly swept into his mother's orbit, away from everything that was usual and comforting; his one cold joy the new license in his pocket, which proved him a pilot of Korval.

It was no inconsiderable thing to be a pilot of Korval. Indeed, he had learned that it was no small thing to be cabin boy on the clan's flagship, true-son and heir of Captain and Master Trader yos'Galan. The child of generations of space-goers, Er Thom had adjusted easily to his duties and to ship-life. He had adjusted less easily to the absence of his fosterbrother, who had been within his arm's reach for the sum of both their lives. Er Thom's earliest memory was of gazing into his brother's face, watching the black eyes watch him in return.

"Good shift to you, young sir."

Er Thom gasped, jolted out of his misery by the quiet greeting, and hastily bowed—junior to senior—to Mechanic First Class Bor Gen pin'Ethil.

"Sir, good shift."

The mechanic considered him out of wide gray eyes. "One remarks that it is the dinner hour," he said delicately.

Er Thom gritted his teeth and bowed again. "One also marks the hour," he said, politely. "However, there is—a book—in one's quarters . . ."

"Ah, but of course." A smile showed briefly. "A cabin boy must always be at study, eh?"

"Just so," Er Thom said and bowed a third time as the other passed by.

Legs none too steady, Er Thom went on, and very shortly thereafter laid his palm against the plate set into the door of his cabin.

He felt the scan crackle across his skin, then the door slid open. He all but jumped through, the lights coming up to show a stark little cubicle made smaller by the built-in folding desk, which was extended to its fullest, and overladen with books, readers, and clipboards. The slender bed was tucked under the lockers in which the rest of his clothing and possessions were stowed, the bed itself occupied by a long, thin figure dressed in a dark long sleeved shirt, vest and leggings of black space leather, booted feet crossed at the ankle, hands crossed over his belt.

Er Thom stared, not quite daring to believe the rather solid evidence before him.

"Daav?" he breathed.

The black eyes opened, the dark head moved on the pillow, and the familiar, beloved smile infused the sharp-featured face with beauty.

"Hullo, *denubia*," he said, swinging his long legs over the edge of the bed and sitting up. "What's amiss?"

Er Thom stared, the skin of his palm still tickling with the after-effect of the scan.

"How," he demanded, rather faintly, "did you get here?"

"Oh, there's nothing to that!" Daav told him. "I can show you the trick, if you like." He tipped his dark head, mischief glinting. "Own that you're glad to see me, beast, or I shall be inconsolable."

"Yes, very likely," Er Thom retorted reflexively, then laughed and threw his arms wide. "In truth, I was just wishing for you extremely."

"Well, there's a proper welcome!" Daav rose and flung himself into the embrace with a will. For a moment, they clung, cheek to cheek, arms each about the other. Er Thom stepped back first.

"But, truly, Daav, how *did* you get here?"

"To the *Passage* you mean?" He moved his shoulders. "I cast myself at the feet of an elder Scout, who was bound for this quadrant." Mischief glinted again. "Surely you don't think I walked?"

"But, the Academy . . ." Er Thom gasped, suddenly struck with a thought almost too horrible to contemplate. "You haven't—they never *rusticated* you?"

"Rusticated me?" Daav looked properly outraged. Which of course proved nothing. "Certainly they did not *rusticate* me! Of all the notions! I suppose you've never heard of term break?"

"Term . . ." Er Thom blinked, counting the relumma backward, and sighed. "I never thought of it," he confessed. "But, surely, our mother . . ."

"Gave her leave, saving only that I find my own way out and back and that I arrive early to my first class at break-end." Suddenly, Daav stretched, and put a hand on his lean middle. "What's the nearest hour for a meal, Brother? I'm not halfway hungry."

Well, and that was no surprise. Er Thom sighed and tried to look stern.

"As it happens, I'm scheduled for dinner this hour. Perhaps I can convince the cook to give you a few dry crackers and a glass of water."

"A feast!" Daav proclaimed gaily, and slid his arm through Er Thom's, turning them both toward the door. "Come, let us test your powers of persuasion!"

"TOOK YOUR LICENSE?" Daav stared, soup spoon halfway to his mouth. It was his second plate of soup. The first had vanished with an alacrity unusual even by Daav's standards, and Er Thom suspected that the elder Scout had not been overgenerous with rations. "Pray, what profit comes of taking your license?"

Er Thom moved his shoulders and looked down at his plate. He had made some inroads into his own meal—at least he would not be called to book for neglecting his duty to stay healthy.

"Master ven'Ducci feels my proper rating is provisional second," he told his plate. "One . . . understands . . . him to believe that the—the strain of carrying a full second class is . . . interfering . . . with one's studies."

"Rot," Daav said comprehensively. "Does he think you're to finish at second class? We're both for master, darling—unless you believe our mother will allow us anything less?"

"No, of course not," Er Thom replied. Chi yos'Phelium had never held shy of telling her sons exactly what she expected them to accomplish on behalf of Clan and kin, and neither Er Thom nor Daav could conceive of failing her.

Daav had another sip of soup. "Do you fly live?"

"Live?" Er Thom blinked. "I fly the dummy board on the inner bridge."

"A second class pilot, practicing at a dummy board?" Daav demanded. "What nonsense!"

"Oh, I suppose you practice live!" Er Thom retorted, stung.

"Of course I do," his brother answered, with a surprising lack of heat. "It's required."

"In fact," he said after swallowing the last bit of soup, "I sat second board to the elder Scout on the trip out. I don't doubt but I'll make the same trade with another pilot for the ride back." He lifted his eyebrows, from which Er Thom deduced that he had allowed his astonishment to show.

"Surely you can't think that the ever-amiable Lieutenant tel'Iquin would lift extra mass where there was no profit to herself?"

"As I have not had the pleasure of the Lieutenant's acquaintance—" Er Thom began, and broke off as a shadow fell across the table between them.

"So," said Captain Petrella yos'Galan, and there was a hard shine in her blue eyes that Er Thom had learned meant the entire opposite of his fostermother's twinkle. "Nephew. Well I had a beam from your mother my sister, desiring me to expect you. When did you think you would come and register your presence with the Captain?" She inclined her head, in mock courtesy. "Or perhaps you believe the ship will feed you for free?"

"Aunt Petrella, my mother sends her love," Daav said with a calm Er Thom envied. "I regret that the desire to see my brother caused me to delay making my bow to the Captain." He smiled one of his sudden, transforming smiles. "And I surely never expected the ship to guest me. I am able and willing to work my passage."

"You relieve me," Er Thom's mother said punctiliously. "And your passage is—?"

"I have ten Standard Days for the ship," Daav said. "At Venture, I will barter for a lift back to Liad."

"And your mother agrees to this." She raised a hand. "No, do not speak. I have her beam. My sister assures me that she reposes faith in both your abilities and in your oath to be early to the first class of the new term. The matter is outside my authority. Within my authority, however . . ." She frowned down at them both.

"Er Thom is not at liberty. He has his studies and his assigned duties, which do not disappear because you have chosen to appear."

Daav inclined his head. "Nor am I at liberty, as we have both agreed that I shall work my passage."

Petrella's lips bent in her pale smile. "So we have. At what work are you able, Nephew?"

"I might be of some small service to the cargo master," Daav said. "I might also be put to use in the mechanics bay or at clerical." He picked up his mug and had a sip of tea before slanting a quick, black glance at Er Thom and looking back to the captain. "I can help my brother with his piloting."

Er Thom felt a jolt. Daav tutor him at piloting? Now, there was turnabout! He felt a glare building, then remembered that Master ven'Ducci held his license hostage and subsided, eyes stinging.

Happily, neither his brother nor his mother seemed to have noticed his near display.

"Oh?" Petrella said, with the ironic courtesy that characterized so much of her discourse with her son. "Last I had heard, you held a second class provisional."

"I now hold a first class provisional," Daav said, with a remarkable lack of preening. "Of course, one requires flight time."

"Which one gains," Er Thom murmured, suddenly enlightened, "by sitting second board to Scout pilots in trade for transport."

Petrella frowned down at him. "Master ven'Ducci has spoken to me," she began.

"Master ven'Ducci," Daav interrupted, against best health, "is an idiot. Come, Aunt! Who ties a second class to a dummy board?"

Both of her eyebrows rose and Er Thom held his breath, waiting for one of her blistering scolds to fall upon Daav's heedless head.

"So, we agree again," Petrella murmured, and there was something less of irony and somewhat more of courtesy in her voice. "You will be pleased to learn then, both of you, that Master ven'Ducci has been instructed to use the Captain's Shuttle for future piloting lessons, beginning tomorrow. I will see to it that your schedules coincide for that lesson, and then—we shall see." She fixed Daav in her eye.

"If I hear aught of mayhem from the master pilot, you will find yourself early indeed for first class, young Daav. Do I make myself sufficiently plain?"

Respectfully, he inclined his head, but Er Thom saw his eyes dancing in mischief. "Aunt, you do."

"It is well." She sighed. "Apply to the first mate for quarters and ship-garb—your brother will show you the way. Your work schedule will be on your screen tomorrow at first hour; pray do not be tardy." Her gaze shifted. "My son . . ."

Er Thom raised his face to hers.

"Mother?"

Her lips bent once more in her slight smile, and she reached into her belt, withdrawing a flat rectangle. Er Thom's hand leapt out, fingers questing, and his mother's smile, strangely, deepened.

"Not a pilot," she murmured, perhaps to herself. "What nonsense." She put the license into his hand and inclined her head.

"Be worthy of it, child of Korval."

HE SAT SECOND board to Daav, Master ven'Ducci a poised, silent presence in the jump-seat at their backs.

"Systems check," Daav murmured, hands moving with precision across his board. Er Thom followed his brother's lead, hands steady and careful, waking that portion of the piloting board which was the responsibility of the copilot. Screens lit, toggles glowed, maincomp beeped. The comm unit likewise beeped as information began to flow in from *Dutiful Passage*. Er Thom fielded the data, translated it, replied and received yet more data.

"The ship wishes us gone, brother," he said, scarcely noting that he spoke. "We are cleared to leave immediately, if that is the pilot's pleasure."

"Nothing more," Daav answered, and threw him a grin. "We have a course, I see, locked to navcomp."

Er Thom looked—a two hour run?—then his brother's voice drew him back to his immediate duty.

"Pray request *Dutiful Passage* to open the bay door."

Er Thom flipped the toggle that opened the voice line. "Captain's Shuttle ready for departure. Request bay door open."

"Bay door open," affirmed the cool voice of the pilot on duty at the starship's main board. "Good lift, pilots."

Screen One showed the bay door iris; Daav laughed, slapped the toggle, and the shuttle rolled free.

"MUCH IMPROVED," Master ven'Ducci said, nearly three hours later, as they stood once again in the bay corridor. He bowed, very slightly. "I am encouraged, Pilot yos'Galan."

Er Thom returned the bow. The lift had been a fine and bewildering thing. The simulations he had been flying were meticulously crafted, but live flight—live flight was different! He was still a-tingle with energy, his thoughts as sharp as fabled Clutch crystal, standing tall in an exhilaration that persisted despite the full knowledge of having several times bungled his board.

"You will both attend me here tomorrow at the same hour," the master pilot said, and with another slight bow strode away down the hall. Er Thom stared after him, frowning.

"Trouble, darling?" Daav was fair glittering himself, black eyes wide in his narrow face.

Er Thom drew a deliberate breath, trying to quiet the exuberant pounding of his heart. "Say, rather, puzzlement. I botched things rather badly at the phase-change and yet he makes no mention of it. Had I made an error one-twelfth as grievous on the practice board, he would not have held shy of apprizing me, never fear it! Yet, today, with three ham-witted errors to my tally, he is 'much encouraged'!"

"Perhaps he means to see if you repeat the errors tomorrow?"

"Repeat them tomorrow?" Er Thom stared. "I should never had made them today! I've been working phase equations in my head since Master Robir showed us the forms, when we were eight."

"Learning curve," Daav said, linking his arm in Er Thom's and beginning to stroll down the hall in the master pilot's wake. "I tremble to tell you how badly I've bungled my math at piloting. We were training on sling landings, you see, and I transposed my vectors."

Er Thom laughed. "Tell me you came in upside down!"

"But of course I came in upside down," Daav said amiably. "And hung upside down in the sling, like seven sorts of fool, while Master dea'Cort used my situation to lesson the rest of the class on the need to thoroughly check one's equations." He sighed and looked briefly mournful, then dropped Er Thom's arm with a grin.

"Enough telling tales out of piloting class!" he said gaily. "It will no doubt astonish you to learn that I am ravenous. If we hurry, I can wheedle an apple out of the cook before reporting to the cargo master for duty. Catch me."

He was gone, running full speed down the hall.

Er Thom bit back a newly acquired curse and hurtled after.

IT WAS WELL into Fourth Shift and both of them should have been long a-bed. Instead, they were in the control room at the heart of the *Passage*. Er Thom was sitting first board. There was no second. Daav was leaving for school on the morrow. He sat, hands folded on his lap, in what would have been the jump-seat in a smaller ship—a passenger on this, their last flight together.

Er Thom's hands moved across the board with swift surety, no wasted motion, no false moves. His face was intent and his shoulders just a bit rigid, but that was expectable, the sim he was flying being somewhat in advance of his skill level.

The screen flashed a familiar pattern—Daav's own particular nemesis, as it happened—and he leaned forward, watching as Er Thom adroitly—one might say, casually—fed in the proper course for an avoid, and the simultaneous adjustment to ship's pressure. Quietly, Daav sighed, leaned back in his chair—and jerked forward the next moment as the screen flared and Er Thom's elegant choreography degenerated into a near random slap at the Jump button, which was entirely wrong and too late besides.

Using the exercise he had been taught by the Scouts, Daav released the tension in his muscles, then put his hand on his brother's shoulder.

"A good run, darling. Don't repine."

Er Thom looked up, blue eyes flashing a frustration of his own ineptitude that Daav understood all too well.

"It can't quite be a good run, can it," he snapped, "when the ship is destroyed around one?"

"Well—no," Daav admitted. "On the other face, you flew further than I have yet to fly."

"Truly?" Er Thom looked so startled that Daav laughed.

"Yes, truly, you lout! Remember me, the ten-thumbed junior brother?"

"All too well, thank you!" Er Thom replied with a gratifying flash of brotherly scorn. He sobered almost immediately. "You have changed, you know. Even in so short a time. I—do you find it at all . . . odd or, or . . . lonely, to, to—" He floundered.

"Do I find it disquieting to be away from all that was usual in my life, and made to stand singleton before the world, when I have no memory but of being half of the whole we two made between us?" Daav said in a serious and quite adult voice. Er Thom took a breath and met bleak black eyes straightly.

"Yes," said Daav, "I do."

"So do I," Er Thom murmured, relieved, in an odd way, that at least this much had not changed—that he found his brother and himself at one on this matter of importance to them both. "One's . . . mother . . . assures one that these feelings will pass. Do you think—"

The door to the control room opened and Petrella yos'Galan strode within.

"Of course I would find you both here," she snapped, but Er Thom thought her face was—not entirely—displeased.

"Good shift, Aunt Petrella," Daav said politely. "Er Thom has just been having a run at the general-flight masters sim."

Petrella's eyebrows rose. "Oh, indeed? And how did he fare, I wonder?"

"Poorly enough." Er Thom spun his chair to face her. "My ship was destroyed two-point-eight minutes into the flight."

Astonishingly, his mother grinned. "No, do you say so? Well I recall that dicey bit of action! Forty-four times, I lost my ship exactly there. The forty-fifth—well, say I survived another minute."

"And I," Daav said mournfully, "am doomed to forever lose my wings at two-point-three."

"There?" Er Thom turned to stare at him. "But that was a mere nothing!"

"So you say!"

"No, but, Daav, all one need do—"

His brother raised a hand. "Yes, yes, I saw you. Perhaps my wretched fingers will have learned their lesson, now I've seen it can be done." He looked up to Petrella, a wry grin on his face. "Fifty-two times."

She smiled back. "I will hear that you've mastered the whole tape soon enough."

Daav inclined his head. "Your certainty gives me courage, Aunt Petrella."

"Now, that, neither of you lacks." She paused, her sharp blue eyes flashing from Er Thom back to Daav. "We raise Venture within the hour, nephew, and tomorrow is the appointed day of your departure. Exert yourself to comfort one who was ever acknowledged as the timid twin: are your arrangements in order and satisfactory to yourself? Better—would your mother my sister express her satisfaction with your arrangements?"

Daav raised his hand. "She and I discussed the scheme in detail before I had her aye. Scout Academy provided a list of pilots who might be receptive to allowing a first class provisional to gain flight time as their second—a list mother studied with some interest before declaring that it would do."

"So." Petrella inclined her head, and glanced again to Er Thom.

"I wonder, my son, if you might not do the captain the honor of ferrying Scout Candidate yos'Phelium to the planet surface tomorrow. I would expect you to stay by him until he has satisfactorily made his contacts, attend to the few small errands you will find listed on your duty screen, and return the Captain's Shuttle to the ship."

Er Thom's breath caught.

"I'm to pilot the Captain's Shuttle alone? Mother—"

She tipped her head, and he thought he detected the beginning of a twinkle in her stern blue eyes.

"Surely that is a task well within the skill of a second class pilot?"

He smiled. "Yes, Captain. It is."

"Good, that is settled, then." She turned. At the door, she looked over her shoulder at them. "The hour has perhaps escaped your notice, pilots. I mention—as elder kin and as a master pilot—that flight is much more enjoyable when one is awake at the board." She inclined her head—"Sleep well"—and was gone.

DAAV WALKED UP to the duty counter, which looked for all the worlds like any counter in any hiring hall one cared to name. Had Er Thom not read the sign as he followed Daav into this place, he would have supposed himself in an office of the Pilot's Guild, rather than the sector headquarters of the Liaden Scouts.

The man behind the counter glanced up from his book, and registered Daav with one quick scout glance. The glance lingered a moment on Er Thom, as if the scout found the appearance into his hall of a halfling in Trader clothes somewhat puzzling.

Daav laid his license on the counter. "One seeks Scout Rod Ern pel'Arot."

"So?" The scout appeared amused. "If one is so ill-advised as to seek Scout pel'Arot on Trilsday, then one must be prepared to seek him at the Spinning Wheel."

Daav inclined his head. "I shall do so. May one inquire the direction of the Spinning Wheel?"

The scout's amusement was almost palpable.

"Down on the blue median, handy to Terraport." He moved his shoulders and picked his book up.

"I am informed," Daav said, which his brother considered nothing more nor less than prevarication, pocketed his license and turned away, Er Thom trailing a respectful two paces behind.

Back on the walkway, Daav paused, face thoughtful. Er Thom looked up the street, down the street, but spied nothing remotely resembling either a blue median or a Terraport.

"Singularly unhelpful, that duty clerk," he grumbled. His brother looked at him, surprise on his sharp-featured face.

"No, do you say so?" He, too, looked up and down the busy thoroughfare. "Now, I think he told us everything we needed to know, if only we apply—ah." He moved forward, stepping off the curb, angling through traffic as if the rushing groundcars were mere figments. Er Thom gasped, then ran after, eyes on his brother's narrow, space-leathered back.

He caught up on the far side of the street, where Daav had paused before a public display-map of Venture Port and near environs.

"Down on the blue median," Daav murmured, "and handy to Terraport." He frowned at the flat display, then reached out and pushed the power-up button.

The display flickered and rolled; colors flashed; flat shapes expanded into three dimensions. The bright pictographs of written Trade appeared last, putting names to this or that building or wayfare.

Daav laughed.

"Here we are," he said, leaning forward and laying his hand wide over a block limned in electric blue. "The blue median, or I'll eat my leathers."

Er Thom leaned forward, squinting at the pictograph identifying a red-lined block just the north of Daav's blue. "Terran Mercantile Association," he read, and Daav laughed again.

"Terraport." He turned his grin on Er Thom. "Now, what was so difficult about that?"

"He might have said 'near the Terran Trade Hall,'" Er Thom pointed out, struggling to keep his lips straight and his face serious.

"Well," said Daav, with a final, calculating stare at the map, "he might have done so. But then he would not have been a Scout." He moved his shoulders, and sent a diffident black glance to Er Thom.

"You have errands to complete for Aunt Petrella, I know, and the blue median does look to be somewhat off your course. Shall we part here?"

Er Thom stared. "I am charged foremost with seeing you safely to the end of your arrangements. You heard her say it." He paused, as another, unwelcome thought intruded. He bit his lip. "Unless you do not wish me with you . . ."

Daav blinked. "What nonsense is this? Of course I want you by me!" He leaned forward, catching Er Thom's arm in a brother's warm grip. "Why else did I come all the way from Liad to see you?"

"Ah." Er Thom glanced aside, blinking, then looked back to his brother and smiled. "Why are we arguing with each other on a public street, then? Let us locate Scout pel'Arot and get you berthed."

"Very well." Daav glanced 'round, then pointed toward the east. "This way, I believe."

THE SPINNING WHEEL was found to be at the end of a short side-way off the main thoroughfare, just half-a-block from the Terran Trade Hall. The Trade pictograph on the corner street sign read "Blueway Cul-de-Sac 12." Below that, a board bearing the hand-painted Terran words "Avenue of Dreams" had been nailed to the post. Daav slipped down the slender way, Er Thom at his side.

A thick-shouldered Terran male sat on a stool beside the door to the casino, watching them with interest. He waved his hand as they approached the door.

"Hold it."

As one, they checked, exchanging a glance. It was Daav who moved a step toward the doorman and inclined his head—proper, as it was Daav's errand they were come upon.

"Yes?" he said.

The man frowned and jerked his thumb at the casino's door. "This here's a gambling hall. No kids allowed, by order of the portmaster."

"I understand," Daav said in his slow, careful Terran. "May one know the local definition of 'kid'?"

"Huh." The doorkeeper showed his teeth. It was perhaps, Er Thom thought, a smile. "A 'kid' is somebody who don't hold a license or a guild-card." The teeth showed again. "So, maybe you got a pilot's license?"

"Indeed." Daav went forward another step, reaching into his pocket. Er Thom moved, too, and put a hand on his brother's arm, halting him just outside the range of the man's Terran-long reach.

The doorkeeper saw the gesture, and laughed—a rusty sound no more cordial than his smile. "Your buddy thinks I'm a chicken-hawk."

"But of course you are no such thing," Daav answered calmly and held his license up for the man to see.

The hostile humor faded from the doorkeeper's face. "First class pilot? How old are you?"

Daav lifted an eyebrow, his face set in haughty lines that reminded Er Thom forcibly of their mother. "Is my age significant? As you see, I hold a valid license. The portmaster's word is met."

"You got that," the man admitted after a moment, and turned a rather more respectful gaze on Er Thom.

"OK, doll. You got a first class card, too?"

"I do not." He showed his license, gripping it as firmly as he might with the tips of his fingers. The doorman sighed.

"Second class. How old are *you*?" He held up his big hand. "It don't make no difference to whether you can go in—your friend's got that pat. Call it curiosity. I don't peg Liaden ages too good, but I'm damned if either one of you looks more'n twelve Standards."

Er Thom slipped his card back into its pocket, glanced at Daav and looked back to the doorman.

"I have fourteen Standard Years," he said courteously.

"And I," said Daav. "Good day to you." He moved toward the door, Er Thom at his shoulder, and the doorman let them go.

Inside at last, they paused, blinking at the muddle of noise, lights and people.

The Spinning Wheel was one large, high-ceilinged room; perhaps at some former time it had been a warehouse. The games of chance were strung out across the thickly carpeted floor, each surrounded by a tangle of players in modes of dress from dock worker coveralls to full evening wear. People were also in motion, drifting between this table and that; still more were busy with the gambling machines lining the back wall.

In the very center of the room was a lighted golden wheel reaching nearly to the ceiling—the device that gave the casino its name. And the cluster of people around that table was equal, Er Thom thought, to the entire crew roster of the *Dutiful Passage*.

Er Thom's heart sank. How were they to find one man—one man whom neither had seen before—in this crush? He glanced at his brother's face and was curiously dismayed to find that even Daav looked daunted.

Er Thom bit his lip. "Perhaps there is a message board?" he suggested, almost certain that there was not. "Or a paging system?"

"Perhaps . . ." Daav murmured, almost inaudible over the din. "I wonder . . ."

"You kids looking for somebody?" The woman who asked it was Terran, tall and willowy; elegant in a red shimmersilk dress. Her hair was yellow—very nearly the same shade as Er Thom's—her eyes a piercing dark brown.

"In fact, we are," Daav said, making his bow as visitor to host. "We were sent here to find Rod Ern pel'Arot."

For a moment, the woman hesitated, and Er Thom was about to despair. Abruptly, her face cleared, and she snapped her fingers.

"Is the week half-gone already?" This was apparently a rhetorical question, since she rushed on without giving either of them opportunity to answer, "The Scout, right? I didn't see him come in, but it's his day, and he hasn't missed one since I've been hostess. He'll be upstairs in the card rooms." She cocked a cogent eye.

"You know what he looks like?"

Daav smiled at her. "Like a Liaden?"

The woman laughed. "Sharp, are you? Yes, like a Liaden. A brown-haired Liaden, going gray, with three fingers missing off his left hand."

Daav bowed. "I am grateful."

"You're welcome," she said cheerfully and pointed across the crowded, noisy room. "You'll find the lift over in the far corner, there. See where there's a break in the line of bandits?"

"Yes," said Daav, politely, Er Thom thought, if without perfect truth.

The woman nodded. "Have a good time—and hope The Scout's winning today." She swept off, the red dress swishing against the carpet.

"Well," said Daav. Er Thom turned to meet his brother's amused eyes. "Still game for the adventure, darling?"

"How could I beg off now?" Er Thom asked. "I'm all agog to meet this Scout of yours. Especially if he's winning."

"Oh, I don't know," Daav said, moving slowly out onto the main floor. "It might prove more informative to discover him at a loss."

Frowning, Er Thom followed.

It was rather like wading through a particularly sticky river, crossing that room. Lights flashed beneath the surface of a table where the dice struck, drawing the eye. Horns blared, uncomfortably loud, announcing a winner at a second table, and claiming the attention of all within earshot. The giant golden wheel in the center of the room *clack-clack-clacked* as it revolved, lights flickering along its edge, the wager marks a bright smear reminiscent of the attenuating light one might glimpse in the second screen in the instant before one's ship entered Jump.

Er Thom paused, captivated by the effect. Gradually, the great wheel slowed, its attendant noises spiraling downward into subdued *clack, clack, clacks,* the wager marks discernible as individual symbols once more. Released, Er Thom's eye fell upon the throng of bettors pressed up against the wheel's table, and caught sight of a familiar badge on the sleeve of a jacket. He followed the sleeve up and discovered the face of Mechanic First Class Bor Gen pin'Ethil, thralled with anticipation, gray eyes pinned to the progress of the wheel, which *clack . . . clack . . . clack . . . CLACKed* to a halt, the lights around its edges flickering like a case lot of lightning bolts.

"Yellow Eleven!" someone called out—possibly the keeper of the machine, but Er Thom was watching Mechanic pin'Ethil, and saw his face change from bespelled to horrified.

"House wins!" called the keeper, and Mechanic pin'Ethil's shoulders sagged within his crew jacket, then firmed. Almost stealthily, he reached into his pocket.

Er Thom went a step forward—and found his arm grabbed.

"There you are!" Daav snapped, bearing him along in his wake with embarrassing ease. "Here I thought you'd been taken by child-stealers between one step and the next, when all that had happened was that you allowed yourself to be caught like a rabbit in a light by that thing!"

"I didn't—" Er Thom began a hot denial, then swallowed it. After all, it *had* been the lights that had pulled him to a halt. He had only seen Mechanic pin'Ethil after.

Daav pulled him onward, past the rest of the tables and the row of mechanicals with their attendant players, straight on to the lift-bank. He punched the summons, keeping a firm grip on Er Thom's arm.

"You may," Er Thom said, with what dignity he could muster, "release me."

"And have you wander off like a kitten after a butterfly and land in some sort of horrid scrape?" his brother inquired. "I think not."

He was saved from having to answer this not altogether unjust assertion by the arrival of the lift. They stepped inside together, Daav punched the button for the next floor above and released Er Thom's arm.

"Mind you, stay by me," he snarled, which really was too much.

Er Thom spun to balance snap with snarl—and stopped.

Daav's face was pale, his lips pressed into a thin line, his brows drawn tightly together—signs Er Thom recognized all too well. His anger melted and he touched his brother on the sleeve

"I hadn't meant to frighten you, darling," he said softly. "I swear I won't stray from your right hand."

Daav sighed and glanced away, then looked back and assayed a smile. "Very well, then." The lift doors slid open, showing a sweetly lit room paneled and carpeted in the first style of elegance, the tables placed with an eye to discretion and art.

Most of the tables were empty. Daav squared his shoulders and left the lift, walking sturdily toward the table where three Terrans in local formal wear played piket with a grizzled man in scout leathers.

Three paces short of the table, at a position equal with the scout's left shoulder, Daav stopped. Er Thom stood at his side, and recruited himself to wait.

They were fortunate that the round had nearly been done. When it was, the scout excused himself to his companions, pushed back his chair and stared them both up and down.

"I expect you're the Dragon cub," he said at last, and none too courteously.

Out of the side of his eye, Er Thom saw Daav's face go entirely bland, in an expression at once unfamiliar and chilling, before he bowed to the scout—junior to senior—the timing coolly precise.

"Daav yos'Phelium Clan Korval," he said, in the High Tongue's mode of introduction. "Do I address Scout Pilot Rod Ern pel'Arot?"

The Scout inclined his head. "You do. I hear you want a ride back home. Why choose me?"

"One's instructor had recommended you as a pilot from whom a novice might learn much," Daav returned, his voice colder, perhaps, than even the High Tongue required.

The Scout cocked his head in what Er Thom read as mock interest. "Now, here's a puzzle. Who teaches you piloting? Boy."

Daav drew a deep breath. "I have the honor of receiving instruction from Master dea'Cort."

Both grizzled brows lifted, and the Scout inclined his head this time with something nearer respect. "Well. And dea'Cort sends you to me." He flicked a glance at Er Thom's face, then looked back to Daav.

"Baggage?"

"One's brother, sent as Captain's escort."

"Wants to make certain you're in good hands?" His glance this time was longer and he spoke directly to Er Thom.

"Well, Trader? Is he in good hands?"

Er Thom frowned, then bowed briefly. "Sir. I hear that my delm has seen your name on the list provided by Master Pilot dea'Cort, which she then approved. How, then, shall your care of my brother be other than excellent?"

The Scout stared, absolutely still, then gave a shout of laughter and slapped his two-fingered hand on the card table.

"Dragons dice early, I learn! Well said." He looked back to Daav.

"These gentles and myself have some business to conclude. I will find you in an hour at the main eatery, belowstairs. They serve a tolerable nuncheon. Tell them you're on The Scout's ticket."

Daav bowed, and Er Thom did, too. "One hour, in the main restaurant," Daav murmured, but The Scout had already turned away, and was reaching for the cards.

THEY PAUSED ON the threshold of the casino's restaurant and embraced without speaking. Daav raised a hand as they let the hug go, and ran his fingers, feather-light, down Er Thom's cheek.

"Keep you safe, *denubia*," he said, light-voiced, as if he did not stand on the edge of parting from his brother—his second self—twice in one scant lifetime, and grinned with more courage than mischief. "Beware of idiots seeking to chain you to a dummy board."

Er Thom smiled, matching Daav's courage, then exceeded it, by taking one step back and raising his hand. "Keep safe, Daav," he murmured, and spun, perhaps too quickly, on his heel and strode off, alone, across the clattering busyness of the casino.

Daav watched him go—a slender, yellow-haired boy in trading clothes and well-made boots, the sleeve of his jacket bearing Korval's venerable Tree-and-Dragon—until he lost him among the tall crowd of gamesters. He bit his lip, then, and blinked hard a time or two to clear his eyes, then went into the restaurant and asked for a table overlooking the floor.

SHOULDERS STRINGENTLY level, Er Thom went across the noisy room. He looked neither left nor right—and most especially he did not look back, being wise enough to know that his fragile seemliness would never withstand the sight of Daav standing at the entrance to the restaurant, watching him safely out the door.

Clack . . . clack . . . clack—as before, the sound drew the ear as insidiously as the flaring lights pulled the eye. Er Thom allowed himself a glance to the left and up, observing the Wheel as it *clack . . . clack . . . clacked* to the end of its course and was still, dark, but for a single wager-mark.

"Blue Seven!" called the croupier, and flourished his wand across the betting table, collecting the losing wagers in a single, precise sweep.

Er Thom discovered that he had stopped walking and frowned, remembering the formidable list of errands he had yet to accomplish in the high town for his parent. He put one foot forward, but his eye had been caught, precisely as before, by the Tree-and-Dragon sigil on the sleeve of Mechanic Bor Gen pin'Ethil's jacket. As he watched, the man reached into his pocket and pulled out a coin, his shoulders rounded as if he stood under some unbearable weight.

Hesitating, Er Thom tried to reckon the time that had passed since he had first passed the Wheel and its cluster of avid players, and then shook himself, crossly. What business was it of his, how a crewman on leave chose to amuse himself?

Bor Gen pin'Ethil placed his coin on the table, his fingers hovering near, as if he might at any moment snatch it away.

Er Thom frowned again, liking that round-shouldered pose of misery less with every heartbeat. He had been several times over the last months assigned to the repair bays, and more than once to Mechanic pin'Ethil himself. A gentle, sweet-natured man, Bor Gen pin'Ethil, skilled in his work and an able teacher, besides. The man who stood with his neck bent at the base of the wheel was as unlike Mechanic pin'Ethil as—as Chi yos'Phellum was unlike her twin.

Er Thom hesitated, and in that moment the croupier extended his glowing wand to the Wheel, thick scarlet sparks flared wetly and the Wheel began to spin, picking up speed until the rimlights were but a foggy smear against the far indigo ceiling.

Alone among the crowd at the table, Bor Gen pin'Ethil did not gaze, entranced, upward into the seductive flare of light. He looked down, staring, or so Er Thom fancied, at the place where he had set his coin.

Er Thom bit his lip. Clearly, something was wrong, and the mechanic was a crewman. *His* crewman, if it came to that; he being the yos'Galan present.

Mechanic pin'Ethil is ill, he decided. In such case, his duty as crew-mate and as yos'Galan was plain. He moved a step toward the man who stood, staring bleakly down at the table.

Clack . . . clack . . .clack. The Wheel came to rest, rim-lights darkening.

The crowd 'round the table sighed as one, saving only Bor Gen pin'Ethil, staring, steadfast, at his coin.

"Yellow Eleven!" called the man with the wand. "The House wins!"

Bor Gen pin'Ethil picked his coin up and turned away from the table.

The thing was done so deftly that it took Er Thom, with his attention close upon the man, a moment to understand what he had seen. Alas, the croupier's wand was more observant.

It began to glow a steady and unalarming amber. The croupier raised it high over his head at the same time directing a courteous, "Your pardon, sir. A word with you, please," at Mechanic pin'Ethil's back.

The mechanic did not heed the gentle summons, but moved steadily away from the table. Heart in mouth, Er Thom plunged forward, certain now that something was earnestly amiss. Even he, the rawest of halflings, knew that a wager once placed upon the table was sacrosanct. The House had won with Yellow Eleven. Mechanic pin'Ethil's coin, covering Green Eight, was forfeit, by all the rules of honor and of play.

He needn't have hurried. The crowd parted for two tall Terrans in formal wear. One reached down and gripped Bor Gen pin'Ethil's arm, holding him still. The second went to the table, carrying another wand to the croupier.

"Malfunction?" she asked, taking the amber-lit wand with a rueful smile. "Ah, well. A spin on the House for everyone."

The croupier bowed and bent, reaching into his tray for coins to put into the questing hands of the players. Er Thom turned away in time to see the other Terran urging Mechanic pin'Ethil forward.

The mechanic balked and twisted, trying to break the Terran's grip. He failed, which could not have been unexpected, and sent a swift, panicked glance about him. Er Thom leapt forward, the man's eye fell upon him and his face closed, becoming the calm, courteous face of an elder crewman. Deliberately, he turned back to the man who held him and inclined his head.

"Hold!" Er Thom had reached the mechanic's side and stared up into the face of the man who held him, and spoke in rapid Trade. "Release him. We will come with you willingly."

"Certainly, I will," said Mechanic pin'Ethil. He drew a deep breath, looked calmly into Er Thom's face, and murmured quickly in Liaden, elder crew to younger. "Halfling, this is not yours. Go now, you should not be in this place."

"These persons will want Balance, will they not?" Er Thom snapped, as if he spoke to Daav, rather than an elder. "Who else from your crewmates is here to support you?"

"No one, gods be praised," the other returned. He paused before inclining his head. "Your actions do you honor, but you must believe me—you want none of this."

"What's the hold-up?" The female Terran was with them, the glowing amber wand cradled in her arm. She glanced over to her mate. "Who's the kid?"

"I am Er Thom yos'Galan," he answered in his slow, careful Terran. "This man," he used his chin to point at Mechanic pin'Ethil, "is of my crew."

"He is, is he?" She looked briefly amused, then shook her head and turned on her heel. "People are staring," she said over her shoulder to the man who held Mechanic pin'Ethil's arm. "Bring them both."

"Right." The man walked after her. Perforce, Mechanic pin'Ethil walked with him, Er Thom keeping pace on his opposite side.

Calmly, the man never loosing his grip on Mechanic pin'Ethil's arm, they walked through the throng of gaily dressed people. Er Thom searched the faces in the crowd, but saw no one he recognized. Apparently, of all the *Passage's* off-shift crew, only Bor Gen pin'Ethil found the Spinning Wheel to his taste.

They passed a knot of Liadens in formal evening wear, the ladies' jewel-toned dresses echoed in the gemstones worn by their escorts. A flicker of black moved at the edge of Er Thom's eye and he turned his head to track it, thinking *Daav*, thinking—but there was no thin, fox-faced boy in scout leather staring at him from the depths of the crowd. Only heedless strangers, intent upon their own pleasure.

Back toward the bandits and the lift bank they went, then turned sharply to the left, went down a short hallway and entered an office, where at last Mechanic pin'Ethil was released by his escort.

Standing beside his crewman, Er Thom heard the door slide closed behind them, looked upon the stern faces of those who awaited them, and wished that he had taken Mechanic pin'Ethil's hint and run.

The next moment, he was ashamed of himself. Run, and leave a crewmate alone to Balance with strangers? Far better to have a mate at one's side in such a wise. Though it would, Er Thom allowed, possibly have been more comfort to Mechanic pin'Ethil, had the mate who stood at his side been Petrella yos'Galan herself.

Their female escort laid the amber wand on the desk before the sternest face of all, murmuring respectfully. "Here's the evidence, Mr. Straudman."

Mr. Straudman neither acknowledged her nor glanced down at the wand. Instead, he stared at Mechanic pin'Ethil his eyes cold in his pale face.

"Stealing, Liaden?" he asked, his Trade flat and rapid. "We don't like to have people stealing from us."

"I understand," said Mechanic pin'Ethil in a calm, if slightly breathless voice. "The error is mine and I will endeavor to repair it."

"Don't trouble yourself," the man behind the desk said. "We know just what to do with thieves." He smiled somewhat, and Er Thom felt his hands curl into fists. He took a breath and moved forward one step. The man who had escorted them here grabbed his arm.

"Stop."

Er Thom inclined his head. "Very well." He waited until he was released, then forced himself to meet the cold eyes of the man behind the desk.

"I am Er Thom yos'Galan Clan Korval. This man is a member of the crew of *Dutiful Passage*. The ship will pay whatever fine is considered just and then we will leave. It is not yours to punish this man, though it is . . . acknowledged . . . that Balance is owed."

Beside him and one step behind, he thought he heard Mechanic pin'Ethil groan.

The man behind the desk blinked, once. He looked to the woman who had carried the wand.

"*Dutiful Passage*? And Clan Korval?"

"Yes, Mr. Straudman."

Mr. Straudman was seen to smile again, a habit Er Thom wished he would give over, and leaned forward, almost companionably.

"And your name is yos'Galan, is it? Well, well." He looked around at the others, some of whom looked less pleased than he—or so Er Thom thought.

"It seems to me we have a profit on the evening," Mr. Straudman said, and pointed his cold eyes at Bor Gen pin'Ethil. "Maybe we ought to pay you a commission, grease-ape."

Mechanic pin'Ethil sighed. "Come, sir. Would you dice with the Dragon?"

"Not in a month of bank days," the Terran replied immediately. "But this isn't dice. This is a simple sale."

He looked at Er Thom. "How much do you think Captain yos'Galan will pay to get you back?"

Er Thom stared, thinking that it was just like his mother's humor, and his fostermother's, too—to declare herself well-pleased to be shut of an irritable, irritating boy, and wish the cold-eyed man joy of him.

And perhaps that was the key.

He moved his shoulders, and showed empty, apologetic hands to man behind the desk.

"One has a brother, sir. I fear you would find the price not to your liking."

The cold-eyed man frowned, and leaned back suddenly in his chair, as if Er Thom had made a particularly clever move in counterchance. Er Thom held his breath, wondering what the man saw.

"So you're worthless, are you?" Straudman said eventually. "Why don't we just call Captain yos'Galan and make sure that's the case before I do anything rash?"

"Because," said a bland voice behind Er Thom, "you will but irritate the good captain, friend Straudman, and bring her eye upon the Juntavas. A poor business all around."

The man behind the desk frowned, his cold gaze leaping beyond Er Thom's shoulder. "The kid says they won't buy him back."

"He tells you nothing but the truth." Scout Pilot Rod Ern pel' Arot strolled into Er Thom's view, then went past him to lean against wall by Straudman's desk. "His brother is the one you want, if you intend to profit by selling Dragon-cubs to the Dragon. This one's the extra."

"So, now what?" said the man behind the desk, for all the worlds as if The Scout were a trusted advisor.

The Scout moved his shoulders against the wall. "While it is true you are unlikely to profit by selling this boy back to yos'Galan, it is also likely that the presumption of offering him will gain you her attention." He snapped upright. "Let them go."

Straudman frowned. "Both of them?"

"A first class mechanic is something the yos'Galan *will* miss," The Scout said simply.

For a moment, there was silence, then Straudman nodded and waved a hand at the room in general.

"Get them out of here."

"I'll take them," said Scout pel'Arot. "It's time I was back at station."

He moved forward, beckoning to Er Thom with his two-fingered hand. "After me, cub. And try not to trip over your own feet."

Which, Er Thom thought, was really uncalled for.

Though it was nothing compared to what Daav had to say to him, some few minutes later, at the head of the Avenue of Dreams.

PETRELLA YOS'GALAN sighed gently, and folded her hands atop her desk. In the chair facing her across the desk, Er Thom recruited himself to await her judgment, the echoes of Daav's thundering scold still ringing in his ears.

In the right hands, silence and stillness were potent tools, as he well knew, his fostermother being past master of both. Whether his true-mother shared that mastery he did not know—though he expected that he was about to learn.

His mother closed her eyes, sighed once more, and opened them.

"Since your *cha'leket* has exercised duty of kin and spoken to you frankly on the subject of endangering yos'Galan's heir by choosing to confront the Juntavas planetary administrator in his very office, we needn't discuss that further." She paused before inclining her head courteously.

"I will say, first, that your instincts do you honor. Your reported assessment of Mechanic pin'Ethil's state—that he was unwell—has been verified by the ship's Healer. I am assured that the compulsion to continue play once one has begun, to the cost even of one's *melant'i*, may easily be lifted by the Master healers at Solcintra Guildhall. Accordingly, Mechanic pin'Ethil will be sent home for Healing." She glanced down at her folded hands, then back to his face.

"I will, of course, write to his delm. It would honor me, if the crewmate who offered him care in his disability would assist me in composing this letter."

Er Thom blinked. He? Almost, he thought he heard Daav, laughing inside his head: *Yes, you, idiot. Who else?*

Hastily, he inclined his head. "I would be honored to assist, ma'am."

"Good." Another pause, another long moment's study of her folded hands.

"All honor to you, also, that you chose to lend Mechanic pin'Ethil your support." She raised one hand, though Er Thom had said nothing. "I know that you have said that there was no choice open to you in this; that your duty was plain, as the mechanic's crewmate and as the sole representative of Korval present. However, it must be recalled that you are but a halfling, and it was perhaps not . . .quite . . . wise of you to go unarmed into an unknown and possibly dangerous situation." She smiled, faintly. "I had said we would not repeat the course flown by your *cha'leket*. Forgive me, that there must be some overlap in approach."

Er Thom inclined his head. "Daav was plain with me, ma'am; I'm an idiot child, unfit to be left alone."

Improbably, her smile deepened. "Ah. Well, perhaps our approaches do not overlap so very much, then. I would say to you that those of the Juntavas are at best chancy and at worst deadly. Korval has an . . . arrangement . . . with the Juntavas, dating back many years—the appropriate citations from the Diaries will be on your screen at the beginning of your next on-shift. Please read them and be prepared to discuss them with me over Prime meal." She did not wait for his seated bow of obedience, but swept on.

"For the purpose of this conversation, let us say that the agreement between Korval and the Juntavas is one of mutual avoidance. The Juntavas does not touch Korval ships. Korval does not interfere with Juntavas business. Matters have stood this way, as I have said, for many years." She frowned over his head, as if she saw something on the opposite wall of her office that displeased her, sighed, and continued.

"The meat of the matter is that, despite this long-standing agreement, despite the fact that the scouts keep watch—the Juntavas is not a safe host. That the gentleman you . . .spoke to . . . would have killed you out of hand is, perhaps, unlikely. For Mechanic pin'Ethil . . ." She moved her shoulders. "Mechanic pin'Ethil is not of Korval, though he serves on a Korval ship. The Juntavas is clever enough to use that distinction to advantage."

His horror must have shown on his face, for his mother gave him another of her faint smiles before asking, "Tell me, my son, what would you have done if any of the armed persons in that office had decided to kill Mechanic pin'Ethil?"

Er Thom stared. Visions fluttered through his head, too rapid to scan, and finally he lifted his hands in exasperation. "I—something. I am a pilot of Korval. I would have done—*something*."

A small pause.

"Ah, yes," his mother said softly. "There is a long history of doing . . . something . . . among the pilots of Korval." She smiled at him and in that instant looked the very image of her twin."I believe we had best accelerate your defense instruction, Pilot."

"Yes, ma'am." He inclined his head.

"Hah." She considered him out of abruptly serious blue eyes, once again unmistakably his true-mother. "I would offer—as elder kin, you know—that we have all of us bid farewell to the comforts and the companions of childhood in order to learn our life-trades and begin to shape adult *melant'i*. I would say that—here is one who recalls the day she watched her sister walk into Scout Academy without her, and who later that same day was shown her quarters aboard the old *Adamant Passage*. I assure you that the ache in one's heart does ease, with time, and with the necessities of daily duty." She raised her hand stilling his start of denial.

"I do not say that you will cease to love, my child. I merely say— you will become an adult." She smiled once more, sweet as Daav. "With luck."

Er Thom grinned, then inclined his head. "I thank you for the instruction of elder kin."

"So." She glanced aside at the clock on her desk. "It is time and past time for you to be a-bed. Come to me at Prime, and mind you have those entries read."

"Yes, Mother." He stood, made his bow and moved toward the door.

He was nearly to the door when he heard her speak his name.

"Ma'am?" He turned to find her standing behind her desk. Slowly, she bowed the bow of honored esteem—

"Sleep you well, pilot of Korval."

✧ Breath's Duty ✧

Delgado, Leafydale Place
Standard Year 1393

IN HIS YOUTH, fishing had bored the professor even more thoroughly than lessons in manners, though he had more than once made the excuse of fishing a means to escape the overly-watchful eyes of his elders. Over time, he had come to enjoy the sport, most especially on Delgado, where the local game fish ate spiny nettles and hence could be hooked and released with no damage to themselves.

It was an eccentricity his neighbors, his mistress, and his colleagues had come to accept—and to expect. Periodically, the professor would set off for the lake region and return, rejuvenated, laden with tales of the ones that had gotten away and on-scale holograms of the ones that had not.

So it was this morning that he parted comfortably from his mistress, tarrying to share a near-perfect cup of locally-grown coffee with her—the search for the perfect cup and the perfect moment being among her chiefest joys—and with his pack of lures, dangles, weights, and rods set off for the up-country lakes.

The car was his other eccentricity—allowed however grudgingly by the collegiate board of trustees, who were, after all, realists. The work of Professor Jen Sar Kiladi was known throughout the cluster and students flocked to him, thus increasing the school's treasury and its status.

The car was roundly considered a young person's car. While fast, it was neither shiny nor new; an import that required expensive replacements and a regimen of constant repairs. Its passenger section had room enough for him, occasionally for his mistress, or for his fishing equipment and light camping gear. Not even the board of trustees doubted his ability to drive it, for he ran in the top class of the local moto-cross club and indulged now and then in time-and-place road rallies, where he held an enviable record, indeed.

The local gendarmes liked him: he was both polite and sharp and had several times assisted in collecting drunk drivers before they could harm someone.

His mistress was smiling from her window. He looked up and waved merrily, precisely as always, then sighed as he opened the car door.

For a moment he sat, absorbing the commonplaces of the day. He adjusted the mirrors, which needed no adjustment, and by habit pushed the trip meter. The sun's first rays slanted through the windshield, endowing his single ring with an instant of silvery fire. He rubbed the worn silver knot absently.

Then, he ran through the Rainbow pattern, for alertness.

The car rumbled to life at the touch of a switch, startling the birds napping in the tree across the street. He pulled out slowly, nodded to the beat cop he passed on the side street, then chose the back road, unmonitored at this hour on an off-week.

He accelerated, exceeding the speed limit in the first few seconds, and checked his mental map. Not long. Not long at all.

HE GRIMACED AS he got out of the car—he'd forgotten to break the drive and now his back ached, just a bit. He'd driven past his favorite fishing ground, perhaps faster there than elsewhere, for there was a lure to doing nothing at all, to huddling inside the carefully constructed persona, to forgetting, well, truly, and for all time, exactly who he was.

The airfield was filled to capacity; mostly local craft—fan-powered—along with a few of the flashy commuter jets the high-born brought in for their fishing trips.

On the far side of the tarmac was a handful of spacefaring ships, including seven or eight that seemed under constant repair. Among them, painted a motley green-brown, half-hidden with sham repair-plates and external piping, was a ship displaying the garish nameplate *L'il Orbit*. The professor went to the control room to check in, carrying his cane, which he very nearly needed after the run in the cramped car.

"Might actually lift today!" he told the bleary-eyed counterman with entirely false good cheer.

As always, the man smiled and wished him luck. *L'il Orbit* hadn't flown in the ten years he'd been on the morning shift, though the little man came by pretty regularly to work and rework the ship's insides. But, who knew? The ship might actually lift one day. Stranger things had happened. And given that, today was as good a day as any other.

Outside the office, the professor paused, a man no longer young, shorter than the usual run of Terran, with soft scholar's hands and level shoulders beneath his holiday jacket, staring across the field to where the starships huddled. A teacher with a hobby, that was all.

An equation rose from his back brain, pure as crystal, irrevocable as blood. Another rose, another—and yet another.

He knew the names of stars and planets and way stations lightyears away from this place. His hands knew key combinations not to be found on university computers; his eyes knew patterns that ground-huggers might only dream of.

"Pilot." He heard her whisper plainly; felt her breath against his ear. He knew better than to turn his head.

"Pilot," Aelliana said again and, half-against his own will, he smiled and murmured, "Pilot."

As a pilot must, he crossed the field to tend his ship. He barely paused during the walk-around, carefully detaching the fake pipe fittings and connections that had marred the beauty of the lines and hidden features best not noticed by prying eyes. The hardest thing was schooling himself to do a proper pilot's walk-around after so many years of cursory play-acting.

L'il Orbit was a Class A Jumpship, tidy and comfortable, with room for the pilot and copilot, if any, plus cargo, or a paying passenger. He dropped automatically into the copilot's chair, slid the ship key into its slot in the dark board, and watched the screen glow to life.

"Huh?" Blue letters formed Terran words against the white ground. "Who's there?"

He reached to the keyboard. "Get to work!"

"Nothing to do," the ship protested.

"You're just lazy," the man replied.

"Oh, am I?" *L'il Orbit* returned hotly. "I suppose you know all about lazy!"

Despite having written and sealed this very script long years ago, the man grinned at the ship's audacity.

"Tell me your name," he typed.

"First, tell me yours."

"Professor Jen Sar Kiladi."

"Oho, the schoolteacher! You don't happen to know the name of a reliable pilot, do you, professor?"

For an instant, he sat frozen, hands poised over the keyboard. Then, slowly, letter by letter, he typed, "Daav yos'Phelium."

The ship seemed to sigh then; a fan or two came on, a relay clicked loudly.

The screen cleared; the irreverent chatter replaced by an image of Tree-and-Dragon, which faded to a black screen, against which the Liaden letters stood stark.

"*Ride the Luck*, Solcintra, Liad. Aelliana Caylon, pilot-owner. Daav yos'Phelium copilot, co-owner. There are messages in queue."

There were? Daav frowned. *Er Thom*? his heart whispered, and he caught his breath. Dozens of years since he had heard his brother's voice! The hand he extended to the play button was not entirely steady.

It wasn't Er Thom, after all.

It was Clonak ter'Meulen, his oldest friend, and most trusted, who'd been part of his team when he had been Scout captain and in command of such things. The date of receipt was recent, well within the Standard year, in fact within the Standard month . . .

"I'm sending this message to the quiet places and the bounce points, on the silent band," Clonak said, his voice unwontedly serious. "I'm betting it's Aelliana's ship you're with, but I never could predict you with certainty . . ."

"Bad times, old friend. First, you must know that Er Thom and Anne are both gone. Nova's *Korval-pernard'i* . . ." Daav thumbed the pause button, staring at the board in blank disbelief.

Er Thom and Anne were gone? His brother, his second self, was dead? Anne—joyful, intelligent, gracious Anne—dead? It wasn't possible. They were safe on Liad—where his own lifemate had been shot, killed in Solcintra Main Port, deliberately placing herself between the fragging pellet and himself . . . Daav squeezed his eyes shut, banishing the horrific vision of Aelliana dying, then reached out and cued the recording.

". . . *Korval-pernard'i*. The name of the problem is the Department of the Interior; their purpose is to eat the Scouts, among other things. One of those it swallowed is your heir, and I don't hide from you that there was hope he'd give them indigestion. Which he seems to have done, actually, though not—but who can predict a Scout commander? Short form is that he's gone missing, and there's been the very hell of a hue and cry—and another problem.

"Shadia Ne'Zame may have discovered his location—but the Department's on the usual bands—monitoring us. Listen to Scout Net, but for the gods' sweet love don't attempt to use it!

"Shadia's due in any time and I'll send a follow-up when she gets here. You'd scarcely know the place, with all the changes since your training.

"If you've got ears for any of us, Captain, now is when we need you to hear." There was a pause, as if Clonak was for once at a loss for words, then: "Be well, old friend. If you've heard me at all . . ."

It ended.

Daav stared for a moment, then punched the button for the next message.

There was no next message. Days had gone by and Clonak had not followed up.

Daav shifted in his seat, thinking.

Desperate and under the shadow of a pursuing enemy, Clonak had found him. And Clonak had not followed up. Suddenly, it was imperative that Daav be somewhere else.

He flicked forward to the microphone.

"This is *L'il Orbit*, ground. I think I've got the problem fixed now. I'm going to be checking out the whole system in a few minutes. If I get a go, I'll need you to move me to a hot pad."

"Hot damn, *L'il Orbit*, way to go!" The counterman sounded startled, but genuinely pleased. "I'll get Bugle over there with the tractor in just a couple!"

"Thank you, ground," Daav said gravely, already reaching for the keyboard.

"Hello," he typed.

"Go," said maincomp.

"Complete run: Flight readiness."

"Working."

So many years. His brother and sister dead. His son in trouble. The son he wasn't going to be concerned with after all. And somehow the Juntavas was mixed around it.

Scout Commander. Daav sighed. Scouts were legendary for the trouble they found. The trouble that might attend a scout commander did not bear thinking upon.

The ship beeped; lights long dark came green. He touched button after button, longingly. Lovingly.

He could do it. He could.

He had left all those battles behind.

"Ground," he said into the mike, the Terran words feeling absurdly wide in his throat, "this bird's in a hurry to try her wings. Everything's green!"

"Gotcha. We'll get you over to the hotpad in a few minutes. Bugle's just got the tractor out of the shed."

Daav laughed then, and laughed again.

It felt good, just the idea of being in space. Maybe he could talk to some of the pilots he'd been listening to for so long—He grimaced; his back had grabbed.

Right. Easy does it.

And then, recalling the circumstances, he reached to the keyboard once more.

"Hello," he typed. "Weapons check."

"I'M NOT A COMBAT pilot, either, Shadia. I think we did as well as might be expected!"

The gesture in emphasis was all but lost in the dimness of the emergency lighting.

"I swear to you, Clonak—they've murdered my ship and if they haven't killed me, I'm going to take them apart piece by piece; and if they have killed me I'll haunt every last one of them to . . ."

The muffled voice went suddenly away and the mustached man raised his hand to signal the separation. The woman shrugged and braced her legs harder against the ship's interior, bringing her Momson Cloak back in contact with his as they sat side by side on the decking behind the control seats, using the leverage of their legs to hold them in place in the zero-g.

"We bested them," the man insisted. "We did, Shadia—since the fact that we're somewhere argues that *their* ship isn't anywhere."

There was a snort of sorts from within the transparent cloak. "I'm familiar with that equation—my instructor learned it from the Caylon herself! But what could they have been thinking to bring a destroyer against a ship likely to Jump? You don't have to *be* a Caylon to know that's . . ."

Her gesture broke the contact again and the near vacuum of the ship's interior refused to carry her words.

Shadia leaned back more firmly against Clonak's shoulder, the slight crinkle sounding from the Cloak not quite hiding his sigh, nor the crinkling from his Cloak.

She glanced at him and saw him shaking his head, Terran-style.

"Next shift, Shadia, recall us both to put on a headset. As delightful as these contraptions are, I'd like us to be able to converse as if we weren't halflings in the first throes of puppy-heart."

She laughed gently, then quite seriously asked, "So you think we'll have a next shift, at least? No one on our trail?"

He sighed, this time turning to look her full in the face.

"Shadia, my love, I doubt not that all is confusion at Nev'Lorn. The bat is out of the bag, as they say, and I suspect the invaders have found themselves surprised and disadvantaged."

He nodded into the dimness, eyes now seeing the situation they'd left behind so suddenly when the Department of the Interior attacked them.

"The ship most likely to have followed was closing stupidly when last we saw it—closing into your fire as well as the sphere of the Jump effect of the hysteresis of our maneuvers. They would have been with us within moments, I think, if they had come through with us."

Clonak gestured as expansively as the Cloak allowed.

"Now—what can I say? We've come out of Jump alive. If we're gentle and lucky the ship may get us somewhere useful. Perhaps we'll even be able to walk about unCloaked ere long; with hard work and sweat much is possible. You *will* remember to tell people that you've seen me sweat and do hard work when this is over, won't you, Shadia? When our present situation is resolved—then we will consider the best Balance we might bring against these murderers."

He sighed visibly, used the hand-sign for "back to work," with a quick undernote of "sweat, sweat, sweat."

She smiled and signaled "work, work, work" back at him.

Clonak stretched then, unceremoniously lifting himself off the floor and away from Shadia. Steadying his feet against the ceiling of the vessel he brought his face near hers and touched left arm to left arm through the Cloaks.

"Shadia, I must give you one more rather difficult set of orders, I'm afraid. I know my orders haven't done much good for you lately, but I pray you indulge me once more."

With his other hand he used the scout hand-talk, signifying a life-or-death situation.

She nodded toward his hand and he closed his eyes a moment.

"If you find that, against chance, we are brought again into the orbit of the Department of the Interior, if they verge on capturing us—you must shoot me in the head."

He flicked an ankle, floated accurately to the floor again, belying the cultivated image of old fool, and he looked into her startled, wide eyes.

"Just dead isn't good enough, Shadia; they'll have medics and 'docs. Do you understand? There must be no chance that they can question me. They cannot know what I know, and they cannot know who else might know it."

Clonak tugged gently on her elbow, and she uncurled to stand beside him, stretching herself and near matching his height.

His hand-talk made the motion demanding assent; she responded in query, his in denial . . . and he leaned toward her until Cloaks touched again.

"I know, Shadia, *neither of us* were raised to be combat pilots. It is thrust upon us both as scouts and as pilots. My *melant'i* is exceedingly clear in this. I can tell you only one thing right now—and little enough it is to Balance my order, I know."

Her hand signaled query again and his flicked the repeated ripple that normally would signify a humourous "all right, all right, already . . ."

"What I know," he said into his Cloak and through the double crinkly life-skins to her ears, "is the name of the pilot they are afraid of. And having made this one pilot their enemy, they now must be the enemy of us all."

THE MATH WAS easy enough, if not quite exact. There were a dozen Momson Cloaks per canister; each of the two installed canisters had eleven left. There were two replacement canisters, and a backup. The emergency kit built into each of the conning seats held a pair of individual Cloaks, as well. Out of an original eight eights to start there were now five dozen and two to go.

Math is a relentless discipline: It took Shadia down the rest of the path almost automatically. Each Cloak was designed to last an average-sized Terran just over 24 hours—Momson Cloaks were, after all, standard issue devices on cruise ships plying the crowded space of the Terran home system—but they were conservatively rated at 30 hours by the scouts.

Perhaps 40 Standard days then, Shadia thought, if usage was equal and none of the units bad, if . . .

She saw the flutter of a hand at the edge of her vision as Clonak signaled for attention; he leaned forward and they touched shoulders as he spoke:

"Not as bad as all that, Shadia—we've got some ship stores too, and the spacesuits themselves, if need be, and there might be a way to . . ." She glanced at him sharply and he pointed toward her right hand.

"I'm not a wizard, child. You were counting out loud."

Shadia rolled her eyes. It was true. She'd been waiting for the battery-powered gyroscope in the auxiliary star-field scope to stabilize with half her mind and with the other half she'd been doing math on her hand.

She bowed carefully amid a sea-noise of crinkling. "Thank you for your notice," she said formally, while her free hand chuckled out the sign for "why me?"

His reply in finger-talk, also with the underlying ripple of a chuckle, was simply "Breath's duty." He pulled away, a rough-trimmed wire conduit clutched carefully through the transparent Momson Cloak, and floated toward the open overhead panel. Shadia likewise turned back to her task in progress.

The ship's tiny forward viewports were automatically sealed by Jump run-up; they were blind unless they could get power back to those motors or use the auxiliary scope to see straight away from the ship.

And now the star-field scope was stable enough to run: Despite Clonak's protestations, he'd managed to perform wizard's work on the back-up electrical system and the device was ready to operate. It was not what one might hope to be using to determine one's position after an interrupted Jump-run, but she'd used less in training.

As she bent to the scope she sighed a breath—and then another. Breath's duty, indeed. Every child on Liad was made by stern Delm or fond grandfather to memorize the passage, which had come virtually unchanged through countless revisions of the Code. Unbidden, portions came to her now, recalled in the awkward rhythms of childish singsong.

"Breath's duty is to breathe for the Clan as the Clan allows, Breath's duty is to breathe the body whole, Breath's duty is to plan for the Clan's increase, Breath's duty is to keep the Balance told, Breath's duty is to . . ."

Carefully, she adjusted the star-field scope. To be useful, she needed to recognize any of the several dozen common Guides—her usual choice was the brilliant blue-white Quarter main giganova—or find a star within disc-view. Disc-view, of course, was optimum. With the auxiliary scope even a basic scan could take a day.

"Breath's duty is to keep the Balance told," she muttered, and noted the gyroscope's base setting. There were a lot of degrees of space to cover, and time moved on.

IT WAS *L'IL ORBIT* and not *Ride The Luck* that docked at Delgado's smallest general-flight orbiting docks; and Professor Jen Sar Kiladi who made a series of transfers to and from accounts long held in reserve. The shuttle trip to the larger commercial center, as well as the various library connections and downloads, were made by a student invented some years before by the professor; and the tools purchased at the local pawn establishment were paid for, in cash, by a man with a brash Aus-Terran accent and super-thin gloves.

"I'M HERE TO FIX your nerligig," the little man told the morning guy behind the bar.

"Ist broke?" the bartender wondered. The device sat in its place, motionless—but it was always motionless at this time of the day, local ordinance requiring the Solemn Six Hours of Dawn to match that of the spiritual city Querna on the planet below.

"Repair order!" said the man, vaguely Aus, waving a flimsy in the air and lugging his kit with him. "I'm good, I'm expensive, and I'm on my night differential."

He looked like one of those semi-retired types: just the kind of guy who'd know how to keep an antique nerligig running.

The bartender shrugged, waved the man and his tools toward the ailing equipment, and poured a legal drink into one glass and its twin into another then gave them both to the customer at the end of the bar.

"Hey, asked for one drink—right?"

"Solemn Six, bud! Can't sell youse that much in one glass this time of the day . . ."

The repairman shook his head, set up his tools, adroitly removed the wachmalog and the bornduggle from the nerligig, and waited patiently for the boss.

THE BOSS was a heavyset Terran, and he traveled today with three guards. He came in looking tired and his guards swept by, checking out the patrons, glancing at the bartender, reconnoitering the restrooms . . .

It was the boss who saw the nerligig guy, professionally polishing one of the inner gimbag joints.

"What's going on here?" he demanded.

The guy glanced at him out of serious dark eyes. "Time to do scheduled maintenance."

The boss grimaced, but gave the correct reply.

"I don't need nothing fancy today."

"Dollar's greener when you do," said the man, polishing away.

"At's awful old."

The repairman looked up, eyes steady—

"I only come out at night, you know."

The boss looked at the bartender, sighed, and watched his guards stand importantly around the bar for a moment.

"You cost me some help today," he said finally, turning back to the nerligig guy.

The man shrugged.

"Good help is hard to find. Better you know before there's a life in it."

The boss sighed again, and waved the repair guy toward his office.

"C'mon back."

THE OFFICE was sparely appointed; a working place and not a showplace. Daav took a supple leather chair for himself, nodding at its agreeability.

The boss sat in his own chair, rubbed his face with his left hand and gestured at his visitor with his right.

"What's your pleasure?"

Daav opened his hands slightly with a half-shrug.

"Information. About that message . . ." The message that shouted the name of Val Con yos'Phelium to all with ears to hear, near-space and far. The message that had shaken him out of his professorial Balancing and brought him into the office of a Juntava, seeking news.

The boss pinched the bridge of his nose and nodded.

"Yeah, I figure every quiet hand in the universe will want to know about that. I think it's the first time the damned 'danger tree' was really used . . ."

Daav sat quietly, watching the man's tired face. No effort to hide how he felt—Daav's greeting, as old as it was, was one recognized by Juntavas on many worlds. The short form was: *Help this person, he has a right to it.* The person in question might be a retired sector boss, an assassin on the way to or from a run—or the whole charade could simply be a test of loyalty.

"What do you need to know?" asked the boss. "What's the aim?"

"Everything you know. I am, let us say, a specialist in people. I can hide them and I can find them. As may be required. I'll need the background as deep as it goes."

The boss man gave a snort.

"I bet you can hide 'em. Standing in my own front room with a whole bag of equipment like you own the place and my guards probably can't tell me the color of your hair or what kind of shoes you wear. Damn smooth . . ." He shook his head in admiration, sighed, and went on, looking straight at Daav.

"Where we are is that there's been—a change of administration. Some of this is official and some's not . . ."

Daav looked on with polite interest, no change on his face.

The boss nodded. "Right. He was asking for it if anyone was, but anyhow, politics aside, we have a Chairman Pro Tem right now, seeing how the Chairman was knifed in his own office by a Clutch turtle."

Daav leaned forward a bit, cocking his head to one side in respectful query.

"Me too! Not what somebody'd expect. A bomb maybe, poison, even just a quiet step-down 'cause somebody had the best of him after all—but no. A pair of Clutch turtles waltzed into his office, had an argument with him, and took him out."

The man's gaze had strayed to his desktop; he looked up, frowning.

"The official thing is—straight from Chair Pro Tem!—that there was a busted deal, resulting from a misunderstanding, and that the former Chairman had made the mistake of threatening a T'carais with a shell-buster."

"With the result that, in defense of his or her superior, a minion used a knife," Daav murmured into the short silence.

The boss looked impressed, but Daav continued. "Perhaps better for all concerned: Most turtles would merely have bitten his head off, or crushed his spine . . ."

The boss blanched, but waved a hand and went on.

"Yeah, well, could have been. Unofficial news is that this turtle crew had come to visit twice; got themselves locked into the Chairman's office and cut their way out through the blast wall with a knife after busting about a thousand gems, and then he had the nerve to try a fast one. Apparently these turtles are the knife clan or something—famous. And by the time the blood's cleaned up, the Chairman Pro Tem finds out the fuss is all about two people."

"That would be the individuals mentioned in the whisper for all worlds . . ." Daav suggested.

The boss smiled wanly.

"Yes, that's them. The turtles—this is official!—claim them to be 'a brother and sister of the Spearmaker's Den' who must be returned unharmed or self-declared free and safe."

Daav looked into the ceiling, momentarily lost in thought. When he looked back, the boss was reaching into a desk drawer for a candy.

"What, may I ask, is the *or*?"

The boss looked grim.

"The *or* is that if they don't turn up safe the Juntavas will be wiped out, starting at the top. This is a promise."

Daav leaned forward, raised his hand to his chin and rubbed it thoughtfully.

"This is," he said after a moment, "a very, very serious problem. No one has ever heard of a Clutch turtle lying. Certainly no one has ever heard of a Clutch turtle or clan breaking a promise. Even I might not be able to hide well enough if the Clutch knew me for an enemy."

The boss snorted again, apparently swallowing his candy whole.

"Right. And so what I have going on, starting about the time you walk out the front door here, is a block-by-block search of every Juntavas holding on Delgado, looking for two of the damnedest trouble-makers you've ever heard of."

Daav, very interested, waved his hand, asking for more information.

"Yeah, OK. One is a First-In Scout Commander! Good, right? Get in the face of somebody who can talk Clutch to the Clutch and just happens to have saved one from a dragon. You know, a nobody, a pushover. Then the other one is a Merc-turned-bodyguard, lived through Klamath and got on—and off!—Cloud."

Daav let out a low whistle. "Do you know how many people lived through Klamath?"

The boss shrugged, tapped his desk. "That's probably in my notes. I got more notes than you can stuff in a garbage can already about this." He broke, searched his desktop, pulled up a flimsy image-flat, and flipped it, casually and quite accurately, to the man in the chair.

Daav listened with half-an-ear as the boss went on—while his eyes measured the photos of his son and his son's companion.

"Getting off Klamath earns you a lifetime 'I'm tough' badge or something. But—this is where we come in—these two started a firefight, in broad daylight, I guess!—between the local Juntavas and the city police in Econsey, back there on Lufkit, just to cover their getaway after they robbed the boyfriend of the local boss' daughter. Then, they managed to get off-planet while the place was under total lock-down, with everybody from the chief of planetary police down to the nightclub bouncer looking for them, and make a leisurely departure from Prime Station in a Clutch spaceship."

Daav continued to look interested, slowly shaking his head as he listened, still taking in the no-nonsense, rather ordinary appearance of both of the missing. A master mercenary who had survived Klamath might be just the person to balance a Scout Commander, he thought.

"Story gets muddled about here," the boss was continuing, "but somehow the local capo managed to grab them. Then he gets the news he can't *do* anything to them. So he sets them off in a spaceship that's been in some kind of a fight and can't go nowhere. Word comes down to make sure these two are really in one piece and to hold 'em, pending the Chairman Pro Tem's personal visit. He goes back . . ."

Daav didn't have to fake the laugh.

"What could he have been thinking?" he asked. "To leave a—what was it, First-In Scout Commander?—in a spaceship and expect it *not* to go away?"

The boss was nodding now and gestured with the piece of candy in his left hand.

"You got it. Exactly how it was. They were gone, the ship was gone and ain't nobody heard nothing about any of 'em since. So now I got to check Delgado and . . ."

Daav raised a palm.

"Please," he said gently. "You mustn't be overly concerned. You'll want to do standard checks on passenger lists and such, but the people you are hunting are not likely to hide out on Delgado. Even if they've *been* here do you think a hardened merc and a First-In Scout are going to set themselves up as shopkeepers or bean farmers?"

Before the boss could answer, Daav stood, demanding a suppleness from his body he did not feel.

"I'll need the name of the new Chairman, copies of whatever transmissions you may have, details of the former location of the missing ship—dupes of your images, as well—and I'll be on my way. Also, I have some things for you . . ." He waved toward the back wall of the office and the bar beyond.

"First, the taller of your security guards stole several of your bartender's tips, and was helping herself to the packaged snacks. That can't be good for your business."

The boss snorted. "Just color them gone. Hey, you're good at what you do—but that don't mean they shouldn't have seen you!"

Daav nodded agreeably. "Also, you'll want to get an explosives expert in here. There's a small package I disconnected and took out of the nerligig—it looks like it might have been connected about six or seven dozen years ago. It may no longer be dangerous, or it may be unstable. In any case, as I am sure you understand, I hesitate to take it with me."

The boss rubbed his forehead and nodded.

"We'll dupe your info for you—and in the meantime I'll call in a specialist."

"Thank you," said Daav and went back to the bar to put his tools away, all the while amazed that a phrase learned so long ago and so far away was still potent enough to make a Juntava jump.

CABIN PRESSURE WAS at one-tenth normal, which should have been counted as good; it signified that Clonak's work was paying off.

Alas, Shadia did not much feel like cheering. She sat lightly webbed to the command chair, patiently doing hours of work by hand and eye that an online computer might do in a blink.

Clonak had left her to the recognition search while he worked on what he called "housekeeping." Housekeeping entailed using a small bubble-bottle to find the worst of the leaks and then seal them with the quick-patch kit.

As for her work, so far she had only three possibles and one probable. Dust in the outer fringes of the Nev'Lorn cluster made some of the IDs difficult and she'd not yet found a near opaque patch or two that might also help her . . .

"Shadia?"

The sound reached her, distorted and distant.

Clonak stood behind her, almost an arm's length away, beckoning her toward a portable monitor hooked to a test-kit. With his other hand he seemed to be fighting a control.

Indeed, the air pressure was building ever so slightly.

Noting her spot, she locked the star-field scope; by the time she got to him he was using both hands on the control. He yelled at her again through the sack-like Cloak; she could barely hear him.

"Please tell me what you see. I'm not sure this will work for long!"

What she saw, besides Clonak wrestling with a wire-filled metal tube, was devastation. The grainy monitor was showing her what would normally be her Screen Five, inspection view.

"The rear portside airfoils are gone," she yelled, schooling her voice to the give the information as dispassionately as possible. "There is damage into the hull; I can see a nozzle—likely it's one of the wing nitrogen thrusters, still attached to a hose—moving as if it is leaking."

Clonak shrugged, did something else with his shoulder, and the image shifted a bit toward the body of the ship.

Shadia blinked, disoriented. The ship didn't have a—Oh.

"The ventral foil has been blown forward and twisted—shredded. The . . ."

The image went blank as Clonak's hands slipped on the tube; the Cloak vibrated with the buzz of his curse.

Shadia continued describing what she had seen.

"There's no sign of any working airfoil components. There are indications of other structural damage. I can't tell you about the in-system engines—the view was blocked by the ventral fin."

Clonak sat down hard.

"That view was blocked by the ventral? Might be something left to work with if we can get some more power going . . ." His last few words were lost as he stared at the blank screen.

"Clonak, I have a feeling that the ship is—bent." Shadia bent close and said it again, this time touching Cloaks shoulder to shoulder.

"Well," he sighed. "That explains why we can't budge the hatch."

They both were silent for a moment; Shadia was glad for the slim comfort offered by touching someone else, even through the plastic.

The ship's spine had taken some of the heat of the attack and the ship was out of true. The rear compartment, including the autodoc, the sleeping alcove, and about 60 percent of the food, was accessible only if they could force the hatch against the bend of the ship.

"We have to assume," Clonak said suddenly, "that we're not airworthy past the hatch; obviously we won't want to be trying any kind of atmospheric descent if we have a choice—Might be missing some hull, too."

He straightened a bit, leaned in to her and said, "Look again. I'll see if I can force this to scan the other side!"

Her fingers answered yes, and Clonak began twisting the cable yet again. The image reappeared and then swung suddenly, showing an oddly unflawed stretch of ship's hull and beyond it the fluted shapes of several nozzles poking out from the blast skirts.

Beyond that was a brightness; three points of light; reddish, bluish, whitish. A local three star cluster—

"The Trio!" she said, but then there was another light, making her blink

"Stop!" she yelled, the noise over loud in her ears.

Clonak let go and the image went away. Shadia stood staring at the blank screen, seeing the stars as they had been.

"We're still in-system," she said, putting her arm against his. "If the Trio and Nev'Lorn Primary are lined up . . ."

"We're somewhat north of the ecliptic," Clonak concluded, "with Nev'Lorn headquarters safely on the other side of the sun."

THE IMAGE OF his son—and of his son's partner—lay on the pilot's seat along with the rest of the information provided by the Juntavas. Daav tried to imagine the boy—a pilot of the first water, no doubt; a scout able to command the respect of a Clutch chieftain, who held the loyalty—and perhaps the love—of the very Hero of Klamath . . .

His imagination failed him, despite the recording furnished by the Juntavas boss.

The boy's voice was firm, quiet and respectful; the information he gave regarding the last known location of his vessel only slightly less useful than a star map. The voice of Miri Robertson was also firm; unafraid, despite the message she'd clearly imparted: All is not as it seems here.

Yet, despite the image, the recording, and the records, his

imagination failed him. Somehow, he thought he had given over the concept of heir, of blood-child. Certainly, he should have been well-schooled by his sojourn on the highly civilized world of Delgado, where the length of all liaisons was governed by the woman and where the decision to have or not to have a child was one the father might routinely be unaware of—witness his mistress's daughter, now blessedly off-planet and in pursuit of her own life.

Daav picked up the flimsy, staring at the comely golden face and the vivid green eyes. A Korval face, certain enough, yet—there was something else. With a pang, he understood a portion of it: the boy, whoever he was, and however he had gotten into the scrape announced to the universe at large, was a breathing portion of Aelliana. Daav projected her face, her hands, her voice at the image of their son, but that did no better for him—what he saw was Aelliana.

The boy was only a boy to him, for all they shared genes and kin.

Daav sighed and laid the picture back on the pilot's chair. Whoever the boy was, elder kin should surely have taught him to stay away from the Juntavas. He should have been given the Diary entries to read. Er Thom knew—who better? Er Thom should have—but Er Thom was gone.

And in the end the duty had not been done, the tale had not been told, and here was the result. Briefly he wondered what other duties he'd left undone . . .

He'd have to find Clonak. Clonak had later news. Clonak would know what needed done, now.

He sighed then, rewebbed himself, scanned the boards, checked the coords he had already keyed in from some recess of his mind, and punched the Jump button.

THEY'D SLEPT FITFULLY in the unnaturally silent craft, each sitting a half-watch in a Scout's Nap. What noises there were, were confined to the Momson Cloaks and their wearers. The Cloaks had a tendency to crinkle when one moved, and though the upper shoulder placement of the air-pack made wonderful sense when standing, it required some adjustment to sleep semi-curled in the command chairs in order not to disturb the airflow.

The wake-up meals were cold trail-packs, laboriously introduced into the Cloaks through the ingenious triple-pocket system, a sort of see-through plastic airlock. Since the Cloaks were basically plastic bags with a few rudimentary "hand spots," the process was awkward, even for two people.

First the trail-packs were located and then held in place with lightweight clamps. Then the outer pocket was opened, with one person pulling lightly on the outer tab and the one inside the Cloak grasping the side wall of the pocket firmly and pulling back. The pocket walls separated, and the resultant bulge had a lip-like seal that was pressed until it opened. The trail-pack went into the newly opened pocket, and the outside was resealed.

The second pocket had a seal at what Shadia thought of as the bottom; by bunching the pocket up from inside it could be made to open, and the trail-pack was moved into that part of the pocket, and that seal to the outside pocket pressed tightly; now there were two seals between vacuum and food. The inner seal, finally, was opened-puffing up the part of the pocket with the trail-pack in it—and finally the food was safely inside the Cloak.

Crumbs being a potential problem, the food bars were handled gingerly and the water squeezed carefully from its bulb.

While she ate, Shadia chewed on the problem of their exact location, with regard to Nev'Lorn 'quarters—and potential rescue.

While knowing that they'd not left the Nev'Lorn system was definitely useful, the camera-monitor wasn't the tool for finding out where they were or, more importantly, where they were headed. It was impossible to guess how much of their intrinsic velocity and flight energy might have been transferred to the attacking destroyer and they had nearly as much chance of being in a tight, highly elliptical orbit as they did in being on the outward leg of a hyperbolic orbit that would throw them out of the system, never to return.

Thus, shortly after breaking her fast, Shadia realigned the gyroscope for the auxiliary instruments and changed her search pattern with the star-field scope. Now that she knew which end was up her job had gone from that of a hopeful pastime to an immediately useful necessity. What they might do about where they were was another matter.

On the other side of the chamber, Clonak busied himself with another semi-disassembled piece of hardware, periodically professing himself or any number of other objects, deities, and people damned, stupid, absurd, or useless.

That she could hear these footnotes to progress clearly proved that the pressure in the ship was slowly rising, in part a result of the action of the layered osmotic membranes that made up much of structure of the Momson Cloak. The finely tuned membranes purposefully released certain amounts of carbon dioxide and hydrogen while retaining some moisture; heavier users might complain of the suit "sloshing" as the moisture reservoirs filled. Far from breathable, the external atmosphere made the Cloaks a little easier to move around in.

The increased pressure also made Shadia aware of an occasional twittering sound she couldn't place. Twice she glanced up to Clonak, hard at work but doing nothing that seemed to make such a noise.

The third time she looked up, Clonak also raised his head. He caught Shadia's eye and smiled ruefully.

"Not rodents, Shadia, with little rat feet. More likely we have micro-sand, scrubbing the hull down to a fine polish. This system has a fine collection of unfinished planets to choose from, I'm afraid.

"Though actually," he continued, "that's not all bad. If the wrong people are looking for us we're better off here than an hour off Nev'Lorn."

"Should we use the monitor to—"

"I've thought of that, but really, the best use of resources is to continue with what we're doing. I may yet get a computer up and running and you may yet find us a safe harbor."

There were several distinct pings and another scrabble of dust on the hull then and Shadia bent back to her charting with a will.

DAAV WOKE WITH a start, certain someone had called his name. About him the ship purred a quiet purr of circulators and the twin boards were green at every mark. The Jump-clock showed he had enough time for breakfast and exercise before he arrived back in normal space. No matter what might befall, he'd be better prepared if he kept now to routine.

He'd been to three systems so far without touching ground at any. Izviet, Natterling, and Chantor were all minor trade ports, ports that usually sported a small training contingent of scouts making use of the nearby space.

At Izviet, a ship a few years out of mode coming from a port rarely heard from was barely gossip, still he'd had the ship come in as *L'il Orbit*, maintaining his professorship as well. The cycle was off—there were no scouts training near the spectacular multi-mooned and multi-ringed gas giant Cruchov. Natterling's usual band of ecologists-in-training were out of session; the wondrous planet Stall with its surface outcroppings of pure timonium had no company. By the time he'd hit Chantor he'd had a lot of news to digest, but there were no cadets practicing basic single-ship in that place, as he had.

Among the news chattered most widely were the rumors attending the Juntavas and their danger-tree broadcast.

Some felt it was trap, aimed at netting the Juntavas. Others explored news-pits and libraries and invented great empires of intrigue: one of these stated that the missing man now ruled a system as a Juntavas boss; another said the merc hero had bagged herself a rich one; yet another swore the pair of them had turned pirate and were staging raids against the scouts.

What was missing in all three places was the back-net chat he would have found in an instant in the old days. In the places he would normally have found scouts he found nothing but notes, signs, recordings: on temporary assignment, on vacation, will return, in emergency please contact . . .

Worse, at Chantor's orbiting Waystation Number 9, in an otherwise dusty maildrop he'd maintained since his training days, was a triple-sealed note with all the earmarks of a demand for payment from a very testy correspondent. The return address meant nothing to him but the message had chilled him to the very bone.

"Plan B is Now in Effect," it said in neat, handwritten, Liaden characters.

No signature. He recognized the handwriting, familiar to him from his former life, when he had been Delm Korval and this man had taken hand-notes of his orders. dea'Gauss. He felt a relief so intense that tears rose to his eyes. dea'Gauss was alive. Or had been. He blinked and looked again at the note. The date was not as recent as Clonak's news.

Plan B: Korval was in grave danger.

He drew a breath and felt Aelliana stir, take note, and finally murmur in his ear: "Whatever has happened? Surely the Juntavas have not caused this?"

The intership chatter had been tense with other rumors; civil wars, Yxtrang invasions, missing spaceships, Juntavas walking openly in midports in daylight.

Daav had debated destinations. Lytaxin—world of a solid ally. Liad itself was surely to be avoided with Plan B in effect!

He sat to board, finally, and, having thought Lytaxin, his fingers unhesitatingly tapped in another code. This was a destination only for scouts and the adventuresome curious; there was no trade there, nor ever had been. Well.

"Well," Aelliana affirmed, and he gave the ship its office.

Now, with an hour yet to Jump-end, Daav hesitated before switching his call signals. No need to give away all his secrets, even to scouts. He set the timer and moved back to begin his exercises. *Ride the Luck* would call him before they arrived at Nev'Lorn.

SHADIA REACHED TO the canister overhead, pulling the red knob that was both handle and face mask. Obligingly the canister gave up its package, the plate descending to shoulder height. Grasping the disk carefully she twisted the red handle. It turned properly in her hand and the initial three minutes of air began flowing from the mask as the Cloak began taking shape. She pushed it toward the floor, stepped into the tube, and as it inflated by her head, she grabbed the blue handle and pulled. That closed the Cloak over her head and with a twist of vapor from the heat seal she was now inside the new Cloak while wearing the old.

Now she reached for the blade on her belt and carefully pierced the diminished Cloak, and writhing awkwardly, stepped out of it, perhaps spicing her language a bit to help, and then a bit more as the old Cloak tangled on her ankle and left her sitting in mid-air. With exasperation she used a few more choice words, asked a couple of pungent questions of the universe at large and cut a bit more with the knife. In another moment, the old Cloak was a mere wrinkle of plastic and a disk, which she handed through the pockets of the new Cloak with relief.

She stuffed it into the waste bin, which was filling rapidly, and surveyed the work area, realizing as she did that she hardly registered the more minor sounds of the space dust on the hull.

Over in the corner, Clonak ter'Meulen, supervisor of pilots, was tampering with a scout issue spacesuit, breaking thereby a truly impressive number of regulations. He had replaced his Cloak nearly a Standard hour before and now sat immersed in carefully deconstructing the suit, with an eye toward keeping the electronics intact.

More or less conversationally—the atmosphere in the ship having gotten up to near 20 percent of normal—he bellowed inside his Cloak.

"Shadia, I hadn't realized you'd spent so much time around Low Port . . ."

She almost laughed and did manage to snort.

"Doubtless, I hurt your ears . . ."

"Well, at least you've hurt my feelings."

She looked at him quizzically.

Clonak glanced away from his work, moving his hand inside the Cloak to pull out a bit of paper towel and mop his brow before continuing.

"I clearly heard you ask whose, ahhh . . . whose *idea* the Cloaks were. Very nearly they are mine!"

Shadia blinked.

"Are you Momson, then?"

"Me, Momson? Not a bit of that, at all." Clonak continued, still busily taking the suit apart. "Momson is some legendary Terran inventor, I gather. No, but the Cloaks—they've only been on scout ships for about 25 years. But then, I guess you could blame Daav yos'Phelium, too, for having the bad judgement to need a Cloak when he didn't have one . . ."

"But I thought the nameplate says that some Terran foundation gave us the money to start installation . . ."

"Right you are. The Richard A. Davis Portmaster Aid Foundation. But I'm afraid that's my fault. They have a wonderful archive—at least equal to the open scout collections!—and I was looking for quick solutions. Headquarters was already moving me into this pilot support track I've ended up in, you see, and dea'Cort himself set me on them.

"When it turned out that we didn't need anything all that esoteric, really, the research librarian was pleased to hand me over to the so-called Implementation Office and they had me walking around in one of these things inside a day. I brought a dozen dozen back for testing and barely a relumma after I had posted off my thank you note, Headquarters sent me off on a secret mission—to pick up a shipload of these things, complete with dispenser canisters."

"Secret mission?" Shadia snorted. "They didn't want other scouts to know you were getting all the plush flights?"

Clonak chuckled briefly at his work.

"Actually, it was far more sinister than that. There's always a faction in the Council of Clans that wants to shut funding for the scouts off, or reduce it. Some of them don't want us doing anything that might benefit Terrans, or they want us to charge for our work, or be turned into pet courier pilots for the High Houses. The idea that we might somehow be in debt to a Terran foundation had to be kept super mum."

Shadia heard the crinkle of the Momson Cloak about her as she shook her head Terran-style and then flipped the hand signal roughly translating as "stupidly assessing the situation, them, as dogs might."

One-handed Clonak replied with "affirm that twice."

Before Shadia could turn back to her work, Clonak stretched himself, permitting his legs to float higher than his head, and held up a series of electronic modules linked by tiny flat cables. At the end of the cables were several tiny power units.

"Shadia, what you see here is the work of a genius."

"Of course," she said politely.

Clonak ignored her. "It's too bad that I nearly destroyed it getting it out of the suit. I can see several more modifications I'll need to make, and then a box-lot of paperwork once we are joyfully returned to Headquarters . . ."

Shadia sighed. "What *is* it?"

"A working transceiver set, of course! What else could it be? Now all we need to do is decide what we might safely say, on what frequency, and how often, for the right people to hear and fetch us away from this lovely idyll of shared pleasure." He moved a shoulder and his feet sank deckward. "I believe we will need your location report by the end of the shift, and since I'm essentailly done with this I'm available to act as your clerk."

RIDE THE LUCK broke into normal space and reported that all was well. Three breaths after, the position report center screen was replaced by a tile of alarms and warnings as the meteor shields went up a notch and the scout's private hailing frequency was crowded by messages and fragments:

". . . ard Jumped out before I could cross-hair him; he definitely took out dea'Ladd!"

". . . was destroyed. Have adequate munitions to continue search pattern . . ."

Daav's hands touched the switches which armed *Ride the Luck*, brought the scans online . . .

". . . have returned fire and am hit. Breath's Duty—notify my clan of our enemy—I have three hours of air, heavy pursuit and no Jump left. Tell Grenada I forgive the counterchance debts. Notify my clan of Balance due these . . ."

Scans showed debris in orbits that should have been clean, and warnaways at Nev'Lorn itself.

Into a battle had come *Ride the Luck*, Tree-and-Dragon broadcasting on all ID ports. No way to tell immediately how old some of the incoming messages might be—

Daav thumbed a switch. "Daav yos'Phelium, Scout Reserve

Captain, copilot of packet boat *Ride the Luck*, requesting berthing information or assignment. Repeat . . ."

Before he was finished, the second iteration he heard a cry of "Korval!" over the open line, and, fainter, "The Caylon's ship!"

The chatter built and by then, *Ride the Luck* had cataloged a dozen objects of note, including two closing tangentially.

On commercial frequency—responding to the ID no doubt— came:

"Freighter *Luck* you are to stand by for boarding by the Department of the Interior; you are under our weapons! Repeat—"

On the scout frequency: "*Luck, Courier 12* here, I have you on my scans. I'm at Breath's Duty, pilot! I have one salvo left before I'm gone. Get away and tell Clan Kia the name of their enemy . . ."

Kia was a Korval trading partner.

Ride the Luck's ranging computer showed the two potential targets and attendant radio frequencies; Daav touched the guidestick and clicked the red circle over one of them. The circle faded to yellow.

Still nothing from Nev'Lorn base.

"Give me my commission, dammit! Are you asleep?" Daav's finger danced over the board. Now he had the ship that had broadcast the duty message identified, and the one that had ordered him to stand by for boarding.

Again the commercial frequency—"Freighter *Luck*, you are under arrest by the Department of the Interior. You are to agree to boarding or we will open fire."

As if to punctuate their demand, the Department's ship fired a beam at *Courier 12*, raking the little vessel from stem to stern. And, finally:

"*Ride the Luck*, this is Nev'Lorn headquarters. Captain yos'Phelium, you are on roster for berth 56A. You are authorized to aid and assist in transit . . ."

"I have conflicting orders," Daav spoke into the mike, both channels open.

The circle on the ranging computer showed orange now.

"This system is under direct supervision of the Department of the Interior," came back the message rather quickly—they were closing fast. "Nev'Lorn Headquarters has been disbanded and is outlawed. Your decision, or we fire, Pilot!"

Nev'Lorn, five light seconds more distant, sent again: "Captain you have a berth waiting . . ."

"Department, " Daav said quietly into the mike, "I am taking your orders under advisement. You have the range on me, I'm afraid."

The image of *Courier 12* seemed to blossom then, as the pilot launched his remaining missiles at the oncoming Department ship. Eight or ten scattered, began maneuvering.

The target circle went dull red.

"Department, please advise best course?" Daav demanded.

That ship, busily lashing out with particle beams at the oncoming missiles, did not reply. The static of those blasts would have torn the transmission out the ether in any case.

The target circle grew a flashing green ring around a bright red center.

With a sigh, Scout Captain Daav yos'Phelium clutched the guidestick and punched the fire button. And again. And again. And again and again until *Ride the Luck* complained about overload and the expanding gases were far too thin to contain survivors.

CLONAK'S GENIAL optimism wasn't sufficient to approve of the ration situation by the time end of shift had come and gone six times, postponed by the simple fact that they still had been unable to achieve complete orbital elements. Between observations and calculations they'd managed to get the test circuit live to the in-system engines and they'd determined that at least a dozen thruster pairs were operable. They might actually be able to go somewhere—if only they knew where to point.

Thanks to the Cloaks, the air supply was good for another thirty days. Food was another matter, since most of it was in storage lockers—if they still existed—in the sealed portion of the ship. They were stretching the interval between meals a little longer each time. At full rations they had food for six days; at their current rate they had fourteen.

⋄⋄⋄

"YOU HAPPENED BY at a fortunate time, Captain," Acting Scout Commander sig'Radia was saying to him. "Not only did you rid us of the last of that infestation, but improved morale merely by appearing, Tree-and-Dragon shouting from your name-points, hard on the heels of rumors that Korval is . . .vanished."

Daav gave her a grave smile. "Korval's luck. May we all walk wary."

She was a woman of about his own age, he estimated, though he did not know her. Obviously, though, she had heard tales of Korval's luck, for she inclined her head formally and murmured, "May it rest peaceful."

"How did this come to pass? An open attack on a scout base by Liadens?"

Scout Commander turned in her chair and pulled a stack of hard-copy messages from under a jar full of firegems.

"Some of it is here," she said, handing him the stack. She seemed about to speak further, but the comm buzzed then; a Healer had been found for the Kia pilot Daav had rescued from the courier boat.

He gave his attention to the messages in his hand. Slowly, a picture built of suspicious activity, followed by conflicting orders and commands from Scout Headquarters and the Council of Clans, muddied by people going missing and a strange epidemic of Scouts being requisitioned—with the assistance of some faction or another within the Council itself—for the mysterious Department of the Interior. Amid it all, a familiar name surfaced.

The commander finished her call and Daav held out the page.

"You may blame Clonak ter'Meulen on my fortuitous arrival—he having sent for me. May I see him? His business was urgent, I gather."

She looked away from his face, then handed him another, much smaller stack of pages. He took them and began leafing through, listening as she murmured, "The Department of the Interior had him targeted. He went down to meet a scout just in from the garbage run—Shadia Ne'Zame. That's when the battle began. They fired on her ship and . . ."

Daav looked up, face bland. Commander sig'Radia shrugged, Terran-style.

"The Department had a warship in-system—say destroyer class. They claimed it was a training vessel. They went after Ne'Zame's ship, fired on her. By then, we were fighting here as well—open firefights and hand-to-hand between us and the Department people here for training."

She showed him empty palms.

"Ne'Zame's ship was hit at least once, returned fire, got some licks in. The Department's ship was closing when she Jumped."

Daav closed his eyes.

"The only wreckage we have is from the destroyer," the commander continued. "There's one piece that might be from a scout ship—but there was other action in that section, and we can't be certain. The destroyer was more than split open—it was shredded—no survivors. If it hadn't been, Nev'Lorn would have been in the hands of the Department of the Interior in truth, when you came in."

Daav opened his eyes. "No word? No infrared beacons? Nothing odd on the off-channels? Clonak is—resourceful. If they went into Little Jump . . ."

Her eyes lit. "Yes, we thought of that. Late, you understand, but we've had tasks in queue ahead. In any case, the chief astrogator gave us this." She turned the monitor on her desk around to face him, touched a button, and a series of familiar equations built, altered by several factors.

Daav blinked—and again, as the numbers slid out of focus. As if from a distance, he heard his own voice ask, courteously, "Of your kindness, may I use the keyboard? Thank you."

Then his hands were on the keyboard. The equation on the screen—changed—in ways both subtle and definitive. He heard his voice again, lecturing:

"The equations are only as good as the assumptions, of course. However, the basic math is sound. This factor *here* will have been much higher, for example, if weapons were being fired—missiles underway in particular would have altered the mass-balance of the system dynamically— and the acceleration of the destroyer—are there recordings of this incident that I may see? I believe there is a significant chance that your astrogator is correct. They may have been *forced* into Little Jump . . ."

The equations danced in his head and on the screen, apart from, but accessible to himself. Moments later, when the acting commander played back the records she had of the encounter, Daav felt an unworldly elation, and watched again as his hands flew along the keypad, elucidating a second, more potent equation.

That done, there was a pause. He heard Aelliana sigh into his ear and found that his body was his own once more.

He looked up from the monitor to meet the scout commander's astonished eyes. She looked away from him, to the construct on the screen, then back to his face.

"Are you," she began. Daav raised his hand.

"Pilot Caylon finds this a very worthy project, Commander. You will understand that Clonak is her comrade, as well." He sighed and looked at the screen. The equation was—compelling, the sort of thing a pilot could make use of. He pointed.

"Your astrogator is to be commended. As you see, we have several congruencies here. This one in particular, which relies on the orbits assumed by the destroyer's fragments, gives us a probability cloud . . ."

The hands on the keyboard were his own this time, the schematic he built from his own store of knowledge.

"Very nearly we have two search bands," he murmured; "one south and one north of the ecliptic, which of course are expanding as we speak. Clonak . . .Clonak is a very stubborn man." He glanced up, meeting the commander's speculative eyes.

"If there is someone you may dispatch to the south, I will search north of the ecliptic." He smiled, wryly. "We may yet retrieve your scouts from holiday."

"ARE YOU READY, Clonak?"

"I am, Shadia."

"Your authorization?"

"The ship is yours."

"As you say."

They'd managed to turn the ship and align it. The idea was simple. They were going to fire what in-system engines they had to decrease the size of their orbit and bring it closer to the more traveled ways of the system. The first time they'd tried, nothing happened, and Clonak had spent another two days tracing wires as Shadia refined the orbit-numbers.

The other necessity was manning the radio, making certain that ship kept an antenna-side to the primary. They were on a round-the-clock talk-and-listen, and would be until—

One of the more raspy bits of space debris in some time distracted them; it sounded almost as if it were rolling along the side of the hull. There was a ping then, and another.

"If we're in cloud of debris—"

"It doesn't sound too bad," Clonak was saying untruthfully, just as a full-sized *clank* ran the hull. Then came more of the scratching sound, almost as if the hull were being sandpapered or—

"Well," Clonak said softly, and then, again. "Well." He moved to the battery-powered monitor and waved his hand at the other scout. "Come along, Shadia. Let's have a look!"

They crowded round the battery-powered monitor and Clonak once more turned it on and twisted the wiring until a connection was made.

The view was altered strangely with a motley green-brown object . . .

Belatedly, Shadia grabbed for the gimmicked suit radio and turned it on—

"Please prepare to abandon ship. This is Daav yos'Phelium and *Ride the Luck*. If Scout ter'Meulen is aboard, it would be kind of him to answer—one's lifemate is concerned for his health."

The hull rang, then, as if *Ride the Luck* had smacked them proper.

"Breath's Duty, but you've the luck," Daav yos'Phelium continued conversationally. "The hull is twisted into the engine back here . . . If I do not receive within the next two Standard minutes an answer of some sort from the resident pilots, I shall have no choice but to force the hatch. Mark. Don't disappoint me, I beg. You can have no idea of how often I've dreamed of forcing open the hatch of a—"

Here, the pilot's mannerly voice was drowned out by Clonak hammering the hull with one of his discarded pieces of piping.

It was Shadia who thumbed the microphone on the makeshift radio and spoke: "We're here, Pilot. Thank you."

✧ The Wine of Memory ✧

"WELL, HERE'S AN IMPROVEMENT," the magician said to his apprentice, watching her walk the red wooden counter across the backs of her fingers. The counter reversed itself, returned along the thin, ringless fingers to the end of the hand, *over* the side, to be deftly caught by that same hand before it had fallen an inch.

Moonhawk looked up with a grin, as proud of mastering this minor bit of hand-skill as she had ever been of learning any of the true-spells taught in Temple. It had taken days of almost constant practice to teach her muscles the rhythm required to move the counter smoothly across her own skin. It was the sort of thing one might do while walking, which was Lute's stated reason for teaching her this skill first. They had been walking for two days.

"I do believe you are ready to learn something a little more difficult," the magician said now, and looked around him.

The road was empty. The road—the track, really, Moonhawk thought—had been empty for two days. Of all the people on Sintia, only Lute and Moonhawk found the village of Karn a destination of interest.

"The season is early," Lute murmured, seeming, as he so often did, to be reading her very thoughts. "When summer is high, this road will be crowded with folk who have business in Karn."

"It will?" Moonhawk frowned after her Temple lessons, recalling the long tales of provinces and products she and the rest of the Maidens had been obliged to memorize. Karn had certainly not been on any of those lists.

She sighed and looked up. Lute was watching her with that particular expression that meant he was receiving the Goddess' own pleasure from her ignorance, which he would not, of course, enlighten until she asked him.

"Very well," she said crossly. "Whatever comes out of Karn, Master Lute, that the world should walk for days to have it?"

"Wine, of course," he answered, setting his bag down in the road with a flourish. "The best wine in all the world that is allowed to those not in Temple."

She blinked. "Wine? But wine comes from Mandiel and Barbary . . ."

"From Astong and Veyru," Lute finished. "Fine vineyards, every one. But the Temples are thirsty. Or greedy. Or both. No drop of wine from those four provinces escapes to a common glass. That wine comes from Karn."

Almost she frowned again, for it was not his place to pass judgement on the Temples—and by extension the Witches who served the Goddess there. But she remembered another lesson from her days as a Maiden in Temple. The wine cellars at Dyan Temple were large and an accurate inventory of vintage and barrel very close to the heart of Merlot, the Temple steward. Inventory was considered the sort of practical, useful work most needed by Maidens who were, perhaps, just a bit prideful of their magics. There had been one season when Moonhawk had spent a good deal of time in the wine cellars, inventory list to hand.

"Attend me now," Lute said, tossing his cloak behind his shoulders.

Moonhawk moved a few steps closer, her irritation forgotten.

"Perhaps you think you have mastered the counter, but the counter may yet be the wiser, eh?" He smiled, but Moonhawk didn't see. All her attention—and all her Witch sense—was focused on his long, clever hands.

"Now we enter the realm of magic, indeed. I am about to reveal to you the method for making a counter disappear." He extended his empty right hand, frowned and flexed the fingers.

"First, naturally enough, one must make a counter appear." And there, held lightly between his first and second fingers was a bright green counter. How it had come there, Lute and his skill knew. Certainly, Moonhawk did not, having seen neither the movement that would have retrieved a cleverly hidden counter nor felt the surge of power that would have been necessary to create a counter. Or the illusion of one.

Lute extended his hand. "Please verify that this is indeed a common wooden counter, such as might be found in any gaming house on Sintia."

She took the disk, felt the smoothness of the paint, the rough edge of wood where the caress of many fingers had worn the paint away. No illusion, this. She handed it back.

"I find it a common wooden counter," she said, for she must also practice the eloquence of his speech, which served, so he said, to divert the attention of an audience and give a magician valuable seconds in which to work. "Such as might be found in any gaming house on the planet."

"Excellent," he said, receiving the token on his callused palm.

"A common counter." He tossed it lightly into the air, caught it on the back of his hand and walked it negligently across his fingers.

"Behaving commonly." He flipped his hand, caught the counter between thumb and forefinger and held it high.

"Now, behold its uncommon attribute."

Moonhawk stifled a curse: There was nothing between the magician's thumb and forefinger but sunshine and cool spring air.

Lute lowered his hand and smiled. "Another lesson that may be practiced as one walks. Though we haven't far to walk now. Tonight, we shall eat one of Veverain's splendid dinners, sample somewhat of last year's vintage and sleep wrapped in soft, sweet-smelling blankets."

Moonhawk stared from him to the red wooden counter in her hand.

"I'm to practice? Pray what am I to practice, Master Lute? I saw neither pass nor Witch power."

Lute smiled. "You saw that it was possible." He bent and retrieved his bag. "Come. Veverain's hospitality tugs my heart onward."

THE TRACK CURVED 'round a grove of dyantrees, and there was Karn, tidily laid out along two main streets and a marketplace. To the east of the village lay the fields; to the west, the winter livestock pens. Behind the village rose a hill, showing terrace upon terrace of leafless brown vines.

There were folk about on the streets, and Lute's stride lengthened. Moonhawk stretched her own long legs to keep the pace, the red counter forgotten for the moment in the pocket of her cloak.

"Ho, Master Lute!" A stocky man in a leather apron raised a hand. "Spring is here at last!"

"And not a moment too soon," Lute agreed with a smile, crossing the street to where the man stood in the tavern's doorway, Moonhawk a step behind him. "How came the village through the winter?"

The man looked sober. "We lost a few to the cold—oldsters or infants, all. The rest of us came through well enough. Except for—." The man's face changed, and Moonhawk caught the edge of his distress against her Witch sense.

"You're bound for Veverain's?" he asked, distress sharpening.

"Of course I am bound for Veverain's! Am I a fool, to pass by the best food, the snuggest bed and the most gracious hostess in the village?"

"Not a fool," the man returned quietly, "only short of news."

Lute went entirely still. Moonhawk, slanting a glance at his face, saw his mouth tighten, black eyes abruptly intense.

"Our Lady of the Snows has taken Veverain?" he asked, matching the other's quiet tone.

The man moved his hand—describing helplessness. "Not—That is to say—Veverain. Ah, Goddess take me for a muddlemouth!" He lifted a hand and ran his fingers through his thinning hair.

"It was Rowan went out to feed the stock one morning in the

thick of winter and when he didn't come back for the noon meal, Veverain went out to find him." He paused to draw a deep, noisy breath. "He'd never gotten to the pens. A tree limb—heavy, you understand, with the ice—had come down and crushed him dead."

Lute closed his eyes. Moonhawk raised her hand and traced the sign of Passing in the air.

"May he be warm, in the Garden of the Goddess."

The tavern-keeper looked at her, startled. Lute opened his eyes, hands describing one of his elegant gestures, calling attention to her as if she were a rare gemstone.

"Behold, one's apprentice!" he said, but Moonhawk thought his voice sounded strained. "Moonhawk, here is the excellent Oreli, proprietor of the justly renowned tavern, Vain Disguise."

Oreli straightened from his lean to make a somewhat inexpert bow. When he straightened, his eyes were rounder than ever.

"Lady."

Moonhawk inclined her head. "Keeper Oreli. Blessings upon you."

He swallowed, but before he could make answer, Lute was speaking again.

"When did this tragedy occur, Friend Oreli? You give me to believe the house is closed. Is Veverain yet in mourning?"

"Mourning," the other man repeated and half-laughed, though the sound was as sad as any Moonhawk had ever heard. "You might say mourning." He sighed, spreading his hands, palm up, for them both to see.

"Rowan died just past of mid-winter. Veverain . . . Veverain shut the house up, excepting only the room they had shared. She turned us away, those of us who were her friends, or Rowan's—turned us away, shunned our company and our aid. And she just sits in that house by herself, Master Lute. Sits there alone in the dark. Her sister's man tends the animals; her niece tilled the kitchen garden and put in the early vegetables. They say they never see her; that she will not even open the door to kin—and you know, *you* know, Master Lute!— that Rowan would never have wanted such a thing!"

"A convivial man, Rowan," Lute murmured. "He and Veverain were well-matched in that."

"Is she still alive?" Moonhawk asked, somewhat impatiently. "Her kin say that they never see her, that she will not open the door. How are they certain that she has not been Called, or that she has not taken some injury?"

"We see the hearth smoke," Oreli said. "We—the care basket is left full by the door in the morning. Some mornings, the basket and the food are still there. Often enough, the basket is empty. She is alive, that we do know. Alive, but dead to life."

Moonhawk frowned. "She has been taking care baskets since Solstice?"

Oreli raised a hand. "A long time, I know. The baskets usually are not sent so long. Forgive me, Lady, but you are a stranger here; you do not know how it was . . . how Veverain cared for us all. When our daughter was ill, we had some of Veverain's baskets—hot soup, fresh bread, tiny wheels of her special cheese—you remember Veverain's cheeses, eh, Master Lute?"

"With fondness and anticipation," Lute replied, somewhat absently. He glanced at the sky. "The day grows old," he murmured.

Abruptly, he bowed to the tavern-keeper, cloak swirling.

"Friend Oreli, keep you well. I hope to visit your fine establishment once or twice during our stay. Immediately, however, the duty of friendship calls. I to Veverain, to offer what aid I might."

"You must try, of course," Oreli said. "When she turns you away, remember that the Disguise serves a hearty supper. And that Mother Juneper will gladly house you and your apprentice."

Lute inclined his head. "I will remember. But, first, let us be certain that Veverain will refuse us." He turned, cloak billowing, and strode off down the street at such a pace that Moonhawk had to run a few steps to catch him.

VEVERAIN'S HOUSE was at the bottom of the village; a long, sprawling place, enclosed by a neat fence, shaded in summer by two well-grown dyantrees. The trees, like their kin at the bend in the track, showed a pale green fuzzing along their limbs; at the roots of each was a scattering of bark and dead branches—winter's toll. When the dyantrees came to leaf, then it would be spring, indeed.

Lute pushed open the whitewashed gate and went up the graveled pathway, Moonhawk on his heels. The yard they passed through seemed neglected, ragged; as if those who had care of it had not come forth with rakes and barrows to clear away the wrack of winter and make the land ready for spring.

There were some indications that neglect was not the yard's usual state; Moonhawk spied mounds which surely must be flowerbeds under drifts of dead leaves, more leaves half-concealing a bird-pool, rocks set here and there with what might prove to be art, once the debris was cleared away.

Gravel crunching under his boots, Lute strode on, to Moonhawk's eye unobservant. He was also silent, which rare state spoke to her more eloquently of his worry than any grandiose phrase.

The path curved 'round the side of the house, and here were the neat rows of the kitchen garden put in by the niece, a blanket over the more tender seedlings, to shield them from the cold of the coming night.

A few steps more, and the path ended at a single granite step up to a roofed wooden porch. A black-and-white cat sat tidily on the porch, companioning a basket covered with a blue checked cloth. Lute paused on the step, bent and offered his finger to the cat in greeting.

"Tween, old friend. I hope I find you well?"

The cat graciously touched his nose to the offered fingertip, then rose, stretched with languid thoroughness, and yawned.

"Tween?" Moonhawk asked quietly. Often, over the months of their travel together, she had deplored the magician's overfondness for words; yet, confronted now with a Lute who walked silent, she perversely wished to have her light-tongued comrade of the road returned.

Lute glanced at her, black eyes hooded. "It was Rowan's joke, see you. The cat is neither all black, which would easily allow of it being named Newmoon; nor all white, which leads one rather inescapably to Snowfall. Indeed, as Rowan would have it, the cat lands precisely between two appropriate and time-honored cat names—an act of deliberate willfulness, so Rowan swore—and thus became Tween."

He looked down at the cat, who was stropping against the care basket.

"Rowan loved a joke—the more complex the jest, the louder he laughed."

He shook himself, then, and mounted the porch, stooping to pick up the basket. The cat followed him to the door, tail high. Lute put his hand on the latch, pushed . . .

"Locked."

"Surely you expected that," Moonhawk murmured and Lute sighed.

"A man may hear ill news and yet still hope that it is untrue. Optimistic creatures, men. I did not hope to find Rowan alive, but . . ." He let the rest drift off, raised his hand and brought sharp knuckles against the wood, then drifted back a step, head tipped inquisitively to one side. The cat settled beside him and began to groom.

At respectful intervals, Lute leaned forward to knock twice, then three times. The door remained closed.

"Well, then." He set the care basket down, slipped his bag from its carry-strap and shook it. Three spindly legs appeared, holding the bag at a convenient height. Moonhawk watched closely while he opened the clasp and put his hand inside: Lute's magic bag held such a diverse and numerous collection of objects that she had lately formed the theory that it was not one bag, but three, attached in some rotating, hand-magical manner undetectable to her Witch senses.

"What are you going to do?" she asked. "Break the lock?"

He looked at her. "Break the lock on the house of one of my oldest friends? Am I a barbarian, Lady Moonhawk? If things were otherwise, it might have been necessary to resort to lockpicks, but I assure you that my skill is such that the lock would have suffered no ill."

She blinked. "Lockpicks? Another hand-magic?"

"A very powerful magic," Lute said solemnly, and withdrew his hand from the bag, briefly displaying a confusing array of oddly contorted wires. "By means of these objects, a magician may learn the shape and secret of a strange lock and impel it to open."

"It sounds like thieve's magic to me, Master Lute."

"Pah! As if a thief could be so skilled! But no matter. We need not resort to lockpicks for this." He replaced the muddle of wires in his bag.

"No?" said Moonhawk, eyebrows rising. "How then will you open the door? Sing?"

"Sing? Perhaps they sing locks at Temple. I have a superior method." He snapped his bag shut and hung it back on the strap.

"Which is?"

"A key." He displayed it: a rough iron thing half the length of his hand.

"A key," she repeated. "And how came you by that?"

"Veverain gave it me. And Rowan gave me leave to use it, if by chance I should arrive during daylight and find the door locked." He gestured, showing her the lowering sun. "It is, I see, still daylight. I find the door—alas!—is locked. Bring the basket."

He stepped up to the door, key at ready. Moonhawk bent and picked up the care basket, settling it over her arm. A sharp snap sounded, Lute pushed the door open and stepped into the house beyond, the cat walking at his knee.

With a deep sense of foreboding, Moonhawk followed.

"VEVERAIN?" LUTE'S VOICE lacked its usual ringing vitality, as if the room's dimness was heavy enough to muffle sound. "Veverain, it's Lute!"

Moonhawk stood by the door, letting her eyes adjust; slowly, she picked out a table, benches, the hulking mass of a cold cookstove.

"Let us shed some light on the situation," Lute said. A blot of darkness in the kitchen's twilight, he moved surely across the room. There was a clatter as he slid back the lock bars and threw the shutters wide, admitting the day's last glimmer of sun.

Details sprang into being. Dusty pots hung neatly above the cold stove; spice bundles dangled from the low eaves; pottery was stacked, orderly and cobwebbed, on whitewashed shelves. The table was dyanwood, scrubbed white; the work surfaces were tiled, the glaze dull with dust.

"Well." Face grim, Lute shed cloak and bag, and dropped them on the table. Crossing the room, he pulled a lamp from its shelf and carried it and a pottery jug to a work table.

Moonhawk walked slowly forward. Despite the light from the windows, the room seemed—foggy. It was also cold—bone-chilling, heart-stopping cold. She wondered that Lute had put aside his cloak.

She set the care basket on the table and pulled her own cloak tighter about her. Lute had filled the lamp and was trimming the wick with his silver knife. Moonhawk shivered, and recalled the neat stack of wood on the porch, hard by the door.

"I'll start the stove," she said to Lute's back. He looked 'round abstractedly.

"Yes. Thank you."

"No," said another voice, from the back of the room. "I will thank you both to leave."

Moonhawk spun. Lute calmly finished with the wick and lit it with a snap of his fingers, before he, too, turned to face his hostess.

"Veverain, have I changed so much in one year's travel? It's Lute."

"Perhaps you have not changed," the woman in the faded houserobe said with a lack of emotion that raised the fine hairs along the back of Moonhawk's neck, "but all else has. Rowan is dead."

"Yes. I met Oreli in the High Street." Lute went forward, hands outstretched. "I loved him, too, Veverain."

She stared at him, stonily, and neither moved to meet him, nor lifted her hands to receive his. Lute stopped, hands slowly dropping to his sides.

"Leave me," the woman said again, and it seemed to Moonhawk that her voice carried an edge this time, as if her stoniness covered an emotion too wild to be confined for long.

Perhaps Lute heard it, too, or perhaps his skill brought him more subtle information. In any wise, he did not leave, but stood, hands spread wide, and voice aggrieved.

"Leave? Without even a cup of tea to warm me? You yourself said that I should never want for at least that of you. The thought of taking a cup of tea at your table has been all that has made the last day's walking bearable!"

"Have you not understood?" And the untamed grief was plain to the ear, now. "I say to you that *Rowan is dead!*"

"Rowan is dead," Lute repeated gently. "He is beyond the comforts of tea and the love of friends. We, however—" He gestured 'round the room, a simple encircling, devoid of stage flourish, and Moonhawk was absurdly relieved to find herself included—"are not."

There was a long moment of silence.

"Tea," Veverain said, and her voice was stone once more. "Very well."

"I'll start the stove," Moonhawk said for the second time, and went out to fetch an armload of wood.

When she came back to the kitchen, some minutes later, Veverain was in Lute's arms, sobbing desperately against his chest.

MOONHAWK IT WAS who made tea in Veverain's kitchen that evening, and served it, silently, to the two who faced each other across the table. She carried her own mug to a wall-bench and sat, quietly watching and listening.

"I cannot," the woman was saying to Lute, "I *must* not forget. I—Rowan—we swore that neither would ever forget the other, no matter what else the future might destroy."

"Yes," Lute murmured, "but surely Rowan would not have wanted this—that you lock yourself away from kin, take from your neighbors' kitchens and give nothing—not even thanks!—in return. Rowan was never so mean."

"He was not," Veverain agreed, her fingers twisting 'round themselves. "Rowan was generous."

"As you are. Come, Veverain, you must stop this. Open your house again to your well-wishers. Tend the garden your niece has started for you, clear the flowerbeds and rake the gravel. Soon enough, the vines will need you, too. It will not be the same as if Rowan worked at your side, but—I promise!—these familiar things will soothe you. In time, you will—"

"In time I will forget!" Veverain interrupted violently. "No! I will *not* forget! Every day, I read his journals. Every day, I sit in his place in our room and I recall our days together. Everything, everything . . . I must not forget a syllable, the timbre of his voice, the lines of his face—"

"Veverain!" Lute reached for her hands, but they fluttered away from capture.

"You do not understand!" Her voice was shrill with agony. "Before you first came to us there was in this village a woman called Redfern, her man—Velix—and their babe. That summer, there was an illness in the village—many died, among them Redfern's man and babe. She grieved and would speak to no one, though she accomplished all her usual business. In the fall, she shut up her house and went to her sister in another village. Two years later, she returned to us, with a new babe and a man she had taken in her sister's village." Veverain's fluttering hands lighted on the cooling mug. Automatically, she raised it to her lips and drank.

"I saw Redfern in the street," she continued, somewhat less shrill. "We spoke of her babe, and of how things had changed in the village in the years she had been gone from us. I mentioned Velix, and she— she *stared* at me, as if I spoke of a stranger. She had forgotten him, Master Lute! It chilled me to the heart, and I vowed I would never so dishonor my love."

"Veverain, this is not the way to honor Rowan." Moonhawk had never heard the magician's voice so tender.

Veverain turned her face away. "You have had your tea," she said, hardly. "There are houses in the high village who will be happy to guest you."

Moonhawk saw Lute's shoulders tense, as if he had taken a blow. He sat silent for a long moment, until the woman across from him noticed either the absence of his voice or the presence of himself, and reluctantly turned her face again to his.

"Lute—"

He raised a hand, interrupting her. "How," he said and there was an electric undercurrent in his voice that Moonhawk did not entirely like. "How if you were shown a way to return to life at the same time you honor your vow to remember?"

There was hesitation, and Moonhawk saw, for just a instant, the woman Veverain had been—vibrant, strong, and constant—through the diminished, grief-wracked creature who sat across from Lute.

"Can you work such a magic?" she asked.

"Perhaps one of us can," Lute replied and stood. "Excuse me a moment, Housemother. I must consult with my apprentice."

"FORGET?" LUTE REPEATED. "But it is the possibility of forgetting that is terrifying her out of all sense!"

"Nonetheless," Moonhawk said, with rather more patience than she felt, "forgetfulness is all I have to offer. I know of no spell or blessing that will insure memory. I only know how to remove such pain as this, which is become a threat to a good and decent woman's life. She suffers much, and I may ease her—will ease her, if she wishes it. But I think she will choose instead to honor her vow." She hesitated, caught by a rare feeling of inadequacy.

"I am sorry, Master Lute."

"Sorry mends no breakage," Lute snapped. Moonhawk felt a sharp retort rise to her tongue and managed, just, to keep it behind her teeth. After all, she reminded herself, Lute, too, had taken losses—not only Rowan, but Veverain, was gone beyond him.

"Your pardon, Lady Moonhawk," his voice was formal, without the edge of irony that often accompanied his use of her title. "That was ill-said of me. I find the Goddess entirely too greedy, that She must always Call the best so soon. How are the rest of us to find the way to grace, when our Rowans are snatched away before their teaching is done?" He sighed.

"But that is matter between myself and the Goddess, not between you and I."

Moonhawk inclined her head, accepting his apology. "It is . . ." she said formally, and bit down on the last word before it escaped, silently cursing herself for fool.

"Forgotten," Lute finished the phrase, tiredly, and looked past her, up into the starry sky. "There must be something," he murmured, and then said nothing more for several minutes, his eyes on the clear glitter of stars, for all the world as if he had entered trance.

Finally, he shook himself, much as a Witch might do when

leaving trance, to re-acquaint herself with the physical body. He brought his eyes down to her face.

"I must try," he said, soberly. "Rowan would want me to try." He extended a hand and touched her lightly on the sleeve. "You are a Witch and have the ear of the Goddess. Now would be a good time to pray."

VEVERAIN SAT AT the table where they had left her, hands tucked around the empty tea cup, shoulders slumped. Her eyes were closed, her cheeks shining with tears in the lamplight.

Seeing her thus, Lute paused, and Moonhawk saw him bring his hands up and move them in one of his more grandiose gestures, plucking a bright silk scarf from empty air. Another pass and the scarf was gone. Lute took a breath.

"There is something that may be attempted," he announced, and it was the Master Magician's full performance voice now. "If you are willing to turn your hand to magic."

Veverain opened her eyes, looking up at him. "Magic?"

"A very old and fragile magic," Lute assured her solemnly. "It was taught me by my master, who had it from his, who had it from his, who had it from the Mother of Huntress City Temple herself. From Whose Hand the lady received the spell, we need not ask. But!" He raised his hand, commanding attention. "For this magic, as for any great magic, there is a price. Are you willing to pay?"

Veverain stared into his face. "I am," she said, shockingly quiet.

"Then let it begin!" Lute's hands carved the air in the same eloquent gesture that had lately summoned the scarf. Stepping forward, he placed an object on the table: a small, extremely supple leather pouch. Moonhawk had seen thousands like it in her life—a common spellbag, made to be suspended from the neck by a ribbon, or a leather cord.

"Into this bag," he intoned, "will be placed five items evocative of Rowan. No less than five, no more than five." He stepped back and looked sternly into Veverain's face. "You will choose the five."

"Five?" she protested. "Rowan was multitudes! Five—"

"Five, a number beloved of the Goddess. No more, no less." Lute was implacable. "Choose."

Veverain pushed herself to her feet, her eyes wide. "How long?" she whispered. "How long do I have to choose?"

"Five minutes to choose five items. Listen to your heart and your choices will be true."

For a moment, Moonhawk thought the other woman would refuse, would crumple back onto the bench, hide her face in her hands and wail. But Veverain had been woven of tougher cord than that. She swayed a moment, but made a good recover, chin up and showing a flash, perhaps, of the woman she had been.

"Very well," she said to Lute. "Await me here." She swept from the room as if her faded houserobe were grand with embroidery and the stone floor not thick with dust.

When she was gone, Lute looked up at the beam with its dangling bunches of herbs, reached up and snapped off a single sprig. It was no sooner in his hand than it vanished; where, Moonhawk could not hazard a guess.

That done, he went over to the table, pulled out the bench and sat, his hands flat, apparently content to await Veverain's return in silence.

Moonhawk drifted over to the wall-bench and settled in to watch.

"HERE," VEVERAIN SAID, and placed them, one by one, on the table before her: a curl of russet-colored hair, a scrap of paper, a gray and green stone, a twig.

"That is four," Lute said, chidingly.

"I have not done," she answered and raised her hands to her neck, drawing a rawhide cord up over her head. Something silver flashed in the lamplight; flashed again as she had it off the cord and placed by the others.

"His promise-ring," she said quietly. "And that is five, Master Lute."

"And that is five," he agreed, hands still palm-flat against the tabletop, in an attitude both quiescent and entirely un-Lute-like.

"What will you do now?" Veverain inquired. Lute raised his eyebrows.

"You misunderstand: it is not I who will do, but you. If you expect that you will sit there and be done to, pray disabuse yourself of the notion."

"But," she stared at him, distress growing, "I am no Witch. I have no schooling, no talent. How am I to build a spell?" Moonhawk could only applaud the housemother's good sense. By her own certain reckoning, it required some number of years to become proficient in spell-craft.

Lute, however, was unworried on this point.

"Have I not said that I have the way of it from my master and all the way back to She who first received the gift of the Goddess? I am here to guide you. But it is you who must actually perform the task, or the spell will have no power."

"I will—put these things in that bag?" Veverain asked. "That is all?"

"Not quite all. Each item must receive its charge. The best technique is to pick up a single item, hold it in your hand and recall—in words or in thought—the connection between Rowan and the object. In this manner, the spell will build, piece by piece, each piece interlocked with and informed by the others."

Which was as apt a description of spell structure as she had ever heard, thought Moonhawk. But Veverain had no glimmer of Witch-sense about her and the tiny flickerings of talent she sometimes caught from Lute were not nearly sufficient to build and bind the spell he described.

Even if such a spell were possible.

At the table, Veverain glanced down among her choices, and put forth a hand. Moonhawk leaned forward, Witch-sense questing, shivering as she encountered the raging gray torrent of Veverain's grief.

Veverain's hand descended, taking up the bright lock of hair.

"This is Rowan's hair," she said tentatively, and Moonhawk felt—something—stir against her Witch-sense. "When we had kept household less than a year, he was chosen by the Master of the Vine to work a season at Veyru in exchange of which we received a vineman of Veyru. The Master of the Vine came with a delegation and petitioned my permission for Rowan—as if I would have denied him such an opportunity! We had been together so short a time, and Veyru is no small journey—I joked that I would not recognize him when he returned. In answer, he cut off this curl and told me that I should always know him, by the flame that lived in his hair."

Carefully, she put the lock into the small leather bag. Lute said nothing, sitting still as a statue of himself.

Veverain chose the gray and green rock.

"When Rowan left home for that season in Veyru, he bore with him this stone from our land so that wherever he was, he would always be home."

The stone joined the lock of hair in the bag and there was definitely something a-building now. Moonhawk could see two thick lines of flame, intersecting at a right angle, hanging just above Veverain's head. She held her breath, staring, and Veverain picked up the scrap of paper.

"The winter after Rowan returned from Veyru was a bitter one. We spent the days in the window, a book between us, while I taught him his letters. He learned to read—and write!—quickly, nor, once he had the skills, did he rest. He read every book in the village, and came back from the vineyards one evening to tell me that he had determined to write a book on the lore of the vine, so that the young vinemen would have a constant teacher and the old a check to their memories. He wrote that book, and others, and kept his journals. More, he passed his skills to other men of the village, who have taught their sons, so Karn need not forget the cure for a vine blight encountered in my mother's time." She hesitated, fingers caressing the scrap.

"This paper bears his signature—the very first time he signed his name."

Lingeringly, the scrap of paper went into the bag and Moonhawk very nearly gasped. The third interlock was a bar of flame as thick as her arm, burning a pure, luminous white.

Carefully, Veverain picked up the scrap of wood.

"This is a piece from our vines on the hill. Rowan loved the vines, the grapes, the wine."

A fourth bar of fire joined the first three, blazing. Stretching her

Witch-sense, Moonhawk found the other woman's grief significantly calmer, less gray, melting, like heavy fog, in the brightness of the spell she built.

For the last time, Veverain reached to the table, and picked up the scarred silver band.

"This is Rowan's promise-ring," she said, so quietly Moonhawk had to strain to hear. "He wore it every day for twenty-five years. If anything on this earth will remember Rowan, this will."

The fifth bar of fire was so bright, Moonhawk's Witch-sense shied from it, dazzled. So, the thing was built, and a powerful spell it was, too. But it wanted binding and it wanted binding now, before the heat of it caught the timbers of the house.

At the table, Lute moved. His right hand rose, the fingers flickered, and there between finger and thumb was the twig he had broken from the herb bundle.

"Rosemary, Queen of Memory," he intoned, solemn as a prayer, "keep Rowan close." He placed the sprig in the bag. Reaching out, he took up the rawhide cord on which Veverain had worn Rowan's ring, and began to tie the spellbag shut.

"In love, memory; in life, love." His hands moved more complexly now, creating two elaborate knots, and half of a third. Sternly, he looked at the woman across from him.

"Once this bag is sealed with the third knot, the spell is made. Once made, it cannot be unmade." He extended the bag, the final knot incomplete, the spell burning, dangerously bright, above the woman's head.

Veverain took the cord in her two hands, and with infinite care made the final knot complete.

"Sealed with my heart, that I never forget," she said, and pulled the cord tight.

Above her head, invisible to all but the staring Witch, the flaming bars wheeled, blurred and vanished, leaving behind, for those who could hear such things, the definitive snap of a spell sturdy-built and bound.

"Stand," Lute said, doing so himself. Veverain rose and he set the bag on its rawhide cord about her neck. "Wear it. And never forget."

From the floor, a flash of white-and-black ascended, landing light-footed on the table. Tween the cat bumped against the housemother's arm, tail held joyously aloft.

Veverain smiled.

"HAVE YOU MASTERED the counter yet?" the magician asked his apprentice as they walked toward the high village in the morning. Behind them, their hostess was already engaged with broom and dust rag, the windows flung open to receive the day.

"You know I haven't!" his apprentice retorted, hotly. "If you must know, Master Lute, I don't think you ever made that counter disappear in the first place—you merely entranced me into believing you had done so!"

"Ah, very good!" Lute said unexpectedly. "You have learned a basic truth of our trade: People make their own magic."

Moonhawk faltered, thinking of what had gone forth last night. "Master Lute, the spell you made last night for Veverain . . ."

"An illustrative case," he said, refusing to meet her eyes.

"No," she said, and put a hand on his arm, stopping him. Determined, she waited until he met her eyes, though she did not compel him do so—indeed, she was not certain that she could compel him to do so, Witch though she was.

The black eyes were on hers.

"I wanted you to know—the spell you made for Veverain was *true*. I saw it building; I saw its binding." She took a breath. "It was well done, Master Lute."

"So." He sighed, then shrugged. "But that does not change the original premise—people *do* make their own magic, just as many see only what they wish to see. Now, about the disappearing counter . . ." He flipped his cloak behind his shoulders and showed her his hands.

"If you wish to make counters appear and disappear, you would do well to supply yourself with several of the same color and hide them about your person. I, for instance, keep several green counters behind my belt—" A flourish, in the grand style, and there they were—four green counters held between the fingers of his left hand.

"Your belt!" protested Moonhawk. "You never—"

"I also," Lute interrupted, implacable, "keep several behind my collar." Another grand flourish and there were four more—yellow this time—between the fingers of his right hand.

"Master Lute—"

"And when you are done with them, why, it's a simple thing to put them away." A shake of both hands and the counters were gone.

Moonhawk drew a deep breath.

"Of course," said Lute, "it is often wise to keep a counter or two elsewhere than upon one's person. Like the one I store behind your ear."

"Behind my ear!" she cried, but there was Lute's hand, brushing past her cheek, and then reappearing, triumphantly displaying a red counter.

Moonhawk sighed.

"Master Lute?"

"Yes, Lady Moonhawk?"

"You're a dreadful master."

"And you," Lute said, turning toward the village, "are an impertinent apprentice. It is a good thing, don't you think, that we are so very well matched?"

✧ Certain Symmetry ✧

THE MORNING OF the sixth and final day of Little Festival dawned in pastel perfection, promising another pellucid day of pleasure for festival-goers.

Pat Rin yos'Phelium Clan Korval, a faithful five-day attendee, had failed through press of pleasure to greet the dawn from the near side—and likewise failed of observing it from the far side, as he was most soundly asleep, and remained so for some hours beyond.

When he did rise and betake himself to his study, he found the day's letters and packets piled neatly to hand, the screen displaying his preferred news service, and a pot of tea gently steaming next to a porcelain cup.

Pat Rin poured for himself and settled into his chair, rapidly scanning the news summary.

The results of yesterday's skimmer races at Little Festival were, inevitably, top news. It could not be otherwise, with both the thodelm of yos'Galan and the nadelm of Korval entire in participation.

Pat Rin sighed, gently, and sipped his tea. One's mother was annoyed, however courteously she had accepted one's cousin's instruction in the matter. He sipped again, savoring the blend, and allowed his gaze to wander from the screen for a moment.

One's cousin had proven . . . unanticipated. One encountered an edge—and a precision of cut—which had not been noted before cousin Val Con's departure for the scouts. It might be that scout training had produced this surprising alteration in the unassuming—even shy—halfling Pat Rin recalled. Or, as one's mother contended, it might simply be that Val Con was coming into his own, that genes would tell, and by the gods it had seemed for a long and telling moment as if her brother Daav himself had stood before her.

Well.

Pat Rin had some more tea, and set the cup aside. He would need to acquaint himself with this new iteration of Val Con. No doubt this skimmer race victory would bring to him any number of gentle inquiries as to the . . . availability . . . of the nadelm. He made a note to speak—unofficially, of course!—to cousin Nova regarding Val Con's current standing with regard to the marriage mart. In the meanwhile, his own business beckoned.

He brought his attention once more to the news screen, noted that several of his more minor investments were performing with gratifying efficiency; read with bored interest the listing of contract-marriages negotiated and consummated; learned of a brawl in mid-Port between the crews of a Terran freighter and a Liaden tug; scanned the list of performances, contests and displays scheduled for this, the last day of Festival, and—blinked.

Fal Den ter'Antod Clan Imtal had died.

Pat Rin called for more information and quickly learned that Fal Den's kin had published a suicide to the Council of Clans and had declined, as was their right, to provide particulars. Business partners and allies of Clan Imtal were advised that the Clan was in full mourning; that the viewing box and pleasure tents held by Imtal would be closed for the remainder of the season; and that those who had been engaged in Balancing accounts with Fal Den should soon find themselves satisfied.

Pat Rin closed his eyes.

He could not name himself a close friend of Fal Den ter'Antod, but he had certainly known the man, and had placed a certain value upon him. Neither a great beauty nor a great intellect, Fal Den possessed charm and an engaging forthrightness of manner that made him an agreeable and even welcome companion. His faults included a belief in the forthrightness of others and a rather thin skin, yet despite these he capably managed both an impeccable *melant'i* and the not-inconsiderable interests of his family on the Port. To believe that Fal Den was dead, and by his own hand . . .

Pat Rin opened his eyes, reached out and touched the discreet pearly button set into his desk.

Fal Den dead. He had seen him only three days past, on the arm of Hia Cyn yo'Tonin, which was deplorable of course, and had Fal Den been the sibling Pat Rin did not possess, he would have been moved to whisper a word in his ear . . .

The door to his office slid open and the excellent pel'Tolian, his general man, stepped within and bowed.

"Good day, Lord Pat Rin."

"Alas, I must disagree," Pat Rin returned. "I find it thus far a singularly distressing day."

"Perhaps matters will improve, as the hours move on," Mr. pel'Tolian suggested.

"Perhaps they will. Certainly, it is possible. In the meantime, however, I must request you to procure a mourning basket and have it delivered to the House of Imtal. I will write the card myself."

"Very good, sir." The man bowed. "Shall you wish to partake of a meal?"

"A light nuncheon. And a glass of the jade."

"Very good, sir," Mr. pel'Tolian said again and went away, the door sliding silently shut behind him.

Pat Rin sat with his eyes closed for perhaps the count of twelve, then turned to deal with his mail.

There were four letters and two packets. Two letters were solicitations of funding for ventures so wonderfully risky that to describe them as "speculative" was to overreach the facts by several magnitudes of wishful thinking. Such letters originated with the same sort of person who thought it . . . fitting . . . to invite him—as multi-season champion at pistol and short arms at Tey Dor's—to join hunting parties on distant outworlds where he might slog through underbrush for days and fire mini-cannons at blameless creatures while enjoying the company of those to whom nothing was more pleasurable . . . He dropped both solicitations into the recycler.

Next was an invitation from Eyan yo'Lanna to make one of her house party, proposed for the middle of next relumma. That was good—sufficient time to have the tailor produce something new and appropriate, perhaps involving the yo'Lanna colors. The sudden fashion of declaring a party within hours or even minutes—the "express" mode, as it was called—made it difficult for one to plan ahead even as it made judging the party's . . . desirability . . . all but impossible.

Eyan's parties, however, were often amusing, correct without being stifling, and always informative. Pat Rin reached into the right hand drawer of the desk, pulled out a stiff ivory card with Korval's Tree-and-Dragon embossed on the front, opened it and wrote the appropriate graceful acceptance. He slid the card into an envelope, penned the direction with his own hand, affixed one of Korval's postage coupons, and placed it in the carved wooden tray that served as his outbox.

The fourth letter was from his fosterfather, Luken bel'Tarda, begging the pleasure of his company that evening for a private dinner at Ongit's.

Pat Rin smiled. The invitation to Ongit's was a joke, by which Luken meant to convey that Pat Rin was arrears in visits. In which complaint, he thought, glancing at the calendar, Luken was entirely justified.

He pulled out a sheet of paper bearing only his name, wrote that he would be pleased to dine with his fosterfather this very evening and begged his pardon for being a light-minded flutter-about-town. He signed himself "Your affectionate son," sealed, directed, stamped, and placed the completed billet in the wooden tray.

The door of his study opened to admit Mr. pel'Tolian, bearing the requested light nuncheon and glass. This, he disposed upon the small table to Pat Rin's left, then picked up the completed mail and, cat-footed, departed,

Pat Rin turned his attention to the first of the two packets. The postage was Aragon's. He had shared several delightful and adventurous Festival hours with a daughter of the House only yesterday. As the adventure had been at the lady's initiative, Pat Rin assumed the packet to contain a Fairing—a gift of gratitude. He broke the seal, unfolded the box, shook out the silken garment enclosed—and very nearly groaned.

He had expected Shan and Val Con's escapade to result in a rash of monstrosities aping Val Con's innovative cloak, the so-called "skimmer" he'd used to such astonishing effect in yesterday's races. He had simply not expected the fashion to have taken so quickly.

Aragon's third daughter had sent him a skimmer—blue, where Val Con's original had been warning light orange—which modification was not, Pat Rin thought, as pleasing as one must have assuredly assumed that it would be. The name of the tailor was impeccable—in fact, his mother's own tailor—and the material flawless. Nor did it seem at all unlikely that the silk had been chosen to precisely match the color of his earring, of which the lady had been most fond. Ah, youth.

He sighed and folded the wretched thing onto his keyboard, and turned back to the opened box. There was no note, which was proper, and told him that Aragon's daughter had breeding, if not taste.

He picked up the second packet, frowned at Imtal's postal mark, broke the seal, and for the second time in a hour found himself at Point Non Plus.

For the packet contained a leather book no larger than Pat Rin's hand, stamped with the sigil of Clan Imtal. Foreknowing, he opened the volume to the first page and verified that what he held was indeed Fal Den ter'Antod's personal debt-book.

There was no note, as of course there would not be, the Code being explicit upon this point. By the act of sending this book, Fal Den had chosen the executor of his will. He, Pat Rin yos'Phelium, was to tend all accounts left unBalanced at the time of Fal Den's death, paying justly where the fault had been Fal Den's; collecting fully where the debt was owed. No light task; this, nor deniable.

And he had precisely thirty-six hours in which to complete it, assuming that all debts were on-planet, which seemed likely.

He did not read past the first page. Not yet. With the patience of a true gambler, he closed the book and settled back into his chair.

First, something to eat, and some wine. His day would no doubt be full.

IN ANOTHER PART of the city of Solcintra, a second late-rising young gentleman rang for his morning-wine and likewise sat down to review his letters and the news.

His correspondence was sparse—two pieces only. The first was a terse page from his man of business, noting receipt into his lordship's portfolio of a substantial gift of stocks and other assets.

The second note was scarcely less terse, and its subject remarkably similar. Betea sen'Equa wished to know when the consideration she had earned would be forthcoming. Happily the young gentleman had lately expended some thought upon just this subject, and knew precisely how to answer her.

From the bottom drawer in his desk, he withdrew a blank sheet of thin paper, of the sort provided to the guests of Mid-Port hotels. On it, he scrawled a few lines with his off-hand, not forgetting to omit his name, nor the sixth-cantra required to hold the reservation, sealed it and slid it into his pocket.

That done, he sipped his wine and perused the news.

His preferred service concerned itself not at all with Port news, so he lacked the account of the disagreement between the Terran and Liaden crews; nor was his latest investment, which had done very well indeed, of the sort to make the board at the Exchange.

Fal Den ter'Antod's suicide though—that news he did take in common with the other tardy young gentleman. He, too, blinked upon encountering the unexpected headline, for he had lately been at pains to become intimate with Fal Den and would not have wagered upon finding him thus weak-willed. In point of fact, he had erred in precisely the opposite direction.

The young gentleman sighed sharply, vexed; the note he had written to Betea sen'Equa absurdly heavy in his sleeve-pocket. He drank off the rest of his wine and sat in his chair, hands folded beneath his chin, staring sightlessly at the news screen.

Long minutes passed, with the gentleman sunk deep in his thoughts. Eventually, he blinked, and sighed a second time, considerably less vexed, and owned that his plans might go forward, unimpeded. The lack of Fal Den was—naturally!—a blow, but life, after all, went on.

Just so.

Satisfied in his reasoning, the young gentleman cleared the news screen, and filed away the letter from his man of business.

The note from Beta sen'Equa he carried over to the recycler. Reaching into his inside pocket he withdrew one of his special sort of cigarillo, and sucked on it twice to light it. He puffed for a moment or two, tasting of the invigorating smoke, until the central embers came to red. Then he touched the tip of the cigarillo gently to one edge of the paper and held it gingerly by the opposite corner. When the quick flames licked toward his fingertips, he dropped the thing into the unit, which extinguished the flames and proceeded to process the carbon.

He puffed again, the sweet smoke rising to join that of the paper and disguise its odor. The cigarillo followed in a few moments, ashes to ashes, to further muddle any trail.

Satisfied with his morning's work, the young gentleman left his rooms, light-footed and whistling.

"THAT'S PREPOSTEROUS." The man who said so was some years Pat Rin's elder; a tea merchant who owned a comfortable establishment in the High Port. Neither Shan nor Shan's father, Er Thom yos'Galan—master traders, both—had been strangers in this place, and Bed War tel'Pyton welcomed Pat Rin in the names of his cousins.

"Alas," Pat Rin said gently, and bowed.

Master tel'Pyton had recourse to his teacup.

"By his own hand? Forgive me, sir, but that's powerful hard to accommodate, for the Fal Den ter'Antod I knew was no such fool."

"I understand your perplexity," Pat Rin murmured. "Indeed, I share it. And yet it is truly said that we cannot know the necessities of another's secret heart."

"True," said the master. "Very true." He sighed, gustily. "So, doubtless you've fallen heir to Fal Den's debt-book, by which circumstance we find him once again to fail of foolishness. Pray name the price of my transgression." He tipped his head, apparently considering this. "I suppose it must have been my transgression, though I'll own there's nothing in my book under Fal Den's name. However, I'll bow to his judgment, for he was nice—very nice—in his measurements."

Pat Rin inclined his head and brought the book from his inner pocket. Carefully, he opened to the proper page—an early entry—and read out the recorded circumstances.

"In the fourth relumma of the year called Tofset, I misspoke in consultation with Master Tea Merchant Bed War tel'Pyton. This misinformation was the direct cause of the master ordering far too many tins of Morning Sunrise tea, which purchase greatly reduced the profits of his business. This fault is mine, and shall be Balanced at my earliest opportunity."

Master tel'Pyton blinked.

"Are you certain—I mean no disrespect!—that this is the matter that lies between myself and Fal Den? For I'll tell you, the incident was trivial when it happened—the tea was stasis sealed for one matter and, for another, your cousin, Er Thom, was trading on port at the time and placed the overbought handily, to his own profit and to mine."

"This entry is the only time that your name appears within the debt-book," Pat Rin said delicately. "Perhaps there is another matter . . . ?"

"Not a bit of it," the tea merchant said sturdily. Abruptly, he bowed, deep and excruciatingly proper. "Fal Den leaves me in perfect harmony, sir, saving only in the matter of his death itself, which cheats me of a friend and a valued colleague. Pray tell his delm so, on my behalf, and write 'paid' to the debt as recorded."

Pat Rin also bowed, closing the battered little book and slipping it away. "I will do so, sir," he said, and added the phrase the Code demanded of those who held this particular death-duty: "Balance has been served—and preserved."

THE SECOND YOUNG gentleman of leisure spent his day

profitably in the City, meeting with certain of his business associates, of whom every one was delighted to learn of the increase in the young gentleman's estate. He was pleased to learn, at a certain, of course impeccable, clerical service that his invitations had been dispatched in accordance with his very explicit instructions. Later in the day, he dined with friends, after which he accompanied them to an exclusive club as their guest, where his luck held at cards and he lost only a very little at dice.

"AND HOW DID you find Little Festival this year, boy-dear? A tedious bore, or a grand adventure?" Luken refilled their glasses from a bottle of Ongit's superlative red.

Pat Rin tipped his head, considering. From anyone else, the question might have been intended as a barb. From one's fosterfather, it surely sprang from a filial interest in himself—and gave one pause. Luken bel'Tarda was not a great intellect, but his *melant'i* was spotless, and he possessed a sweet, sure subtlety that Pat Rin found he treasured more deeply as the years passed. It behooved one, always, to give serious consideration to Luken's questions.

So: "I found Little Festival to be . . . largely agreeable," Pat Rin said, slowly. "Though I will own to some moments where one's mind wandered from the pure pursuit of pleasure to matters of business. And of course, some bits were nothing short of terrifying." He picked up his glass and swirled the wine, idly, eyes on the movement of the dark red liquid. "Of course, you've heard of Shan and Val Con's victory at the skimmer field?"

Luken grinned. "From the newspaper and from your mother, too. *She* predicts a wastrel lifetime for both, sinking ever further from Code and kin." He sipped his wine. "No fear there, I think. Young Val Con tells me *he's* no intention of continuing along the line of skimmers—too wearing by half! And Shan has put the craft up for sale, now that his point's been taken."

He did not say, as one's mother would assuredly have done, "No doubt with his eye already upon some other mad enterprise."

"You've seen Val Con, then?" This was interesting; had the young cousin left the wiles of Festival to do family duty?

"Oh, aye, he was by this morning. We shared a bite of breakfast and a catch-up." Luken sipped.

Last seen, Val Con had been engaged to attend a piece of business that must assuredly have kept him until very late in the evening, if Pat Rin had read the set of the lady's face a-right. To have arisen from the double exertions of the race and the pleasure tents early enough to share breakfast with dawn-rising Luken—well. Surely, the young cousin became a paragon.

"He's a good lad," Luken said comfortably. "The scouts agree with him, which was the same with his father."

"One's mother swears him the spit of her brother."

"Does she, now?" Luken paused, doubtless considering the issue from all sides, and finally moved a hand in negation. "I won't say there isn't an edge here and there—especially upon an ascent to the boughs, you know—but I do believe Er Thom has achieved other than a facsimile of Daav. No disrespect meant to your mother, dear."

Pat Rin smiled. "Certainly not."

The service door opened at that juncture, admitting their waiter, bearing deserts. By the time these were accommodated, and the finishing wine poured, Luken had introduced the subject of Pat Rin's current projects.

He sighed. "Alas, I've been named an instrument of Balance."

Luken looked at him, glass arrested halfway to his lips. "I wonder that you took the time to dine with me. You could have set another day, boy-dear. Thirty-six hours is little enough to right all the wrongs that might be made in a lifetime."

"Happily, I'm set to Balance the life of a meticulous man," Pat Rin said. "There were only four outstanding debts, and I've managed to lay three today." He inclined his head, self-mocking. "Behold me, industrious."

"I allow that to be tolerably industrious," Luken said, apparently quite serious. "Most likely you'll stop on your way home this evening and put paid to the last."

"Would that I were that fortunate. The fourth is likely to be the end of my own *melant'i*, if you will have it."

"As knotty as that?" Luken put his glass aside. "You might honorably consult an elder of your clan. I happen to be an elder of your clan, in case you had forgot it."

"Yes, very likely. In the meanwhile, I've no idea how knotty the thing may be, the notation being somewhat . . . murky. You might say I should simply throw myself upon the honor of the debt-partner, which I might do, had I one idea of who she may be."

"Surely you've checked the Book of Clans—ah!" Luken caught himself up. "Perhaps the lady is Terran, boy-dear. You'll want the Census."

"The lady's name appears to be Liaden," Pat Rin said, "though I do have a request in to Terran Census, so every wager is covered." He pulled Fal Den's debt book from his sleeve pocket and flipped to the page.

"Betea sen'Equa is the person for whom—" He glanced up at a slight sound from Luken, who seemed to have lost color. "Father?"

"For whom do you Balance?" Luken asked, and his tone was much cooler than Pat Rin was wont to hear from his foster father.

"For Fal Den ter'Antod Clan Imtal, found dead by his own hand last evening. The book arrived in this morning's mail."

"Hah." Luken relaxed visibly. "I had read that. Bad business. And he notes a Balance with sen'Equa? Boy-dear, I must ask if you are certain of the notation."

Wordlessly, Pat Rin handed him the debt-book.

For several heartbeats, Luken frowned down at the note, then sighed, closed the book and handed it back.

"Betea sen'Equa, certain enough, though how one of Imtal came to—there, it's none of mine. And distressed I am to find it one of yours, lad."

"I apprehend that you are familiar with the lady—or at the least, the lady's kin."

"Oh, I know who they are—there was a time when everyone knew who they were, though I see that's no longer the case. They had used to be Terran—I recall being told that the family name is ancient Terran—*Seneca*. They set up in Port, and carried on just as if they were still on any Terran world you like—which meant they married oddly, mostly of Terrans, you see, and took no care to establish their clan."

"Which is why I don't find them in the Book of Clans."

"Nor in Terran Census, either." Luken sighed. "In anywise, boy-dear, if it's sen'Equa you want, it's to Low Port you'll go."

"Ah, will I? How delightful." Pat Rin slipped Fal Den's debt-book into his sleeve and absently took up his wineglass. "I wonder what trade it is that Family sen'Equa follows?"

Luken moved his shoulders. "Why, they began in mechanical and electronics repair, with a side in the gaming business. The repair work led them to vending machines, you see, and an exclusive contract with dea'Linea. Then, when dea'Linea incepted that tedious scandal and got ruined by way of it, sen'Equa sued for such holdings as remained—in payment of their contract. I was myself involved as a trustee of the dissolution, and saw the paperwork. sen'Equa received only the most meager of settlements—well, they had no one to speak for them. So, unless they have moved far forward—or backward—sen'Equa owns properties in Mid-Port and in Low-Port, in the form of several small gambling houses."

"Oh," Pat Rin said, and very nearly smiled. "Do they?"

SHE HAD READ the letter thrice, more alarmed each time. A *party*, here, at House of Chance? Worse, a party composed, or so he would have her understand, entirely of those who made High Port—aye, and the city beyond it—their home? All very well and good to bring in one or three at a time, filling the private rooms, to her profit. But, a party of three to four *dozen* lord-and-ladyships? It was . . .

. . . frightening.

Betea sen'Equa was not a woman of fragile nerve, nor was hers an imaginative nature. Yet this latest letter from Hia Cyn—this proposed—engaged—event—*felt wrong*. Gods' mercy that her grandmother was dead, and Betea did not have to go before her with such feeble misgivings in her heart.

"Hitch your fortune to the High-Port," that redoubtable old lady had been wont to say, "and the cantra will flow into your pocket."

Which had doubtless been true in the old days, when her

grandmother, with the assistance of various patrons, added three houses to the sen'Equa holdings—one in High Port itself.

Grandmother's wisdom had likewise served Betea's mother, who had added another Mid Port house to the chain before a drunken quarrel with her latest patron left her dead.

After that came Betea's aunt, who decreed that sen'Equa had no need of patrons; that sen'Equa houses would henceforth pay for themselves, with no dependence on those who sat high.

It had been a worthy dream, Betea thought so even now. But her aunt in her grief over the loss of her sister had reckoned without worldly realities. sen'Equa had no standing among the clan-bound, nor ever had. Oh, they paid taxes, in return of which they were guaranteed the protections and services of the Port. But they had no *social* standing, and no one was obliged to either sell, or treat with them at fair cost.

Or pay a death-price, for kin who were murdered.

It had been fair market prices and rent that the names of the wealthy patrons had purchased for sen'Equa, and by the time her aunt realized that, the house in High Port had faltered and was closed.

Her aunt then did what no other of their family had done—she left the Port and went into the city, to apply for a Name from the Council of Clans.

But to become a Name, there must be a Name willing to sponsor the applicant to the Council. A patron, in fact—and Betea's aunt would have none of patrons.

So, now it was Betea and two houses left—their starting place in Low Port, where Uncle Tawm ruled, and the House of Chance in the Terran section of Mid Port. Terrans scarce cared what your name was—or if you had a name at all, so long as your cantra was good. They sold to Betea as they would to any other business on the street— yes, and came by in the evening or ahead of their morning shifts, to wager a bit on the wheel, perhaps, or buy into a game of cards.

She'd been doing well enough, or so she told herself now, and had no need to return to the patron model. Only that the loss of those two houses in her aunt's time and another on her aunt's death—had eaten at Betea and made her dream, too, dream of the days when sen'Equa held five houses and there was talk of building a sixth . . .

Betea sighed, dropped the letter to her desk for the fourth time, slipped the sixth-piece into her pocket, and, restless, went down the ramp into the main room, to see how the play went on.

Which is how she came to be there when he walked in the door: High Port, sure enough, with his pretty brown hair and a blue gemstone in one ear; dressed in a sober, expensive jacket and shiny boots. She saw the hint of the pistol beneath the jacket and approved his good sense, even as she went forward to intercept him.

"May I assist you, lordship?" she inquired, coming up on him from the right, her hands plainly in sight, out of respect for the pistol.

Velvet brown eyes considered her at some length, and then he inclined his head, very slightly.

"Do you know, perhaps you can?" he said, and his voice was pleasant on the ear. "I am looking for Betea sen'Equa."

Her stomach clenched, but she put the silly start of fear aside and bowed deeply, which the high ones cared about.

"You have found her," she said. "How may I assist you?"

"I am here on a matter of Balance," the pretty man told her, "which stands between yourself and Fal Den ter'Antod."

Betea felt the blood drain from her face. She might have known that the game would fold someday, and one who was perhaps a little bolder than the others would send his man of business, or his delm, or his elder kinsman to Balance the matter—with her. She touched her tongue to lips suddenly gone dry.

"Why does he not come himself?" she asked.

"Because he is dead," the other said, and moved a hand, showing her the ramp up to the office in her own establishment.

"Perhaps this is not a discussion you wish to continue on the open floor?"

Dead? But . . . Betea clutched at her disintegrating courage, straightened her back and looked boldly into the man's dark eyes.

"Please come with me," she said, and turned away without looking to see if he followed. Somehow, she didn't doubt that he would.

❖❖❖

THE OFFICE WAS comfortably appointed, the screens that monitored the playing floor set into the wall above the manager's cluttered desk.

A quick and subtle glance at the clutter revealed to Pat Rin the sorts of papers one might find on the desk of any manager, High Port or Low—invoices, bills of lading, lists, and the various correspondence of business. A handwritten letter on plain paper lay askew in the center of the desk, as if it had been flung down in haste. A blank comm screen sat to the right of the general disorder, the keyboard shoved away beneath.

At the center of the room, Betea sen'Equa turned to face him. She was tall, Pat Rin noted—a little above his own height, though nothing near Shan's—and lithe, with a girl's pretty, soft face. Her eyes were as blue and as ungiving as sapphire—and it was to the woman who had earned those eyes that he made his bow.

"I am Pat Rin yos'Phelium Clan Korval. I come to you as the instrument of Fal Den ter'Antod's will. Your name is written in his debt-book. It falls to us to Balance that which lies between you."

The hard blue eyes considered him, emotionless; the round, girl's face betrayed only youth.

"Please tell me how Fal Den came to die," she said, and her voice did waver, just a little. "I saw him only days ago . . ."

"He died by his own hand," Pat Rin told her and used his chin to point at the dark screen. "If you permit, I will call up the report from news service."

She glanced at the screen, and stepped to one side. "If you please."

He moved to the desk, tapped the power key, called up the public archive, and stood aside.

Betea sen'Equa came forward, frowned at the synopsis, reached down and called for more information, then stood looking at it for far longer than it should have taken her to read it. Eventually, however, she recalled herself and turned to Pat Rin, her face somewhat paler than it had been.

"What is written next to my name," she asked steadily, "in Fal Den's debt-book?"

She had offered him neither a chair nor refreshment, which discourtesy was irritating. Pat Rin discovered himself more inclined to believe the debt lay on the lady's side, which did no honor to his duty. If Fal Den himself had not known which of the two of them was owing and owed . . .

Pat Rin inclined his head. "I regret. Only your name appears. It is the very last notation in the book, written on the day of his death, and it is very possible that the process that ended with his self-murder was even then at work."

She stared at him, eyes and face without expression.

Pat Rin sighed. "Perhaps if we speak together of your dealings with Fal Den on the occasion of your last meeting, we may discover between us both the fault and the Balance owed."

Still she stared at him, and she was not, by Pat Rin's judgment, either a half-wit or a fool . . .

"Self-murder," she said abruptly. "Are they certain of that?"

He frowned. "It is what his kin has sworn to the Council. Have you reason to believe that Fal Den came by his death in another fashion?"

"Perhaps. I don't . . ." She spun aside, rudely, and paced to the far end of the room, where she stood for the slow count of six heartbeats, facing the wall, showing him her back.

At last, she took a deep breath, turned and walked back to the center of the room. She stopped several paces away and looked boldly into his eyes.

"I know why my name is written in Fal Den's book," she said, and her voice was as hard as her eyes. "I know who owes and who is owing. I will tell you these things. For a price."

"A price?" Pat Rin raised his eyebrows. "Madam, your name is written in a dead man's book. You do not bargain price with *me*."

"But I do," she said sharply. "You may be bound to play by High Port rules, lordship, but *I* am not. My mother died at the hand of a High Port lord. She had no book nor no other high friends to call in her debt, and the lord himself said the thing was outside of lawful Balance, for she had no Name to protect her." She crossed her arms under her breasts and now the bold gaze was a glare.

"I am selling the information you need. You will buy it, or you will not." She inclined her head, brusquely. "Your throw, lordship."

It was on the end of his tongue to tell her that he had no need to buy anything from her—but that was only pique, such as would make Luken laugh and bid him to climb down from the high branches.

Mastering his irritation, he looked at her, standing tall and stern before him.

The lady has the winning hand, he told himself, wryly, which rubbed ill against his pride as a gamester. And he was not come here, he reminded himself, as a gamester, but as the agent of Fal Den's will, upon which the petty prides and irritations of Pat Rin yos'Phelium had no right to intrude.

He bowed to the lady, very slightly.

"What is your price?"

VIEWED CORRECTLY, Pat Rin thought, shaking his lace into order and frowning at his reflection in the dressing-glass, the situation was piquant. Indeed, one was persuaded that one's deplorable cousin Shan would find it rich in hilarity. And, to be just, had it been Shan dressing just now to attend, of all things, an *express*, Pat Rin might have found himself more inclined toward laughter.

His partner in this evening's enterprise could not be dislodged from her conviction that he attended such affairs as a matter of course on every quarter-day, nor from the equally demented belief that his very presence held her proof against whatever predations she imagined that Hia Cyn yo'Tonin intended to visit upon her.

Though, Pat Rin allowed, fixing the sapphire in his ear, to be wary of Hia Cyn yo'Tonin proved Betea sen'Equa to be a woman of sense, however late in her life.

It had taken all of his powers of persuasion, and not a little High House hauteur, to wring the information he required from Betea after he had given his word to attend this evening's festivities.

The tale she had told was a simple one, nor was Fal Den the first to come away from an acquaintance with Betea sen'Equa lighter by certain equities and certificates of stock.

It would have seemed simple thievery, and the lady herself the final culprit, yet there was another player in the game, whose presence muddied the score considerably.

As Betea told it, her first meeting with Hia Cyn yo'Tonin was mere chance. Pat Rin, who knew the man, doubted this, but had not thought it appropriate to interrupt the lady's account with his private speculations.

In any case, Hia Cyn, through design or mischance, came into the orbit of Betea sen'Equa and very quickly showed her how she might increase profits. Betea had ambitions, Pat Rin learned, but not much understanding of the ways of what she termed "the high world."

Hia Cyn brought to her young people—mostly young men—who were slightly in awe of the gaming world, and slightly in awe of her, she who was tall and exotic, and who held modest court within her own houses.

The games were—initially—honest, with small friendly wagers. But after a time, the stakes would alter. In the private parlors, the victims would play for small sums until some point of *melant'i* or other would be brought into the conversation and slowly the net would be drawn about them. Carefully, then, while served sympathetic portions of wine, or perhaps one of Hia Cyn's special cigarillos, the mark would be brought to promise against their quartershare, or against their inheritance. Especially, Hia Cyn liked them to promise something that would come to them only when the person immediately before them in their clan's line of succession came to die.

Thus the stakes were things like quitclaims to islands, access codes to small and private lodges, the desperately secret formula of some proprietary process.

This, she learned later; she had delivered the first few keywords and certificate numbers to Hia Cyn without ever knowing what they were, earning thereby what he was pleased to call a "finder's fee." In cash.

No one ever came back to her and confronted her with their loss, which for a time fed the comforting illusion that what she dealt in were "might-happens" of no value.

Alas, she was not a lady who allowed herself to repose long in ignorance. If what she gained for Hia Cyn was worthless, she reasoned, why then was she paid to procure it?

And so she finally learned that these items promised at late night in the heat of play were more than a gambler's losses. They became the very evidence of a threat—perhaps a mortal threat!—to a person of *melant'i*. As such, they were bought back with ridiculous ease, often with items or in amounts the victims themselves suggested— things that were in one way or another extremely liquid and little prone to tracking.

Knowledge should have set her free, for surely even Nameless Port-folk might report larceny to the Proctors. However, Betea weighed the risk of being implicated along with Hia Cyn and the all-too-probable outcome of being found the sole offender, and did not call the Proctors. In any wise, she said, the trade was slowing down. Indeed, for several relumma, Hia Cyn introduced her to no one new.

And then, at the beginning of the present relumma, he had brought Fal Den ter'Antod to her attention.

"And now he has died," Betea had said, stone-faced in the office above her modest gambling house. "None of the others cared so much."

She had named those others in the course of her narration and Pat Rin had taken those names to the redoubtable dea'Gauss, Clan Korval's man of business, who was even now in the process of checking accounts with various of the masters of the Accountants Guild.

Which left Pat Rin free to attend a party in the deplored and deplorable express mode, with only six hours left him to correctly place and Balance the error that had brought Fal Den to his death.

It was well here to reflect upon Fal Den, Pat Rin thought, and the nicety of his honor, which had not allowed him to place a debt of which he was uncertain.

Pat Rin sighed and gave his lace a last, unnecessary, shake. Time and past time to get on with the pursuit of pleasure.

Express, indeed.

✧✧✧

THE ADDRESS WAS in Solcintra Mid-Port, on a street well-known to a certain set of self-styled adventurers and high rollers. An adventurer he was not, but in the course of learning to be a high roller, it had sometimes been necessary for Pat Rin to attend parties on this street. Now an acknowledged player, he still received invitations to such parties, but of late he had more and more often discovered himself, regretfully, with a conflicting engagement. To be seen in the area during a business day was unexceptional, of course, but to be seen here in the evening, dressed in all his finery . . .

At least he was not alone. He saw several vaguely familiar faces in the distance, all of them younger than he, each carrying their sealed red packet inscribed with the legend, "To Be Opened Expressly at the House of Chance."

He bowed distantly in the direction of a young lady whose name escaped him—her face notable in that Pat Rin had witnessed the end of a match at Tey Dor's in which this gentle became the dozen dozenth of the current year's list. Pat Rin sighed—no doubt he would be singled out during the express to give hints and best wishes, if not to lend countenance to the rather interesting costume that the lady had found appropriate to wear to an event that might turn out to be nothing more than an evening of light play. Indeed, she gained his side as he came up to the gaudily painted doorway, and just in time he recalled her name—Dela bel'Urik Clan Shelart.

Together, they entered the sen'Equa's House of Chance, he in his evening lace, and she as she might appear for an evening among friends to her house; or even friends to her bed. Assuredly, someone ought to speak to the lady regarding the attire generally held to be proper for public outings—but it would not be he.

A servant, bland-faced, admitted them to the house, and waved them to a small room to the right of the entranceway.

"You may open your envelopes and don your accessories in this chamber," he said. "After you have appropriately adorned yourselves, you may find the rest of the guests in the larger room. Buffets will be laid in the private parlors at mid-revel."

It was at this point that Betea sen'Equa herself appeared, slightly breathless, as if she had run down from her office the moment the monitor showed his arrival. Immediately, was Dela bel'Urik's costume discovered to be mere commonplace, quite cast into the shade by Betea's choice of flame-red shirt, cut low across her breasts, form-fitting leather trousers, and soft-soled leather houseboots.

Nor was the young bel'Urik's address sufficient to assure her place at Pat Rin's side. Betea swept forward, using her height much as he sometimes used his, to clear a path through a crowd and arrive at his destination unrumpled and unimpeded.

"He has not yet arrived," she said, leading the way into the accessory chamber. Pat Rin followed, but not without a wistful thought to the bel'Urik.

"I have been through our records," she said, pulling what appeared to be a small square of leather from between her breasts. "Never has the House of Chance hosted such an event. Why *must* it be here—"

"—Is something that we shall perhaps discover of Hia Cyn, when we have an opportunity to speak," Pat Rin interrupted, striving for patience. He was here, he reminded himself, as an instrument of Balance. His personal pets and peeves had no brief here. Looking down, he broke the seal on his Express packet, and, wonderingly, pulled out a folded bit of leather, much like the one Betea had . . .

The leather unfolded, revealing its form: A half-mask in supple black leather, with ribands of the same color.

Betea's mask was flame-red. As he watched, she tied it into place and let the ribands fall over one shoulder, the tasseled ends kissing the swell of her breast.

Pat Rin's uncle, Daav yos'Phelium—Val Con's very father—had once told Pat Rin a story about a world where all went masked and revealed themselves only to their most intimate kin. The story had turned upon a man with whom Uncle Daav had sworn to be acquainted, who had one day formed a desire to go about his daily business unmasked, and the unlooked-for and increasingly distressful situations that arose from taking that single, seemingly correct, decision.

The story had a lesson at its heart, of course—a scout lesson, with which one's mother most emphatically disagreed. The lesson was that custom was arbitrary and oft-times nonsensical, and that the superior person was one who was not shackled by the custom of his homeworld, but moved freely from one set of traditions to another, without offense to any.

To wear a mask on Liad was, of course, to be very wicked. Masks were erotic, intoxicating and entirely outside of Code.

"Well?" Betea sen'Equa asked, not a little snappish. "Are you going to put that on, or are you not?"

THE HOUR WAS growing late.

Not that the young gentleman of leisure was at all concerned for the final outcome of the evening, he only wished that Betea would approach him so that the matter could be settled, finally and for all. She oversaw for a time the room's small spin-wheel, and joined a party at cards, making certain that the money and the drink flowed, as a proper hostess must do.

Indeed, he would quite miss Betea, and where he would find another cat's paw so perfectly situated, he could not predict. However, he was a young man of an optimistic cast of mind and rarely allowed the problems of tomorrow to oppress him today. He did not doubt for a moment that Betea would find herself able to accommodate the arrangements he had made for her. After all, what could it matter to a clan-less where she lived or to whom she owed duty?

If only she would she would stop circulating and come within his orbit so the evening could go forward . . .

IT WAS . . . disconcerting . . . to enter a room filled with people dressed with entire propriety, saving only that their features were masked. Pat Rin, master of any social situation described in the Code, felt ill-at-ease, which sensation he found unsatisfactory in the extreme.

By contrast, Betea strolled into the room as if she had gone masked all her life, moving among people whose motives and desires were hidden from her. Which, Pat Rin thought, the echoes of Uncle Daav's old story suddenly ringing in his ears, perhaps she had.

He raised his head and moved into the room, ignoring, as best as he was able, the supple caress of leather against his cheeks. A masked servant offered him wine from a tray, which he accepted, and, sipping, moved even further into the room.

Betea, he saw, was well advanced of him, her crimson shirt a beacon among the pastel evening colors of the Festival season.

Strolling through the room, Pat Rin recovered somewhat of his equilibrium. He had a good ear for voices, and he found that he recognized the accents of more than one social acquaintance in conversation, mask to mask.

So acclimated did he become, in fact, that when hailed by a yellow-haired lady in an emerald-green mask, he inclined his head gravely and murmured, "Good evening, Eyan. I hope I find you well?"

The lady gave a startled laugh and moved forward to lay her hand on his arm.

"Quick, my friend. Very quick. A word in your ear, however: We name no names here."

Pat Rin sipped his wine. "Whyever not?"

"Oh, it adds to the mystery, the intrigue, the naughtiness! Is it not absurd?"

"Perhaps. But it is possible that you will change my mind. I am not accustomed to finding you engaged in the absurd."

"Prettily said," smiled the lady. "Alas, I am here at the whim of a friend, who had heard of such affairs being all the rage from her *cha'leket*. I must seek her soon, to find if the telling matches reality, or if we may go and find a less . . . *mclant'i* challenging . . . gathering." She had recourse to her own glass, eyes quizzing him over the crystal rim.

"But how do I find you present at such an exercise? Pay-off on a wager? Never say that you lost!"

Pat Rin inclined his head. "I find my situation similar to your own; and am here at the necessity of another." He swept a glance across the room, looking for the crimson shirt—and failing to find it.

"Pat Rin?" Her hand was on his sleeve once more. "What's amiss?"

"I—am not certain," he replied, and turned sharply on his heel. "Perhaps nothing is amiss. Your pardon, Eyan . . ." He moved off into the crowded room, leaving her frowning behind him.

IT HAD BEEN absurdly easy. Betea had all but literally walked into his arms, and it had been simplicity itself to guide her into the parlor where his business associate awaited them.

"This is she?" The man behind the table asked, while Hia Cyn held Betea firmly by her arm.

"It is," he said, adroitly avoiding the kick she aimed at his shins.

"And you have the right to sell her into indenture?"

"Sir, I have," said Hia Cyn. "There is a debt between us of long standing, which she makes not the slightest push to settle. I certainly—"

"That," snarled Betea, twisting against his grip, "is a lie! I owe you nothing!"

"Yes, well . . ." Hia Cyn shifted his grip and got her arm up behind her, hand between her shoulder-blades, which quietened her quick enough. "I have the papers, sir, which you've seen. The Council itself acknowledges my right to redeem my money through the sale of this woman's work for a period of seven Standard years."

"He's a wizard with papers, this one!" Betea snarled. "Look twice at any signatures he shows you, lordship—Ah!"

"Respect for your betters, Betea," Hia Cyn said pleasantly, but the man behind the table frowned.

"She's worth less to me with a broken arm," he said, sternly. "Nor do I wish to buy at hazard."

"Sir—"

"You are wise," came a cool voice from behind. "Sir, release that woman. She is neither your chattel nor your debtor."

The man behind the table moved a hand, beckoning. "Who are you, sir?"

Pat Rin yos'Phelium stepped into the room, impeccable in high-town lace; his face covered by a supple black mask; blue gem blazing in his right ear.

"I was told we name no names here, sir," he said calmly.

"However, I have business and a name for the man who has attempted to sell you that which does not belong to him." He turned and raised his hand, pointing.

"Hia Cyn yo'Tonin, release that person, and prepare to answer me in a matter of Balance."

"Balance?" Hia Cyn's grip loosened, from pure amaze, so Betea thought, though she was quick to take advantage of his lapse.

"We are in the midst of social pleasure," Hia Cyn protested. "How may Balance go forth here?"

"Balance goes forth in the name of Fal Den ter'Antod, whom your actions slew. Do you deny that you are Hia Cyn yo'Tonin?"

"I neither deny nor acknowledge! You, sir, are not anonymous. I know your voice. I know that ear-stone—as who does not? I've seen you deep in the cards—and shooting, at Teydor's!"

Betea, forgotten in the argument, moved swiftly to the side, raised her hand and pulled the bright ribands.

"What!" Hia Cyn raised his hand too late. The mask had slipped, fallen, and was held useless in his left hand. He stood revealed, his face seeming curiously naked, the skin slightly damp where the leather had cuddled his cheeks.

Pat Rin raised a hand, showing the battered debt-book, Imtal's sigil to the fore.

"I have a book from the hand of a dead man, Hia Cyn yo'Tonin. Balance goes forth, here and now. What Balance is just, for the loss of a life?"

"I repudiate this. I will not accept Balance from a masked robber."

"But do you know," said a feminine voice from the door, "I think you will?" A smallish lady with gray hair, and wearing a mauve mask stepped into the room, closely followed by Eyan yo'Lanna's emerald. The mauve mask inclined her head to Pat Rin.

"I have only this afternoon had a message from dea'Gauss, sir. I believe I am in your debt for the very welcome information he imparted." She raised a hand. "Your duty takes precedence over my own. Pray continue. I believe we may be in a situation where witnesses may be . . . appropriate."

Pat Rin inclined his head. "Ma'am." He looked again to Hia Cyn yo'Tonin, and it was anger he felt. Anger, that this man lived where Fal Den ter'Antod—twelve dozen times more worthy!—had died. Died for the cause of this man's greed. And he was to Balance this wrong? There was no Balance fitting. Even death . . .

The man behind the table cleared his throat.

"I do not wish to trespass into a private affair," he said calmly. "However, I think it relevant to point out to those concerned that I came here to buy seven years' of hard labor in my company's mine. It matters not at all to me whose labor I buy, so long as the contract is valid."

Pat Rin turned and looked at the man behind the table.

"Seven?"

The man inclined his head. "The contract can, of course, be renewed, at seller's option. I am limited to the purchase of seven-year blocks."

"I see." Pat Rin held looked again at Hia Cyn yo'Tonin, pale and sweating. "Let us say seven years initially, renewal to depend upon Fal Den ter'Antod's delm."

"The Council!" yelped Hia Cyn.

"I don't think that the Council will find it difficult to name you beholden," the lady in the mauve mask said. "And if Imtal does not impose additional terms of service, you may warm yourself by the certainty that you will have pel'Varn to reckon with on the day your indenture is done."

It was too much. Hia Cyn spun, knocking Eyan aside, and vaulted into the main room, Betea in hot pursuit.

"Card-sharp!" she cried. "Stop him!"

The pleasure-seekers—gamesters and High Houselings alike— turned to stare at the one so hideously accused; several young gentlemen were seen to cast down their dice or their cards and move in pursuit.

Hia Cyn slammed to a halt, staring at the room full of masks, the avid eyes focused on him. He glanced down at his left hand, fingers still uselessly clutching his mask. Revealed, he thought. Revealed and ruined.

"Do not run from the lordship's Balance, Hia Cyn," Betea's voice was quite near. He jerked his head up and stared at her. "It was wrong, what we did. And now a man has died of it."

"A fool has died of it," he snarled, snatching his hidden pistol free. "And not the only one."

He raised the weapon and pulled the trigger.

Betea fell; someone in the crowd of pleasure-seekers screamed, someone else shouted. And Hia Cyn turned, seeking the way out—

And found instead a tall man dressed all in evening lace and jewels, the blue stone in his ear blazing. He was showing empty hands, which marked him a third fool.

"Put the gun aside," Pat Rin said, pitching his voice for gentleness. "Put the gun aside and stand away, Hia Cyn. You hold no winning cards here."

"No?" The gun came around, the eyes wild and the face aflame with some fever of madness.

There was no time to warn the crowd, no time to think. Pat Rin brought his right hand down, felt the little gun slide into his palm. The target . . .

Hia Cyn fired as he fell; the pellet from Pat Rin's palm gun had already shattered his heart.

There was silence among the pleasure-seekers, and Pat Rin, shaking, slipped his weapon away. Several of the young gentlemen were bending over what was left of Hia Cyn yo'Tonin. He went to kneel beside Betea sen'Equa, discovering a heartbeat, and a wound to the upper arm. She opened her eyes as he bent over her.

"Lord," she said breathily to Pat Rin as he stooped near her, "the masks!"

"Yes."

It was absurdly difficult to untie the ribands that held his own mask in place. If only his fingers wouldn't shake so . . .

Finally, the thing was done and he stood, raising his hand for silence against the sudden storm of chatter: "yos'Phelium!" "Suicide to draw against a yos'Phelium!" "He must have been in his cups!" "Card-sharp! The hostess herself accused him!"

Someone—he thought it was Dela bel'Urik—called, stridently, for silence.

It fell, and Pat Rin cleared his throat.

"If someone would be so good as to call the Port Proctors? Also, it would be well to remove your masks."

These things were done, and when the Proctors did arrive, in goodly time, since they also knew the street, the only mask in the room was held in the death grip of Hia Cyn yo'Tonin.

IMTAL HERSELF RECEIVED the debt-book from his hands, riffled the pages, and read the four accountings, lingering over the fourth. She lay the book aside.

"Our House is honored," she said, bowing.

"It was an honor to serve," Pat Rin replied, properly, and bowed even lower.

"Hah." She considered him out of tired brown eyes. "And what else do you bring me, child of Korval?"

Pat Rin moved his hand and Betea came forward, bowing as he had shown her.

"This is Betea sen'Equa; her name appears in the last entry in the book. Alas, Fal Den wrote neither a plus nor minus beside her name, nor any other elaboration; and I am unable to precisely reconstruct his will regarding her."

The brown eyes narrowed. "I have read the last entry, and found it unilluminating. 'In consideration of the *melant'i* of all involved, all debts in this pairing must be considered satisfied, pending the delm's acceptance of the matter'."

Pat Rin bowed acknowledgment. "Just so. Betea took part in the scheme which caused Fal Den's death; it was something in which I feel she was also a victim. Your kinsman could not himself squarely place the debt, nor can I. The best Balance I may craft is to suggest that you speak with this person, candidly and at length, and that a new Balance be struck if need be, to Balance the loss of Fal Den's worth." He paused, then added, with utmost delicacy, "I also suggest that you consult most closely with your business advisors about the matters this woman may reveal before setting that worth. Had it not been for the unfortunate public suicide of Hia Cyn . . ."

"yo'Tonin. I have heard the news of that, and I have—as you may understand—heard other news of that. I would not have had such a necessity forced opon you."

"The necessity was mine, Imtal. I could hardly have refused to serve Fan Del's wishes."

There was a short silence, then an inclination of the head. "As you say. I assume that this is the young person who was wounded in the service our House?"

"Imtal, it is."

"Hah." The brown eyes now frankly swept Betea. "My father knew your grandmother. Well."

Betea managed a strong voice: "My grandmother knew many people. Well."

It was the correct response. Imtal smiled. "Assuredly, we shall need to talk—candidly and at length."

To Pat Rin she inclined her head. "My thanks for your service to our House."

That was a dismissal. Pat Rin bowed. "My thanks for the forbearance of the House. I grieve for your loss, as well as my own."

That said, and most properly, he allowed himself to be ushered from the room.

✧ BALANCE OF TRADE ✧

Gobelyn's Market
Standard Year 1118

"IF YOU TRADE WITH Liadens, trade careful, and for the gods' love don't come sideways of honor."

This set of notes was old: recorded by Great-Grand-Captain Larance Gobelyn more than forty Standard years ago, dubbed to ship's library twenty Standards later from the original deteriorating tape. Jethri fiddled with the feed on the audio board, but only succeeded in lowering the old man's voice. Sighing, he upped the gain again, squinting in protest of the scratchy, uneven sound.

"Liaden honor is—active. Insult—any insult—is punished. Immediately. An individual's name is his most important possession and he will kill to preserve its integrity. Think twice before trading with—"

"Jethri?" Uncle Paitor's voice broke across the tape's recitation. Jethri sighed and thumbed "pause."

"Yessir," he said, turning his head toward the intercom grid set in the wall.

"Come on down to the trade room, will you? We need to talk over a couple things."

Jethri slipped the remote out of his ear. His uncle was senior trader on *Gobelyn's Market* and Jethri was senior apprentice. Actually, he was the only apprentice trader, his sibs and cousins being well above him in years and rank, but the ladder was immutable.

"Yessir," he said again. Two quick fingertaps marked his place in the old notes file. He left the common room at a brisk walk, his thoughts half on honor.

HIS UNCLE NODDED him into a chair and eased back in his. They were coming in on Ynsolt'i and next hour Paitor Gobelyn would have time for nothing but the feed from the port trade center. Now, his screen was dark, the desktop barren. Paitor cleared his throat.

"Got a couple things," he said, folding his hands over his belt buckle. "On-Port roster: Dyk an' me'll be escorting the payload to central hall and seeing it safe with the highest bidder. Khat's data, Grig's eatables, Mel's on tech, Cris'll stay ship-side. You . . ."

Paitor paused and Jethri gripped his hands together tight on his lap, willing his face into a trader's expression of courteous disinterest. They had textile on board—half-a-dozen bolts of cellosilk that Cris had taken on two stops back, with Ynsolt'i very much in his mind. Was it possible, Jethri wondered, that Uncle Paitor was going to allow . . .

"Yourself—you'll be handling the silk lot. I expect to see a cantra out of the six. If I was you, I'd call on Honored Sir din'Flora first."

Jethri remembered to breathe. "Yes, sir. Thank you." He gripped his hands together so hard they hurt. His own trade. His own, very first, solo trade with no Senior standing by, ready to take over if the thing looked like going awry . . .

His uncle waved a hand. "Time you were selling small stuff on your own. Now." He leaned forward abruptly, folded his arms on the desk and looked at Jethri seriously. "You know we got a lot riding on this trip."

Indeed they did—three-quarters of the *Market's* capital was tied up in eight Terran pounds of *vya*—a spice most commonly sold in five-gram lots. Jethri's research had discovered that *vya* was the active ingredient in *fa'vya*, a Liaden drink ship's library classified as a potent aphrodisiac. Ynsolt'i was a Liaden port and the spice should bring a substantial profit to the ship. Not, Jethri reminded himself, that profit was ever guaranteed.

"We do well with the spice here," Paitor was saying, "and the captain's going to take us across to Kinaveral, do that refit we'd been banking for *now*, rather than two Standards from now."

This was news. Jethri sat up straighter, rubbing the palms of his hands down the rough fabric of his work pants.

"Refit'll keep us world-bound 'bout a Standard, near's we can figure. Captain wants that engine upgrade bad and trade-side's gonna need two more cargo pods to balance the debt." He grinned suddenly. "Three, if I can get 'em."

Jethri smiled politely, thinking that his uncle didn't look as pleased with that as he might have and wondering what the downside of the trade was.

"While refit's doing, we figured—the captain and me—that it'd be optimum to restructure crew. So, we've signed you as senior 'prentice with *Gold Digger*."

It was said so smoothly that Jethri didn't quite get the sense of it.

"*Gold Digger*?" he repeated blankly, that much having gotten through, by reason of him and Mac Gold having traded blows on last sighting—more to Jethri's discomfort than Mac's. He came forward in his chair, hearing the rest of it play back inside the whorlings of his ears.

"You've signed me onto *Gold Digger*?" he demanded. "For how long?"

Paitor raised a hand. "Ease down, boy. One loop through the mines. Time they're back in port, you'll be twenty—full adult and able to find your own berth." He nodded. "You make yourself useful like you and me both know you can and you'll come off *Digger* a full trader with experience under your belt—"

"Three *Standards*?" Jethri's voice broke, but for once he didn't cringe in shame. He was too busy thinking about a converted ore ship smaller than the *Market,* its purely male crew crammed all six into a common sleeping room, and the trade nothing more than foodstuffs and ore, ore and mining tools, oxy tanks and ore . . .

"Ore," he said, staring at his uncle. "Not even rough gem. *Industrial ore*." He took a breath, knowing his dismay showed and not caring about that, either. "Uncle Paitor, I've been studying. If there's something else I—"

Paitor showed him palm again. "Nothing to do with your studying. You been doing real good. I'll tell you—better than the Captain supposed you would. Little more interested in the Liaden side of things than I thought reasonable, there at first. No harm in learning how to read the lingo, though, and I will say the Liadens seem to take positive note of you." He shook his head. "'Course, you don't have your full growth yet, which puts you nearer their level."

Liadens were a short, slight people, measured against Terran averages. Jethri wasn't as short as a Liaden, but he was, he thought bitterly, a damn sight shorter than Mac Gold.

"What it is," Paitor said slowly. "We're out of room. It's hard for us, too, Jethri. If we were a bigger ship, we'd keep you on. But you're youngest, none of the others're inclined to change berth, and, well— Ship's Option. Captain's cleared it. Ben Gold states himself willing to have you." He leaned back, looking stern. "And ore needs study, too, 'prentice. Nothing's as simple as it looks."

Thrown off, thought Jethri. *I'm being thrown off of my ship!* He thought that he could have borne it better, if he was simply being cast out to make his own way. But the arranged berth on *Gold Digger* added an edge of fury to his disbelief. He opened his mouth to protest further and was forestalled by a *ping!* from Paitor's terminal.

The Senior Trader snapped forward in his chair, flipping the switch that accepted the first of the trade feeds from Ynsolt'i Port. He glanced over at Jethri.

"You get me a cantra for that silk, now."

That was dismissal. Jethri stood. "Yessir," he said, calm as a dry mouth would let him, and left the trade room.

Ynsolt'i Port
Textile Hall

"PREMIUM GRADE, honored sir," Jethri murmured, keeping his eyes modestly lowered, as befit a young person in discourse with a person of lineage and honor.

Honored Sir din'Flora moved his shoulders and flipped an edge of the fabric up, frowning at the underweave. Jethri ground his teeth against an impulse to add more in praise of the hand-loomed Gindoree cellosilk.

Don't oversell! he could hear Uncle Paitor snap from memory. *The trader is in control of the trade.*

"Half-a-cantra the six-bolt," the buyer stated, tossing the sample cloth back across the spindle. Jethri sighed gently and spread his hands.

"The honored buyer is, of course, distrustful of goods offered by one so many years his inferior in wisdom. I assure you that I am instructed by an elder of my ship, who bade me accept not a breath less than two cantra."

"Two?" The Liaden's shoulders moved again—not a shrug, but expressive of some emotion. Amusement, Jethri thought. Or anger.

"Your elder misinstructs you, young sir. Perhaps it is a testing." The buyer tipped his head slightly to one side, as if considering. "I will offer an additional quarter-cantra," he said at last, accent rounding the edges of the trade-tongue, "in kindness of a student's diligence."

Wrong, Jethri thought. Liadens did nothing for kindness, which he knew from the tapes and from crew-talk. Liadens lived for revenge, and the stories Khat told on the subject kept a body awake on sleep-shift, praying against the mistake that would earn him nitrogen in his back-up oxy tank in payment of a Liaden's "balance."

Respectful, Jethri bowed, and, respectful, brought his eyes to the buyer's face. "Sir, I value your kindness. However, the distance between three-quarter cantra and two is so vast that I feel certain my elder would counsel me to forgo the trade. Perhaps you had not noticed—" he caught himself on the edge of insult and smoothly changed course—"the light is poor, just here . . ."

Pulling the bolt forward, he again showed the fineness of the cloth, the precious irregularities of weave, which proved it hand-woven, spoke rapturously of the pure crimson dye.

The buyer moved his hand. "Enough. One cantra. A last offer."

Gotcha, thought Jethri, making a serious effort to keep his face neutral. One cantra, just like Uncle Paitor had wanted. In retrospect, it had been an easy sell.

Too easy? he wondered then, looking down at the Liaden's smooth face and disinterested brown eyes. Was there, just maybe, additional profit to be made here?

Trade is study, Uncle Paitor said from memory. *Study the goods, and study the market. And after you prepare as much as you can, there's still nothing says that a ship didn't land yesterday with three holds full of something you're carrying as a luxury sell.*

Nor was there a law, thought Jethri, against Honored Buyer din'Flora being critically short on crimson cellosilk, this Port-day. He took a cautious breath and made his decision.

"Of course," he told the buyer, gathering the sample bolt gently into his arms, "I am desolate not to have closed trade in this instance. A cantra . . . It is generous, respected sir, but—alas. My elder will be distressed—he had instructed me most carefully to offer the lot first to yourself and to make every accommodation . . . But a cantra, when his word was two? I do not . . ." He fancied he caught a gleam along the edge of the Liaden's bland face, a flicker in the depths of the careful eyes, and bit his lip, hoping he wasn't about to blow the whole deal.

"I don't suppose,"— he said, voice edging disastrously toward a squeak "—my elder spoke of you so highly . . . I don't suppose you might go a cantra-six?"

"Ah." Honored Sir din'Flora's shoulders rippled and this time Jethri was sure the gesture expressed amusement. "One cantra-six it is." He bowed and Jethri did, clumsily, because of the bolt he still cradled.

"Done," he said.

"Very good," returned the buyer. "Set the bolt down, young sir. You are quite correct regarding that crimson. Remarkably pure. If your elder instructed you to hold at anything less than three cantra, he was testing you in good earnest."

Jethri stared, then, with an effort, he straightened his face, trying to make it as bland and ungiving as the buyer's.

He needn't have bothered. The Liaden had pulled a pouch from his belt and was intent on counting out coins. He placed them on the trade table and stepped back, sweeping the sample bolt up as he did.

"One cantra, six dex, as agreed. Delivery may be made to our warehouse within the twelve-hour." He bowed, fluid and unstrained, despite the bolt.

"Be you well, young sir. Fair trading, safe lift."

Jethri gave his best bow, which was nowhere near as pretty as the buyer's. "Thank you, respected sir. Fair trading, fair profit."

"Indeed," said the buyer and was gone.

Ynsolt'i Port
Zeroground Pub

BY RIGHTS, he should have walked a straight line from Textile Hall to the *Market* and put himself at the disposal of the Captain.

Say he was disinclined just yet to talk with Captain Iza Gobelyn, coincidentally his mother, on the subject of his upcoming change of berth. Or say he was coming off his first solo trade and wanted time to turn the thing over in his mind. Which he was doing, merebeer to hand, on the corner of the bar he'd staked out for his own.

Buyer din'Flora, now—that wanted chewing on. Liadens were fiercely competitive, and, in his experience, tight-fisted of data. Jethri had lately formed the theory that this reluctance to offer information was not what a Terran would call spitefulness, but *courtesy*. It would be—an *insult*, if his reading of the tapes was right, to assume that another person was ignorant of any particular something.

Which theory made Honored Sir din'Flora's extemporaneous lecture on the appropriate price of crimson cellosilk—interesting.

Jethri sipped his beer, considering whether or not he'd been insulted. This was a delicate question, since it was also OK, as far as his own observations and the crewtapes went, for an elder to instruct a junior. He had another sip of beer, frowning absently at the shipboard above the bar.

"'Nother brew, kid?" The bartender's voice penetrated his abstraction. He set the glass down, seeing with surprise that it was nearly empty. He fingered a Terran bit out of his pocket and put it on the bar.

"Merebeer, please."

"Coming up," she said, skating the coin from the bar to her palm. Her pale blue eyes moved to the next customer and she grinned.

"Hey, Sirge! Ain't seen you for a Port-year."

The dark-haired man in modest trading clothes leaned his elbows on the counter and smiled. "That long?" He shook his head, smile going toward a grin. "I lose track of time, when there's business to be done."

She laughed. "What'll it be?"

"Franses Ale?" he asked, wistfully.

"Coming up," she said and he grinned and put ten-bit in her hand.

"The extra's for you—a reward for saving my life."

The barkeeper laughed again and moved off down-bar, collecting orders and coins as she went. Jethri finished the last of his beer. When he put the glass down, he found the barkeeper's friend—Sirge—looking at him quizzically.

"Don't mean to pry into what's none of my business, but I noticed you looking at the board there. Wouldn't be you had business with *Stork*?"

Jethri blinked, then smiled and shook his head. "I was thinking of—something else," he said, with cautious truth. "Didn't really see the board at all."

"Man with business on his mind," said Sirge good-naturedly. "Well, just thought I'd ask. Misery loves company, my mam used to say—Thanks, Nance." This last as the barkeeper set a tall glass filled with dark liquid before him.

"No trouble," she assured him and put Jethri's schooner down. "Merebeer, Trader."

"Thank you," he murmured, wondering if she was making fun of him or really thought him old enough to be a full Trader. He raised the mug and shot a look at the ship-board. *Stork* was there, right enough, showing departed on an amended flight plan.

"Damnedest thing," said the man next to him, ruefully. "Can't blame them for lifting when they got rush cargo and a bonus at the far end, but I sure could wish they waited lift a quarter-hour longer."

Jethri felt a stir of morbid curiosity. "They didn't—leave you, did they, sir?"

The man laughed. "Gods, no, none of that! I've got a berth promised on Ringfelder's *Halcyon*, end of next Port-week. No, this was a matter of buy-in—had half the paperwork filled out, happened to look up at the board there in the Trade Bar and they're already lifting." He took a healthy swallow of his ale. "Sent a message to my lodgings; of course, but I wasn't at the lodgings, I was out making paper, like we'd agreed." He sighed. "Well, no use crying over spilled wine, eh?" He extended a thin, calloused hand. "Sirge Milton, Trader at leisure, damn the luck."

He shook the offered hand. "Jethri Gobelyn, off *Gobelyn's Market*."

"Pleasure. *Market's* a solid ship—Arin still senior trader?"

Jethri blinked. The routes being as they were, there were still some who'd missed news of Arin Gobelyn's death. This man didn't seem quite old enough to have been one of his father's contemporaries, but . . .

"Paitor's Senior Trader," he told Sirge Milton steadily. "Arin died in a loading accident, seven Standards back."

"Sorry to hear that," the man said seriously. "I was just a 'prentice, but he impressed me real favorable." He took a drink of ale, eyes wandering back to the ship-board. "Damn," he said, not quite under his breath, then laughed a little and looked at Jethri. "Let this be a lesson to you—*stay liquid*! Think I'd know *that* by now." Another laugh.

Jethri had a sip of beer. "But," he said, though it was none of his business, "what happened?"

For a moment, he thought the other wouldn't answer. Sirge drank ale, frowning at the board, then seemed to collect himself and flashed Jethri a quick grin.

"Couple things. First, I was approached for a closed buy-in on— futures." He shrugged. "You understand I can't be specific. But the guarantee was four-on-one and—well, the lodgings were paid until I shipped and I had plenty on my tab at the Trade Bar, so I sunk all my serious cash into the future."

Jethri frowned. A four-on-one return on speculation? It was possible—the crewtapes told of astonishing fortunes made Port-side, now and then—but not likely. To invest all liquid assets into such a venture—

Sirge Milton held up a hand. "Now, I know you're thinking exactly what I thought when the thing was put to me—four-on-one's way outta line. But the gig turns on a Liaden Master Trader's say-so, and I figured that was good enough for me." He finished his ale and put the glass down, waving at the barkeeper.

"Short of it is, I'm cash-poor 'til tomorrow mid-day, when the pay-off's guaranteed. And this morning I came across as sweet a deal as you'd care to see—and I know just who'll want it, to my profit. A cantra holds the lot—and me with three ten-bits in pocket. *Stork* was going to front the cash, and earn half the profit, fair enough. But the rush-money and bonus was brighter." He shook his head. "So, Jethri Gobelyn, you can learn from my mistake—and I'm hopeful I'll do the same."

"Four-on-one," Jethri said, mind a-buzz with the circumstance, so he forgot he was just a 'prentice, talking to a full Trader. "Do you have a paper with the guarantee spelled out?"

"I got better than that," Sirge Milton said. "I got his card." He turned his head, smiling at the bartender. "Thanks, Nance."

"No problem," she returned. "You got a Liaden's card? Really? Can I see?"

The man looked uneasy. "It's not the kind of thing you flash around."

"Aw, c'mon, Sirge—I never seen one."

Jethri could appreciate her curiosity: he was half-agog, himself. A Liaden's card was as good as his name, and a Liaden's name, according to Great-Grand-Captain Larance, was his dearest possession.

"Well," Sirge said. He glanced around, but the other patrons seemed well-involved in their own various businesses. "OK."

He reached into his pouch and pulled out a flat, creamy rectangle, holding it face up between the three of them.

"Ooh," Nance said. "What's it say?"

Jethri frowned at the lettering. It was a more ornate form of the Liaden alphabet he had laboriously taught himself off the library files, but not at all unreadable.

"Norn ven'Deelin," he said, hoping he had the pronunciation of the name right. "Master of Trade."

"Right you are," said Sirge, nodding. "And this here—" he rubbed his thumb over the graphic of a rabbit silhouetted against a full moon—"is the sign for his Clan. Ixin."

"Oh," Nance said again, then turned to answer a hail from up-bar. Sirge slipped the card away and Jethri took another sip of beer, mind racing. A four-on-one return, guaranteed by a master trader's card? It was possible. Jethri had seen the rabbit-and-moon sign on a land-barge that very day. And Sirge Milton was going to collect tomorrow mid-day. Jethri thought he was beginning to see a way to buy into a bit of profit, himself.

"I have a cantra to lend," he said, setting the schooner aside.

Sirge Milton shook his head. "Nah—I appreciate it, Jethri, but I don't take loans. Bad business."

Which, Jethri acknowledged, was exactly what his uncle would say. He nodded, hoping his face didn't show how excited he felt.

"I understand. But you have collateral. How 'bout if I buy *Stork's* share of your Port-deal, pay-off tomorrow mid-day, after you collect from Master ven'Deelin?"

"Not the way I like to do business," Sirge said slowly.

Jethri took a careful breath. "We can write an agreement." The other brightened. "We can, can't we? Make it all legal and binding. Sure, why not?" He took a swallow of ale and grinned. "Got paper?"

Gobelyn's Market

"NO, MA'AM," Jethri said as respectfully as he could, while giving his mother glare-for-glare. "I'm in no way trying to captain this ship. I just want to know if the final papers are signed with *Digger*." His jaw muscles felt tight and he tried to relax them—to make his face trading-bland. "I think the ship owes me that information. At least that."

"Think we can do better for you," his mother the Captain surmised, her mouth a straight, hard line of displeasure. "All right, boy. No, the final papers aren't signed. We'll catch up with *Digger* 'tween here and Kinaveral and do the legal then." She tipped her head, sarcastically civil. "That OK by you?"

Jethri held onto his temper, barely. His mother's mood was never happy, dirt-side. He wondered, briefly, how she was going to survive a whole year world-bound, while the *Market* was rebuilt.

"I don't want to ship on *Digger*," he said, keeping his voice just factual. He sighed. "Please, ma'am—there's got to be another ship willing to take me."

She stared at him until he heard his heart thudding in his ears. Then she sighed in her turn, and spun the chair so she faced the screens, showing him profile.

"You want another ship," she said, and she didn't sound mad, anymore. "You find it."

Zeroground Pub

"NO CALLS FOR Jethri Gobelyn? No message from Sirge Milton?"

The barkeeper on-shift today was maybe a Standard Jethri's elder. He was also twelve inches taller and outmassed him by a factor of two. He shook his head, so that the six titanium rings in his left ear chimed together, and sighed, none too patient. "Kid, I told you. No calls. No message. No package. No Milton. No nothing, kid. Got it?"

Jethri swallowed, hard. "Got it."

"Great," said the barkeep. "You wanna beer or you wanna clear out so a paying customer can have a stool?"

"Merebeer, please," he said, slipping a bit across the counter. The keeper swept up the coin, went up-bar, drew a glass, and slid it down the polished surface with a will. Jethri put out a hand—the mug smacked into his palm, stinging. Carefully, he eased away from the not-exactly-overcrowded counter and took his drink to the back.

He was on the approach to trouble. Dodging his senior, sliding off-ship without the captain's aye—approaching trouble, right enough, but not quite established in orbit. Khat was inventive—he trusted her to cover him for another hour, by which time he had better be on-ship, cash in hand and looking to show Uncle Paitor the whole.

And Sirge Milton was late.

A man, Jethri reasoned, slipping into a booth and setting his beer down, might well be late for a meeting. A man might even, with good reason, be an hour late for that same meeting. But a man could call the place named and leave a message for the one who was set to meet him.

Which Sirge Milton hadn't done, nor sent a courier with a package containing Jethri's payout, neither.

So, something must have come up. Business. Sirge Milton seemed a busy man. Jethri opened his pouch and pulled out the agreement they'd written yesterday, sitting at this very back booth, with Nance the bartender as witness.

Carefully, he smoothed the paper, read over the guarantee of payment. Two cantra was a higher buy-out than he had asked for, but Sirge had insisted, saying the profit would cover it, not to mention his "expectations." There was even a paragraph about being paid in the event that Sirge's sure buyer was out of cash, citing the debt owed Sirge Milton, Trader, by Norn ven'Deelin, Master Trader, as security.

It had all seemed clear enough yesterday afternoon, but Jethri thought now that he should have asked Sirge to take him around to his supplier, or at least listed the name and location of the supplier on the paper.

He had a sip of beer, but it tasted flat and he pushed the glass away. The door to the bar slid open, admitting a noisy gaggle of Terrans. Jethri looked up, eagerly, but Sirge was not among them. Sighing, he frowned down at the paper, trying to figure out a next move that didn't put him on the receiving end of one of his uncle's furious rakedowns.

Norn ven'Deelin, Master of Trade . . .

The words looked odd, written in Terran. Norn ven'Deelin, who had given his card—his name—into Sirge Milton's keeping. Jethri blinked. Norn ven'Deelin, he thought, would very likely know how to get in touch with a person he held in such high esteem. With luck, he'd be inclined to share that information with a polite-talking 'prentice.

If he wasn't inclined . . .Jethri folded his paper away and got out of the booth, leaving the beer behind. No use borrowing trouble, he told himself.

Ynsolt'i Upper Port

IT WAS LATE, but still day-Port, when he found the right office. At least, he thought, pausing across the street and staring at that damned bunny silhouetted against the big yellow moon, he hoped it was the right office. He was tired from walking miles in gravity, but worse than that, he was scared. Norn ven'Deelin's office—if this *was* at last his office—was well into the Liaden side of Port.

Not that there was properly a Terran side, Ynsolt'i being a Liaden world. But there were portions where Terrans were tolerated as a necessary evil attending galactic trade, and where a body caught the notion that maybe Terrans were cut some extra length of line, in regard to what might be seen as insult.

Standing across from the door, which might, after all, be the right one, Jethri did consider turning around, trudging back to the *Market* and taking the licks he'd traded for.

Except he'd *traded for* profit to the ship, and he was going to collect it. That, at least, he would show his senior and his captain, though he had long since stopped thinking that profit would buy him pardon.

Jethri sighed. There was dust all over his good trading clothes. He brushed himself off as well as he could, finger-combed his hair, and looked across the street. It came to him that the rabbit on Clan Ixin's sign wasn't so much howling at that moon, as laughing its fool head off.

Thinking so, he crossed the street, wiped his boots on the mat, and pushed the door open.

❖❖❖

THE OFFICE BEHIND the door was airy and bright, and Jethri was abruptly glad that he had dressed in trading clothes, dusty as they now were. This place was high-class—a body could smell profit in the subtly fragrant air, see it in the floor covering and the real wooden chairs.

The man sitting behind the carved center console was as elegant as the room: crisp-cut yellow hair, bland and beardless Liaden face, a vest embroidered with the moon-and-rabbit worn over a salt-white silken shirt. He looked up from his work screen as the door opened, eyebrows lifting in what Jethri had no trouble reading as astonishment.

"Good-day to you, young sir." The man's voice was soft, his Trade only lightly tinged with accent.

"Good-day, honored sir." Jethri moved forward slowly, taking care to keep his hands in sight. Three steps from the console, he stopped and bowed, as low as he could manage without falling on his head.

"Jethri Gobelyn, Apprentice Trader, *Gobelyn's Market*." He straightened and met the bland blue eyes squarely. "I am come to call upon the Honored Norn ven'Deelin."

"Ah." The man folded his hands neatly upon the console. "I regret it is necessary that you acquaint me more nearly with your business, Jethri Gobelyn."

Jethri bowed again, not so deep this time, and waited 'til he was upright to begin the telling.

"I am in search of a man—a Terran," he added, half-amazed to hear no quaver in his voice—"named Sirge Milton, who owes me a sum of money. It was in my mind that the Honored ven'Deelin might be willing to put me in touch with this man."

The Liaden frowned. "Forgive me, Jethri Gobelyn, but how came such a notion into your mind?"

Jethri took a breath. "Sirge Milton had the Honored ven'Deelin's card in pledge of—"

The Liaden held up a hand, and Jethri gulped to a stop, feeling a little gone around the knees.

"Hold." A Terran would have smiled to show there was no threat.

Liadens didn't smile, at least, not at Terrans, but this one exerted himself to incline his head an inch.

"If you please," he said. "I must ask if you are certain that it was the Honored ven'Deelin's own card."

"I—the name was plainly written, sir. I read it myself. And the sigil was the same, the very moon-and-rabbit you yourself wear."

"I regret." The Liaden stood, bowed and beckoned, all in one fluid movement. "This falls without my area of authority. If you please, young sir, follow me." The blue eyes met his, as if the Liaden had somehow heard his dismay at being thus directed deeper into alien territory. "House courtesy, Jethri Gobelyn. You receive no danger here."

Which made it plain enough, to Jethri's mind, that refusing to follow would be an insult and the last thing he wanted to do . . .

He bowed slightly and walked forward as sedately as trembling knees allowed. The Liaden led him down a short hallway, past two closed doors, and bowed him across the threshold of the third, open.

"Please be at ease," the Liaden said from the threshold. "I will apprise the master trader of your errand." He hesitated, then extended a hand, palm up. "It is well, Jethri Gobelyn. The House is vigilant on your behalf." He was gone on that, the door sliding silently closed behind him.

This room was smaller than the antechamber, though slightly bigger than the *Market's* common room, the shelves set at heights he had to believe handy for Liadens.

Jethri stood for a couple of minutes, eyes closed, doing cube roots in his head until his heartbeat slowed down and the panic had eased back to a vague feeling of sickness in his gut.

Opening his eyes, he went over to the shelves on the right, half-trained eye running over the bric-a-brac, wondering if that was really a piece of Sofleg porcelain and, if so, what it was doing set naked out on a shelf, as if it were a common pottery bowl.

The door whispered behind him, and he spun to face a Liaden woman dressed in dark trousers and a garnet colored shirt. Her hair was short and gray, her eyebrows straight and black. She stepped energetically into the center of the room as the door slid closed behind her, and bowed with precision, right hand flat against her chest.

"Norn ven'Deelin," she stated in a clear, level voice. "Clan Ixin."

Jethri felt the blood go to ice in his veins.

Before him, Norn ven'Deelin straightened and slanted a bright black glance into his face. "You discover me a dismay," she observed, in heavily accented Terran. "Say why, do."

He managed to breathe, managed to bow. "Honored ma'am, I— I've just learned the depth of my own folly."

"So young, yet made so wise!" She brought her hands together in a gentle clap, the big amethyst ring on her right hand throwing light off its facets like purple lightning. "Speak on, young Jethri. I would drink of your wisdom."

He bit his lip. "Ma'am, the—person—I came here to find—told me Norn ven'Deelin was—was male."

"Ah. But Liaden names are difficult, I am learning, for those of Terran Code. Possible it is that your friend achieved honest error, occasioned by null-acquaintance with myself."

"I'm certain that's the case, Honored," Jethri said carefully, trying to feel his way toward a path that would win him free, with no insult to the Trader or her House, and extricate Sirge Milton from a Junior's hopeless muddle.

"I—my friend—did know the person I mistakenly believed yourself to be well enough to have lent money on a Port-week investment. The—error—is all my own. Likely there is another Norn ven'Deelin in Port, and I foolishly—"

A tiny hand rose, palm out, to stop him. "Be assured, Jethri Gobelyn, of Norn ven'Deelin there is one. This one."

He had, Jethri thought, been afraid of that. Hastily, he tried to shuffle possibilities. Had Sirge Milton dealt with a go-between authorized to hand over his employer's card? Had—

"My assistant," said Norn ven'Deelin, "discloses to me a tale of wondering obfusion. I am understanding that you are in possession of one of my cards?"

Her assistant, Jethri thought, with a sudden sharpening of his wits on the matter at hand, had told her no such thing. She was trying to throw him off-balance, and startle him into revealing a weakness. She was, in fact, *trading*. Jethri ground his teeth and made his face smooth.

"No, ma'am," he said respectfully. "What happened was that I met a man in Port who needed loan of a cantra to hold a deal. He said he had lent his liquid to—to Norn ven'Deelin, Master Trader. Of Clan Ixin. He said he was to collect tomorrow—today, mid-day, that would be—a guaranteed return of four-on-one. My—my payout contingent on his payout." He stopped and did not bite his lip, though he wanted to.

There was a short silence, then, "Four-on-one. That is a very large profit, young Jethri."

He ducked his head. "Yes, ma'am. I thought that. But he had the—the card of the—man—who had guaranteed the return. I read the name myself. And the Clan sign—just like the one on your door and—other places on Port . . ." His voice squeaked out. He cleared his throat and continued.

"I knew he had to be on a straight course—at least on this deal—if it was backed by a Liaden's card."

"Hah." She plucked something flat and rectangular from her sleeve and held it out. "Honor me with your opinion of this."

He took the card, looked down and knew just how stupid he'd been.

"So wondrously expressive a face," commented Norn ven'Deelin. "Was this not the card you were shown, in earnest of fair dealing?"

He shook his head, remembered that the gesture had no analog among Liadens and cleared his throat again.

"No, ma'am," he said as steadily as he could. "The rabbit-and-moon were exactly the same. The name—the same style, the same spacing, the same spelling. The stock was white, with black ink, not tan with brown ink. I didn't touch it, but I'd guess it was low-rag. This card is high-rag content . . ."

His fingers found a pattern on the obverse. He flipped the card over and sighed at the selfsame rabbit-and-moon, embossed into the card stock, then looked back to her bland, patient face.

"I beg your pardon, ma'am."

"So." She reached out and twitched the card from his fingers, sliding it absently back into her sleeve. "You do me a service, young Jethri. From my assistant I hear the name of this person who has, yet does not have, my card in so piquant a fashion. Sirge Milton. This is a correctness? I do not wish to err."

The ice was back in Jethri's veins. Never insult a Liaden. Liadens lived for revenge, and to throw another Terran into Liaden revenge was about the worst—

"Ma'am, I—please. The whole matter is—is my error. I am the most junior of traders. Very likely I misunderstood a senior and have annoyed yourself and your household without cause. I—"

She held up a hand, stepped forward and lay it on his sleeve.

"Peace, child. I do nothing fatal to your *galandaria*—your countryman. No pellet in his ear. No nitrogen replacing good air in an emergency tank. Eh?"

Almost, it seemed to Jethri that she smiled.

"Such tales. We of the clans listen in Port-bars—and discover ourselves monsters." She patted his arm, lightly. "But no. Unless he adopts a mode most stupid, fear not of his life." She stepped back, her hand falling from his sleeve.

"Your own actions reside in correctness. Very much is this matter mine of solving. A junior trader could do no other, than bring such at once before me.

"Now, I ask, most humbly, that you accept Ixin's protection in conveyance to your ship. It is come night-Port while we speak, and your kin will be distressful for your safety. Myself and yourself, we will speak additionally, after solving."

She bowed again, hand over heart, and Jethri did his best to copy the thing with his legs shaking fit to tip him over. When he looked up the door was closing behind her. It opened again immediately and the assistant stepped inside with a bow of his own.

"Jethri Gobelyn," he said in his accentless Trade, "please follow me. A car will take you to your ship."

Gobelyn's Market

"SHE SAID SHE wouldn't kill him," he said hoarsely. The captain, his mother, shook her head and Uncle Paitor sighed.

"There's worse things than killing, Son," he said and that made Jethri want to scrunch into his chair and bawl, like he had ten Standards fewer and stood about as tall as he felt.

What he did do, was take another swallow of coffee and meet Paitor's eyes straight. "I'm sorry, sir."

"You've got cause," his uncle acknowledged.

"Double-ups on dock," the captain said, looking at them both. "Nobody works alone. We don't want trouble. We stay close and quiet and we lift as soon as we can without making it look like a rush."

Paitor nodded. "Agreed."

Jethri stirred, fingers tight 'round the coffee mug. "Ma'am, she— Master Trader ven'Deelin said she wanted to talk to me, after she—settled—things. I wouldn't want to insult her."

"None of us wants to insult her," his mother said, with more patience than he'd expected. "However, a master trader is well aware that a trade ship must trade. She can't expect us to hang around while our cargo loses value. If she wants to talk to you, boy, she'll find you."

"No insult," Paitor added, "for a junior trader to bow to the authority of his seniors. Liadens understand chain of command real well." The captain laughed, short and sharp, then stood up.

"Go to bed, Jethri—you're out on your feet. Be on dock second shift—" she slid a glance to Paitor. "Dyk?"

His uncle nodded.

"You'll partner with Dyk. We're onloading seed, ship's basics, trade tools. Barge's due Port-noon. Stick *close*, you understand me?"

"Yes, ma'am." Wobbling, Jethri got to his feet, saluted his seniors, put the mug into the wash-up and turned toward the door.

"Jethri."

He turned back, thinking his uncle's face looked—sad.

"I wanted to let you know," Paitor said. "The spice did real well for us."

Jethri took a deep breath. "Good," he said and his voice didn't shake at all. "That's good."

Gobelyn's Market
Loading Dock

"OK," SAID DYK, easing the forks on the hand-lift back. "Got it." He toggled the impeller fan and nodded over his shoulder. "Let's go, kid. Guard my back."

Jethri managed a weak grin. Dyk was inclined to treat the double-up and Paitor's even-voiced explanation of disquiet on the docks as a seam-splitting joke. He guided the hand-lift to the edge of the barge, stopped, theatrically craned both ways, flashed a thumbs-up over his shoulder to Jethri, who was lagging behind, and dashed out onto the *Market's* dock. Sighing, Jethri walked slowly in his wake.

"Hey, kid, hold it a sec." The voice was low and not entirely unfamiliar. Jethri spun.

Sirge Milton was leaning against a cargo crate, hand in the pocket of his jacket and nothing like a smile on his face.

"Real smart," he said, "setting a Liaden on me."

Jethri shook his head, caught somewhere between relief and dismay.

"You don't understand," he said, walking forward. "The card's a fake."

The man against the crate tipped his head. "Is it, now?"

"Yeah, it is. I've seen the real one, and it's nothing like the one you have."

"So what?"

"So," Jethri said patiently, stopping and showing empty hands in the old gesture of goodwill, "whoever gave you the card wasn't Norn ven'Deelin. He was somebody who *said* he was Norn ven'Deelin and he used the card and her—the honor of her name—to cheat you."

Sirge Milton leaned, silent, against the cargo bail.

Jethri sighed sharply. "Look, Sirge, this is serious stuff. The Master Trader has to protect her name. She's not after you—she's after whoever gave you that card and told you he was her. All you have to do—"

Sirge Milton shook his head, sorrowful, or so it seemed to Jethri. "Kid," he said, "you still don't get it, do you?" He brought his hand out of the pocket and leveled the gun, matter-of-factly, at Jethri's stomach. "I know the card's bogus, kid. I know who made it—and so does your precious master trader. She got the scrivener last night. She'd've had me this morning, but I know the back way outta the 'ground."

The gun was high-g plastic, snub-nosed and black. Jethri stared at it and then looked back at the man's face. *Trade*, he thought, curiously calm. *Trade for your life.*

Sirge Milton grinned. "You ratted another Terran to a Liaden. That's stupid, Jethri. Stupid people don't live long."

"You're right," he said, calmly, watching Sirge's face and not the gun at all. "And it'd be real stupid for you to kill me. Norn ven'Deelin said I'd done her a service. If you kill me, she's not going to have any choice but to serve you the same. You don't want to corner her."

"Jeth?" Dyk's voice echoed in from the dock. "Hey! Jethri!"

"I'll be out in a second!" he yelled, never breaking eye contact with the gunman. "Give me the gun," he said, reasonably. "I'll go with you to the master trader and you can 'make it right.' "

" 'Make it right'," Sirge sneered and there was a sharp snap as he thumbed the gun's safety off.

"I urge you most strongly to heed the young trader's excellent advice, Sirge Milton," a calm voice commented in accentless Trade. "The master trader is arrived and Balance may go forth immediately."

MASTER VEN'DEELIN'S yellow-haired assistant walked into the edge of Jethri's field of vision. He stood lightly on the balls of his feet, as if he expected to have to run. There was a gun, holstered, on his belt.

Sirge Milton hesitated, staring at this new adversary.

"Sirge, it's not worth dying for," Jethri said, desperately.

But Sirge had forgotten about him. He was looking at Master ven'Deelin's assistant. "Think I'm gonna be some Liaden's slave until I worked off what she claims for debt?" He demanded. "Liaden Port? You think I got any chance of a fair hearing?"

"The Portmaster—" the yellow-haired Liaden began, but Sirge cut him off with a wave, looked down at the gun and brought it around.

"No!" Jethri jumped forward, meaning to grab the gun, but something solid slammed into his right side, knocking him to the barge's deck. There was a *crack* of sound, very soft, and Jethri rolled to hisfeet—

Sirge Milton was crumbled face down on the cold decking, the gun in his hand. The back of his head was gone. Jethri took a step forward, found his arm grabbed and turned around to look down into the grave blue eyes of Master ven'Deelin's assistant.

"Come," the Liaden said, and his voice was not—quite—steady. "The master trader must be informed."

Gobelyn's Market
Common Room

THE YELLOW-HAIRED assistant came to an end of his spate of Liaden and bowed low.

"So it is done," Norn ven'Deelin said in Trade. "Advise the Portmaster and hold yourself at her word."

"Master Trader." The man swept a bow so low his forehead touched his knees, straightened effortlessly and left the common room. Norn ven'Deelin turned to Jethri, sitting shaken between his mother and Uncle Paitor.

"I am regretful," she said in her bad Terran, "that solving achieved this form. My intention, as I said to you, was not thus. Terrans—"

She glanced around, at Paitor and the captain, at Dyk and Khat and Mel. "Forgive me. I mean to say that Terrans are of a mode most surprising. It was my error, to think this solving would end not in dyings." She showed her palms. "The counterfeit-maker and the, ahh— *distributor*—are of a mind, both, to achieve more seemly Balance."

"Counterfeiter?" asked Paitor and Norn ven'Deelin inclined her head.

"Indeed. Certain cards were copied—not well, as I find—and distributed to traders of dishonor. These would then use the—the—*melant'i*—you would say, the *worth* of the card to run just such a shadow-deal as young Jethri fell against." She sat back, mouth straight. "The game is closed, this Port, and I come now to Balance young Jethri's service to myself."

His mother shot a glance at Paitor, who rose to his feet and bowed, low and careful. "We are grateful for your condescension, Master Trader. Please allow us to put paid, in mutual respect and harmony, to any matter that may lie between us—"

"Yes, yes." She waved a hand. "In circumstance far otherwise, this would be the path of wisdom, all honor to you, Trader Gobelyn. But you and I, we are disallowed the comfort of old wisdom. We are honored, reverse-ward, to build new wisdom." She looked up at him, black eyes shining.

"See you, this young trader illuminates error of staggering immensity. To my hand he delivers one priceless gem of data: Terrans are using Liaden honor to cheat other Terrans." She leaned forward, catching their eyes one by one. "Liaden honor," she repeated, "to cheat other Terrans."

She lay her hand on her chest. "I am a master trader. My—my *duty* is to the increase of the trade. Trade cannot increase, where honor is commodity."

"But what does this," Dyk demanded, irrepressible, "have to do with Jethri?"

The black eyes pinned him. "A question of piercing excellence. Jethri has shown me this—that the actions of Liadens no longer influence the lives only of Liadens. Reverse-ward by logic follows for the actions of Terrans. So, for the trade to increase, wherein lies the proper interest of trader and master trader, information cross-cultural must increase." She inclined her head.

"Trader, I suggest we write contract between us, with the future of Jethri Gobelyn in our minds."

Uncle Paitor blinked. "You want to—forgive me. I think you're trying to say that you want to take Jethri as an apprentice."

Another slight bow of the head. "Precisely so. Allow me, please, to praise him to you as a promising young trader, of learned instinct and strongly enmeshed in honor."

"But I did everything wrong!" Jethri burst out, seeing Sirge Milton laying there, dead of his own choice, and the stupid waste of it . . .

"Regrettably, I must disagree," Master ven'Deelin said softly. "It is true that death untimely transpired. This was not your error. Pen Rel informs to me your eloquence in beseeching Trader Milton to the path of Balance. This was not error. To solicit solving from she who is most able to solve—that is only correctness." She showed both of her hands, palms up. "I honor you for your actions, Jethri Gobelyn, and wonder if you will bind yourself as my apprentice."

He wanted it. In that one, searing moment, he knew he had never wanted anything in his life so much. He looked to his mother.

"I found my ship, Captain," he said.

✧ A Choice of Weapons ✧

The number of High Houses is precisely fifty.
And then there is Korval.
—From the Annual Census of Clans,
on file with the Council of Clans, Solcintra, Liad

"I AM NOT worthy."

Daav yos'Phelium bowed low. When he straightened, it was not to his full height, but with carefully rounded shoulders and half-averted face: a lesser being, faint with terror at his own audacity.

His mother would have laughed aloud at such obvious mummery. His delm—Korval Herself, she who held the future and life of each clanmember in her sedately folded hands—merely lifted an elegant golden eyebrow.

Daav schooled himself to stillness—small challenge for one who was a scout—face yet averted. He did not quite bite his lip, though the inclination was strong. Not all of his present display was artifice; it was no inconsiderable thing to bring Korval's Own Eye upon onself, true-son though he be.

A full Standard minute passed before Korval shifted slightly in her chair.

"In the one face," she said, reflectively, and in no higher mode than that of parent to child, "the question of how long you might stand there, cowed and silent, beguiles my closest interest. On the other face, it is *Daav* before me, and one cannot be certain but that this is a ploy engineered to rob us both of the pleasure of attending Etgora's certain-to-be-tedious evening gather." The mode shifted, and she was his Delm once more, chin up and eyes no warmer than ice.

"Elucidate this sudden unworthiness. Briefly."

Mode required that a petitioner accept the Delm's Word with a bow. Daav did so, forehead brushing knees, and returned to the round-shouldered pose of inferiority.

"I have today received my quartershare accounting from dea'Gauss and with it certain documents needful of my attention. One of those documents was the Delm's Formal Declaration of Heir, in which I discover myself named Korval-in-future." He moved his shoulders, easing tension that was born not only of the unnatural posture.

"The information amazes?" Korval-in-present inquired. "Surely you are aware that you have been trained for the duty since you had sense of language."

Daav inclined his head. "But I was not trained alone. Er Thom has been at my side, schooled as I was, word and gesture. We studied the same diary entries. We learned our equations at the same board. All in accordance with Delm's Wisdom—that two be conceived and trained to the duty, to insure that Korval *would* have its delm, though yos'Phelium's genes twice proved inadequate."

He paused, daring a quick glance at his delm's face from beneath modestly lowered lashes. No sign—of irritation, impatience, boredom. Or humor. Chi yos'Phelium had been a scout herself before duty called her to delmhood, forty Standard years ago. *Her* face would reveal whatever she wished to show.

"Er Thom," Daav murmured, "has a steady nature; his understanding of our history and our present necessities is entirely sound. Of course, he is a master pilot—indeed, his skill over-reaches my—"

Korval raised her hand.

"A discussion of your fosterbrother's excellencies is extraneous to the topic." She lowered her hand. "Daav yos'Phelium professes himself unworthy to assume the duty he was bred and trained for, thus calling a Delm's Decision into question—that is your chosen theme. Speak to it."

Daav took a deep breath, bowed. She was correct—of course she was correct. A delm could not be wrong, in matters of clan. That the delm had mischosen her heir was no fault of her judgement, but his own error, in withholding information she required. He had intended to speak ere she had chosen, but he had not expected her to have chosen so soon.

He came to his full height and met his delm's chill eyes squarely.

"Perhaps, then, I should have put it that I am unfit for the duty. While I am off Liad, performing even the most tedious of tasks required by Scout Headquarters, my temper is serene and my judgement sound. I am scarcely a day on the homeworld and I am awash in anger. People annoy me to the edge of endurance. Mode and measure grate my patience. I cannot say with any certainty that my judgement is sound. Indeed, I fear it is dangerously unsound." He bowed again, buying time, for this next was difficult, for all it needed to be said.

"I had been to the Healers, last leave, and asked that the distemper be mended."

"Ah," said Korval. "And was it so?"

Daav felt his lips twitch toward a smile—most inappropriate when one was in conversation with one's delm—and straightened them with an effort..

"Master Healer Kestra," he said, "was pleased to inform me that many people find Liadens irritating."

"So they do," his delm agreed gravely. "Most especially do yos'Pheliums who have not yet attained their thirtieth Name Day find Liadens annoying. If you will accept the experience of one who is your elder, I will certify that the annoyance does ease, with time."

Daav bowed acceptance of an elder's wisdom. "I would welcome instruction on how not to do a murder in the interim."

Korval tipped her head, looking into his eyes with such intensity he thought she must see into his secret soul. It required effort, to neither flinch nor look away, but less effort—noticeably less effort—than had been required, even five years ago.

"As concerned as that," Korval murmured and looked down at her folded hands, releasing him. She was silent for a few moments, then looked back to his face.

"Very well. The delm will take her Decision under review."

Daav felt his knees give, and covered the slight sag with a bow of gratitude.

"All very fine," said Korval. "But I will not start you in the habit of questioning Delm's Decision."

"Of course not." He bowed again, every line eloquent of respect.

"So very well-trained," Korval murmured, rising from her chair. "It's nothing short of marvelous."

FROWNING, DAAV CONSIDERED the gun.

It was not a pretty gun, in the way meant by those who admired jeweled grips and platinum-chased cylinders. It was a functional gun, made to his own specifications and tuned by Master Marksman Tey Dor himself. It was also small, and could be hidden with equal ease in Daav's sleeve or his palm.

Etgora's evening-gather, now. It might please his mother to dismiss this evening's affair as tedious, but the papers forwarded by dea'Gauss had shown that it was not so long ago that Clan Etgora and Clan Korval had come at odds—and when Balance was done, it was Korval who showed the profit.

Etgora had pretensions. A clan with its profit solidly in the star-trade, they had strained after High House status, and fell but a hand's breadth short before the loss to Korval set them a dozen Standard years further back from the goal. There was bitterness in the House on that count, Daav did not doubt.

However, if Etgora wished to secure its teetering position as a high-tier Mid House, they must show a smooth face to adversity. *Of course* they would place Korval upon the most-honored guest list. They could not do otherwise and survive.

By the same logic of survival, Etgora would take utmost care that no slight or insult befell Korval while she was in their care.

Which meant that Daav, chancy tempered as he knew himself to be, might safely leave his hideaway in its custom-fitted box.

And yet . . .

"Might," he murmured, slipping the little gun into his sleeve, "is not ought."

He glanced to the mirror, smoothed the sleeve, twitched the lace at his throat, touched the sapphire in his right ear and made an ironic bow. His reflection—black-browed, lean and over-long—returned the salutation gracefully.

"Do *try* not to kill anyone tonight, Daav," he told himself. "Murder would only make the evening more tedious."

THEY WERE ADMITTED to Etgora's townhouse and relieved of their cloaks by a supernaturally efficient servant, who then bowed them into the care of a child of the House.

She had perhaps twelve Standards, hovering between child and halfling, and holding herself just a bit stiffly in her fine doorkeeper's silks.

"Kesa del'Fordan Clan Etgora," she said, bowing prettily in the mode of Child of the House to Honored Guests. She straightened, brown eyes solemn with duty, and waited for them to respond, according to Code and custom.

"Chi yos'Phelium," his mother murmured, bowing as Guest to House Child, "Korval."

The brown eyes widened slightly, but give her grace, Daav thought; she did not make the error of looking down to see Korval's ring of rank for herself. Instead, she inclined her head, with composure commendable in one of twice her years, and looked to Daav.

He likewise bowed, Guest to House Child, and straightened without flourish.

"Daav yos'Phelium Clan Korval."

Kesa inclined her head once more and completed the form.

"Ma'am and sir, be welcome in our house." She paused, perhaps a heartbeat too long, then bowed. "If you would care to walk with me, I will bring you to my father."

"Of your kindness," his mother murmured and followed the child out of the welcoming parlor, Daav walking at the rear, as befit one of lesser rank who was likewise his delm's sole protection in a House not their own.

Kesa led them down a short, left-tending hallway, through an open gateway of carved sweetstone and out into an enclosed garden, and the full force of the evening gather.

Etgora, Daav observed, as he followed his mother and their guide down cunning, crowded walkways, was a clan which addressed its projects with energy. Challenged to display a clean face to the world, it did not hesitate to bring the world together immediately for the purpose.

A more conservative clan, Daav thought, his quick, scout-trained eyes catching glimpses of an astonishing number of High Houselings among the crowd, would have invited Korval, of course, to this first gather since its failure, and perhaps one or two others of the High Houses, at most. Not so Etgora, who seemed to have formed the guest list almost entirely from the Fifty, with a few taken from the ranks of the higher Mid-Level Houses, for the purpose, Daav supposed, of filling out odd numbers.

Progress along the pathways was slow, what with so many acquaintances who must be acknowledged with a bow. Both Daav and his mother several times had to duck under gay strings of rainbow-colored streamers and the imported oddity of Terran-made balloons.

At long last, they achieved the center of the garden, where a man slightly younger and a good deal less elegant than his mother was speaking with apparent ease to no other than Lady yo'Lanna. Daav owned himself impressed. Lady yo'Lanna was his mother's oldest friend among her peers in the High Houses, and he held her in quite as much awe now as he had at six.

"Father," Kesa bent deeply, the full bow of clanmember to Delm, and straightened self-consciously, shoulders stiff beneath her finery.

"Your pardon, good ma'am," the gentleman murmured, and, receiving Lady yo'Lanna's half-bow of permission, turned to face them.

"Kesa, my child. Who have you brought me?"

"Father, here is Chi yos'Phelium and Daav yos'Phelium Clan

Korval," the child said in the very proper mode of Introduction. She turned and bowed, Housechild to Guests. "Honoreds, here is my father, Hin Ber del'Fordan, Etgora."

So Kesa's father was Etgora Himself. It explained much, Daav thought, from the unexpected youth of the door guardian to her stiff determination to observe every mode precisely.

"Korval, you do me honor!" Etgora swept the bow between equals—theoretically true, between delms, Daav thought wryly—and augmented it with the trader's hand-sign for "master," a nice touch, drawing on the common trading background of both Houses while publically acknowledging Korval's superiority.

His mother, Daav saw, was inclined to be amused by their host's little audacity. She bowed just short of full Equal, accepting the master status Etgora acknowledged.

"To be welcome in the house of an ally is joy," she said clearly into the sudden nearby silence. She straightened and extended a hand to touch Daav's sleeve.

"One's son, Etgora."

"Lord yos'Phelium." The bow this time was Delm to Child of an Ally's House: High Mode, indeed, but carried well, and necessitating, alas, the rather tricksy Child of a Delm to an Ally as the most precise response. He straightened in time to see his mother incline her head to Lady yo'Lanna.

"Ilthiria, I find you well?"

"As well as one can be in this crush. Etgora is proud of his achievement—and justly so!—but you and I know how to value an empty garden."

Had he been less well-trained, Daav would have winced in sympathy for Kesa's father. Lady yo'Lanna, it seemed, was not *entirely* at one with her host.

The pale eyes moved, pinning him. "Young Daav, newly at leave from the scouts."

He bowed, lightly. "I have no secrets from you, ma'am."

"Do you not?" Her eyebrows rose. "Then come to me tomorrow and whisper in my ear the tale of how a certain mutual acquaintance came to break his arm in Mid-Port evening before last."

Damn. He bowed again, aware of his mother's gaze on the side of his suddenly warm face.

"If that is your wish, then how can I deny you?"

"Very properly said," Etgora interjected. "And who better to know Port gossip than a scout, who are said to have ears in every cranny?" He turned, spied his daughter, yet standing stiffly to one side.

"Kesa, my jewel. Lord yos'Phelium will wish to reacquaint himself with his age-mates, as he is just returned from the scouts. Pray show him to the Sunset Garden—and then you may refresh yourself."

He turned to Daav.

"Card tables have been set out, sir, and other light amusements. Please, be easy in our House."

He flicked a glance at his mother, who inclined her head.

"Amuse yourself, Daav, do. Etgora will wish to walk Ilthiria and myself through his garden. I will require your arm in two hours."

"Ma'am." He bowed obedience to the delm, then a general leave-taking to Lady yo'Lanna and Etgora. This done, he bowed once more, very gently, and offered his arm to Kesa del'Fordan. "Lady Kesa, will you walk with me?"

She hesitated fractionally, brown eyes lifting to his face in a child's straight look of assessment. Whatever she saw convinced her that he was not having fun at her expense, for she stepped forward and put her hand lightly on his sleeve.

"Certainly, I will walk with you," she said, unself-consciously. "How else may I show you to the Sunset Garden?"

"Very true," Daav replied gravely. From the edge of his eye, he saw Etgora offer an arm and his mother take it. "In which direction shall we walk, then, Lady?"

"This," she said, moving a hand to the west, belatedly adding, "Of your goodness."

The pathways toward sunset were somewhat less crowded than those they had followed from the house. That was not to say, Daav thought, that the paths were empty or that the garden reposed in tranquility.

He bowed briefly to Lady pel'Nyan and moved on, Kesa

del'Fordan silent on his arm. Etgora, he considered, had come a fair way to making a recover. Lady yo'Lanna's attendance had of course assured the attendance of several other Houses of rank. And if *she* were inclined to smile upon Etgora . . .

Or, Daav thought suddenly, if Ilthiria yo'Lanna attended at the request of her old friend Chi yos'Phelium, delm of the ancient ally of her House? Oh, yes, that fit well. Especially when one heard one's mother declaring herself comforted in the presence of an ally. Korval had never taken allies easily, to the benefit, mostwise, of the more conservative clans.

Daav made a mental note to review the Summary of Balance dea'Gauss had sent more closely. He had missed the reason that Etgora was thought necessary to the interests of Korval. Presumption had, of course, been answered, but it seemed that the upstart clan could not be allowed entirely to sink. Thus, this gather, with its theme of courteous and charming commonsense, and everyone of consequence in attendance.

In consideration of which, Daav said to himself, *you are in arrears of your duty.*

He tipped his head, assessing his companion from beneath his lashes. She looked pale, he thought, and her jaw was definitely clenched too tightly for fashion. Her shoulders moved like boards beneath the pretty silk tunic and the hand that rested against his sleeve put no pressure on his arm at all.

He cleared his throat gently and smiled when she looked up, startled.

"I hope you will allow me to commend your performance as House Guard," he murmured. "I am persuaded that you stand the duty often."

Kesa blushed, lashes flickering. "Not," she said, somewhat faintly, "so very often." She paused, glancing aside, then looked back to his face.

"In fact," she said, rather breathlessly, "this evening is the first time I have stood between the House and the world. It is—it has been my brother's duty, you know—he is the elder—but, this evening, he . . . He asked our father for other work."

"Very proper in him," Daav murmured, noting her hesitation and drawing the conclusion that Kesa's brother's "ask" had very little of "if-you-please" about it. "So this was your first time a House Guard? I am all admiration. Well I remember my first time at the door—a mere dinner party, nothing like what we have here!—and I was wishing for nothing but my bed before even half the guests were arrived!"

She actually laughed, and Daav ducked as they passed beneath a string of balloons and streamers.

Kesa paused, frowning up at him and the balloons just behind his head.

"I do not—you are very tall, are you not? I recall my father said that Korval is a tall clan. He—Jen Dal was to have made certain the lines were strung well above—but I am certain." she said in a sudden rush, "that he could not have realized that, that—"

"That the pickpocket who wishes to rob Korval must bring his own stepladder," Daav said lightly, rescuing her from what could only be an unfortunate culmination of her sentence.

Kesa frowned. "I do not entirely—"

"Ah, Daav! I had heard the scouts had released you to us!"

The voice was lovely, as was the lady. Two years ago, he had been besotted with both. He was no longer besotted, but he was indebted to her for a lesson well-delivered and equally well-learned, and so he bowed, with courtesy.

"Bobrin, good evening to you."

She returned his bow, eyes teasing his face, then straightened, one hand rising to her flower-braided hair. Her eyes left his face, and found Kesa.

"It is Etgora's daughter, is it not?"

Kesa bowed low—Child of the House to Honored Guest. "Kesa del'Fordan, Lady del'Pemridj."

"Just so." Bobrin inclined her beflowered head, then shot Daav a glance of pure mischief. "Take advice and walk carefully with this one, Housedaughter. Daav—" She paused, likely on the edge of more specific mischief. Daav met her eye squarely, and had the satisfaction of seeing her look aside.

"Daav," she said. "Good evening."

She swept down the path and Daav became aware that he was gritting his teeth. Deliberately, he relaxed his jaw and looked down at his companion.

Kesa was staring after Bobrin, brown eyes wide. After a moment, she sighed and glanced up at Daav.

"She is a very beautiful lady. I—do you think when I am grown I might wear flowers in my hair?"

When you are grown, Daav thought, *my hope is that you will care more for other matters—even for what I deduce is your scapegrace brother—than for the dressing of your hair.*

Her look, however, was appealing—and she was, after all, a child—so he swallowed his initial answer and instead looked about with wide amaze, flinging his arm out.

"Why, here we are in the very heart of a garden! What is to prevent you from having flowers in your hair this instant, if you wish it?"

"I—" She, too, stared about, as if she just now realized their setting, then looked back to his face.

"No one, that is, I have yet to learn the—the proper manner in which to place flowers in the hair."

"Ah, there you are fortunate," Daav said gaily. "I have some training in the placement of hair-ornaments. Perhaps you will allow me to be of service to you."

The brown eyes took fire. "Would you? I—I would be in your debt."

"Not a bit of it." Daav said stoutly. "It is a pleasure to share my skill. Now, which flowers will you have?"

She moved to the edge of the walk, staring at the orderly rows of blossom. "That, if you please," she said, pointing to a low, spike-leafed shrub. Its indigo blooms were flat and multi-petalled, noteworthy without being ostentatious, and a good match for the silk Doorkeeper's tunic.

"Excellent," Daav murmured approvingly and bent to pluck one. The stem was woody, but broke easily. "Yes, very good. Now, my Lady, if you will step over here, so that we do not impede traffic while this very delicate operation is performed . . ."

Kesa stepped to his side, Daav inclined his head to Lord Andresi—another of his mother's cronies—who smiled and passed on without comment.

"Now, then," Daav said. "I will wish you to stand very tall, but not at all stiffly. True beauty is never ill at ease. Very good. A moment, now, while I discover the perfect placement—yes, I believe so." He hesitated, flower poised. "Be easy, Lady Kesa, but as still as you may—"

He moved, scout-quick, smoothing her thick brown hair with one hand while he slid the flower home just above her right ear.

"Let us be certain that it is well-anchored," Daav said, hands hovering. "Move your head now—look up at me. Ah—"

"Stand away from my sister!"

The voice was, of course, too loud. Had the phrase been whispered it would have been too loud, at this gather. Daav sighed and glanced up.

The young man bearing down on them had something of Etgora's look to him, albeit Etgora in an ugly pet. He had, Daav judged, about twenty Standard years.

"Calm yourself, sir," Daav said moderately. "I am doing your sister no harm."

"I will be the judge of that, sir!" the other snapped. "As kinsman, I—"

"Jen Dal, be still!" Kesa flung about—the flower stayed firmly in place, Daav saw with pleasure. "There's nothing amiss." She swallowed and glanced back to Daav. "Lord yos'Phelium, here is my brother, Jen Dal del'Fordan. Jen Dal, here is Daav yos'Phelium Clan—"

"I know who he is," Jen Dal said awfully. "Sir, you have not yet put yourself at a decent distance from my sister." Kesa made a sound rather like a splutter, which Daav interpreted as outrage. Her brother spared her a single withering glance.

"Be still, Kesa. This is a matter of honor."

"If it's a matter of *my* honor," Kesa said, with spirit, "then I should judge the damage and the price, not you."

"Completely by Code," Daav said, uneasily aware that they were attracting a crowd.

The young gentleman stared at him, eyes hard with hatred. *So,* thought Daav, *the balloons were not strung so low by accident. Here's one who has taken Etgora's fall as a blow to his heart, and cannot see 'round his anger to the greater good of the House.*

"My sister is a child, sir. It is as ludicrous to expect her to know proper Code as it is to expect her to know all the faces of harm."

Daav drew a breath, trying to still the quick flare of anger. For Kesa's sake, for the sake of Etgora's value to Korval, he would *not* lose his temper. He would quell this self-important upstart and dismiss him, then disperse the growing crowd of the curious. He was Chi yos'Phelium's son. These things were not beyond him.

"Sir, your concern for your kin does you credit. However, I feel that you have allowed an elder sibling's natural partiality—"

Jen Dal del'Fordan turned his face away.

"Kesa," he said, as if Daav had finished speaking—no, as if Daav had never begun to speak!—"pray remove yourself from the proximity of this—person."

Tears filled the brown eyes. "Jen Dal, he is our *guest*! I am quite unharmed, Lord yos'Phelium was only placing a flower in my hair, as I asked him to do!" There was a ripple through those gathered at that, but Jen Dal was unmoved.

"This man is son of a House with a long history of predation among the lesser Houses. I will not see him attack my kin. He will—"

Oh, gods, Daav thought, suddenly seeing the destination of the farce. *You fool!* He leaned forward and touched Kesa lightly on the sleeve.

"Lady, your brother is correct. You cannot stay this."

For a heartbeat, the brown eyes searched his face, then she stepped back, bowed fully—House Child to Honored Guest—and turned. She walked away as sedately as one with years of negotiation behind her, and the crowd parted to let her through.

"You, sir," Jen Dal del'Fordan cried, "will satisfy the honor of my House!"

"Don't be absurd," Daav said, voice stringently calm, despite the anger trembling within. "The honor of your House is intact, as you well know."

"I know nothing of the sort. Korval destroys clans as casually as I pluck a flower." The last was said with a sneer and Daav caught his breath at the sheer, blinding stupidity of the man. Did he not know that even now Korval and Etgora were mending the damage given his clan? Did he not know that with Korval's patronage and the smiles of the High Houses, Etgora would recover its loss and reap new profits before Kesa signed her first Contract lines?

"You do your sister an injustice—you call her honor and her understanding into question before all these."

He threw an arm out, showing the so-quiet crowd damming the pathway. "Is this the path a brother treads, in the task of keeping his kin safely? Your understanding is at fault in this, sir. Neither Etgora nor Etgora's children has taken lasting harm from Korval. Have done and stand away."

Jen Dal del'Fordan smiled. "And I say," he returned, voice, without doubt, pitched to carry far into the gardens, "that Korval has tainted Etgora's honor. Everyone here has heard me. I will have satisfaction, sir!"

Fool! Daav raged, forcing himself to breathe deeply. He bowed, deliberately, in the mode of Master to Novice, taking a savage satisfaction in the gasp from the crowd.

"Call the House's dueling master," he said, and his voice was not—quite—steady. "I will satisfy you."

From the corner of his eye, he saw the crowd waver and reform with Etgora and his mother in the first rank. His mother's face was very calm.

THE CARD TABLES in the Sunset Glade had been hastily removed to make room for the combatants. Clan Etgora's dueling master bowed to Daav.

"My Lord yos'Phelium, as the one challenged, you may choose the weapons of the duel. The House can provide pistols, swords, knives, or Turing forks from its own arsenal. If you wish a weapon we do not own, the House will acquire a matched set of the weapon of your choice, within reason. If it appears, in the judgement of the Master of the Duel, that your weapon has been chosen with an eye to indefinitely postponing this duel, you will be required to choose another weapon. Is this understood, sir?"

"It is." Daav closed his eyes, briefly considering edges and explosives, bludgeons, the perfectly tuned gun in his sleeve, but—no. Such weapons were insufficiently potent; they limited one to the infliction of mere physical damage. He required—*he would have*—a fuller Balance.

Daav opened his eyes and pointed at the gaily colored balloons, strung on their strings at the edge of the glade.

"There is my weapon of choice, sir. If the House is able, let a dozen of those be filled with water and let both my opponent and I choose three. Can this be done?"

The dueling master bowed. "Indeed it can. And the distance?"

"Twelve paces, I believe," Daav said, counting the moves. "Yes, that will do."

"Very well," said the dueling master and went away to give instructions.

The balloons arrived in very short order and were placed, carefully, on the lawn. A murmur rose up from the crowd—and an outcry from Daav's opponent.

"What is this? Toys? Do you consider a challenge from Etgora a matter for mockery, sir? Dueling master! Take these insults away, sir, and bring us the matched set in the mahogany case!"

The dueling master bowed. "The rules of the duel state clearly that weapons are the choice of the challenged, sir. Lord yos'Phelium has chosen balloons filled with water, at twelve paces. He is within both his rights and the bounds of the duel."

"I will not—" began Jen Dal, but it was Etgora who spoke up from the sidelines.

"Do you know, my son, I think you will? Lord yos'Phelium has made his choice. Plainly, he is a man who stands by his decisions, no matter how foolish they may appear. I would counsel you to do the same."

"Lord yos'Phelium," said the Master of Duel, "choose your weapons."

Daav stepped forward, knelt in the grass and picked up the first balloon. It was not quite as firm as he wished and he set it aside. The second pleased him and he cradled that one in his arm. The third . . .

"Will you hurt him?" Kesa asked from his side. He glanced at her, unsmiling.

"I do not think these will hurt him, though that is always a danger, in a duel."

"But you will make him ridiculous," said Kesa. "Jen Dal hates to be laughed at."

"Many people do," Daav said, finding his third weapon in the seventh balloon. He tucked it neatly in the cradle of his left arm and rose to his feet. "Stand clear of the firing range, Lady Kesa. Of your kindness."

She hesitated a moment longer, throwing one of her disconcertingly direct looks at his face. Then she bowed, simply, as between equals, and walked sedately to her father's side, in the first rank of spectators.

Daav waited while his opponent randomly picked his weapons, then stomped to the center of the field, the balloons wriggling and threatening to leap from his ineptly crossed arms.

The dueling master held his hands over his head.

"The contestants will count off six paces each, turn and stand steady. First shot to the challenged. A hit is counted only on a strike to the body of one's opponent. The affair is finished when each contestant has expended his ammunition. The win goes to the contestant who has taken the least hits, or to he who draws first blood. In case of tie, Lady yo'Lanna shall decide the victor." He lowered his hands and stepped back.

"Gentlemen, turn. Count off. One! Two! Three! Four! Five! Six! Turn! Lord yos'Phelium, fire at will."

Deftly, Daav plucked a balloon from the cradle of his arm, gauged its flow, probable spin and mass—and threw.

The balloon elongated, caught up with itself, tumbled once and hit Jen Dal's tunic, dead center, with a satisfying splat. Someone in the crowd laughed, and quickly stopped.

"This is a farce!" shouted Jen Dal.

"It is a duel," the master returned sternly. "Attend, if you please, sir. The shot is yours."

Jen Dal clumsily tipped his balloons onto his off-hand, snatched one free, holding it firmly—as it happened, a bit too firmly, for the sphere exploded, showering him with water.

Ignoring the resulting curses, the dueling master looked to Daav, who sent his next balloon high into Jen Dal's left shoulder.

The dueling master had scarcely given his sign before the sodden young man had snatched up his second balloon, somewhat less robustly—and hurled it in Daav's direction.

It was a good throw, only missing by twelve or fifteen inches.

Daav weighed his last balloon in his hand and considered deloping.

"A duel with toys and water," Jen Dal del'Fordan called from his position. "Korval takes good care that it spills no blood for honor."

The balloon was airborne before Daav had taken conscious thought. It sped, hard and true, and struck his opponent precisely in the nose.

Jen Dal howled, dropped his remaining balloon and bent double, both hands rising to his face. Med-techs rushed in from the sidelines and the dueling master raised his hands above his head.

"Lord yos'Phelium has drawn first blood! The duel is done!"

"HOWEVER DID YOU hit upon water balloons?" his mother inquired some time later, in the privacy of Jelaza Kazone's upstairs parlor.

"Something I read of Terran custom," Daav said hazily. "You know what scouts are, ma'am!"

"Indeed I do," she replied, sipping wine and looking out into the peaceful night-time garden.

Abruptly, she turned from the window. "Daav, I am persuaded you did right to speak to the delm about your worthiness to stand Korval."

He froze, heart rising into his throat. She had seen! Observing the duel with Korval's Own Eyes, she had seen his error. She understood that at the moment of decision he had not acted for the good of the clan but from his own sense of injury, exacting a Balance—a Balance brutal of a halfling's dignity.

Worse, he had gained an enemy of his own rank—for he had heard, later, that Jen Dal was Etgora's heir—who hated him now, and would surely hate him when they both came delm-high. All his mother's careful work, undone. Undone, because Daav could not put the good of all before his own bad temper.

It must be Er Thom, now, he thought. *With Er Thom as Korval, Etgora may deal without malice, saving only I'm kept sanely out of sight . . .*

Belatedly, he became aware of his mother's eyes upon him, and bowed. "Ma'am . . .."

She raised her hand. "Speak not. I will tell you that the delm has reviewed her Decision, based on what she has seen of your understanding and judgment this evening. You acted as well as inexperience might, preserving both Etgora's heir and the peace between our Houses. With age will come . . .tidier . . .solutions." She smiled faintly.

"You are na'delm, my son. Korval-to-be. I trust you will not feel it necessary to revisit the matter. I doubt you will find the delm so accommodating again."

He stared, speechless. She had seen with Delm's Eyes, but she had not understood. Korval Herself had erred in a matter of clan. He moved his head, trying to clear his vision, which was abruptly indistinct.

His mother moved forward, smile deepening. "Don't look so stricken, child," she said gently. "You'll do very well." She raised a hand to cup his cheek.

"Or at least as well as any of us have."

✧ Changeling ✧

THE FIRST THING THEY told him when he emerged from the catastrophic healing unit was that his wife had died in the accident.

The second thing they told him was that her Clan was pursuing retribution to the fullest extent of the Code.

They left him alone, then, the med techs, with instructions to eat and rest. The door slid closed behind them with the snap of a lock engaging.

Out of a habit of obedience, he walked over to the table and lifted the cover from the tray. The aroma of glys-blossom tea rose to greet him and he dropped the cover, tears rising.

He had not known his wife well, but she had been pretty and bold and full of fun—one found it inconceivable, newly healed from one's own injuries and with the scent of her preferred blend in the air, that she was—that she was—

Dead.

The tears spilled over, blinding him. He raised his hands to cover his face and wept where he stood.

His name was Ren Zel dea'Judan Clan Obrelt. He was twenty-one Standard years old and the hope of all his kin.

THEY WERE SHOPKEEPERS, Clan Obrelt. It scarcely mattered what sort of shop, as long as it wanted keeping. In the hundreds of years since the first dea'Judan took up the trade, Obrelt had kept flower shops, sweet shops, hardware shops, book shops, wine shops, green groceries, and shops too odd to mention. The shops they kept were never their own, but belonged to other, wealthier clans who lacked Obrelt's genius for management.

Having found a trade that suited them, Obrelt was not minded to change. They settled down to the work with a will and achieved a certain reputation. Eventually, it came to be Obrelt managers that the High Clans sought to manage the stores the High Clans owned. In the way of commerce, the price that Obrelt might ask of clans desirous of employing their shopkeepers rose. The House became—not wealthy, not in any Liaden terms—but comfortably well-off. Perhaps not nearly so well-off by the standard of the far homeworld, Liad itself; but comfortable enough by the easy measure of outworld Casia.

A Clan of shopkeepers, they married and begat more shopkeepers, though the occasional accountant, or librarian, or Healer was born. These changelings puzzled the clan elders when they appeared, but honor and kin-duty were served and each was trained to that which he suited, to the increase and best advantage of the clan.

Into Clan Obrelt, then, in the last relumma of the year called Mitra, a boychild was born. He was called Ren Zel, after the grandfather who had first taken employ in a shop and thus found the clan its destiny, and he was a normal enough child of the House, at first, second and third counting.

He was quick with his numbers, which pleased Aunt Chane, and had a tidy, quiet way about him, which Uncle Arn Eld noted and approved. No relative was fond enough to proclaim him a beauty, though all allowed him to be neatly made and of good countenance. His hair and eyes were brown; his skin a rich, unblemished gold.

As befit a House in comfortable circumstance, Obrelt was wealthy in children. Ren Zel, quiet and tidy, was invisible amid the gaggle of his cousins. His three elder sisters remembered, sometimes, to pet him, or to scold him, or to tease him. When they noticed him at all, the adults found him respectful, current in his studies, and demure—everything that one might expect and value in the child of a shopkeeper who was destined, himself, one day to keep shop.

It was Aunt Chane who first suspected, in the relumma he turned twelve, that Ren Zel was perhaps destined to be something other than a shopkeeper. It was she who gained the delm's permission to take him down to Pilot's Hall in Casiaport. There, he sat with his hands demurely folded while a lady not of his clan tossed calculations at him, desiring him merely to give the answer that came into his head.

That was a little frightening at first, for Aunt Chane had taught him to always check his numbers on the computer, no matter how certain he was, and he didn't like to be wrong in front of a stranger and perhaps bring shame to his House. The lady's first calculations were easy, though, and he answered nearly without thinking. The quicker he answered, the quicker the lady threw the next question, until Ren Zel was tipped forward in his chair, face animated, brown eyes blazing in a way that had nothing tidy or quiet about it. He was disappointed when the lady held up her hand to show she had no more questions to ask.

Also that day, he played catch with a very odd ball that never quite would travel where one threw it—at least, it didn't the first few times Ren Zel tried. On his fourth try, he suddenly understood that this was only another iteration of the calculations the lady had tossed at him, and after that the ball went where he meant it to go.

After the ball, he was asked to answer timed questions at the computer, then he was taken back to his aunt.

She looked down at him and there was something . . . odd about her eyes, which made him think that perhaps he should have asked the lady's grace to check his numbers, after all.

"Did I do well, Aunt?" he blurted, and Aunt Chane sighed.

"Well?" she repeated, reaching to take his hand and turning toward the door. "It's the delm who will decide that for us, youngling."

Obrelt Himself, informed in private of the outcome of the tests, was frankly appalled.

"Pilot? Are they certain?"

"Not only certain, but—enthusiastic," Chane replied. "The Master Pilot allows me to know that our Ren Zel is more than a step out of the common way, in her experience of pilot-candidates."

"Pilot," the Delm moaned and went over to the table to pour himself a second glass of wine. "Obrelt has never bred a pilot."

Chane pointed out, dryly, that it appeared they had, in this instance, bred what might be trained into a very fine pilot, indeed. To the eventual increase of the clan.

That caught Obrelt's ear, as she had known it would, and he brightened briefly, then moved a hand in negation. "All very well to say the *eventual* increase! In the near while, have you any notion how much it costs to train a pilot?"

As it happened, Chane did, having taken care to possess herself of information she knew would lie near to Obrelt's concern.

"Twenty-four cantra, over the course of four years, apprentice fees for two years more, plus licensing fees."

Obrelt glared at her. "You say that so calmly. Tell me, Sister, shall I beggar the clan to educate one child? I allow him to be extraordinary, as he has managed to become your favorite, though we have prettier, livelier children among us."

"None of whom is Ren Zel," Chane returned tartly. She sighed then and grudgingly showed her lead card. "A first class pilot may easily earn eight cantra the Standard, on contract."

Obrelt choked on his wine.

"They say the boy will achieve first class?" he managed a few moments later, his voice breathless and thin.

"They say it is *not impossible* for the boy to achieve first class," she replied. "However, even a second class pilot may earn five cantra the Standard."

"'May'," repeated obrelt.

"If he brings the clan four cantra the Standard, he will pay back his education right speedily," Chane said. Observing that her brother wavered, she played her trump.

"The Pilot's Guild will loan us his first two year's tuition and fees, interest-free, until he begins to earn wages. If he achieves first class, they will write paid to the loan."

Obrelt blinked. "As desirous of the child as that?"

"He is," Chane repeated patiently, "more than a step out of the common way. Master Pilot von'Eyr holds herself at your pleasure, should you have questions for her."

"Hah. So I may." He walked over to the window and stood

looking down into the modest garden, hands folded behind his back. Chane went to the table, poured herself a glass of wine and sipped it, recruiting herself to patience.

Eventually, Obrelt turned away from the window and came forward to face her.

"It is a strange path we would set the child upon, Sister, to a place where none of his age-mates may follow. He will sail between stars while his cousins inventory stock in back storerooms. I ask you, for you have given him his own room in your heart: Do we serve him ill or well by making him a stranger to his kin?"

And that was the question that needed to be asked, when all considerations of cantra costs were ended. What was best done for Ren Zel himself, for the good of all the clan?

Chane set her glass aside and met her Delm's eyes straightly.

"He is already a stranger among us," she said, speaking as truly as she knew how. "Among his age-mates he is a cipher—he is liked, perhaps, but largely ignored. He goes his own way, quiet, tidy, courteous—and invisible. Today—today, when the pilots returned him to me, it was as if I beheld an entirely different child. His cheeks glowed, his eyes sparkled, he walked at the side of the master pilot visible and proud." She took a breath, sighed it out.

"Brother, this boy is not a shopkeeper. Best for us all that we give him the stars."

And so it was decided.

REN ZEL ACHIEVED his first class piloting license on the nineteenth anniversary of his Name Day. He was young for the rank, especially for one who had not sprung from a piloting House, but not precocious.

Having thus canceled out half of his tuition and fees, he set himself to paying off the balance as quickly as possible. It had been plain to him for several years that the clan had gone to extraordinary expense on his behalf and he did not wish his cousins to be burdened by a debt that rightly belonged only to himself. That being so, he had the Guild accountant write a contract transferring the amount owed from Clan Obrelt to Ren Zel dea'Judan Clan Obrelt, as a personal debt.

He was young, but he had a reputation among the elder pilots with whom he'd flown for being both steady and level-headed, a reputation they were glad to broadcast on the Port.

That being so, contracts came his way—good contracts, with payouts in the top percentage of the Guild's rates. Often enough, there was a bonus, for Ren Zel had a wizard's touch with a coord string— or so his elders praised him. Those same elders urged him to go for Master, and he thought he would, someday.

After he cleared his debt.

IT WAS NIGHT-PORT at Casia by the time he finished shutdown and gave the ship into the keeping of the client's agent. Ren Zel slung his kit over a shoulder and descended the ramp, filling his lungs with free air. World air tasted different than ship air, though he would have been hard put to say which flavor he preferred, beyond observing that, of world air, he found Casia's the sweetest.

At the bottom of the ramp, he turned right and walked leisurely through the night-yard, then out into the thoroughfare of Main Port.

The job he had just completed had been profitable—an exhilarating run, in fact, with the entire fee paid up front and a generous bonus at the far end. A half-dozen more like it would retire his debt. Not that such runs were common.

Night-port was tolerably busy. He saw a pilot he knew and raised a hand in greeting. The other waved and cut across the crowded walkway.

"Ren Zel! I haven't seen you in an age! There's a lot of us down Findoir's—come and share a glass or two!"

He smiled, but moved his hand in a gesture of regret. "I'm just in. Haven't been to Guild Hall yet."

"Well, there's a must," the other allowed cheerfully. "Come after you've checked in, do, for I tell you we mean to make a rare night of it. Otaria's gotten her first."

"No, has she? Give her my compliments."

"Come down after you've checked in and give them to her yourself," his friend said, laying a hand briefly on his sleeve. "Until soon, Ren Zel."

"Until soon, Lai Tor."

Warmed, he continued on his way and not many minutes later walked up the stairs into Casiaport Guild Hall.

The night clerk took his license, scanned it and slid it back across the counter. "Welcome home, Pilot." She tapped keys, frowning down at her readout. Ren Zel put his card away and waited while she accessed his file.

"Two deposits have been made to your account," she said, scrolling down. "One has cleared, and twelve percent clan share has been paid. Eleven-twelfths of the balance remaining has gone against the Pilots Guild Tuition Account, per standing orders. No contracts pending . . ." She paused, then glanced up. "I have a letter for you, Pilot. One moment." She left the console and walked to the back.

Ren Zel frowned. A letter? A *paper* letter? Who would—

The clerk was back, holding a buff-colored envelope. She used her chin to point at the palm reader set into the surface of the counter.

"Verification, please, Pilot."

Obediently, he put his palm over the reader, felt the slight tingle, heard the beep. He lifted his hand and the clerk handed him the envelope. His fingers found the seal embossed on the sealed flap— Obrelt's sign.

Ren Zel inclined his head to the clerk.

"My thanks."

"Well enough," she replied and looked once more her screen. "Status?"

He paused on the edge of telling her "on call," feeling the envelope absurdly heavy in his hand.

"Unavailable," he said, fingers moving over the seal.

She struck a last key and inclined her head.

"So recorded."

"My thanks," he said again and, shouldering his kit, walked across the hall to the common room.

As luck would have it, the parlor was empty. He closed the door behind him, dropped his kit and slid his finger under the seal.

A letter from Obrelt? His hands were not quite steady as he

unfolded the single sheet of paper. Paper letters had weight, and were not dispatched for pleasantries.

Has someone died? he wondered, and hoped that it might not be Chane, or Arn Eld or—

The note was brief, written in Obrelt's Own Hand.

Ren Zel dea'Judan was required at his Clan House, immediately upon receipt of this letter.

His delm judged it time for him to wed.

IT WAS MORNING WHEN the taxi pulled up before Obrelt's House. Ren Zel paid the fare, then stood on the walkway until the cab drove away.

He had not come quite "immediately," there being no reason to rouse the House at midnight when so many were required to rise early and open the various shops under Obrelt's care. And he was himself the better for a shower, a nap and a change of clothes, though it was still not easy to consider the reason he had been summoned home.

Home.

Ren Zel turned and looked up the walk, to the fence and the gate and the tall town house beyond them. He had grown up in this House, among the noisy gaggle of his sibs and cousins; it was to this House that he had returned on his brief holidays from school. Granted, he had come back less often after he had finished with his lessons, but there had been flight time to acquire, techniques to master and the first class to win.

Once he held first class, of course, there had been contracts to fulfill, the debt to reduce. Between contracts, he had routinely kept his status on "on call," which required him to lodge at the Guild Hall. The debt shrunk, but so, too, did his contact with his family.

He looked at the gate, and took a deep breath, steeling himself as if for some dreaded ordeal. Which was nonsense. Beyond the gate were only his kin—his clan, which existed to shelter him and to care for him and to shield him from harm.

He took a step up the walkway.

The gate in the wall surrounding Obrelt's house sprang open and a woman emerged from the fastness beyond, walking briskly in her neat, shopkeeper's uniform and her sensible boots, a manager's clipboard cuddled against her breast.

She saw him and checked, eyes widening for the leather-jacketed stranger on Obrelt's very walk. Ren Zel held out his hands, palms showing empty.

"Eba," he said softly to his next eldest sister, "it is I."

"Ren Zel?" Her gaze moved over his face, finding enough of Obrelt there to soothe her into a smile and a step forward, hand extended. "Brother, I scarcely knew you!"

He smiled in his turn and went to take her hand.

"The jacket disarmed you, doubtless."

She laughed, kin-warm. "Doubtless. Jump-pilot, eh? It suits you extremely."

Eba had been his favorite sister—young enough not to entirely despise the childish projects of a younger brother, yet old enough to stand as sometimes ally against the more boisterous of the cousins. Ren Zel pressed her fingers.

"I find you well?"

"Well," she conceded, and then, playfully, "And well you find me at all, rogue! How many relumma have passed since you last came to us? I suppose it's nothing to you that I am tomorrow sent to Morjan for a twelve-day? I was to have left today, but necessity calls me to the shop. Say at least you will be at Prime!"

"I believe I shall," he said. "The delm calls me home, on business."

"Ah!" She looked wise. "One had heard something of that. You will be pleased, I think." She dropped his hand and patted the leather sleeve of his jacket. "Go on inside. I must to the shop."

"Yes, of course." She read his hesitation, though, and laughed softly, shaking her glossy dark hair back.

"You cannot stand out on the walk all day, you know! Until Prime, Ren Zel!"

"Until Prime, Eba," he replied, and watched her down the walk. She turned at the corner without looking back. Ren Zel squared his shoulders, walked up to the gate and lay his palm against the plate.

A heartbeat later, he was within Obrelt's walls. Directly thereafter, the front door accepted his palmprint and he stepped into the house.

His nose led him to the dining room, and he stood on the threshold several minutes before one of the cousins caught sight of him, touched the arm of the cousin next to him, who turned, then spoke quickly—quietly—to the cousin next to *her* until in no time the whole busy, bustling room was still, all eyes on the man under the archway.

"Well." One stirred, stood up from her place at the table.

"Don't dawdle in the doorway, child," said Aunt Chane, for all the stars as if he were ten again. "Come in and break your fast."

"Yes, Aunt," he said meekly and walked forward. The cousins shook themselves, took up the threads of their conversations, poured tea and chose slices of sweet toast. Ren Zel came to the table and made his bow.

"Ma'am."

"Ren Zel." She held out a hand, beckoning, and he stepped to her side. Chane smiled, then, and kissed his cheek. "Welcome home."

AUNT CHANE SAT ON the short side of the table across which Ren Zel and Obrelt Himself faced each other, in the Advocate's Chair. The wine was poured and the ritual sip taken; then the glasses were set aside and Obrelt laid the thing out.

"The name of the lady we propose for your wife is Elsu Meriandra Clan Jabun," he said, in his usual bluff way.

Ren Zel blinked, for Jabun was a Clan old in piloting. Certainly, it was not Korval, but for outworld Casia it was very well indeed— and entirely above Obrelt's touch.

The Delm held up a hand. "Yes, they are beyond us absolutely— pilots to shopkeepers. But Obrelt has a pilot of its own to bring to the contract suite and Jabun was not uninterested."

But surely, Ren Zel thought, surely, the only way in which Obrelt might afford such a contract was to cede the child to Jabun—and that made no sense at all. Jabun was a Clan of pilots, allied with other of the piloting Houses. What use had they for the seed of a child of

Obrelt, bred of shopkeepers, the sole pilot produced by the House in all its history? He was a fluke, a changeling; no true-breeding piloting stock such as they might wish to align with themselves.

"The child of the contract," his Delm continued, "will come to Obrelt."

Well, yes, and *that* made sense, if Obrelt found pilot wages to its taste and wished to diversify its children. But, gods, the expense! And no guarantee that his child would be any more pilot than Eba!

"No," Aunt Chane said dryly, "we have not run mad. Recruit yourself, child."

Ren Zel took a deep breath. "One wishes not to put the clan into shadow," he said softly.

"We have been made to understand this," Obrelt said, of equal dryness with his sister. "Imagine my astonishment when I learned that a debt contracted by the House for the good of the House had been reassigned to one Ren Zel dea'Judan Clan Obrelt. At his request, of course."

"My contracts are profitable," Ren Zel murmured. "There was no need for the House to bear the burden."

"The clan receives a tithe of your wages," Aunt Chane pointed out.

He inclined his head. "Of course."

He looked up in time to see his aunt and his delm exchange a look undecipherable to him. The delm cleared his throat.

"Very well. For the matter at hand—Jabun and I have reached an equitable understanding. Jabun desires his daughter to meet you before the lines are signed. That meeting is arranged for tomorrow evening, at the House of Jabun. The lines will be signed on the day after, here in our own house. The contract suite stands ready to receive you."

The day after tomorrow? Ren Zel thought, feeling his stomach clench as it did when he faced an especially tricksy bit of piloting. Precisely as if he were sitting board, he took a breath and forced himself to relax. Of course, he would do as his delm instructed him—obedience to the delm, subservience to the greater good of the clan, was bred deep in his bones. To defy the delm was to endanger the clan, and without the clan there was no life. It was only—the matter came about so quickly . . .

"There was a need for haste," Aunt Chane said, for the second time apparently reading his mind. "Pilot Meriandra's ship is come into dock for rebuilding and she is at liberty to marry. It amuses Jabun to expand his alliances—and it profits Obrelt to gain for itself the child of two pilots." She paused. "Put yourself at ease: the price is not beyond us."

"Yes, Aunt," he said, for there was nothing else to say. Two days hence, he would be wed; his child to come into clan, to be sheltered and shaped by those who held his interests next to their hearts. The Code taught that this was well, and fitting, and just. He had no complaint and ought, indeed, feel honored, that the clan lavished so much care on him.

But his stomach was still uncertain when they released him at last to settle his business at the Port and to register his upcoming marriage with the Guild.

THE LINES WERE signed, the contract sealed. Elsu Meriandra received her delm's kiss and obediently allowed her hand to be placed into the hand of Delm Obrelt.

"Behold, the treasure of our clan," Jabun intoned, while all of Clan Obrelt stood witness. "Keep her safe and return her well to us, at contract's end."

"Willingly we receive Elsu, the treasure of Jabun," Obrelt responded. "Our House stands vigilant for her, as if for one of our own."

"It is well," Jabun replied, and bowed to his daughter. "Rest easy, my child, in the House of our ally."

The cousins came forward then to make their bows. Ren Zel stood at the side of his contract-bride and made her known to each, from Obrelt Himself down to the youngest child in the nursery—his sister Eba's newest.

After that, there was the meal of welcoming. Ren Zel, who held lesser rank in Obrelt than his wife held in Jabun, was seated considerably down-table. This was according to Code, which taught that Obrelt could not impose Ren Zel's status on Elsu, who was accustomed to sitting high; nor could her status elevate him, since she was a guest in his House.

He had eaten but lightly of the meal, listening to the cousins on either side talk shop. From time to time he glimpsed his wife, high up-table between his sister Farin and his cousin, Wil Bar, fulfilling her conversational duty to her meal partners. She did not look down-table.

The meal at last over, Ren Zel and Aunt Chane escorted Jabun's treasure throughout Obrelt's house, showing her the music room, the formal parlor and the tea room, the game room and the door to the back garden. In the library, Aunt Chane had her place a palm against the recording plate. This registered her with the House computer and insured that the doors allowed to contract-spouses would open at her touch.

Departing the library, they turned left down the hall, not right toward the main stair, and Aunt Chane led the way up the private stairway to the closed wing. In the upper hallway, she paused by the first door and bowed to Elsu Meriandra.

"Your room, contract-daughter. If you find aught awry, only pick up the house phone and call me. It will be my honor to repair any error."

Elsu bowed in turn.

"The House shows me great kindness," she said, most properly, her high, sweet voice solemn. She straightened and put her hand against the plate. The door slid open and she was gone, though Ren Zel thought she looked at him, a flickering glance through modestly lowered lashes, in the instant before the door closed behind her.

Though it was not necessary, Aunt Chane guided him to the third and last door on the hallway. She turned and smiled.

"Temporary quarters."

This sort of levity was not like his aunt and Ren Zel was startled into a smile of his own. "Thank you, ma'am."

"Thank us, is it?" She tipped her head, considering him in the hall's dim light. "Let the flowers aid you," she said softly. "It will be well, child."

He had his doubts, in no way alleviated by the few words he had actually exchanged with his wife, but it would serve no useful purpose to share them with Aunt Chane. The clan desired a child borne of the union of pilots: His part was plainly writ.

So, he smiled again and raised her hand, laying his cheek against the backs of her fingers in a gesture of kin-love. "It will be well," he repeated, for her comfort.

"Ah." She seemed on the edge of saying something further, but in the end simply inclined her head before walking, alone, back the way they had come.

After a moment, Ren Zel put his hand against the door and entered his temporary quarters.

He had been here yesterday, moving in his clothes and such of his books as he thought would be prudent. He had even opened the inner door and gone into the middle room—into the contract-room itself—walking lightly on the lush carpet.

The bed was ornate, old, and piled high with pillows. The flowers twined up two bedposts and climbed across the connecting bars, spilling down in luxuriant curtains of green and blue. Sunlight poured down from the overhead window, heating the blossoms and releasing the aphrodisiac scent. Standing by the wine-table, Ren Zel had felt his blood stir and taken a step away, deliberately turning his back on the bed.

The rest of the room was furnished but sparsely: there was the wine-table, of course; and a small table with two chairs, at which two might take a private meal; and a wide, yellow brocade sofa facing a fireplace where sweet logs were laid, awaiting the touch of a flamestick. The solitary window was that above the bed; the walls were covered in nubbled silk the color of the brocaded sofa.

Across the room—directly across the room from the door by which he had entered—was another door. Beyond, he knew, was another room, like the room he had just quit, where his sisters were laying out those things Elsu Meriandra had sent ahead.

Some trick of the rising heat had filled his nostrils with flower-scent again and Ren Zel had retreated to his own quarters, locking the door to the contract-room behind him.

Now, showered and dressed in the robe his sisters had given him in celebration of his marriage, he paused to consider what little he knew of his wife.

She was his elder by nearly three Standards, fair-haired, wide-eyed, and comely. He thought that she was, perhaps, a little spoilt, and he supposed that came of being the true-daughter of a High Clan delm. Her manners were not entirely up in the boughs, however, and she spoke to Aunt Chane precisely as she ought. If she had little to say to him beyond those things that the Code demanded, it was scarcely surprising. He was in all things her inferior: rank, flight-time, age, and beauty. And, truth be told, they had not been brought together to converse.

That which had brought them together—well. He had taken himself to the sleep learner, to review the relevant section of Code, for the contract-bed was a far different thing than a breakshift tumble with a comrade—and there his wife had the advantage of him again. She had been married once already, to a pilot near her equal her rank, and Jabun had her child in its keeping.

Sighing, he straightened his garment about him, catching a glimpse of himself in the mirror: ordinary, practical Ren Zel, got up in a magnificent indigo-and-silver marriage robe that quite overwhelmed his commonplace features. Sighing again, he glanced at the clock on the dresser.

The hour was upon him.

Squaring his shoulders under their burden of embroidery, Ren Zel went to the inner door, and lay his palm against the plate. The door opened.

Elsu Meriandra was at the wine-table, back to him. Her hair was loose on her shoulders, her robe an expensive simplicity of flowing golden shadowsilk, through which he could plainly see her body. She heard the door open and turned, her eyes wide, lustrous with the spell of the bed-flowers.

"Good evening," she said, her high voice sounding somewhat breathless. "Will you drink a glass with me . . . Ren Zel?"

His name. A good sign, that. Ren Zel took a breath, tasting the flowers, and deliberately drew the scent deep into his lungs. He smiled at the woman before him.

"I will be happy to share a glass with you, Elsu," he said softly, and stepped into the contract-room.

REN ZEL WOKE IN the room he had been allotted, and stretched, luxuriating in his solitude even as he cataloged his various aches. The lady was not a gentle lover. He thought he could have borne this circumstance with more equanimity, had he any indication that her exuberance sprang from an enthusiasm for himself. To the contrary, she had brushed his attentions aside, as one might dismiss the annoying graspings of a child.

Well, he thought ruefully, he had heard that the flower did sometimes produce . . . unwarranted . . . effects.

So thinking, he rolled neatly out of bed, showered, and dressed in his usual plain shirt and pants. He stamped into his boots and picked up his latest book—a slender volume of Terran poetry. The habit of taking a book with him to breakfast had formed when he was a child and it had come to his notice that the cousins let him be, if he were diligently reading.

He was passing the game room on his way to the dining hall when the sound of child's laughter gave him pause.

It was not entirely . . . comfortable . . . laughter, he thought. Rather, it sounded breathless, and just a little shrill. Ren Zel put his hand against the door and, quietly, looked inside.

Elsu Meriandra was playing catch with young Son Dor, who had, Ren Zel remembered, all of eight Standards. She was pitching the ball sharply and in unexpected directions, exactly as one might do when playing with a pilot—or one destined to be a pilot.

Son Dor was giving a good accounting of himself, considering that he was neither a pilot nor the child of a pilot. But he was clearly at the limit of both his speed and his skill, chest heaving and face wet with exertion. As Ren Zel watched, he dove for the ball, reacting to its motion, rather than anticipating its probable course, actually got a hand on it and cradled it against his chest. He threw it, none too steadily, back to Elsu Meriandra, who fielded the toss smoothly.

"That was a good effort," she said, as Ren Zel drifted into the room, meaning to speak to her, to offer her a tour of the garden and thus allow Son Dor to escape with his *melant'i* intact.

"Try this one," Elsu said and Ren Zel saw her hands move in the familiar sequence, giving the ball both velocity and spin. Dropping his book, he leapt, extended an arm and snagged the thing at the height of its arc. He danced in a circle, the sphere spinning in a blur from hand to hand, force declining, momentum slowing, until it was only a ball again—a toy, and nothing likely to break a child's fragile fingers, extended in a misguided attempt to catch it.

"Cousin Ren Zel!" Son Dor cried. "I could have caught it! I *could* have!"

Ren Zel laughed and danced a few more steps, the ball spinning lazily now on the tips of his fingers.

"Of course you could have, sweeting," he said, easily. "But you were having so much fun, it was more than I could do not to join in." He smiled, the ball spinning slowly. "Catch now," he said to Son Dor, and allowed the toy to leave his fingers.

The child rushed forward and caught it with both hands.

"Well done!" Ren Zel applauded. Son Dor flushed with pleasure and tossed the ball back. Ren Zel caught it one-handed, and allowed his gaze to fall upon the wall clock.

"Cousin," he said, looking back to the child, "is it not time for history lessons?"

Son Dor spun, stared at the clock, gasped, and spun back, remembering almost at once to make his bow.

"Ma'am, forgive me. I am wanted at my studies."

"Certainly," Elsu said. "Perhaps we might play ball again, when your studies free you."

Son Dor looked just a bit uneasy about that, but replied courteously. "It would be my pleasure, ma'am." He glanced aside. "Cousin . . ."

Ren Zel waved a hand. "Yes, all you like, but do not, I implore you, be late to Uncle Arn Eld. You know how he grumbles when one is late!"

Apparently Son Dor knew just that, and the knowledge gave his feet wings. The door thumped closed behind him and Ren Zel let out his breath in a long sigh before turning to face Elsu Meriandra.

She was standing with her head tipped, an expression of amused curiosity upon her face.

"He is not," Ren Zel said, stringently even, "a pilot. He will never be a pilot."

She frowned slightly at that and motioned for the ball. He threw it to her underhanded and she brought it, spinning hard, up onto her fingers.

"Are you certain of that, I wonder? Sometimes, when they are young, they are a little lazy. When that is the case, the spinball may be depended upon to produce the correct response."

Ren Zel moved his shoulders, letting the tension flow out of him. She did not understand—how could she? Pilot from a House of pilots. He sighed.

"The children of this House are shopkeepers. They have the reactions and the instincts of shopkeepers." He paused, thinking of Son Dor, laboring after a toss that a pilot's child would find laughably easy.

"He was striving not to disappoint," he told Elsu Meriandra. "What you see as 'a little lazy' is Son Dor's best reaction time. The spinball—forgive me—damage might well have been done."

Her face blanked. She caught the ball with a snap and bowed, unexpectedly low. "It was not my intention to endanger a child of the House."

She straightened and looked at him out of the sides of her eyes. "One was told, of course, but it is difficult to recall that this is not a House of pilots. Especially when there is yourself! Why, one can hardly hold a conversation in Guild Hall without hearing of your accomplishments!" She bowed again, more lightly this time. "You do our Guild great honor."

She did not wait for his reply, but turned and crossed the room to put the ball away. After a moment, Ren Zel went to pick up his fallen book.

"What have you?" she asked from just behind him. He turned and showed her the cover.

She frowned at the outlandish lettering. "That is Terran, is it not?"

"Indeed. *Duet for the Star Routes* is the title. Poetry."

"You read Terran?" She seemed somewhat nonplused by this information.

"I read Terran—a little. I am reading poetry to sharpen my comprehension, since I find it a language strong in metaphor."

Elsu moved her gaze from the book to his face. "You *speak* Terran."

That was not a question, but he answered it anyway. "Not very well, I fear. I meet so few to practice against that my skill is very basic."

"Why," she asked, the frown back between her eyes, "would you wish to learn these things?"

Ren Zel blinked. "Well, I am a pilot. My craft takes me to many ports, some of them Terran. I was . . . dismayed . . . not to be able to converse with my fellows on those ports and so I began to study." He paused. "Do you not speak Terran?"

"I do not," she returned sharply. "I speak Trade, which is sufficient, if I am impelled into conversation with—with someone who is not able to speak the High Tongue."

"I see," Ren Zel murmured, wondering how to extricate himself from a conversation that was growing rapidly unpleasant for them both. Before he arrived at a solution, however, the lady changed the subject herself.

"Come, we are both pilots—one of us at least legendary in skill!" she said gaily. "What do you say we shake the House dust from our feet and fly?"

It sounded a good plan, he owned; for he was weary of being Housebound already. There was, however, one difficulty.

"I regret," he said, his voice sounding stiff in his own ears. "Obrelt does not keep a ship. One is a pilot-for-hire."

"As I am," she said brightly. "But do not repine, if you haven't your own ship. I own one and will gladly have you sit second board."

Well, and that was generous enough, Ren Zel thought. Indeed, the more he thought about it, the better the scheme appeared. They were, as she said, both pilots. Perhaps they might win through to friendship, if they sat board together. Only look at what had lain between himself and Lai Tor—and see what comrades they had become, after shared flight had made their minds known to each other.

So—"You are generous," he told Elsu Meriandra. "It would be pleasant to stretch one's wings."

"Good. Let me get my jacket. I will meet you in the front hall."

"Well enough," he said. "I will inform the House."

ELSU'S SHIP WAS A small middle-aged packetspacer, built for intra-system work, not for hyperspace. It would also, Ren Zel thought, eyeing its lines as he followed his contract-wife toward the ramp, do well in atmospheric flight. The back-swept wings and needle-nose gave it an eerie resemblance to the raptors that lived in the eaves of the Port Tower, preying on lesser birds and mice.

"There," Elsu used her key and the ship's door slid open. She stepped inside and turned to make him an exaggerated bow, her blue eyes shining.

"Pilot, be welcome on my ship."

He bowed honor to the owner and stepped into the ship. The hatch slid shut behind him.

Elsu led the way down the companionway to the piloting chamber. She fair flung herself into the chair, her hands flying across the board, rousing systems, initiating checks. From the edge of the chamber, Ren Zel watched as she woke her ship, her motions nearer frenzy than the smooth control his teachers had bade him strive to achieve.

She turned in the pilot's chair, her face flushed, eyes brilliantly blue, and raised a hand to beckon him forward.

"Come, come! Second board awaits you, as we agreed! Sit and make yourself known to the ship!" Her high voice carried a note that seemed to echo the frenzy of her board-run and Ren Zel hesitated a moment longer, not quite trusting—

"So an intra-system is not to your liking?" she inquired, her voice sharp with ridicule. "Perhaps the legendary Ren Zel dea'Judan flies only Jump-ships."

That stung, and he very nearly answered in kind. Then he recalled her as she had been the night before, inflicting her hurts, tempting him, or so it seemed, to hurt her in return—and he made his answer mild.

"Indeed, I took my second class on just such a ship as this," he said and walked forward at last to sit in the copilot's chair.

She glanced at him out of the edge of her eyes. "Forgive me, Pilot. I am not usually so sharp. The lift will improve my temper."

He could think of nothing to say to that and covered this lapse by sliding his license into the slot. There was a moment's considering pause from the ship's computer, then his board came live with a *beep*. Ren Zel initiated systems check.

Elsu Meriandra was already on line to the Tower, requesting clearance. "On business of Clan Jabun," Ren Zel heard and spun in his chair to stare at her. To characterize a mere pleasure-lift as—

His wife cut the connection to the Tower, looked over to him and laughed. "Oh, wonderful! And say you have never told Tower that a certain lift was just a little more urgent than the facts supported!"

"And yet we are not on the business of Clan Jabun," Ren Zel pointed out, remembering to speak mildly.

"Pah!" she returned, her fingers dancing across the board, waking the gyros and the navcomp. "It is certainly in the best interest of Jabun that one of its children not deteriorate into a jittercase, for cause of being worldbound." She leaned back in the pilot's chair and sighed. "Ah, but it will be fine to lift, will it not, Pilot?"

"Yes," Ren Zel said truthfully. "Whither bound, Pilot?"

"Just into orbit, I think, and a long skim down. Do you fancy a late-night dinner at Head o'Port when we are through?"

Ren Zel's entire quartershare was insufficient to purchase a dinner at Head o'Port, which he rather thought she knew.

"Why not a glass and a dinner at Findoir's? There are bound to be some few of our comrades there."

She moved her shoulders. The comm beeped and she flipped the toggle.

"*Dancer.*"

While she listened to Tower's instruction, Ren Zel finished his board checks and, seeing that she was feeding coords into her side, reached 'round to engage the shock webbing.

"Pilot?" he inquired, when she made no move to do the same.

"Eh?" She blinked at him, then smiled. "Oh, I often fly unwebbed! It enhances the pleasure immeasurably."

Perhaps it did, but it was also against every regulation he could think of. He opened his mouth to say so, but she waved a slim hand at him.

"No, do not say it! Regulation is all very well when one is flying contract, but this is pleasure, and I intend to be pleased!" She turned back to her board. The seconds to lift were counting down on the center board. Ren Zel ran another quick, unobtrusive check, then Elsu hit the engage and they were rising.

It was a fine, blood-warming thing, that lift. Elsu flew at the very edge of her craft's limits and Ren Zel found plenty to do as second board. He found her rhythm at last and matched it, the two of them putting the packet through its paces. They circled Casia twice, hand-flying, rather than let the automatics have it. Ren Zel was utterly absorbed by the task, caught up entirely in the other pilot's necessity, enwrapped in that state of vivid concentration that comes when one is flying well, in tune with one's flight-partner, and—

His board went dead.

Automatically, his hand flashed out, slapping the toggle for the back-up board.

Nothing happened.

"Be at ease, Pilot!" Elsu Meriandra murmured, next to him. "I have your board safe. And now we shall have us a marvelous skim!"

She'd overridden him. Ren Zel felt panic boil in his belly, forced himself to breathe deeply, to impose calm. He was second board on a ship owned by the pilot sitting first. As first, she had overridden his board. It was her right to do so, for any reason, or for none—regulations and custom backed her on this.

So, he breathed deeply, as he had been taught, and leaned back in his chair, the shock web snug around him, watching the descent on the screens.

Elsu's path of re-entry was steep—Ren Zel had once seen a tape of a scout descent that was remarkably like the course she had chosen. She sat close over the board, unwebbed, her face intent, a fever-glitter in her eyes, her hands hurtling across her board, fingers flickering, frenzy just barely contained.

Ren Zel recruited his patience, watching the screens, the descent entirely out of his hands. Gods, how long since he had sat *passenger*, wholly dependent on another pilot's skill?

The ship hit atmosphere and turbulence in the same instant. There was a bump, and a twitch. Ren Zel flicked forward, hands on his useless board—and sat back as Elsu made the recover and threw him an unreadable look from over-brilliant blue eyes.

"Enjoy the skim, Pilot," she said. "Unless you doubt my skill?"

Well, no. She flew like a madwoman, true enough, but she had caught that boggle just a moment ago very smoothly, indeed.

The skim continued, and steeper still, until Ren Zel was certain that it was the old scout tape she had fashioned her course upon.

He looked to the board, read hull-heat and external pressure, and did not say to the woman beside him that an old packet was never the equal of a scout ship. She would have to level out soon, and take the rest of the skim at a shallow glide, until they had bled sufficient momentum to safely land.

She had not yet leveled out when they hit a second bit of turbulence, this more demanding than the first. The ship bucked, twisted—again Ren Zel snapped to his dead board, and again the pilot on first corrected the boggle and flew on.

Moments passed, and still Elsu did not level their course.

Ren Zel leaned forward, checking gauges and tell-tales, feeling his stomach tighten.

"Pilot," he said moderately, "we must adjust course."

She threw him a glance. "Must we?" she asked, dulcet. "But I am flying this ship, Ren Zel dea'Judan."

"Indeed you are. However, if we do not level soon, even a pilot as skilled as yourself will find it—difficult—to pull out. This ship was not built for such entries."

"This ship," she stated, "will do what I wish it to do." Incredibly, she kept her course.

Ren Zel looked to the screens. They were passing over the ocean, near enough that he could see the v-wakes of the sea-ships, and, then, creeping into the edge of screen four, towering thunderheads where the water met the land.

"Pilot," he said, but Elsu had seen them.

"Aha! Now you shall see flying!"

They pierced the storm in a suicide rush; winds cycled, slapping them into a spin, Elsu corrected, and lightning flared, leaving screen three dead.

"Give me my board!" Ren Zel cried. "Pilot, as you love your life—"

She threw him a look in which he had no trouble reading hatred, and the wind struck again, slamming them near into a somersault in the instant her hand slapped the toggle. The cabin lights flickered as Ren Zel's board came live, and there was a short, snapped-off scream.

Poised over the board, he fought—fought the ship, fought the wind, fought his own velocity. The wind tossed the ship like so many flower petals, and they tumbled again. Ren Zel fought, steadied his craft and passed out of the storm, into a dazzle of sunlight and the realization that the ground was much too close.

He slapped toggles, got the nose up, rose, rose—

His board snapped and fizzed—desperately, he slapped the toggle for the secondary back-up.

There was none.

The ship screamed like a live thing when it slammed into the ground.

ON THE MORNING OF his third day out of the healing unit and his second day at home, his sister Eba brought him fresh clothes, all neatly folded and smelling of sunshine. Her face was strained, her eyes red with weeping.

"You are called to the meeting between Obrelt and Jabun next hour, Brother," she said, her voice husky and low. "Aunt Chane will come for you."

Ren Zel went forward a step, hand outstretched to the first of his kin he had seen or spoken to since the accident. "Eba?"

But she would not take his hand, she turned her face from him and all but ran from the room. The door closed behind her with the wearisome, too-familiar sound of the lock snapping to.

Next hour. In a very short time, he would know the outcome of Jabun's pursuit of Balance, though what Balance they might reasonably take remained, after three full days of thought on the matter, a mystery to him. The Guild would surely have recovered the flight box. They would have run the tape, built a sim, *proven* that it had been an accident, with no malice attached. A tragedy, surely, for Jabun to lose a daughter. A double tragedy, that she should die while in Obrelt's keeping. There would be the life-price to pay, but— Balance?

He considered the computer in its alcove near the window. Perhaps today he would be allowed to access the nets, to find what the world knew of this?

But no, he was a pilot and a pilot's understanding was quicker than that. He knew well enough the conditions of his tenure here. All praise to Terran poetry, he even knew the proper name for it.

House arrest.

Escorted by med techs, he'd arrived home from the Medical Center, and brought not to his own rooms, but to the Quiet Suite, where those who mourned, who were desperately ill—or dying— were housed. There was a med tech on-call. It was he who showed Ren Zel the computer, the call button, the bed; he who locked the door behind him when he left.

There was entertainment available if one wished to sit and watch, but the communit reached only the med tech and the computer accessed only neutral information—no news, no pilot-net; the standard piloting drills did not open to his code, nor had anyone brought his books, or asked if he wished to have them. This was not how kin cared for kin.

Slowly, Ren Zel went over to the pile of clean clothes. He slipped off the silver-and-indigo robe, and slowly, carefully, put on the modest white shirt and dark trousers. He sat down to pull his boots on and sat a little longer, listening to the blood singing in his ears. He was yet low of energy. It would take some time, so the med tech told him—perhaps as long as a relumma—to fully regain his strength. He had been advised to take frequent naps, and not to overtire himself.

Yes, very good.

He pushed himself to his feet and went back to the table. His jacket was there. Wonderingly, he shook it out, fingering the places where the leather had been mended, pieced together by the hand of a master. As he had been.

The touch and smell of the leather was a reassuring and personal commonplace among the bland and antiseptic ambiance of the quiet suite. He swung the jacket up and on, settling it on his shoulders, and looked at the remaining items on the table.

His piloting license went into its secret pocket. For a moment, he simply stared at the two cantra pieces, unable to understand why there should be so much money to his hand. In the end, still wondering, he slipped them into the pocket of his jacket.

Behind him, he heard the lock snap, and turned, with a bare fraction of his accustomed speed, staggering a little on the leg that had been crushed.

Chane dea'Judan stepped into the room, the door sliding silently closed behind her. He stood where he was, uncertain, after Eba and two days of silence, what he might expect from his own kin.

If Aunt Chane will not speak to me, he thought, *I will not be able to bear it.*

She paused at the edge of the table and opened her arms. "Ren Zel."

He almost fell into the embrace. His cheek against her shoulder, he felt her stroke his hair as if he were small again and needing comfort after receiving some chance cruelty from one of his cousins.

"It's gone ill, child," she murmured at last and he stirred, straightened, and stood away, searching her solemn face.

"Ill," he repeated. "But the life-price of a pilot is set by the Guild. I will take the—" He stopped, struck dumb by the impossible.

Aunt Chane was weeping.

"Tell me," he said then. "Aunt?"

She took a moment to master herself, and met his eyes squarely.

"A life for a life," she said. "Jabun invokes the full penalty. Council and Guild uphold them."

He stared at her. "The flight box. Surely, the Guild has dumped the data from the flight box?"

"Dumped it and read it and sent it by direct pinbeam to a Master Pilot, who studied it and passed judgement," Aunt Chane said, her voice edged with bitterness. "Jabun turned his face from the Master Pilot's findings—and the request to hold open review at Casiaport Hall! He called on three first class pilots from Casiaport Guild to judge again. I am told that this is his right, under Guild law." She took a deep breath and looked him squarely in the eye.

"The honored pilots of Casiaport Guild find you guilty of negligence in flight, my child, the result of your error being that Pilot Elsu Meriandra untimely met her death."

But this was madness. They had the box, the actual recording of the entire flight, from engage to crash.

"Aunt—"

She held up her hand, silencing him.

"I have seen the tape." She paused, something like pride—or possibly awe—showing in her eyes. "You will understand that it meant very little to me. I was merely astonished that you could move so quickly, recover so well, only to have the ship itself fail you at the last instant . . ." Another pause.

"I have also read the report sent by the Master Pilot, who makes points regarding Pilot Meriandra's performance that were perhaps too hard for a father to bear. The Master Pilot was clear that the accident was engineered by Pilot Meriandra, that she had several times ignored your warnings, and that she had endangered both ship and pilots by denying you access to your board during most of the descent. That she was not webbed in . . ." Chane let that drift off. Ren Zel closed his eyes.

"I heard her scream, but I could not—the ship . . ."

"The Master Pilot commends you. The others . . ."

"The others," Ren Zel finished wearily, "are allied to Jabun and dare not risk his anger."

"Just so. And Obrelt—forgive us, child. Obrelt cannot shield you. Jabun has demonstrated that we will starve if we reject this Balancing."

"Demonstrated?"

She sighed. "Eba has been released from her position, her keys stripped from her by the owner before the entire staff of the shop. Wil Bar was served the same, though the owner there was kind enough to receive the keys in the privacy of the back office. Both owners are closely allied with Clan Jabun."

Gods. No wonder Eba wept and would not see him.

"We will mourn you," Aunt Chane said softly. "They cannot deny us that." She glanced at the clock, stepped up and offered her arm.

"It is time."

He looked into his aunt's face, saw sorrow and necessity. Carefully, tender of the chancy leg, put his hand on the offered arm and allowed himself to be led downstairs to die.

THE HOUSE'S MODEST ballroom was jammed to overflowing. All of Clan Obrelt, from the eldest to the youngest, were present to witness Ren Zel's death. Fewer of Clan Jabun were likewise present, scarcely a dozen, all adult, saving one child—a toddler with white-blonde hair and wide blue eyes that Ren Zel knew must be Elsu's daughter.

On the dais usually occupied by musicians during Obrelt's rare entertainments was a three-sided table. On the shortest side stood Ren Zel; Aunt Chane and Obrelt Himself were together at one of the longer sides; Jabun and his second, a gray-haired man with steel-blue eyes, stood facing them.

In the front row of witnesses sat a figure of neither House, an old and withered man who one might see a time or two a year, at weddings and funerals, always wearing the same expression of polite sadness: Tor Cam tel' Vana, the Eyes of Casia's Council of Clans.

"We are here," Jabun lifted his voice so that it washed against the far walls of the room, "to put the death upon the man who murdered Elsu Meriandra, Pilot First Class, daughter of Jabun."

"We are here," Obrelt's voice was milder, but no more difficult for those in the back to hear, "to mourn Obrelt's son Ren Zel, who dies as the result of a piloting accident."

Jabun glared, started—and was restrained by the hand of his second on his sleeve. Thus moderated, he turned his hot eyes to Ren Zel.

"What have you in your pockets, dead man? It is my Balance that you go forth from here nameless, rootless and without possessions."

Slowly, Ren Zel reached into his jacket pocket and withdrew the two cantra pieces.

"Put them on the table," Jabun hissed.

"He will return them to his pocket," Obrelt corrected and met the other's glare with a wide calmness. "Ren Zel belongs to Obrelt until he dies. It is the tradition of our clan that the dead shall have two coins, one to an eye." He gestured toward the short side of the table, still holding Jabun's gaze. "Ren Zel, your pocket."

Obediently, he slipped the coins away.

Once again, Jabun sputtered; once again, he was held back by his second, who leaned forward and stared hard into Ren Zel's face.

"There is something else, dead man. We will see your license destroyed ere you are cast away."

Ren Zel froze. His license? Were they mad? How would he work? How would he live?

"My nephew gave his life for that license, Honored Sir," Aunt Chane said serenely. "He dies because he was worthy of it. What more fitting than it be interred with him?"

"That was not our agreement," the second stated.

"Our agreement," said Obrelt with unbreached calm, "was that Ren Zel dea'Judan be cast out of his clan, and made a stranger to his kin, his loss to Obrelt to precisely Balance the loss of Elsu Meriandra to Clan Jabun. Elsu Meriandra was not made to relinquish her license in death. We desire, as Jabun desires, an exact Balancing of accounts."

Jabun Himself answered, and in such terms that Ren Zel would have trembled, had there been room for fear beside the agony in his heart.

"You think to buy him a life? Think again! What ship will employ a dead man? None that Jabun knows by name." He shifted, shaking off his second's hand.

In the first row of witnesses, the aged man rose. "These displays delay and impair the death," murmured the Eyes of Council. "Only his delm may lay conditions upon a dying man, and there is no death until the delm declares it." He paused, sending a thoughtful glance to Jabun. "The longest Balance-death recorded stretched across three sundowns."

Jabun glared briefly at the Eyes, then turned back to the table.

"He may retain the license," he said, waving his hand dismissively. "May it do him well in the Low Port."

There was silence; the Eyes bowed toward the Balancing table and reseated himself, hands folded on his knee.

Obrelt cleared his throat and raised his voice, chanting in the High Tongue.

"Ren Zel dea'Judan, you are cast out, dead to clan and kin. You are nameless, without claim or call upon this House. Begone. Begone." His voice broke, steadied.

"Begone."

Ren Zel stood at the small side of the table, staring out over the roomful of his kin. All the faces he saw were solemn; not a few were tear-tracked.

"Begone!" snarled Jabun. "Die, child killer!"

In the back of the ballroom, one of the smallest cousins began to wail. Steeling himself, not daring to look at Chane, nor anywhere save his own feet, Ren Zel walked forward, down the three steps to the floor; forward, down the thin path that opened as the cousins moved aside to let him gain the door; forward, down the hallway, to the foyer. The door stood open. He walked on, down the steps to the path, down the path to the gate.

"Go on!" Jabun shouted from behind. Ren Zel did not turn. He pushed the gate open and walked out.

The gate crashed shut behind him and he spun, his heart slamming into overaction. Shaking, he flattened his palm against the plate, felt the tingle of the reader and—

Nothing else. The gate remained locked. His print had been removed from the House computer. He was no longer of Obrelt.

He was dead.

IT WAS FULL NIGHT when he staggered into the Pilots Guildhall in Casiaport. He'd dared not break a cantra for a taxi-ride and his clan-credit had proven dead when he tried to purchase a news flimsy with the headline over his photograph proclaiming "Pilot Dead in Flight Negligence Aftermath." His sight was weaving and he was limping heavily off the leg that had been crushed. He had seen Lai Tor in the street a block or an eternity over, raised his hand—and his friend turned his face aside and hurried off in the opposite direction.

Dead, Ren Zel thought, and smiled without humor. *Very well, then.*

A ghost, he walked into the Guildhall. The duty clerk looked up, took him in with a glance and turned her face away.

"You are not required to speak to me," Ren Zel said, and his voice sounded not quite . . . comfortable . . . in his own ears. "You are not required to acknowledge my presence in any way. However." He pulled his license from its secret pocket and lay it face down on the reader. "This license—this *valid license*—has a debt on it. This license will not be dishonored. List the license number as 'on call,' duty clerk. The debt will be paid."

Silence from the clerk. No move, toward either the license or the computer.

Ren Zel took a ragged breath, gathering his failing resources. "Is Casiaport Guildhall in the practice of refusing repayment of contracted loans?"

The clerk sighed. Keeping her eyes averted, she turned, picked up the license and disappeared to the back.

Ren Zel gasped, questioning the wisdom of this play, now that it was too late, his license possibly forfeit, his life and his livelihood with—

The clerk reappeared. Eyes stringently downturned, she placed a sheet of printout and his license on the countertop. Then she turned her back on him.

Ren Zel's heart rose. It had worked! Surely, this was an assignment. Surely—

He snatched up his license and slipped it away, then grabbed the paper, forcing his wavering sight to focus, to find the name of the client, lift time, location.

It took him all of three heartbeats to realize that he was not looking at flight orders, but an invoice. It took another three heartbeats to understand that the invoice recorded the balance left to be paid on his loan, neatly zeroed out to three decimal places, "forgiven" stamped across the whole in tall blue letters, and then smaller blue letters, where the Guildmaster had dated the thing, and signed her name.

Tears rose. He blinked them away, concentrating on folding the paper with clumsy, shaking fingers. Well and truly, he was a dead man. Kinless, with neither comrades nor Guildmates to support him. Worldbound, without hope of work or flight, without even a debt to lend weight to his existence.

The paper was folded, more or less. He shoved it into his jacket pocket, squared his aching shoulders and went out into Night-Port.

On the walk, he turned right, toward Findoir's, taking all of two steps before recollecting himself. Not Findoir's. Every pilot on Port had news of his death by now.

His comrades would turn their faces away from him, as Lai Tor had. He might speak to them, but they would not answer. He was beyond them—outcast. Nameless. Guildless. Clanless.

Dead.

The tears rose again. He blinked them away, aghast. To weep openly in the street, where strangers might see him? Surely, even a ghost kept better Code than that.

He limped a few steps to the left and set his shoulders against the cool stone wall of Casiaport Guildhall. His chest hurt; the bad leg was a-fire, and the street scene before him seemed somewhat darker than even night might account for.

Ren Zel took a breath, imposing board-calm. Dispassionately, he cataloged his resources:

A first class piloting license. A Jump-pilot's spaceleather jacket, scarred and multiply patched. Two cantra.

He leaned his head against the stone, not daring to close his eyes, even here, in the relative safety of Main Port.

They expected that he would go to Low Port, Clan Jabun did. They expected him to finish his death there. Obrelt had cast against that, winning him the right to hold his license; winning him, so he must have thought, a chance to fly. To live.

And how had Jabun countered? Briefly, Ren Zel closed his eyes, seeing again the three-sided table, the crowd of cousins, weeping and pale; heard Jabun snarl: "What ship will employ a dead man? None that Jabun knows by name."

And that was his doom. There was no ship on Casiaport that Jabun could not name.

Or was there?

Ren Zel opened his eyes.

Jabun's daughter—had not spoken Terran.

Perhaps then her father did not know the names of *all* the ships on port.

He pushed away from the wall and limped down the walk, heading for Mid Port.

THE MAN BEHIND the desk took his license and slid into the computer. His face was bored as he scrolled down the list of Ren Zel's completed assignments.

"Current," he said indifferently. "Everything in order, except . . ." The scrolling stopped. Ren Zel's mouth went dry and he braced himself against the high plastic counter. Now. Now was when the last hope died.

The duty cler—no. The roster boss looked down at him, interest replacing boredom in his face.

"This note here about being banned from the big hall. That temporary or permanent?"

"Permanent," Ren Zel answered, and was ashamed to hear his voice shake.

"OK," the boss said. He pulled the license out of the slot and tossed it across the counter. Exhausted though he was, still Ren Zel's hand moved, snatching the precious thing out of the air, and sliding it safely away.

"OK," the boss said again. "Your card's good. Fact is, it's too good. Jump-pilot. Not much need for Jump-pilots outta this hall. We get some intersystem jobs, now and then. But mostly the Jumps go through Casiaport Guild. Little bit of a labor tax we cheerfully pay, for the honor of being allowed on-world."

It was an astonishment to find irony here. Ren Zel lifted his eyes and met the suddenly knowing gaze of the roster boss, who nodded, a half-smile on his lips.

"You got that, did you? Good boy."

"I do not," Ren Zel said, careful, so careful, of the slippery, modeless Terran syllables, "require a Jump-ship, sir. I am . . . qualified . . . to fly intra-system."

"Man's gotta eat, I guess." The boss shook his head, stared down at the computer screen and Ren Zel stood rooted, muscles tense as if expecting a blow.

The boss let his breath out, noisily.

"All right, here's what. You wanna fly outta here, you gotta qualify." He held up a hand, though Ren Zel had said nothing. "I know you got a first class card. What I don't know is, can you run a Terran board. Gotta find that out before I turn you loose with a client's boat." He tipped his head. "You followin' this, kid?"

"Yes, sir." Ren Zel took a hard breath, his head aching with the effort of deciphering the man's fluid, idiomatic Terran. "I am . . . required . . . to, to demonstrate my worth to the hall."

"Close enough," the boss allowed, crossing his arms atop his computer. "The other thing you gotta do, after you pass muster, is post a bond."

Ren Zel frowned. "Forgive me, I do not—'bond'?"

"Right." The boss looked out into nothing for a moment, feeling over concepts, or so Ren Zel thought. "A bond is—a contract. You and me sign a paper that basically says you'll follow the company rules and keep your face clean for a Standard, and to prove you're serious about it, you give me a cantra to keep. At the end of the year,

if you kept your side of the contract, I give you your money back."
Again, he held up his hand, as if he expected Ren Zel's protest.

"I know your word binds you, you being all honorable and
Liaden and like that, but it's Gromit Company policy, OK? You don't
post bond, you don't fly."

"O . . . Kay," Ren Zel said slowly, buying himself a thimbleful of
time while he worked the explanation out. He gathered, painfully,
that the hall required him to post earnest money, against any
misfortune that might befall a client's goods while they were under
his care. In light of what had happened to the last item entrusted to
him in flight, it seemed that the hall was merely prudent in this.
However . . .

"If the . . . Gromit Company? . . . does not fulfill its side of the
contract?"

The boss gave a short laugh. "Liadens! If the company don't fulfill
its side of the contract, kid, we'll all be lookin' for work."

That didn't quite scan, but he was tired, and his head ached, and
his leg did, and if he did not fly out of the Terran hall, who else on all
of Casiaport would hire him? He inclined his head.

"I accept the terms," he said, as formally as one could, in Terran.

"Do you?" The boss seemed inclined to find that humorous as
well. "OK, then. Report back here tomorrow Port-noon and we'll
have you take the tests. Oh—one more thing."

"Yes."

The man's voice was stern. "No politics. I mean that. I don't want
any Liaden Balances or vendettas or whateverthehell you do for fun
coming into my hall. You bring any of that here and you're out, no
matter how good a pilot you are. Scan that?"

Very nearly, Ren Zel laughed. Balance. Who would seek Balance
with a dead man?

He took a shaky breath. "I understand. There is no one who . . .
owes . . . me. Anything."

The boss held his eyes for a long moment, then nodded. "Right.
Keep it that way." He paused, then sighed. "You got a place to
sleep?"

Ren Zel pushed away from the counter. "I . . . not . . ." He sighed in his turn, sharply, frustrated with his ineptitude. "Forgive me. I mean to say—not this evening. Sir."

"Huh." The boss extended a long arm and hooked a key off the board by his computer. "This ain't a Guildhall. All we got here is a cot for the willfly. Happens the willfly is already in the air, so you can use the cot." He threw the key and Ren Zel caught it between both palms. "You pass the entry tests, you find your own place, got it?"

Not entirely, no. But comprehension could wait upon the morrow.

"Yes, sir," Ren Zel said respectfully, then spent two long seconds groping for the proper Terran phrase. "Thank you, sir."

The man's eyebrows rose in apparent surprise. "You're welcome," he said, then jerked his head to the left. "Second door down that hall. Get some sleep, kid. You're out on your feet."

"Yes," Ren Zel whispered, and managed a ragged approximation of a bow of gratitude before turning and limping down the hall. He slid the key into the slot and the second door whisked open.

The room beyond was no larger than it needed to be to hold a Terran-sized cot. Ren Zel half-fell across it, his head hitting the pillow more by accident than design. He managed to struggle to a sitting position and pulled off his boots, setting them by long habit where he would find them instantly, should he be called to fly. After sober thought, he removed his jacket and folded it under the pillow, then lay down for a second time.

He was asleep before the timer turned the room lights off.

ON ITS FACE, the case had been simple enough: A catastrophe had overtaken two first class pilots. First board was dead, second nearly so, and Guild law required that such matters be reviewed and judged by a master pilot. So the Guild had called upon Master Pilot Shan yos'Galan Clan Korval, Master Trader and Captain of the tradeship *Dutiful Passage*.

Shan had, he admitted to himself, ridden the luck long enough, having several times during the last three Standards been in *precisely* the wrong place to be called upon to serve as Master of Judgment, though his name had been next on the roster.

This time he was the only Master Pilot near, and in fact had already filed a flight plan calling for him to be *on*, the planet on which the fatal incident had occurred. Thus the Guild snared him at last, and offered a budget should he need to study what was left of the ship, or convene a board to do so.

A budget was all very good, but it did nothing to lessen Shan's dislike of this particular duty. Still, he had read the file, reviewed the raw data from the flight box and, finally, in a state of strong disbelief, flew the sim.

Even in simulation, flying fatals is—unpleasant. It was not unknown that master pilots emerged weeping from such flights.

Shan emerged from flying the Casia fatal in an all-but-incandescent fury.

First board was dead because she was a fool—and so he stated in his report. More—she had allowed her stupidity to endanger not only the fine and able pilot who had for some reason found it necessary to sit second to her, but unnamed and innocent civilians. That the ship had finally crashed in an empty plain was due entirely to the skill of the pilot sitting second board, who might have avoided the ground entirely, had only the secondary backup board required by Guild regulations been in place.

Shaking with rage, Shan pulled the ship's maintenance records.

The pilot-owner had not even seen fit to keep to a regular schedule of routine maintenance. Several systems were marked weak in the last recorded mechanic's review—three Standard years past!—at which time it was also noted that the copilot's backup board was non-operational.

Typing at white heat, Shan finished his report with praise for the copilot, demanded an open hearing to be held at Casiaport Guildhall within a day of his arrival on-Port, and shunted the scalding entirety to the Tower to be pinbeamed to Guild Headquarters, copy to Casiaport Guildmaster.

He had then done his best to put Casia out of his mind, though he'd noted the name of the surviving pilot. Ren Zel dea'Judan Clan Obrelt. *There* was a pilot Korval might do well to employ.

✧✧✧

"REN ZEL, GET YOUR ass over here." Christopher's voice was stern.

Ren Zel checked, saw the flicker of anger on his copilot's face and waved her on toward the gate. "Run system checks. I will be with you quickly."

"Yah," she said, grumpily. "Don't let Chris push you around, Pilot."

"The schedule is tight," Ren Zel returned, which effectively clinched the argument and sent her striding toward the gate. Ren Zel altered course for the counter and looked up at the roster boss.

"Christopher?"

The big man crossed his arms on top his computer and frowned down at him. "What'd I tell you when you first signed on? Eh? About what I didn't want none of in this hall?"

"You wished no vendettas, Balance or whateverthehell I might do for fun to disturb the peace of the hall," Ren Zel recited promptly, face betraying nothing of the puzzlement he felt.

An unwilling grin tugged at the edge of Christopher's mouth. "Remember that, do you? Then you remember that I said I'd throw you out if you brought anything like that here."

"Yes . . . ." What was this? Ren Zel wondered. Half-a-relumma he had been flying out of the Terran hall. And now—

"Guy come in here last night, looking for you," the boss said now. "Fancy leather jacket, earrings, uptown clothes. Blonde hair going gray; one of them enameled rings, like the House bosses wear. Talked Trade, and I wouldn't call him polite. Seemed proud of his accent. Reeled off your license number like it tasted bad and wanted to know if it was registered here." Christopher shrugged. "Might've told him no—ain't any business of his who flies outta this hall—but your number was right up there on the board, with today's flight schedule. He didn't talk Terran, but he could read numbers quick enough."

Jabun? was Ren Zel's first thought—a thought he shook away, forcefully. There was no reason for Jabun to seek him; he was *dead* and it was witnessed by the Eyes. Surely Jabun, of all the Clans on Casia, knew that.

In the meantime, Christopher was awaiting an explanation, and his copilot was awaiting him at the ship they were contracted to lift in a very short while.

"I—do not know," he told the roster boss, with what he hoped was plain truth. "There is no one—*no one*—who has cause to seek me here. Or to seek me anywhere. I am . . . outside of Balance." He hesitated, recalled his copilot's phrase and offered it up as something that might be sensible to another Terran: "I am *no longer a player*."

"Huh." The boss considered that for a moment, then shook his head. "OK, but it better not happen again." He glanced to one side. "Look at the clock, willya? You gonna lift that ship on time, Pilot?"

"Yes," said Ren Zel, taking that for dismissal. He turned and strode quickly toward the gate. The leg that had been crushed had not—entirely—healed, and was prone to betray him at awkward moments, so he did not quite dare run, though he did move into a trot as he passed the gate onto the field.

The client's ship—a packet somewhat older than the one that had belonged to Elsu Meriandra—was mercifully near the gate, the ramp down and the hatch open. Ren Zel clattered up-ramp, slapped the hatch closed as he sped through and hit the pilot's chair a heartbeat later, automatically reaching over his shoulder for the shock strap.

"Tower's online," Suzan said, her fingers busy and capable on the second's board. "We got a go in two minutes, Pilot."

"Yes." He called up his board, flickering through the checks; reviewing the flight plan and locking it; pulling in traffic, weather and status reports. "Cargo?"

"Port proctor's seal on it."

"Good. Please tell Tower we are ready."

He and Suzan had flown together before—indeed, they were already seen as a team among certain of the clients, who had made a point to ask Christopher to "send the pilots we had last time." This was good; they made a name for themselves—and a few extra dex.

Suzan was a solid second classer with more flight time on her license than the first class for whom she sat copilot. She flew a clean, no-nonsense board, utterly dependable; and Ren Zel, cautiously, liked her. From time to time, she displayed a tendency to come the elder kin with him, which he supposed was natural enough, considering that she overtopped him, outmassed him, and could easily have given him twelve Standards.

"Got the go," she said now.

"Then we go," Ren Zel replied, and engaged the gyros.

NIGHT-PORT WAS IN its last hours when Ren Zel and Suzan walked through the gate and into the company's office. Christopher's second, a dour person called Atwood, waved them over to the counter.

"Guy in here looking for you, Ren Zel."

His blood chilled. Gods, no. Let it not be that Christopher was forced to send him away.

Some of his distress must have shown on his face, more shame to him, for Suzan frowned and put her big hand on his sleeve. "Pilot?"

He shook her off, staring at Atwood, trying to calm his pounding heart. "A—guy. The same who asked before?"

Atwood shook her head. "New. Chris says," she glanced down, reading the message off the computer screen: "Tell Ren Zel there's another guy looking for him. This one's a gentleman. Asked for him by name. Might be a job in it." She looked up. "It says he—the guy—will be back here second hour, Day-Port, and wants to talk to you."

He took a breath, imposing calmness. *By name*? And who on Casia would speak his name, saving these, his comrades, Terrans, all. Ah. Christopher perhaps would . . . understand . . . a *Terran* gentleman. How such a one might have the name of Ren Zel dea'Judan was a mystery, but a mystery easily solved.

He glanced at the clock over the schedule board: last hour, Night-Port, was half gone. Too little time to return to his room, on the ragged edge of Mid-Port. Too long to simply wait on a bench in the hall . . .

"'Bout enough time to have a bite to eat." Suzan grinned and jerked her head toward the door. "There's a place couple streets down that actually brews real coffee," she said. "C'mon, Pilot. My treat."

COFFEE, REN ZEL thought, some little while later, was clearly an acquired taste.

The rest of the meal was unexceptional—even enjoyable—in its oddness. The one blight was the lack of what Suzan styled 'poorbellows'. An inquiry after this unknown and absent foodstuff gained Ren Zel the information that poorbellows were a kind of edible fungus, after which the coffee tasted not quite as bitter as he had at first thought it.

The meal done, Suzan drained her third cup and went to the front to settle the bill, stubbornly refusing his offer to pay for his share with a, "Told you it was my treat, didn't I?"

Ren Zel shrugged into his jacket and followed her slowly. "Treat" was a Terran concept, roughly translating into "a gift freely given," with no Balance attending. Still, it went against his sense of propriety, that his copilot should give him a gift. Perhaps he might search out some of these poorbellows elsewhere on port and make her a gift in return? He considered it, then found his thoughts drifting elsewhere, to the mysterious "gentleman" whom he was, very soon now, to meet.

That the "gentleman" was Terran seemed certain. That he would, indeed, offer Ren Zel dea'Judan a Jump-pilot's contract, as Christopher seemed to think, was—not so certain.

But if the offer was made? Ren Zel wondered, stepping out onto the walkway and slipping his hands in the pockets of his jacket. If the unknown gentleman offered a standard Jump contract, with its guarantee of setting the pilot on the world of his choice after the terms were fulfilled, then Ren Zel might yet prosper, though in a solitary, Terran sort of way. If he chose his port wisely, he—

"There!" The unfamiliar voice disrupted his thoughts, the single word in Liaden. He looked toward the sound, and saw a gaggle of five standing halfway to the corner. All were dressed in Low Port motley; four also wore the leather jackets of Jump-pilots.

And not one of them, to Ren Zel's eye, was anything like a pilot.

The foremost, perhaps the one who had spoken, bowed, slightly and with very real malice.

"Dead man," he said with mock courtesy, "I am delighted to find you so quickly. We are commissioned to deliver you a gift."

Yes—and all too likely the gift was a knife set between his ribs, after which his jacket would become a prize for the fifth in the pack.

"All right, Pilot, let's get us back to hall and see this mystery man of—" Suzan froze, the door to the restaurant still balanced on the ends of her fingers, looking from Ren Zel to the wolf pack.

"Friends of yours?"

He dared not take his eyes from the face of the leader, who seemed dismayed by the advent of a second, much larger, player in the game.

"No," he told Suzan.

"Right," she said, and pushed the door wider, rocking back on her heel. "There's a back door. After you."

Keeping his back to the wall, he slithered past her, then followed as she sped through the main dining room, down a short hallway and into the kitchen. She raised a hand to a woman in a tall, white hat, and opened the door in the far wall. In keeping with a copilot's duty, she stepped through first, then waved him after.

"OK. Down this alley about two blocks, there's a beer joint. Tom and Gina hang out there on their downshifts. We'll pick 'em up and all go back to the hall together."

It was prudent plan, Tom and his partner being no strangers to street brawls, if even half of their stories were to be believed. Ren Zel inclined his head. "Very well."

"Great. This way."

They had gone perhaps a block in the direction of the tavern, when Ren Zel heard a noise behind them. A glance over his shoulder showed him the wolf pack just entering the alley by the rear door to the restaurant.

Suzan swore. Ren Zel saw the gleam of metal among the pack as they moved into a ragged run nothing like the smooth flow of pilot motion. Though it would serve. And when they were caught, the wolf pack would not care whether they killed one or two.

He already had one death on his hands.

"Go on," he said to Suzan. "I will speak with them."

She snorted, "Pilot, I thought you knew I wasn't as big a fool as I look. Those boys don't want talk—they want blood." She reached down and grabbed his arm.

"Run!"

Perforce, he ran, stretching to match her pace, willing the bad leg not to betray him. Behind, he heard their pursuers, chanting—"Dead man! Pilot slayer! Dead man!"—and found time to be grateful, that Suzan did not speak Liaden.

"Here," she gasped and pulled him with her to the right. One massive shoulder hit the plastic door, which sprang open, and they were eight running paces into a dark and not overcrowded room before Suzan let him go, shouting, "Vandals right behind us! Call the Watch!"

Several of the patrons of the room simply dropped the long sticks they had been holding and bolted for the front door, for which Ren Zel blamed them not in the least. Left on his own, he spun, fire lancing the bad leg, which held, thank the gods, and looked about him for a weapon.

There were several small balls on the green covered table just beside him. Before he had properly thought, he had snatched the nearest up. The ball was dense for something so small, but that was no matter. His hands moved in the familiar pattern, the thing was spinning and then airborne as the first of the wolf pack charged into the room.

The ball caught the fellow solidly in the nose. He went down with a grunt, not quite tripping the man immediately behind him. That one, quick enough, if not Pilot-fast, leapt his comrade and landed on the balls of his feet, a chain dangling from his hand.

He saw Ren Zel and smiled. "Dead man. But still alive to pain, eh?" The chain flashed as the man jumped forward. Ren Zel ducked, heard metal scream over his head, grabbed one of the fallen long sticks and came up fast, whirling, stick held horizontal between his two hands.

The chain whipped again. Ren Zel threw the stick into the attack. The chain wrapped 'round the gleaming wood twice, and Ren Zel spun, trying to pull the weapon from his adversary's grip.

With a laugh, the wolf jumped forward, grabbed the stick and twisted. Ren Zel hung on, then lost his grip, danced back a step, and then another as the man raised the weapon in both hands and swung it, whistling, down.

Once again, action preceded thought. Ren Zel dove, rolling under the green covered table, heard chain and stick hit the floor behind him, and came up on the far side of the table just in time to see Suzan place a well-considered bar stool into the back of his opponent's head.

Elsewhere in the room, the remaining three of the pack were engaged with those of the patrons who had not run. Suzan waded back into the melee, swinging her bar stool with abandon. Thinking that he might yet have use for a weapon, Ren Zel, went 'round the table to retrieve the long stick. The thing was shattered, the pieces still wrapped in chain. That he let lie, judging he was more likely to harm himself than any adversary, should he try to wield such an unfamiliar weapon. He straightened, ears pricked. Yes—from the open front door came the sound of a siren, growing rapidly louder. The Port Proctors would soon arrive, Ren Zel thought, with a sinking sense of relief. All would be—

Across the room, the pack leader dropped his man with a flickering knife thrust. He spun, seeking new blood, saw Suzan's unprotected back—

"Ware!" Ren Zel screamed, but the word was in Liaden; she would not know . . .

Ren Zel jumped.

The knife flashed and he was between it and his copilot, one shoulder, covered in tough spaceleather, taking the edge and turning it. Ren Zel spun with the force of the blow, deliberately using it as he came back around—

And the bad leg failed him.

Down he went, the wolf leader atop, and it was a muddle of shouts and blows and kicks before the quick shine of the knife, snaking past the leather this time, slicing cloth and flesh. Ren Zel lashed out, trying to escape the pain. The knife bit deeper, twisting. He screamed—and was gone.

"MASTER PILOT, I REGRET," Casiaport Guildmaster was all but stuttering in distress. "Notification should have been sent. I swear to you that I will learn why it was not. However, the fact remains that no hearing has been scheduled. The case was adjudicated by three first class pilots, fault has been fixed and the matter is closed."

Shan lifted his eyebrows, feeling the woman's guilt like sandpaper against his skin, and she rushed on, babbling.

"Guild rule is plain, as the Master Pilot surely knows. Three first class pilots may judge, in the absence of a Master—and may overturn, in the case of a disputed judgment."

"Guild rule is plain," Shan agreed, in the mode of master to junior, which was higher than he usually spoke with another pilot. "Though it is considered good form to allow the Master Pilot in question to know that his judgement has been disputed.

"Since I am here in any wise," he continued, "I will see the file."

The Guildmaster gasped; covered the lapse with a bow.

"At once, Master Pilot. If you will step down to the private parlor, the file will be brought."

Shan inclined his head. "Bring also Pilot dea'Judan, if he is on-Port."

"Pilot dea'Judan?" the Guildmaster repeated, blankly.

"Pilot Ren Zel dea'Judan Clan Obrelt," Shan explained, wondering how such a one had risen to the rank of Guildmaster of even so backward a port as Casia. "Surely you recall the name?"

"I—Indeed I do." She drew a deep breath and seemed to recruit her resources, bowing with solemn precision. "I regret. Ren Zel dea'Judan Clan Obrelt is dead."

Shan stared. "And yet I ran the license number through the port's own database just before departing my ship and found it listed as valid and active."

The Guildmaster said nothing.

"I see," Shan said, after several silent moments had elapsed. "I will review the case file now, Guildmaster." He turned and walked down the hall to the private parlor.

The file, brought moments later by a pale-faced duty clerk, was thin enough, and Shan was speedily master of its contents. True enough, his judgement had been set aside in favor of the cooler findings of three first class pilots, all of whom flew out of Casiaport

Guildhall. Shan sighed, shaking his head as his Terran mother had sometimes shaken hers, expressing not negation so much as ironic disbelief.

There was a computer on the desk. He used his Master Pilot's card to sign onto the news net and spent a few minutes tracking down the proper archives, then shook his head again.

The legal notices told the story plainly: Obrelt had been cruelly Balanced into banishing their only pilot and naming him dead. None that kept strict Code would deal with a man who had no clan to stand behind his debt and honor . . .

It was the description of the circumstances surrounding death, fully witnessed by the Eyes of Council, that sent him once again into the public ways of Casiaport and finally to the Gromit Company's shabby Mid Port office.

There, the luck was slightly out, for Pilot dea'Judan was flying. The man behind the counter, one Christopher Iritaki, had suggested he return early next morning and had promised to let the pilot know that an appointment had been set in his name.

Shan presented himself at Gromit Company slightly in advance of the appointed hour, to find Mr. Iritaki's second on duty.

"I'm sure they'll be back any minute, sir," Ms. Atwood said, sending a faintly worried look at the clock. "They just went a couple streets over for a bite and a cup of coffee. Ren Zel's solid. He wouldn't miss an appointment for anything short of catastrophe."

"I'm sure you're right," Shan said soothingly. He smiled at the roster boss and had the satisfaction of seeing the worry fade from her face.

"I could fancy some coffee myself," he confided. "Do you happen to know which shop the pilots favor? Perhaps I won't be too late to share a cup with them."

It happened that Atwood did know which shop, which was a favorite among the company's pilots. "Only place on Casia you can get real coffee," she said, and Shan would have sworn there were tears in her eyes.

A few moments later, possessed of directions to this mecca, and having extracted Ms. Atwood's promise to hold Pilot dea'Judan, should he arrive back at the Hall in the meantime, Shan sauntered out into the sharp air and rumble of early morning Casiaport.

Though there was nothing in his face or his gait to betray it, Shan was in a fever to shake the dust of Casia from his feet. His evening had been spent delving deeper than was perhaps good for his peace of mind into the affairs of Casiaport Guildhall and a certain Clan Jabun. The information he uncovered was disturbing enough that he found he had no choice, as a Master Pilot who owed duty to the Guild, but to call Jabun before a full board of inquiry.

However, he thought, stretching his long legs and turning into the street where he would find the "best damn coffee on Casia," that job of form-filing would certainly wait until he had Ren Zel dea'Judan safely in hand.

The coffeeshop hove into view on his left, precisely as promised. Shan checked his long stride, but did not approach the door, which was crowded around with people, all staring up-street, where a commotion was in progress.

Shan felt the hairs shiver on the nape of his neck. What was it that the Ms. Atwood had said? That nothing would keep Ren Zel from an appointment except calamity?

The scene up-street had every trapping of calamity, including the white trucks and flashing blue lights of Casiaport Rescue, clustered in such abundance that the Port Proctor's sun-yellow scooters were scarcely noticeable.

Shan stretched his legs again, moving quickly toward the hubbub.

He had no trouble walking through the cordon thrown up by the Proctors—he was never stopped by guards if he did not wish to be—and into what the sign by the door dignified as "Wilt's Poolroom and Tavern."

Inside—well.

All about were knots of med techs, attending the wounded. Elsewhere, Proctors questioned several unmistakable grounders who were for some reason wearing pilots' leathers. Toward the back of the room, a figure was shrouded in a white plastic sheet. Not far distant lay another figure, blood a black pool on the floor. Shan touched a stud on his belt, alerting every *Dutiful Passage* crewmember on Port that there was a comrade down and in danger. Help was on the way. Now . . .

Directly before him, a Terran woman was shouting at a med tech.

"Hey!" she yelled in Trade, grabbing the tech's arm. "There's somebody over there who needs you."

The tech turned, glanced along the line of the Terran's finger, then slid his arm free, sighing slightly.

"I am not allowed to tend that one."

"What?" the Terran gaped. "You just patched up four of the worst desperadoes I've seen on this Port in a long time and you ain't allowed to tend a pilot who was wounded while protecting his copilot?"

"He is clanless," the tech said, with a note of finality in his soft, Liaden voice.

"He'll be *lifeless* if you people don't do something for him soon!"

The tech turned his back.

The Terran pilot raised her hand, and Shan swung forward, catching her lightly 'round the wrist.

"Precisely how will being arrested for assault help your pilot?" he inquired in Terran.

The woman spun, pulling her wrist free. She stared at him; took a deep breath.

"He's gonna *die*."

Shan glanced at the still figure in its pool of black blood, noting the ragged breath, and the sweat on the pale, unconscious face. He looked back to the Terran pilot.

"Perhaps not. Just a moment." He stepped forward, claiming the med tech's attention with a genteel cough and bowed when the man turned.

"Good-day. I am Shan yos'Galan Clan Korval, Captain of *Dutiful Passage*."

Recognition moved in the tech's eyes. "Captain yos'Galan, I am honored." He bowed, deeply.

Shan inclined his head, then pointed across the room to the downed pilot.

"That person is one of my crewmen, med tech. His contract started today. I understand that you may not tend him, but my *melant'i* is clear. I require the use of your kit."

Relief flickered across the tech's face; he held the kit out with alacrity. "Certainly, sir. Please return it when you are through."

"I will," Shan inclined his head once again and turned, gathering the Terran pilot with a glance and lifted eyebrow.

"What'd you say?" she asked, following him to where her pilot lay, alone in the midst of all the official bustle.

"That I required the use of his kit in order to perform first aid on my crewman." Shan knelt down, heedless of the blood, and began to remove the towels she had used to try to staunch the blood.

"He ain't your crew," she protested.

"Ah, but he is a pilot, and I am partial to pilots. Besides, he might well have *been* mine, if he'd managed to stay out of trouble long enough to . . ." His breath caught. The wound was bad—deep and ragged. Immediately, reflexively, he ran a quick mental sequence to relax and focus himself.

"Knife," the Terran said, succinctly. "He took it for me. At least," she amended, as Shan opened the med kit and poked among the various tools of the tech's trade, "the first strike was meant for me. Got between me and the blade—I coulda handled it, but he's so *damned* fast. He'd've been OK, except the bum leg went out on him and the hood was on him like a terrier on a rat . . ."

Shan had found what he was looking for—a suture gun. "Unpleasant, but effective," he commented, fingering the settings. "At least he's unconscious. We'll just do a quick patch, I think—something to hold him together until we can get him up to the *Passage*."

The Terran blinked. "You're the guy the pilot was supposed to meet at the hall this morning."

He met her eyes. "In fact, I am—and I am remiss. My name is Shan yos'Galan Clan Korval."

She sucked air, eyes going wide. "Tree-and-Dragon," she said, possibly to herself, then inclined her head, roughly, but with good intent. "I'm Suzan Fillips."

Shan nodded. "Suzan Fillips, your pilot needs you. Please hold him while I do the patch."

She did and Shan bent to the unpleasant task, sending up indiscriminate petitions to all the gods of mercy, that the boy beneath his hand remain unconscious.

At last the thing was done. He set the suture gun aside and sat back on his heels. Suzan Fillips took her hands slowly from the downed pilot's shoulders and looked up.

"Tell me about this 'bad leg'," Shan said. "Had he been injured before today?"

"He was in a crash not too long ago and the leg never healed right," Suzan said, meeting the eyes straitly. "You know about the crash—you're the master pilot. I remember your name from the report."

"Do you?" He look at her with renewed interest. "Where did you get the report, I wonder?"

She snorted. "I'm a registered pilot on this port. I used my card and pulled the file. Even Terrans hear rumors—and we'd heard one about a crackerjack pilot who'd been drummed outta the local Guild for not having the good taste to die in a crash. I read the reports—yours and the one they liked better. Tried to get the sim, too, but the Guild won't lend it."

The slanted white brows pulled together. "Won't lend it? Yet you are, as you point out, a pilot on this port."

"Jabun." The voice was faint and none too steady. Both Shan and Suzan jumped before staring down at the wounded pilot. His eyes were open, a dilated and glittering black, the brown hair stuck to his forehead in wet, straggling locks.

"Jabun," he repeated, the Liaden words running rapidly and not altogether in mode. "Not enough that they had me cast out. I must die the true death, if he must hire a wolf pack to the task. Dishonor. Danger! They must not find—" He struggled, trying to get his good arm around.

Shan put his hands firmly on the boy's shoulders. "Pilot. Be at ease."

The unseeing black eyes met his. "When will they have done?" he demanded. "When will they—"

Shan pushed, exerting force as well as force of will. "Lie *down*," he said firmly, in a mode perilously close to that he would use with a feverish child. "You are wounded and will do yourself further injury."

"Wound—" Sense flickered. "Gods." He twisted, weakly; Shan held him flat with no trouble.

"Suzan!"

She snapped forward, touching his unwounded shoulder. "Here, Pilot. I'm OK, see?"

Apparently, he did. The tension left him and he lay back, understanding in his eyes now. Shan frowned.

"You accuse Clan Jabun seriously," he said, in the Liaden mode of comrade, and thinking of his own discoveries of the evening before. "Have you proof?"

"The pack leader . . ."

He glanced at Suzan, who jerked her head to the left, where two Port Proctors were talking to sullen man in a scarred leather jacket.

"All right," he said, in Terran, for Suzan Fillips' benefit. "I will speak to the pack leader. Pilot dea'Judan, you will remain here *quietly* with your copilot."

The glittering eyes stabbed his. "Yes."

One of the proctors looked up as he approached and came forward to intercept him. "Master Trader?" he inquired courteously.

Shan considered him. "One hears," he said, delicately, "that yon brigand was hired by a House to deal death to a dead man."

The Proctor sighed. "It produces the name of Jabun—but this is not unusual, you know, sir. They grasp at anything they hope will win them free of the present difficulty."

"Just so," Shan murmured, and drifted back toward Suzan Fillips and Ren Zel dea'Judan.

"I believe you," he said to the wounded pilot's hot eyes, and looked thoughtfully at the Terran.

From the entrance came the sounds of some slight agitation among the guards, who parted to admit a pilot of middle years, his pale hair going to gray, his leather gleaming as if new-made.

"It's him!" shouted the man who had been the wolf pack leader, and was silenced by his guards.

A Proctor moved forward, holding his hands up to halt the newcomer.

"Sir, this is the scene of a death by misadventure; I must ask you to leave unless you—"

"Ah, is it a death?" The man's face displayed such joy that Shan swallowed, revolted. "I must see for myself!"

The Proctor moved his hand as if to deny, but another signed assent and the three of them strode across the room to the covered form.

"Your lordship is to understand that this is . . . unpleasant," the first Proctor said. "The nose has been forcibly crushed into the brain by a blow . . ."

"That is of no matter," the newcomer snapped. "Show me!"

The Proctors exchanged glances, then bent and lifted the covering back. Shan rose to his feet, eyes on His Lordship's proud, eager face, glowing with an anticipation so—

"What nonsense is this?" the man shouted. "This is not he!"

"I am here . . . Suzan, help me stand. Jabun, I am here!"

The voice was barely a croak, nearly inaudible. The bloodied figure gained his feet, more than half-supported by his grim-faced copilot.

"The dead man you want . . . the dead man you want is here!" Ren Zel gritted out, and Shan stepped back, giving Jabun clear sight of his victim.

"You!" Jabun flung forward one step, hatred plain in his comely face, then froze, as if he had abruptly understood what he had done.

"Speaking to a dead man?" Ren Zel rasped. "Out of Code, Jabun." He drew a sobbing breath. "Look on me—dead by your malice. One death was not enough, one Balance insufficient . . ." He swayed and Shan moved to offer his support as well. Ren Zel gasped.

"You, who deal in life and death—you will be the death of all you are pledged to hold!"

A gasp ran through the room, and Shan felt a tingle in the close air of the poolroom, as if a thunderstorm were charging.

Jabun stood as if struck; and Shan heard a med tech mutter, "*Dramliza*, you fool! Will you play Balance games against a wizard?"

Ren Zel straightened, informed by an energy that had nothing to do with physical strength.

"Jabun, you are the last delm of your House. The best of your line shall lifemate a Terran to escape your doom. The rest of your kin will flee; they will deny their name and their blood, and ally themselves with warehousemen and fisherfolk for the safety such alliances buy!

"Hear me, Jabun! In my blood is told your tale—witness all, all of you see him! See him as he is!"

"Pilot—" began Suzan, but Shan doubted Ren Zel heard her worried murmur, lost as he was in the dubious ecstacy of a full Foretelling.

"It is Jabun the pod-pirate," he cried, and Shan felt the hairs raise on his arms, recalling his own researches. "Jabun the thief! Jabun the murderer! Beware of his House and his money!"

The poolroom was so completely quiet that Shan heard his own heartbeat, pounding in his ears.

Jabun was the first to recover, to look around at the faces that would not—quite—return his regard.

"Come, what shall you? This—this is a judged and Balanced murderer, dead to Code, clan and kin. It is raving, the shame of its station has no doubt broken its wits. We have no duty here. It is beneath our *melant'i* to notice such a one."

"Then why," came the voice of the man Suzan had identified as the wolf pack leader, "did you give us a cantra piece to beat him to death?"

Jabun turned and stared at his questioner, moved his shoulders under the bright leather. "Proctors, silence that person."

"Perhaps," murmured one of the two who had shown him the dead brigand. "I fear I must ask you to remain here with us, your lordship. We have some questions that you might illuminate for us."

"I?" Jabun licked his lips. "I think not."

"We have authority here, sir," the second Proctor said, and stepped forward, beckoning. "This way, if you will, Your Lordship."

"Of your kindness, Pilots," Ren Zel dea'Judan said, his Liaden slurring and out of mode, "I would sit . . ."

Shan and Suzan got him into a chair, where he sagged for a moment before reaching out none-too-steadily to touch his copilot's sleeve.

"Tell Christopher," he managed, and his Terran was blurred almost out of sense. "I—apologize. The hall—his pilots—I did not know. It is not done . . ."

Suzan patted his knee. "It's OK, Pilot. You leave Chris to me."

Shan nodded, reached into his sleeve and pulled out a card. He held it out to Suzan Fillips, who blinked and shook her head.

Patiently, he held the card extended, and looked seriously into her eyes.

"Should you find yourself at risk over this incident," he said, "use the beam code on the card."

She licked her lips. "I—"

"Take. It." The wounded pilot's voice was barely audible, but the note of command was strong. The woman's hand rose. She slipped the card out of Shan's fingers and slid it immediately into her license pocket.

"Good," said Ren Zel, and Shan saw now only a wounded pilot, with no trace of the power of Foretelling, nor voice of command . . .

There was a clatter at the door. Shan looked around and spied Vilt and Rusty of his own crew, raised a hand, and then glanced down at Ren Zel dea'Judan.

"Pilot, I offer you contract: a Standard year's service on the *Dutiful Passage*, after which we will renegotiate or, if you wish, you will be set down on the world of your choice."

Ren Zel swallowed, and looked up to meet his gaze firmly. "You are Liaden," he managed. "I am dead."

"No," Shan said, in earnest Terran. "You really must allow my skill to be better than that."

Almost, it seemed that the wounded boy smiled. The lids drooped over the fevered eyes.

"I accept," he murmured. "One Standard year."

✧ A Matter of Dreams ✧

ON SINTIA, it's the dreaming that first marks a witch.

A child will dream the minutiae of life, relate the sending in the morning, all innocent and dewy-eyed; astonished when the dream events turn true next day—or next one.

She's watched then, for grandma will have contacted Temple, never doubt it; and after a time the child will dream the name of the one she had been Before. Then she'll be brought to Circle and trained to be one with the Dream.

I know the way because Jake used to talk about his Mam, my gran'mam, who'd Dreamed a Dream and had the training and then left the Temple and who she'd been—for love, Jake said, and for stars.

I've never dreamed the Naming-Dream, being outworlder, even though witch-blood. I figure only the damned come to me—those who died unquiet or outside the love of the Holy; those who somehow lost their Name. I figure that, but I don't say it. I dream the dreams and I let them go. Sometimes they come back. Sometimes they come true.

The first time I saw Her was dreamsight.

She was in a port side bar—too coarse a place for Her to be—standing straight in her starry blue robe, with her breasts free and her face shining with power, black hair crackling lightning and spread around her like an aurora. Her eyes—her eyes were black, and in the dream she saw me. At her feet was broken glass; the shine of a knife.

She was young—not above fifteen—with the silver bangles hiding half of one slim arm. But for all that, I wanted to go down on my knees in front of her and lay my cheek against her mound from which had sprung the worlds and the stars and the deep places between. That's how it was, in the dream.

But then the dream ended, as they do, and there was Lil, yelling about orbit and was I coming or not, so it was out of the cot and let the dream go and get about the business of making a living.

I never talked to Lil about the dreams. They scared her, and there's nothing worth that. Still, she's witch-blood too and knows as sure I do when I've dreamt, though she never dreams at all.

"Well?" she spat at me, spiteful the way sisters are, within the protection of Us against Them. "Was it wet this time?"

"Keep it down and keep it clean," I answered, no more gentle, because there was the flutter in the nine-dial I didn't like, which meant relying on number eight, a thing that had been a bad idea since I was copilot and Mam on prime.

"Where's the passenger?" I asked, because there was a certain amount of care taken, when you'd been paid hard coin to deliver someone intact to a place.

"Webbed in gentle as a roolyet," Lil said and I gave a grin for the old adventure, though putting *Mona Luki* through the orbiting sequence was proving more of a problem than usual.

"Shit," muttered Lil, hands over her part of the business. "We gotta get that reset before we lift, Fiona."

"On Sintia?"

"Federated port," she answered, which was true. And, "Credit's good," which was not.

"Yeah," I said, not wanting to argue the point and have her start to worry. "We'll let our passenger off and see if we can't patch it. Bound to be junkyards."

"Flying a junkyard," she answered, which I should have known she would. "Mam'd have a fit, Fiona . . ."

And that was another line of thought better left alone.

"Mind your board," I growled, and she sighed, and looked rebellious, and turned her head away.

Tower came on in another few seconds, with an offer of escort, if we had equipment trouble. I turned down the escort, which was expensive, but requisitioned a repair pad, which came gratis, they having noted trouble, and we got her down without any bad glitches.

Our passenger, that was something else.

Cly Nelbern got her first sight of Sintia Port there in screen number one, looked sour and flung herself into prime pilot's chair like she had a right to it. Lil had her mouth half-opened before she caught my headshake, but I doubt Nelbern would have heard a shout just then.

I finished making my coffee-toot and ambled over, leaned a hip against the chair-back and spoke over her head. "We can give you a hand with your baggage," I said, "or you can leave it stored. We'll be here a day or two. Repairs."

Nelbern gave one of those snorts we'd decided between us passed for her laughing and shook her head, real gentle, eyes still and always on that screen.

"So eager to lose me, Captain?"

"Not to say," I answered, calm, like Mam'd taught us to talk to dirtsiders. "It's just that you paid cash money for Jumps in a hurry. I figured you had an appointment."

"An appointment," she repeated and snorted. "An appointment." She licked her lips like the phrase tasted sweet and glanced up at me out of wide blue eyes.

"As it happens, Captain, I do have an—appointment. Yes." She smiled, which I had never liked in her, and nodded. "I wonder if I might impose upon the good natures of yourself and your sister just a bit further."

I gritted my teeth and brought the cup up to keep it from showing; feeling Lil tense up behind me. I was mortally sick of dirtside manners and a stranger on our ship, whether she carried an ambassador's ransom in Terran bits or no. It was on the tip of my tongue to say so, though not as blunt as that, when she turned full around to face me.

"I noticed a bit of a boggle on the way in, I thought," she said, in that conversational way officials use when it's bound to cost you plenty. I stared down at her and shrugged.

"Told you we'd be here a day or so."

"Indeed. Repairs, I think you said." She stared, sizing me up, maybe, though I was sure she'd done that long ago. "Repairs to the central mag coil don't come cheap, Captain; and it's hardly anything you'd like to trust to the junkyard and a gerryrig." She smiled. "If you had a choice."

I felt Lil behind me like a wound spring, and in my heart I cursed all dirtsiders—especially this one. I gritted my teeth and then bared them, not caring a whit for manners.

"So now I've got a choice, have I?"

"Certainly you have a choice." She brought her hand up, and I focused on the thing that gleamed there; did a double-stare and nearly dumped my drink in her lap.

She was holding a Liaden cantra piece.

I stared, not at the coin—enough money for several choices and maybe a luxury, too—but at her face—and read no more there than I ever had, save it was the first time I thought her eyes looked mad.

"What in starlight do you *want*?" That was Lil, coming up like she was stalking tiger, bent at the waist, her eyes on the shine of the money.

Cly Nelbern looked up at me and she smiled before turning to face my sister and hold the coin up high.

"An escort," she said softly. "Just an escort, Ms. Betany, as I walk around the town. In case the natives are restless."

"An escort," I scoffed, around the cold dread in my belly. "On Sintia, a woman needs no escort—unless you'll be breaking into the Temple?"

The mad eyes gleamed my way, though she forbore to smile again. "Not the Temple, Captain. Of course not." She did smile then, her eyes going back to Lil. "That would be foolish."

"Then us not being fools—" I began, short-tempered with something near terror.

But Lil shot a glance that silenced me long enough for her to gabble: "A cantra, *Fiona*! *New* parts, backups, a new 'doc, *coffee . . .*"

Her eyes were back on Cly Nelbern and I knew right then I'd lost her.

"Lillian!" I snapped, as much like Mam as I could.

Too late. "I'll do it," she told the dirtsider. And held out her hand for the money.

I sat down slow on the arm of the copilot's chair and brought the tepid coffee-toot up to sip. There was nothing else to do, the word having been given. Nothing except:

"I'll be coming along as well, then. If that coin's so wide a treasure, I reckon it'll pay berth-cost while we *escort* this lady 'round town."

Nelbern laughed, a half-wild sound no more pleasant than her smile. "Think I won't pay, Captain?" She sent a brilliant glance into my face, and flicked the coin to Lil.

"Order your repairs," she said, standing up. "And you'll—both—be ready to come with me in one hour."

She sauntered off toward her cabin and I looked at my sister, standing there with her hand clenched 'round that money, and her cheeks flushed with lust of it and I sighed and hovered a second between sad and mad; figured neither would mend it and stood up myself.

"I'll take first shower," I said, tossing the cup into the unit as I went past.

At the door I looked back, but she was showing back to me, head half-tipped, like she hadn't even noticed that I'd gone.

WE WANDERED, that endless afternoon, visiting tradebars, dives, and talking-booths on both sides of the river. Some places folk eyed us; some places they eyed our employer. Other places they ignored us entirely, and those I liked least of all.

The last was near the city-line, close enough to the Temple that the evening chant echoed off the dirty windows and the tawdry buildings, making even Cly Nelbern look up for a moment before turning down the short, ill-kept walk.

This place at least made some pretense of cleanliness: the window was clear enough to let the evening light come through; the bar was chipped but polished; the tender's tattered apron had recently been washed.

I was three steps into the room before I realized why it felt so comfortable. It reminded me of *Mona Luki*: desperately shipshape and tidy, and showing the worn spots despite it.

It hadn't always been so. When Mam and Jake had run her, back when I was little enough to be strapped in a net slung between their seats, watching baby-eyed while they worked the Jumps between them—then *Mona Luki'd* gleamed, oiled and cared-for and prosperous as you like. Then there'd been coffee—yes, and chocolate—and repairs when they were needed and spare parts in third hold. Lil was too young to remember those days—too young, just, to remember Jake, killed in the same mishap that had taken Mam's leg.

I'd dreamed that accident; I'd even told Mam. They'd gone out to make the repair anyway, of course, as who, save on Sintia, would not? I'd climbed into the netting with the baby and held her 'til Mam started to scream.

Six years old, I was then, but it got me thinking hard about dreams.

"So!" That was Cly Nelbern and here was the present. I came alert to both, sending my gaze along hers to the man in Sintian town clothes—shabby, bright blue overshirt, bold with raveling embroidery, darker blue pants, worn wide and loose in respect of the heat, with matching fancy-work around the hems.

He had a tired face, used honestly, I thought, with eyes showing desperation far back. Likely I looked the same: respectability balanced on the knife-edge of despair, needing only one more disaster to send us all over into thieves.

He gulped, brown eyes darting from her face to mine, barely glancing from me to Lil before his face softened a touch and he bowed, gesturing toward the rear of the little room.

"I have a table, La—ma'am." His voice was agreeable, though it quavered. Nelbern shrugged and pushed forward.

"Delightful," she said, and the edge in her voice put the shine of fear in his eyes. "Lead on."

It was a small enough table in a snug, ill-lit corner, tight seating for four, but he'd clearly been expecting only her.

"My—companions," Cly Nelbern said to his startled glare. "Captain Fiona and Ms. Lillian Betany, of the *Mona Luki*."

It gave me a chill, being named there, and by the sudden dart of Lil's eyes, I could see it chilled her, too. But she stayed tight where she was, perched on a chair crammed next to the man—and Cly Nelbern smiled.

"Well?" she said, and the icy edge was back in her voice. "Where is it?"

He gulped, sent a hunted glance around the room at my back and firmed his face to look at her.

"In the office at the Port House, Lady. And that's where it's going to stay."

Nelbern didn't frown, which was what I expected. She picked up her drink and had a sip, eyeing him over the chipped rim.

"Indeed." She set the glass aside. "That wasn't our agreement."

Mild as it sounded, it was evidently bad enough. The man stared at her dumbly, pale to the lips.

"Our agreement," she pursued, still in that mild-as-milk voice, "was that you provide me with a certain item, in return for which I provide you with a particular sum of money." She stared at him. "That *was* the agreement?"

He gulped. "Yes, Lady."

"'Yes, Lady'," she repeated softly, then leaned suddenly across Lil, to put her face right up to his and hiss: "Then what in the name of the Last Hell do you mean by telling me you don't have that file?"

"I—" he tried to pull back, but there was nowhere to go. He licked his lips. "There is a—a Maiden out of Circle House, come to study and catalog the files. She—Lady, I dare not! If Circle House finds me—"

"What I'll leave for the Temple to find if I don't have that file within the day will be far beyond worrying about Witches," Cly Nelbern snarled. "Do you mark me, Pirro Velesz?"

If he hated the speaking of his name, in that place and in such company, he gave no sign other than the roll of an eye.

"The Maiden," he said, "is named Moonhawk."

Nelbern leaned back and reached for her glass. "What do I care for her name? If you can't match wits with a half-grown chit out of Circle House—"

"Moonhawk," the man interrupted, with an intensity that raised the hairs along the back of my neck, "is the oldest Name in Circle. Moonhawk is the most powerful servant of the Goddess—every life she lives is exceptional—historic . . ."

"Don't prate at me like an abo! So the girl had the wit to pick an elite name—she's still in school. Come to Port House to study the records, you said. Where's the danger—"

"The girl," Velesz interrupted again, "is Moonhawk's incarnation in this life, Lady. Fact. She is young, but the power abides within her. The danger is that she has not yet relearned control. The training her elders-in-world provide is to ensure that she will not—accidentally— use more force than might be necessary."

"Loose cannon." That was Lil, unexpected and great-eyed, but still well away from fright.

The man turned his head, eyes easier for looking at her again. "Loose cannon," he repeated and nodded, a smile coming and going in the second before he looked back to Cly Nelbern. "Power without guidance."

"Well, then we'll see to it that she has no need to expend her powers." Nelbern finished her drink and put the glass away. "I have a client, can you understand that? An—organization—that has paid me to—collect—a certain fact. The only place this fact has come to light is Sintia. My client has paid for proof. I *will* provide proof, whether you earn your fee or not." She looked closely at Velesz.

"My client is not easily thwarted, you see? Satisfaction earns reward. The wages of inefficiency are destruction and disgrace." She leaned forward, and I saw fear bloom at last in my sister's eyes and saw the sweat bead on the man's face.

"Disappoint me and be sure that your name will pass higher."

"Lady—" he began, but Cly Nelbern had pushed back her chair and turned away, carelessly flinging a handful of coins to the table.

"Tomorrow midday," she said softly. "At Diablo's, in the port. Have it." And she was gone.

I half-rose, but Lil stayed put, the fear like lunacy in her eyes. If she wasn't ship and blood I'd have left her but—

"Let's move," I said, gruff-like, so not to spook her, but she stared at me like she had when Mam died, and never moved a hair.

"Lil—"

"Lady Lillian," that was Pirro Velesz, leaning over to take her hand, oh so gently. His voice was soft, and I seemed to hear it, like a cat's burr, somewhere in the middle of my brain. "You cannot stay here, Lady Lillian. Go with your captain."

Incredibly, the fear subsided and she turned her eyes to him. "What're you gonna do?" she asked, matter-of-fact as if they were old shipmates and she had every right of an answer.

He smiled and pressed her hand, speaking as if to a child, "Why, I will go to the Port House and do what I may, and trust that the Goddess is good."

It seemed to satisfy her, who never had patience with my dream-tellings. She nodded and rose, Velesz with her, and he gave her hand into mine with a little bow, as if all were right and tight with him.

But the eyes he lifted to mine in the moment he gave Lil over were blighted with dread. His lips held the ghost of the smile he'd shown her, but his eyes were the eyes of a man looking at his death, or worse.

I hesitated, thinking to offer—what? I had no aid to give, trapped likewise by Cly Nelbern's coin. I nodded my thanks and went away, my sister's hand warm in mine.

IT'S A MARVEL how many repairs can be done to a ship, in the course of six short hours. A marvel, too, how much it all cost: enough to put a sizable dent in Cly Nelbern's cantra-piece. Though, truth told, the leavings of money would be enough to give *Luki* some semblance of credit again—enough, even, to claim a small amount of interest, if Lil would agree to forego real coffee for a time.

I had just thought that comfortable thought, musing among the itemizations on the screen, when I caught a sound behind me and spun the chair, fast.

Cly Nelbern smiled her ugly smile and came forward another step, to lean companionably against the copilot's chair and nod at the bill on the screen.

"Everything put to right now, Captain?"

"Everything'd take a deal more than a cantra," I said, reluctantly honest, "but we're set to fly."

"Good," she said, somewhat absent, and I asked the next question even more reluctantly.

"You'll be wanting our escort tomorrow?"

She looked up at that, alert as a dock-rat. "But of course—and a lift out, too. If we're up against the Temple—if that fool out there trips up . . ." The words faded and she focused on me again. "Have us moved to a hot-pad, Captain."

I looked at her hard. "We're ready to fly, I said. I didn't say we were champing on it. Plan to look around, take on cargo."

"You have a passenger." The voice was milk-mild and I felt my heart shudder, remembering her at the tavern.

I shook my head. "We're through with passengers. Trade's what we were born to; trade's what we'll stay with."

"Indeed." She pointed at the screen, at the invoice still visible, waiting for my thumbprint so the funds could leave *Luki*'s account. "I demand return of my loan, Captain Betany."

I stared at her. "That was no loan, and you well know it. Payment for escort, was what you said."

"Really?" she purred and then I knew how far Lil had lost us. "Do you have a contract stating so, Captain?"

I held onto my glare with an effort. "No."

"No." She smiled. "But I have a contract stipulating that I offered a cantra in loan for needful repairs, payable upon demand, else the ship resolves to me."

My mouth dried and my heart took up thumping so hard I thought the scans might read it. "You have no such thing."

"Oh, I do," she assured me; "and so do you. Right there in the daily log." She leaned away from the chair and started back toward the companionway. "Do move us to a hot-pad, Captain; there's a good girl."

It took me a long time to move, after she was gone. The first thing I did was open the log and read the thing she'd put there, sealed with my own codes.

Ship and blood. Mam'd told me to save things in that order, always. Ship first, then blood. I'd never in life have signed such a thing, nor agreed for the sake of a cantra . . .

Ship and blood. I thumbprinted the invoice and put the call through for the ready-pad. I okay'd those charges, too, forgetful of the meaning of the numbers; and then I went to my bunk to lie down, sealing the door and detaching the bell.

After a time of lying there in cold terror, eyes screwed shut against the awful sight of the ceiling, I fell asleep and I dreamed.

The dream was a confusion of pointing fingers and harsh voices making accusations that echoed into meaninglessness. At the center of it all stood my goddess of the barroom, her hair quiescent, though her eyes were not; and the one word that echoed clearly from the finger-pointers was "Recant!"

The word that I woke with among pounding head was hers, shaping my mouth with Her will: "No."

THE SHIP WAS QUIET. World clock showed midnight, straight up. Ship clock showed 0200.

I made myself a cup of 'toot and slid into the pilot's chair, worry gnawing at my gut. Cly Nelbern was surely mad, with more than grounder lunacy. No simple dockside bully, she; but a dangerous woman, and on more levels than gave me comfort.

The man? The man was desperate, and that carried its own brand of danger. But he seemed sane enough, and perhaps might be turned a card—made a pawn. Sacrificed for ship and blood.

It was snatching at starlight, of course, and madness in its own way, but I had to try something, there in the dark quiet; had to make some stab at saving my ship, my sister.

Curiously, it was Nelbern's money that bought me a way to make that stab, sorry as it might be. I set aside my cold drink and cycled the chair forward. I'd never had the credit to tap into a current planetary data bank before. We'd always bought old records—last week's cargo movements, yesterday's closing prices, and left it at that—but not this time.

I typed in Pirro Velesz' name. I tapped the dot for full database inspection. I offered up a prayer to whatever gods might be awake and listening, there in the deep heart of the night.

Then I went to sleep.

CLY NELBERN WOKE me by laughing, waving a hand at the screen where Velesz' information glittered like an unexplored star system.

"That's close to the way I found him, Captain, except that I didn't have a name—I just looked for a desperate person."

She laughed again, harder.

"That's how I found *Mona Luki*, too. Hard as you try to hide it, the information's there. I *know* how to read that spiral. Dreamers like you and that greengrocer—always thinking you'll find a way to beat the universe.

"I've seen it over and over again. You think you're something special. Think luck'll be with you. Well, you got lucky, Captain. I found you, thought you'd be useful and pulled you out of your downspin. *I'm* your luck, and if you're a smart girl, you'll ride easy with me, no arguments."

She waved at the screen again.

"But you want to know all about Senor Velesz—go ahead—read it. It's not a secret, is it?" Her words bit, deep and bitter, but I couldn't think of anything useful to say to a dirtsider who held mortgage to my ship and my kin, so I spun the chair back around and I read.

THE SHORT OF IT was that Pirro Velesz got himself suckered into a contract to supply some upcountry Temple with vittles for a year. When he couldn't make delivery the Temple took his business and put him to work at the rate of a Standard year for each month the Temple had to buy its food from someplace else. He had the option of buying himself out, of course—but he'd rolled everything on that losing deal—and no one on Sintia would lend money to a Temple debtor.

I sagged back into the pilot's chair, yanked two ways: pity and despair. So much for the stab to save us. Pirro Velesz was in worse case than *Mona Luki* or either of her sorry crew.

MIDDAY AT DIABLO'S. Too far from the city to hear the Temple chanting. Too close to the port to see anything but outworlders, half of them drunk and the other half out of luck, hunched over the bar like their last hope of salvation, eyes blurred like the middle of Jump.

Not one of them took note of us at all.

Lil was jumping terrified—the move to the hot-pad in the middle of our night and the guilt that came with knowing she'd sold our ship, however unknowing, had her in a state already. The bar filled with chancy spacers wired her even higher.

Pirro Velesz was nowhere to be seen.

Cly Nelbern found us a ringside table, ordered up a round of drinks and leaned back. She sipped from her glass now and then, and her hands were steady when she did, but for all of that I thought she looked tense and I tried not to think what she'd do, if she were forced into hunting him out.

The crowd thinned soon enough, as my drink sat untouched on the table. Lil's was long swallowed and Nelbern had all but finished her own.

She had just waved her hand for the waiter when there was a flicker at the doorway and a ripple of city-clothes in the corner of my eye. Nelbern came to her feet in one smooth flow, moving through the knot of patrons.

Lil charged to her feet the next second, wailing something inarticulate under her breath.

"Lillian!" I cried as she went by, but her eyes were full of anguish and she never heard me at all.

A circle had opened around them—Cly Nelbern and Pirro Velesz—a circle of the dead-eyed incurious, who turned back to drinking after a glance determined the business was none of theirs.

"Well?" I heard her say, as Lil pushed a way to his side.

"Well." He looked tired, his shabby blue tunic draggled and dirty. He swayed where he stood and Lil put a hand under his elbow to steady him.

I saw a smile come and go on his face, like a whisper of might-have-been; then he reached in his sleeve and pulled out a thin white envelope of the kind used for dirtsider's mail and handed it to Cly Nelbern.

She shook her head toward a table and we moved that way, Lil bright in the reflection of the man's wan smile.

"So." A purr of satisfaction as Nelbern opened the folder and pulled out a strip of film. "The original?"

He nodded. "As agreed."

"Delightful. And I have payment for you." She patted her own sleeve. Something in the gesture chilled me, and I saw Lil clutch after the man's arm, her eyes showing white at the edges.

It was then that I saw Her, in life as in dreaming, walking into that place in Her cleanness and her power, as if nothing evil could ever touch Her.

"Witch!" screamed one of the drunks at the bar, and threw a glass, which fell, stone-heavy, and broke on the floor at Her feet.

She turned Her head and there was silence at the bar; raised a hand and drew a sign in the fetid air. The silence shimmered, then broke apart, as the one who had thrown the glass lay his head upon the bar top and wailed.

She turned back then, fixed us with those eyes, which saw us and saw through us.

"Pirro Velesz." Her voice was deep, not ungentle; I heard it in my heart.

He licked his lips. "Mercy, Lady."

"Return what you have stolen."

"Lady, I cannot."

The smooth brow creased; then those eyes moved again, pinning Cly Nelbern.

"Return what you have stolen."

The older woman smiled, and bowed a trifle, one hand over her heart. "Why certainly, child," she said agreeably, and reached into her sleeve.

Lil cried out—a single wild shriek of protest. The man flung out a hand, too late, to stop the throw. I jumped half-forward, not sure if my mark was Lil or Nelbern, and saw the knife arc silver-bright, straight for Moonhawk's breast.

It fell, as had the glass; there was a clatter of shards where it struck. Cly Nelbern was already moving, the shine of another blade in her hand, swinging for an undercut that would take the girl out as Nelbern charged on—

"STOP!"

The world rocked and the stars shook in their places. I froze where I was, unable to do otherwise, my muscles commanded by Her will, not mine. I saw Cly Nelbern fall, and Lil. I saw Pirro frozen upright like myself, and heard the silence; wondered if everyone in the bar were like froze . . .

Moonhawk lifted a hand, bangles tinkling like carnival, and pointed a slender finger at Pirro.

"Return what you have stolen."

He moved, wooden-like, and went to his knees at Nelbern's side. He pulled the envelope from her belt, but tarried, his fingers straying to her wrist. Slowly, he stood and bowed to the girl.

"Lady, this woman is dead."

The power shimmered, and I saw the girl through the Goddess; frightened by what she had done, and saddened. She bent her head and when she raised it again, the girl was gone.

Pirro bowed, offered the envelope with its strip of film.

She took it and slipped it away, her eyes, black and brilliant, boring into his. In a moment, she had moved, turning like attention to me, so that I felt Her hovering over my soul; felt Her touch on my heart; felt, at last, the loosening of Her will and blurted out: "My sister is dead!"

The black eyes seared into me. "Your sister is alive, Fiona Betany. Give thanks to the Goddess and honor your gifts. All of them."

She went to Lil then, and spoke two words which my ears somehow refused to hear. Then she reached down Her own hand to help my sister rise, and stepped back to survey the three of us.

"You will return to your ship and you will leave this world. You are forbidden to return, on pain of punishment from the Circle."

She motioned, drawing burning signs within the air. "Go now!

Be prosperous and true." A tip of a hand toward what had been Cly Nelbern. "Leave that one here."

She paused, looking at us with those eyes, that saw us and saw through us and forgave everything they saw.

"Goddess bless," she said. "Now run!"

It might have been that easy, had the others not come just then: Temple robes of starry blue, cowls half-hiding faces that woke the echo of "Recant!" within me. There were three, or five, or eight of them. Their magics so shimmered air and truth that I could not count the number.

"HOLD!" demanded one of the group, and, perforce, we did.

One witch pointed at me; I heard the word "Talent!" and nothing else until a second witch pointed at Lil, and me, and Pirro and waved us all into a circle with the word "Conspiracy" binding us together like rope.

A third snatched open the envelope that Moonhawk had meekly given her and let out a smoking curse. "They would have stolen the secret of the catalyst molecule!"

There was charged silence, as if a great secret had been revealed, and the oldest among them laughed, all brittle.

"So, someone seeks to manufacture witches. Little enough success would have attended them! The Temple way is best. As all know— and believe."

She glanced about and took a brisker tone. "The wrong is that they dared to steal from us—the Temple! Retribution is demanded."

She gestured at us, and there was certainty in my heart: Ship and blood—and a good man, too . . . doomed.

The shortest witch raised a hand, began to trace a sign—and stopped because Moonhawk was abruptly there, meek no longer, slashing across the other's sorcery with a jangle of bracelets.

"Let be!" she snapped. "Moonhawk has looked and Moonhawk has forgiven. This was a dream-matter! Their way is clear, guaranteed by the Goddess!"

The shorter witch gaped, hand suspended in mid-sign. "*Moonhawk* has forgiven! Heresy, Maiden. By what right—"

The argument raged, words unsayable were said and then sign against sign was raised and the witches contended there—

But I found my limbs were my own again and I grabbed Lil's arm with one hand and Pirro's with the other and we took Moonhawk's last advice—we ran, and none chased after.

JUST AS WELL THAT MOONHAWK banned us from her world, for *Mona Luki's* lift-off and out-travel that day is now legend among traders and Port Masters (who all too often add an extra watch-minder to our bill), and most likely we'd be shot down on approach for traffic violations alone. But Moonhawk had told us to *run*!

And we did what she told us—all of what she told us; and we're as prosperous as a three-crew ship can be.

Pirro calms Lil as none since Mam did; she has found the best truth possible. I have found Pirro practical, a man of his word, always.

We share shifts or switch about to cover the boards. It works well, two sisters and their husband—not an odd arrangement, among small traders. Two babies on the way, which will fill the ship nicely and give us all too much to do.

I take the Dreaming seriously now, which accounts for some of our luck in trade—and in other things.

Now and again over the months I dreamt of her—Moonhawk. Not happy dreams. A burning. A hacking away of her long black hair. A mort of hard times among strangers, too much work, not enough food—things I remember all too well myself, so could be those dreams weren't true. Sometimes I'd wake and find myself with my arms pushed tight against the cabin's wall as if I'd tried to push those hard times away . . .

Just lately, though, I dreamed her again, after a long time of no dreams at all. It woke me and I lay there, listening to Pirro breathe and considering what I'd seen: Moonhawk, short hair all curly, dressed in prosperous trader clothes, bending to embrace a fair-haired boy while a tall man looked on, smiling.

The dream had felt true, I thought, and turned over to nudge Pirro awake and tell him.

He smiled sleepily and hugged me, the motion of his hands a comfort.

"Will our daughter be a Dream-Witch, too?" he asked and I had no quick answer, for of our daughter the dreams are just beginning.

—Standard Year 1375

✦ Phoenix ✦

CYRA HURRIED THROUGH the bustle of the pre-dawn, head down, and face hidden.

She traveled early, when the friendly shadows helped hide her deformity, allowing her to negotiate the eight chancy blocks from the anonymous apartments she kept in a nondescript building—where the floor numbering was in fresher paint in Terran numerals than in the older Liaden—to the streets she depended upon for her living.

Once on those streets no one remarked her, and few noticed her passing or her business, except those who had need to buy or sell this or that bauble of stone or made-stone or metal. The half-light suited her purpose, and even so she sometimes found herself automatically facing away from the odd passerby of Liaden gait and stature who would consider her worthless, or less.

On some worlds, Cyra would have been valued for her intelligence and her skills. On others, her demeanor and comeliness would surely have been remarked.

On others—but none of that mattered, for here on Liad she was marked for life by the knife of her Delm, and guaranteed a painful existence without the support of clan or kin for at least the remaining ten years of the dozen she'd been banned from clanhouse and the comforts of full-named society.

At one time, of course, she'd been Cyra chel'Vona Clan Nosko.

343

Now, on the streets where she was seen most, she was "that Cyra," if she was anything at all.

The marks high on her cheeks were distinctive, but hardly so disfiguring or repulsive in themselves to have people of good standing turn their heads or their backs on her until she passed. Yet, those of breeding did . . ..

This was scarcely a problem any longer, for she had long ago moved the shambles of her business from the streets of North Solcintra, where she had served the Fifty, to the netherworlds of Low Port, where her clientele were most frequently off-worlders, the clanless, outlaws, and the desperate.

Her own fortunes had fallen so far that she opened and closed her small shop by herself, working daily from east-glow to mid-day, and then again from the third hour until whatever time whimsey-driven traffic in the night faltered. Occasionally even these hours were insufficient to feed her, and she would work in the back-house at Ortega's—cleaning dishes, turning sheets, cooking, pushing unruly drunks out the back door—where her face would not be remarked—and thereby eating and sometimes earning an extra bit or two.

That was the final indignity. Very often her purse was so shrunken that she measured her worth not in cantra or twelfths but in bits—Terran bits!—and was pleased to have them. For that matter, being employed by a pure-blood Terran was, by itself, enough to turn any of the polite society from her face, no matter that the Terran was a legal landholder.

Things had been somewhat better of late; the new run of building on the east side of the port gave many of her regulars a chance at day labor and those of sentimental bent often returned in hope for the items they'd sold last week, or even last year.

This morning she was tired, having spent much of the evening at Ortega's, filling in for a cook gone missing. Shrugging her way into the store after touching the antiquated keypads she caught a glimpse of someone standing huddled against the corner of the used clothing store.

Closing the door behind her, leaving behind the sound of the morning shuttles lifting under the clouds, and the jitneys in the streets, she settled into the quiet of the thick-walled old building, checking the time to see that she was early enough to set tea to boil, and to warm and wolf the leftover rolls she carried from last night's work. She started those tasks, glancing through the scratched flex-glass of the door as she moved the few semi-valuable pieces from their hiding places to the case, and uncovered the special twirling display that held her choice Festival masks behind a clear plastic shield.

Cyra admired the green feathered mask as it twirled by, recalled the evening her aunt had brought her the ancient box and said, "This green does not become me, and I doubt I'll go again to Festival. This was *my* aunt's, after all, and is much out of style—but if you wish it, it is yours."

And so she'd worn it to her first Festival, finding delight in the games of walking and eyeing, the while looking for people she might know and seeking one who might not know her . . ..

Later, she'd been doubly glad of that Festival, for the marriage her uncle found for her was without joy *or* success, which had scandalized him despite the medic's assurance that she was healthy— and quashing her chance at full time study at the Art Institute.

Now, of course, she was denied the Festival at all.

She took her hand from beneath the plastic shield, where it had strayed, unbidden, and returned to routine, eyes drawn to the sudden flash of color outside the window, as the light began to rise with real daybreak.

He—at the distance the wildy abundant Terran beard was about all she could be sure of, aside from the bright blue skullcap he wore to hide his hair—*he* was dressed in what may have once been fine clothes, but which looked somewhat worse than they ought. She doubted he could see her, but his face and eyes seemed to spend about half their time watching her shop door and the other half watching chel'Venga's Pawnshop.

She sighed gently. The ones who had not the good sense to wait until the store was respectably open were the ones who were selling something. She wasn't sure which sort was worse—the ones who needed something they wouldn't be able to afford or the ones who couldn't afford to sell what they had to offer for a price she was able to give. At least he'd be out soon, no doubt, and she'd be able to keep the fantasy she held to heart from being overly tarnished yet again, the fantasy that Port Gem Exchange was yet a jewelry store and not yet a pawnshop in truth.

The clock stared back at her. Once upon a time she had slept until mid-day when she wished. Now she used each hour as if there was not a moment to waste. And for what this early morning? So that she might eat without being observed, and without companions. No need to rush—chel'Venga's Pawnshop rarely opened on time.

THE TERRAN STOOD at his corner, left hand in pocket, watching across the way as the increasing jitney traffic blocked his view from time to time, his beard waving in the wind. He'd seen her work the door and had straightened; and was there when she went back inside to get the rope-web doormat that welcomed her visitors. The pawnshop had no such amenities as rugs or mats. Perhaps it made no difference to her customers, but such were among the few luxuries she had these days.

He was not on the corner when she straightened from placing the mat in doorway and a quick glance showed him nowhere on the street. The lights had gone on in the pawnshop. They'd likely stolen the man away. Now Cyra regretted not giving in to the impulse to beckon to him as she unlocked the door, no matter the poor manners of it. It was hard to keep good *melant'i* in this part of the city, after all.

And then he was back, this time carrying a large, flat blue package of some kind, and he was hurrying, fighting the wind and the traffic, threatening at one point to run into a jitney rather than risk his burden.

Then he was there, larger than she'd realized, his relative slenderness accentuating his height, the dense beard distorting and lengthening his already long face, and his plentiful dark brown hair, brushed straight back from the high forehead, making him seem that much taller now that he'd taken the hat respectfully off to enter her store.

He came in quietly, with the noise of a large transport lifting from the port masking not only his sounds but those of the door until it closed, leaving his breathing—and hers—loud in the room.

He glanced down at her, nodded Terran-style, and looked over the shop carefully. Somehow she felt he might be looking at the tops of the cases—it had been many days since she'd thought to dust them, for who ever climbs a stool to inspect them?

He smiled at her, his light brown eyes inspecting her face so quickly that she hadn't time to flinch at the unexpected attention; nodded again, and said in surprisingly mannered Liaden, "I regret it has taken me so long to find your operation. I suspect we are both the poorer for it. "

At that he pulled from his pocket a large handful of glittery objects, some jeweled, some enameled or overlaid; pins, rings, earrings, necklaces . . .

And, she suspected quickly, all of them real.

"These are for sale," he said, "for a reasonable return. Since I am very close to crashing I will not haggle nor argue. I will simply accept or reject your offers on each. I would hope to get more than scrap value. You are a jeweler, however, and will know what you need."

His hands were the competent hands of an artisan, she decided as he turned the items out on her sales cloth. Despite the items he sold, he was ringless and despite the worn look of his clothes the marks on his hands were those of someone who worked with them regularly, not one who was careless or unemployed. Indeed, there were spatters, or patterns of colors on his skin, masked somewhat by the unusual amount of hair on his wrists, on the back of his hands, even down to his knuckles. Cyra was distracted, yes, even shocked: she had never seen a man with hair so thick it looked like fur!

"Indeed, we shall look," she managed, fretting at herself for the incivility of staring at someone's hands.

Quickly she sorted, finding far too many items of real interest. A dozen earrings—some of them paired and some not—all of quality. A strangely designed clasp pin, set with diamonds, starstones, and enamel work. A necklace, of platinum she thought, set with amethyst. Then the glass was in her hand, and the densitometer turned on, and the UV light, as well.

In a twelve day she would rarely expect to see so many fine pieces, much less at once.

"The pin," she said finally, "is obviously custom work. I suspect it of more value to the owner or designer than to me . . ."

"My great-uncle designed that himself," said the man, "and he is always one for the gaudy. Set it aside and we can talk about it later. Else?"

Cyra looked up—way up—into those brown eyes. He looked at her without sign of distress, and so she continued, oddly comforted.

"I would offer to buy the lot if we were closer to Festival," she admitted, "even the pin. But these are all quality items, as you do know, and they are somewhat more—extravagant, let us say—than I might usually invest in at this season."

"That's not an offer," the Terran returned, his face suddenly strained. "And I will need something for later, too."

"Perhaps," she suggested, "you should choose those least dear to you and point them out to me. I will offer on them."

His hands carefully moved the earrings to a small pile, and the necklace, leaving the pin by itself, and retrieving deftly other pins and the two rings. He leaned his hands on the counter then, as if tired.

"An offer," he said, "with and without the pin. You know that it is platinum; know that it is platinum from the very Amity object— and the provenance can be proved . . ."

Cyra grabbed up the pin, admiring its weight and the clasp design. Impulsively, she touched his hand, the one that held the other retrieved objects, and turning it over, pressed the pin into it.

"In that case, this is better placed with someone among the High Houses. They fail to arrive here in sufficient number to make my purchase worthwhile . . ."

And then she named a price which was far more of her available capital than she normally risked—but far less than the value she perceived before her—and was oddly annoyed by the man's rather curt, "That will do."

She was even more annoyed by the rapt attention he paid as she counted the cash out—as if each coin was in doubt. The she realized he was looking at her face. Involuntarily, she colored, which made her angry. Too long among the Terrans if she could blush so easily . . .

"No," he said suddenly, his Liaden gone stiffly formal. "I did not mean to disturb you. I sought—I was trying to see if I might read or recognize the etchings or tattoos on your face."

Cyra felt her face heat even more. She covered the scars with close-held fingers, looking up.

"Our transaction is finished. You may go."

He reached his hand toward her face and she flinched.

"Ah," he said, wisely. "The rule is that you may reach and touch my hand, but I, may not reach and touch yours. When the crash is coming I see things so clearly . . ."

Startled, she stepped back.

"Forgive me," she managed, and paused, seeking the proper words. Indeed, *she* had overstepped before he had; it was folly to assume that one who was Terran had no measure of manners.

Then: "But why this crash? Crash? You do not seem to be on drugs or drink, and . . ."

Now she was truly flustered; more so when he laughed gently.

"In truth, I am very much on drugs right now. I have been drinking coffee constantly for the last three days. Starting last night, I have been drinking strong tea, as well. It has almost been enough, you see, but I could tell it would not continue to work, so I need to buy food—I should eat very soon—I need to write the notes, though, and look once more before the crash."

Cyra held her hands even closer to her face.

"You need not look at all. These are none—"

But he was shaking his head, Terran-wise.

"No, you misunderstand. I need to look at the art so I remember what comes next . . . sometimes it is not so obvious to me when I start moving again."

Cyra was sure she *must* be misunderstanding—but before she could reply he pocketed the coins from the counter top and hefted the fabric-covered blue case or portfolio he'd brought in, laying it across the counter and reaching quickly for the seals.

"You, you love beautiful things—you must see this!" he said, nearly running over his words in his haste. "This one is my best so far! This is the reason I have come to Liad . . . this is where the Scouts are!"

Now he wasn't staring at Cyra at all, and she found the willpower to bring her hands down and come forward to see what might be revealed.

Some kind of tissue was swirled back from inside the case and before her was a photograph of a double star—with one redder and the other bluer—taken from the surface of an obviously wind-swept desert world with tendrils of high gray clouds just entering the photograph.

But sections were missing or else the photo-download had been incomplete or—

Now the odor came to her, eerily taking her back to the brief time she studied painting before turning to jewelry.

"You painted this? You are painting it now?" She looked up into his face and rapidly down to the work again. The detail was amazing, the composition near perfect, the—

"Yes," he was saying, "yes, it is my work. But I must not paint *now,* because now I am tired and spent and will only ruin what I have done. For now, the work is not safe near me!"

Cyra recalled working long and hard on her first real commission, so long and hard in fact that she'd finally fallen asleep in the midst, and woke to find the beaten metal scratched and chewed in the polishing machine, destroyed by the very process which should have perfected it.

She heard her voice before she realized she was speaking—

"If you need a place—I can keep it here. It will be safe! Then, when you are awake and ready, you can claim it."

He laughed, sudden and short, and with an odd twist of amusement pulling his grin into his beard.

"When I wake. Yes, that is a good way to put it. When I wake."

With a flourish he waved his hand over the tissue, swept it back over the painting, and sealed the portfolio.

"My name," he said quite formally, "is Harold Geneset Hsu Belansium. Among my family, I am known as Little Gene. To the census people I am BelansiumHGH, 4113." He paused, smoothed his beard, and smiled wryly before continuing.

"When I'm lucky, the pretty ladies of the universe call me Bell. Please, Lady, if I may have your name, I would appreciate it if you would call me Bell."

With that he handed the portfolio into her care.

She bowed. "Bell you wish? Then Bell it is. I am Cyra the Jeweler to the neighbors here, or simply Cyra. I will see you when you wake."

SOUND RUMBLED THROUGH the walls and rattled the room around Cyra, who involuntarily looked toward the ceiling. This one was an explosion then—more blasting, for the expansion—and not a rerouted transport flying low overhead. Rumor had it that several of the older houses two streets over were settling dangerously, but that was just rumor as far as she was concerned. Her store would be fine. It *would*.

She tried to tell herself it was just the noise that was making her skittish, but she knew it wasn't so. She had moved the stool behind the counter to gain a better vantage of the street, and had developed a nervous motion—nearly a shake of the head it was—when surveying the street.

The knowledge that she had a masterwork of art in her back room awaiting the return of the absent Bell frightened her deeply.

Suppose he didn't return? Suppose he had "crashed" in some fey Terran way and was now locked in a quiet back room at Healers Hall, or worse?

A smartly dressed businessman carrying a bag from the pastry shop strode by and Cyra found herself looking anxiously past him toward the corner where she'd first spotted Bell. It didn't help—the businessman had slowed, eyes caught by one of her displays, perhaps—and now was peering in and reaching for the door, carefully wiping feet, and bringing the brusque roar of a transport in with him as he entered. He closed the door and the sound faded . . .

Cyra slid to her feet.

"Gentle sir." She bowed a shopkeeper's bow. "How may I assist you today?"

He bowed, and now that she did not have the advantage of the stool, she saw that he was very tall, with sideburns somewhat longer than fashionable and—no, it was a very thin Terran-style beard, neatly trimmed and barely covering chin.

"Cyra, I am here to bring you a snack and to collect my painting."

She gawked, matching the height, and the color of the beard, and the voice—

"Bell!"

He laughed, and said mysteriously "You, too?"

"Forgive me," she said after a moment. "You gave me great pause. I have been watching for you—but I did not . . ."

He put the bag on the counter and began rooting through it, glancing at her as if calculating her incomplete sentence to the centimeter.

"I clean up well, eh? But here—if you'll make some tea, the lady at the pastry shop assures me you're partial to these . . ."

"Pastry shop? What does that have to do with anything?" She sputtered a moment, and— "Eleven days!" She got out finally, which was both more and less than she wished to say.

He lived very much in his face, the way Terrans do; his eyes were bright and his smile reached from the corners all the way to his bearded chin. He laughed gently, patting the counter, where there were now half-a-dozen pastries for her to choose from.

"Yes," he acknowledged. "Eleven. Not too bad. The worst was twenty-four, but that was before I knew enough to keep food by, and I'd been partying instead of painting."

"But what did you do for eleven days?"

He shook his head and the grin dissolved. He glanced down, then looked back to her, eyes and face serious.

"I crashed. I slept and I tried to sleep. I spent hours counting my failures, numbering my stupidities. I counted transports and the explosions and watched the crack in the wall get larger with each. Every so often I knew I'd never see my painting again, and I would know that I'd been taken and that you'd fled the city and I would never see you again, either."

He raised his hand before she could protest. "And then I would pull myself together and say 'Fool! Bewitched by beauty again!' And that way I'd recall your face and the painting, and try to sleep, knowing you'd be here, if only I could recall the shop name when I walked by. I nearly didn't, you know. I had to focus on that set of ear cuffs that match yours before I was sure."

She nearly reached for her ear, and then she laughed, somehow.

"Forgive me. I am without experience in this *crashing* you do. I was concerned for you, for your health, for your art!"

He smiled slowly. "We're both concerned for my health then, which I'm sure will be greatly improved if I can eat. My stomach has been growling louder than the shuttles! Please, join me! Afterward I will need to visit the port—it would be good if you could do me the favor of retaining my art until I return." The smile broadened. "I promise—I will not be gone eleven days, this time."

The noise of the street invaded their moment then, as two young and giggling girls entered. They stopped short, staring at the towering, bearded figure before them.

"Please," said Cyra to Bell. "If you will come back here, we can let my patrons look about!"

He nodded, and moved without hesitation.

She opened the counter tray to let him pass, indicated a low stool for him (his knees seemed almost to touch his ears!), and moved the pastries to the work table where they would both be able to reach them.

He smiled at her as she lifted a pastry to her lips. She felt almost giddy, as if she'd discovered some new gemstone or precious metal.

DEBBIE, THE HALF-TERRAN pastry maker from the shop four doors down was in, again, when Cyra returned from apartment hunting. It didn't improve her mood much; the girl hardly seemed as interested in the goods as in Bell, and her language was sprinkled with Terran phrases Cyra could just about decipher on the fly. Likewise the assistant office manager from the Port Transient Shelter. Didn't they realize that—she shushed her inner voice, nodding, Terran fashion, to Bell in his official spot behind the trade counter. He winked at her and she sighed. Were Terrans always so blatant?

The conversation continued unabated and there on the counter were actual goods; an item she didn't recognize, so it was for sale to the shop.

"Now," Bell was saying carefully, "I've seen places that these might have been in the absolute top echelon."

The women gazed at him.

Drawn to the story and the voice despite the crowd, Cyra leaned in to hear.

"Of course, that would only be if the local priestess had purified the stone before it was cut, blessed the ore the silver had come from, sanctified the day the ring was assembled, and then prayed over the ring-giver and scried the proper hour for giving.

"In other corners of the universe," he went on, "as, say, on Liad or Terra, the flaws in the stone might mark it ordinary. If I were you, I would ask Cyra if she'll set a price, knowing it for a *nubiath'a* hastily given . . ."

Cyra moved behind the counter to take up the office of buyer, but the women had both apparently heard tall tales from Terrans in the past—

"Bell, now really, were you on that planet," asked the assistant office manager, "—or have you merely heard of it?"

He rolled his eyes and surprised Cyra with a discreet pat as she squeezed by him.

"What, am I a spaceman, or a scout, to have all my stories disbelieved?"

They laughed, but he continued, assuming a serious air.

"Actually, it was almost all a disaster. The planet you should never go to is Djymbolay. I arrived just after I finished a painting on board the liner, and was pretty well spent. I had my luggage searched twice for contraband, and then they confiscated the painting as an unauthorized and unsanctified depiction of the world."

He shook his head, then tapped it with his finger. "They wanted to have me put away for blasphemy or something, I think. It took a scout who happened by—all thanks to little John!—to let me keep my papers and my paint and my freedom. Off with my head or worse, I expect was the plan! But the scout was there on another matter and interceded. The locals walked me across the port under armed guard, and the scout came, too, to be sure that it was gently done—and they kept me confined to the spaceport exit-lounge for the twelve days the ship was there. If several kind ladies hadn't taken pity, and brought me meals and blankets, I might well have starved and froze."

Cyra bit back a comment halfway to her lips; after all she knew not where he'd slept before she met him, nor, for that matter, that he always returned to his own rooms on the afternoons and evenings he went to the lectures at Scout Academy. She only knew he returned to the store with sketches and ideas and full of hope that he might eventually be permitted to visit a new world, to be the first painter, the first interpreter . . .

In a few moments more, the transaction was made; she paid a fairly low price for the emerald ring—the one suggested by the seller—and agreed to look at earrings that might be a match.

The two women gone, Bell looked at her carefully.

"You're tired—and you've been angry."

Exasperated by his grasp of the obvious, Cyra waved her hands in the air in a wild gesture, and snapped, "How else?"

"You might be pleased, after all. The emeralds were got at a decent price."

"Yes, a decent price. But if I'm going to afford you, my friend, we'll need to do better."

He looked at her with the same air of frankness he'd used when talking about the disaster that had cost him a painting, and shook his head.

"Yes, I know; I am hardly convenient for myself, much less for anyone else."

"That's not what I meant!" she protested. "I mean that—I mean that it is difficult to find a larger place to live hereabouts, and nearer to my apartment there are those who will not rent to someone who—"

"Someone who might bring a Terran home of a night," Bell finished, as she faltered. "Inconvenient I said, and I meant!" he insisted with heat. "I don't mind sleeping here in the store, after all, though the light is not always good. Perhaps you can offer to rent the corner place the next street over."

They had been over that before, too. Bell's situation was so changeable that neither knew how long they might find each other's company pleasant, useful, or convenient. He could hardly sign a lease, with his "transient alien" status in the port computers assuring that any who looked would laugh at his request. Even getting a room beyond the spaceport was difficult for him, except here in the Low Port area. Mid Port was too dear for his budget in any case.

He could hardly co-sign with her, either. The conditions her delm had set were strict and might well bear on that—if she wished to ever return to the House, she would, during her time of exile, refrain from forming formal alliances; she must not buy real estate; she was forbidden to marry, or to have children . . .

There could be no co-signing; she could speak for none other than herself. But to add a place where some of his paintings could be shown—this close to the port, they might gain a better clientele with such a gallery.

Truth told, though, Bell's sometime presence permitted Cyra to cut her dependence on Ortega's chancy employ; in fact, twice recently they'd been there as patrons.

He looked at her, snatched the ring to his hand and began tossing it furiously into the air. This, after three previous ragged forty-day cycles, she recognized. Any day, perhaps any moment, he would drag out the rough sketches and ideas, choose one, and then hardly see her, even should she stand naked before him, while he took plasboard and tegg-paint and the secret odds and ends from his duit box and transformed them by touch of skilled hand and concentration and willpower unmatched to art as fine as ever she'd seen. Days, he would be one with the art.

And then he would crash; folding into a hollow and dispirited being barely willing to feed himself, with a near-fear of sunlight and a monotone voice and no plans to speak of . . . until the cycle came full and from the gray, desperate being emerged Bell, fresh and whole and new. Again.

He shook the ring, tossed it, glanced anxiously to his art kit where it was stashed near the door to the back room.

"I know," he said. "I know! It's almost time. I think we should close early, perhaps, and go someplace fine to eat—I'll pay!—and plan on a bottle of good wine and snacks—I've chosen them already—and a night, a glorious night, my beauty. And then, we can talk at breakfast, if the art's not here yet, and if it is, we'll talk in a few days."

In front of her then, the choice—and she knew already she'd take it, or most of it. Had she a clan to call on she would pledge her quartershare—to make this work, she'd—but what she would do *if* was no matter, now. Her quartershare would go—till the twelfth year, at least—into the account of a dead child, just as her invitations—large and small—would go to her delm, and be returned with the information that she was in mourning and not permitted.

She recalled the discreet caress a few moments earlier, her blood warming . . .

Tonight she would forget the she was poor and outcast. Bell would take them somewhere with his stash of cash and they would spend as if he were a visiting ambassador instead of an itinerant artist, and then he would—

"Bell," she said gently, "perhaps we should stay until nearer closing. My friend. I followed your instructions last time, you know—there are three prepared boards waiting—and I have already an extra cannister of spacer's tea and you gave me enough for two tins of Genwin Kaffe last time, so we have that. That is, if you are certain that you won't talk to the Healers this time."

He looked at her then and his eyes were hungry; she doubted that hers were not.

"I'll check the boards, Cyra, and make sure that you have room to work this time, too."

CYRA TASTED THE SALT on her lips, and nearly wept as she relaxed against him. He was so inexhaustible and inventive a lover, she thought, that perhaps she should have invited the office manager to help out—and she laughed at the silliness, and he heard her, Bell with his hands still willing and eager, and his quirky Terran words dragged out of him in the midsts.

"Now I'm funny. Oh, woe, oh woe . . ."

She could see him in the half-light he preferred for lovemaking;

just bright enough that the mirrors on the wall might tell an interesting tale to a glancing eye. She remembered that he'd brought beeswax candles, along with wine and flowers that first evening after his very first return, when he'd somehow parlayed her concern—

She laughed again, this time finding his hair and beard wooly near her face, and she gently moved to brush them orderly. He had something more on his mind though, as her hands came in contact with his cheek; but she held him a moment and he was willing to be calmed.

Of course, she should not stroke his beard and his cheek; she should not kiss his nose, nor lay her palm on his face, this Terran who never knew the taboo of it . . .

"Let's trade," he said, very gently. "A story for a story, a touch for a touch."

Then he laid his hand on her cheek, spreading his wide hand so that his thumb and his forefinger spanned her face.

It was late in the night, very nearly morning; the sounds from the road were not yet impinging on their lair. His breathing, and hers, and his touch.

"I," he said after a moment. " I cannot go to the Healers, because when someone in my family is cured, we loose the art. My father, my grandfather, my uncle—myself. I tried, there once—"

He paused, brushed her hair away from her eyes, kissed her on her nose, covered the marks on her face as if he would wipe them away. "After that painting was stolen from me I could have been locked up forever there, but for the good luck of a scout's intercession. So, I thought I should get over the crash. I spoke to a doctor and he seemed to make sense, and they gave me a therapy and drugs and an implant . . ."

"Here!"

He guided her hand and held it against that long scraggly scar on his leg. She'd found that scar before, but never dared question—there were things lovers were not to ask, after all; the Code was clear on that.

"Three months," he said very quietly. "Let me say about two of my usual cycles, though they change sometimes—be warned!—and

I had not even the slightest twinge of being able to paint, and what I drew was stick figures and bad circles and patterns, and I spoke politely to people and one night I went home and picked up a cooking knife and thought that I would cut my throat."

He took her hand and placed it under his beard, where it was just above his throat, and let her feel the pulse of him, and the smaller, more ragged scar.

"I'd made a start, actually, when I realized that what I wanted was not my throat cut, but my art back. And so I took the knife and opened my leg and took the thirty-four months' worth of implant that was left out of me, and I washed it down the drain."

She stared at him, at once fascinated and horrified, not knowing what to say.

"My cousin," he went on, after a moment. "My cousin Darby. He took the cure and has stayed on it. He's married, he goes to work, comes home, goes to work, comes home—and I have the last piece of sculpture he did before the implant. He was brilliant. He made me look like a bumbling student. But it is gone. Five years and he can't draw a face much less model one; he can't see the images in the clouds!"

He brushed his lips over the mark under her left eye, then kissed the one under her right eye.

"You know," he said quietly, "you are beautiful. I have known beautiful ladies, my friend, and you are very beautiful."

The realization hit her—what he would ask, in exchange for this tale from his soul. Very nearly, she panicked, but he caught her mouth with his, and in a few moments she relaxed against him.

"My friend," she said, "you can be as cruel as you are wonderful. To cut yourself so—the pain! But I am not so brave as you. I took the cuts from my delm, in punishment—cut with the blade my family keeps from the early days. Then I wept and cried, and was cast from the House . . ."

"Does this person yet live?" Not in his deepest despair had she heard his voice so cold.

Cyra looked into his face and saw he meant it—that he contemplated Balance or revenge or—

"No, Bell, you cannot. My delm was doing duty. I was cut to remind me and to warn others."

He said nothing, but kissed her face again, gently, waiting.

"We are not as rich a house as some others, Clan Nosko; and my delm, my uncle, is not so easy a spender as you or I. As I was youngest of the daughters of the house—and lived at the clan seat, it being close to my shop—it fell my duty sometimes to spend an afternoon and a night, or sometimes two, doing things needful. And so . . ."

Here she paused a moment, gently massaging Bell's neck under the beard, imagining all too well . . .

"So it was," she went on very quietly, with the blood pounding in her ears, "that I was briefly in charge of the nursery, the nurse having been given a discharge for cost or cause, I know not. I had put the child Brendar to bed; a likely boy come to the clan through my sister's second marriage. I changed him once, but he was otherwise biddable. I was trying for my Master Jeweler's license, so I was at study with several books. I read, and read more, hearing no fuss. Then my sister came home, and the child was not asleep, but had died sometime in the night."

There was quiet then.

Finally, he kissed her again, each scar, very carefully.

"I'd thought there must be more, but I see the story now, and I am near speechless. The child died of an accident—

"My incompetence and negligence . . ."

He pressed a finger to her lips so hard it nearly hurt.

"I am a fool, Cyra, my beautiful friend. I thought it was your own anger, or your own desire, that placed those marks on your face; that you had rebelled against the rules of this world and even now wore them as badges. That they were inflicted by your family to humiliate and destroy you never came to mind . . ."

He brushed the hair out of her face again.

"I will paint your picture one day, I promise. Your face will be known as among the most beautiful of this world. And they will see that they have lost you, for I'll not let them have you back!"

She had no quick answer for this, and then he said, "Here!" and placed her hand again on the long leg scar.

She felt the welt there—he laughed, nibbled on her earlobe, and moved her hand a bit, murmuring, "Now, Lady, *here* if you wish to be pleased!"

She did, and she was.

THREE DAYS LATER, Cyra was not so very pleased.

To begin, Bell had become inspired sometime in the night of their pillow talk and when she awoke alone in the dawn she found him sketching like a madman on her couch, barely willing to drag himself away from his work long enough to share a breakfast with her.

He packed his sketches and walked with her to the shop, his eyes as elsewhere as his mind. Twice she had to repeat herself while she spoke with him, and then he disappeared into the back room to work as soon as they reached the store.

In the afternoon he had rushed out of the back room, complaining that she'd not told him the time, and stormed out, on his way to a lecture he particularly wanted to see. Worse, he stormed back, having left his sketchbook and wallet, and dashed off with nary a backward glance. When he didn't return by closing—he sometimes went to discussion groups after the lectures—she'd not expected him to come by her apartment, and he didn't, which grated mightily.

In the morning, he wandered in very late, hung over and exhausted, explaining that he'd met a pack of scouts at the lecture and talked with them until the barkeep announced shift-change at dawn. He was animated, nearly wildly so, explaining that he might "have a line on" the scout who had helped him at Djymbolay; that his conversations of the evening had revealed that he owed Balance to that scout; that he might have an idea for yet another painting; and that when he had more money there was a world he'd have to travel to and—

"I have an appointment, Bell," Cyra said abruptly. "Tell me later!"

She rushed out the door, barely confident—and barely caring—that he'd heed the advent of a customer.

Her appointment was with her tongue—had she stayed and heard more she surely would have said hurtful words.

So she walked, nearly oblivious to the sounds of transports— more this day than others since a portion of the port would be closed late in the afternoon for some final tricksy bit of work for the expansion—and found herself several blocks from her usual streets, in a very old section, where the buildings and the people were barely above tumbledown.

Surprisingly, she saw Debbie-the-pastry-girl hurrying from one of the least kept brick-fronts; Number 83 it was, a regrettable four-story affair sporting ungainly large windows and peeling paint. The peaked, slate roof suggested that the building was several hundred Standards old, and it looked like it had no repair since the day it was built.

Heart falling, she reached into her card case, and removed the slip of paper she had from Bell the day he'd agreed to share his direction with her: Number 83 Corner Four Ave, Room 15.

A shuttle's long rumble began then; she could feel the sidewalk atremble as she watched the pastry girl's blue-and-green hair disappear in the distance. Also on the paper was the pad combination, and with the whine of the shuttle rising behind her, and then over, she stood, and for a moment was tempted to enter Number 83 and find Room 15, open the door, and see if—if . . .

She turned and walked all the way home for lunch, grasping the paper tightly in her fist.

When she got back to the store, calmer, but heartsore, there was Bell's back vaguely visible in the back room. He heard her enter and yelled out over his shoulder "Any luck?"

"No," she said, quietly. "No luck, Bell."

She slept badly alone, and the rumble of the transports, joined with the not entirely foreign sounds of proctor-jitneys blaring horns as they answered a nighttime summons hadn't helped.

And now, on her store step across the road in the dawn light?

Debbie, cuddling Bell's good jacket in her arms.

"BELL'S OK," THE GIRL said quickly, shaking her absurd hair back from a remarkably grimy face. "He wasn't bleeding all that much and the medic said he'll do. The proctor, now, he'll be okay, too, other'n his pride's pretty well hurt by getting really whomped—I mean *decked* in front of all his buddies. But there's gonna be some fines to pay, I guess, and he's gotta have a place to live and—"

Cyra stood staring, hard put to sort this tumbled message, clinging at last to the simple, "Bell's OK . . ."

Debbie was looking at her with desperate eyes. "Cyra, you're a lucky girl, you know? But you're gonna have to get someone down to the jail to get him *out*. He's not the kind of guy that'll get along there, and hey—what it'll take is 'a citizen of known *melant'i*, moral character, and resources.' I sure don't qualify for the resources part, the *melant'i* I ain't got and I'm not sure if I qualify for the character part . . ."

Cyra wasn't too sure about the character part either, though the fact that the girl was here with so many of Bell's belongings argued for her. Arrayed on the step was a ship bag with "Belansium" printed on a tag, four or five studies—paintings and sketches of a woman, who Cyra realized must be herself by the detail of the face—nude in different positions, some small odds and ends in boxes, a small paint kit, a picnic box . . .

"Tell me again," Cyra demanded. "After we get these inside. From the beginning. I'll make tea."

DEBBIE RUSHED OFF while the tea was heating and returned with pastries, and a damp towel, which she was using on the dust and grime on her bare arms.

"I was having company over and wasn't much paying attention to other stuff when I heard one of the transports go over. Things started trembling and—well, wasn't at the stage I thought, then the next thing I know there was a big *cherunk* kind of noise and the front wall just fell out into the street. The whole place got shaky and we all got out. Bell come dashing out from his room carrying something big and square and rushing down the steps with it whiles bricks and roof-stuff falling all around.

"We was outside standing and staring—most everyone out by then, when the whole building kind of slanted over backwards and leaned into the alley. My guy, he's pretty smart, he'd grabbed a bottle of wine on the way out, and we all had a sip, and when it looked like there wasn't any more *up* to fall *down* we went in to see what we could save and to make sure no one was inside—and a bunch of snortheads showed up. One grabbed one of them sketches of you and yelled for some of the others—

"That Bell picked up part of a drainpipe and started hitting and bashing at them guys, and then my guy hit one of 'em with the empty bottle, and then the proctors showed up and Bell wasn't letting no one near his stuff. Proctor kind of waved something in his direction and Bell did this neat little dance step and brought his hand out and lifted the proctor right off his feet. Right quick they was all on him . . . and I had to explain—see it was my Ma's building, and all—but they still got Bell for drunk-and-disorderly, striking a proctor, and I don't know what else. And I can't speak for him!"

"Neither can I," Cyra said. admitted, staring down into her tea and trying not to think of Bell at the hottest part of his cycle, locked away from his paints and pens. "Neither can I."

"YOU HAVE ARRIVED," the receptionist told Cyra, "at a bad time. I have no one to spare to listen to your story, as interesting as it must be. The scouts are not in the habit of interfering with the proctors on matters of Low Port drunk-and-disorderly . . ."

Cyra glared. "He was not drunk—not at this time in the cycle. Disorderly—he did strike a proctor, but—" she stopped, suddenly struck by a thought, and came near to the counter again.

"Have you a scout named Jon?" she asked.

"Only several," a female voice said from close behind her. Cyra spun, face heating. The scout tipped her head, eyes bright and manic, as the eyes of scout's so often were. "Would you wish us to know that it is a scout named Jon whom the proctors discovered to be drunk and disorderly? I don't find that impossible. Why, I myself have been drunk and disorderly in Low Port. It is excellent practice for the dining situations found on several of the outworlds."

"Captain sig'Radia . . ." the receptionist began, but the scout waved a hand.

"Peace. Someone has arrived with time to spare for a story about a drunk and disorderly in Low Port." She cocked a whimsical eyebrow in Cyra's direction, looking her full in the face, as if the disfiguring scars were invisible, or non-existent. "The acoustics of this hallway are quite amazing, but allow me to be certain—I did hear you say 'struck a proctor'?"

Cyra admitted it dejectedly. "But it is not the scout Jon who did this," she continued, feeling an utter fool. "I had merely thought, since my friend—Bell—was known to the scout . . ."

"Ah. And something more of your friend—Bell—if you please? For I do not believe, despite our abundance of Jons, that we have any scouts named Bell."

Cyra bit her lip. "He is a Terran—an artist. Last night, the apartment house he lived in fell down, and—"

"Now I have the fellow!" Captain sig'Radia cried, and grinned with every appearance of delight. "What we heard on the Port is that he knocked down a prepared, on-duty proctor, barehanded. Quite an accomplishment, though I don't expect the proctors think so. No sense of humor, proctors."

"It must be unpleasant," Cyra murmured, "after all, to be knocked down."

"Oh, wonderfully unpleasant," the scout agreed happily. "Especially with the rest of your team looking on."

"Yes," Cyra bit her lip, wondering how possibly to explain the cycles, and the tragedy of Bell being without his paints *now*. "If you please, Bell—it is very bad . . ." she stammered to a halt.

"Complicated, eh?" the scout said sympathetically. "Come, let us be private."

She took Cyra's arm as if they were long friends, and escorted her out of the main room and down a hall.

"Ah, here we are," the scout said, and put her palm against a door, which opened willingly, utterly silent.

The lights came up as they walked down the room to the table and chairs. Cyra looked about, marveling at the size of the chamber, her eye caught and held by a projection on the front wall—a planetscape, it was, showing a sun and a great-ringed planet in the distance and a close up portion of bluish-green atmosphere—

Cyra gasped, recognition going through her like a bolt, though she had never seen this painting, but the composition, the eloquence the *work*—it could only be—

"That is Djymbolay, is it not?" She asked the scout captain, her voice shaking.

The woman looked at her in open wonder. "It is, indeed. How did you know?"

"My friend Bell painted the original of that." She used her chin to point.

The captain looked, face very serious now. "I see. You will then be comforted to know that the original is safe in the World Room." She looked back to Cyra, her smile crooked.

"And your friend Bell is by extrapolations no more nor no less than Jon dea'Cort's glorious madman. Allow me to see if the scout is within our reach."

SUMMONED, Jon dea'Cort arrived quickly and heard the tale out with a grin almost as wide as Bell's could be, when he stood at the height of his powers. When all was said, he looked to Cyra, and inclined his head.

"Your Bell, he is at what stage in his continuing journey?"

She blinked against the rise of unexpected tears and made herself meet his eyes squarely. "He is painting. Please—"

He held up a hand. "Yes. You were right to come to us." He looked to Captain sig'Radia, who lifted an eyebrow.

"A change of custody, I think," he said to her. "Certainly, they will insist that he be heard, and fined, but he must be got out of the holding tank at once and allowed to paint before drunk-and-disorderly becomes cold murder."

Cyra sat up, horrified. "Bell would not—" A bright glance stopped her.

"Would he not? Perhaps you are correct. But let us not put him to the test, eh?" He grinned suddenly, scout-manic. "Besides, I want to see what magic flows from his brush this time."

THEY GAVE HER a room, and a meal, and promised to fetch her, when Bell was arrived. She ate and lay down on the bed, meaning to close her eyes for a moment only . . .

"Cyra?" The voice was quiet, but unfamiliar. "It is I, Jon dea'Cort. Your Bell is safe."

She sat up, blinking, and found the scout seated on the edge of her bed, face serious.

"Is he well?" she demanded. "Is he—"

He held up a hand. "Would you see him? He is painting."

"Yes!"

"Come then," he said, and he led her out and down the hall to a lift, then down, down, down, perhaps to the very core of the planet, before the doors opened, and there was another hall, which they walked until it intersected another. They turned right. Jon dea'Cort put his hand against a door, which slid, silently, open, and they stepped into a large and well-lit studio.

Bell at the farther end of the room, his easel in the best light and he was working with that focused, feverish look on his face that she had come to know well—and to treasure.

The scout touched her hand, and tipped his head toward the door. Cyra followed him out.

"Thank you," she said, feeling conflicting desires to sing and weep. "He will crash—sometime. Often, he knows when, but in a strange place, with this interruption—I do not know. Someone— someone should pay attention to him."

"Surely," the scout said amiably. "And that someone ought to be yourself, if you are able?"

She hesitated for a moment, thinking of the shop in Low Port, and then inclined her head. "I am able."

"CYRA?" SHE LOOKED UP from her work, smiling, and found Bell gazing seriously down at her.

Having gained her attention, he went to a knee, and raised his hand to her face. She nestled her cheek into the caress.

"Are you sorry, Cyra? To leave your home, to be rootless, companioned to inconvenient Bell, and in the sphere of scouts . . ."

She laughed and turned her face, brushing her lips against his palm, and straightening.

"What is this? You will be painting tomorrow, my friend; do not try to tease me into believing that you are on the down-cycle!"

He smiled at that, and touched a fingertip to her nose before dropping his hand to his knee. "You know me too well. But, truly, Cyra . . ."

She put the pliers down and reached out, placing her hands on his shoulders and gazing seriously into his eyes.

"I am not sorry, Bell. Did you not say that you would take me away? You have done so, and I am not sorry at all."

He had kept the other part of that pillow-sworn vow, as well, and the portrait of herself that he had completed in Scout Headquarters remained there, on display in the reception area, with other works of art from many worlds.

"I have the original," he had said to Jon dea'Cort. "Take you the copy, and let us be in Balance."

And so it had been done, and now they were—attached to scouts, spending time on this research station, or that surveillance ship, while Bell painted, and sketched, and fed his art. Cyra fed her own art, and her jewelry was sought after, when they came to a world where they might sell, or trade.

"We do well," she said, leaning forward to kiss his cheek. "I am pleased, Bell."

He laughed gently and leaned forward, sliding his arms around her and bringing her on to his knee.

"You're pleased, are you?" he murmured against her hair. "But could you not be—just a little—*more* pleased?"

She laughed and wrapped her arms closely around his neck, rubbing her cheek against the softness of his beard.

"Why, yes," she said, teasing him. "I might be—just a *little*—more pleased."

He laughed, and rose, bearing her with him, across their cabin to the bed.

—Standard Year 1293

✧ Naratha's Shadow ✧

For every terror, a joy. For every sorrow, a pleasure.
For every death, a life. This is Naratha's Law.
    —From, *Creation Myths and Unmakings:*
        A Study of Beginninng and End

"TAKE IT AWAY!" The Healer's voice was shrill.

The scout leapt forward, slamming the lid of the stasis box down and triggering the seal in one smooth motion.

"Away, it is," she said soothingly, as if she spoke to a child, instead of a woman old in her art.

"Away it is *not*," Master Healer Inomi snapped. Her face was pale. The scout could hardly blame her. Even with the lid closed and the seal engaged, she could feel the emanation from her prize puzzle—a grating, sticky malevolence centered over and just above the eyes, like the beginnings of ferocious headache. If the affect was that strong for her, who tested only moderately empathic, as the scouts rated such things, what must it feel like to the Healer, whose gift allowed her to experience another's emotions as her own?

The scout bowed. "Master Healer, forgive me. Necessity exists. This . . . object, whatever it may be, has engaged my closest study for—"

"Take. It. Away." The Healer's voice shook, and her hand, when she raised it to point at the door. "Drop it into a black hole. Throw it

369

into a sun. Introduce it into a nova. But, for the gods' sweet love, *take it away*!"

The solution to her puzzle would not be found by driving a Master Healer mad. The scout bent, grabbed the strap and swung the box onto her back. The grating nastiness over her eyes intensified, and for a moment the room blurred out of focus. She blinked, her sight cleared, and she was moving, quick and silent, back bent under the weight of the thing, across the room and out the door. She passed down a hallway peculiarly empty of Healers, apprentices and patrons, and stepped out into the mid-day glare of Solcintra.

Even then, she did not moderate her pace, but strode on until she came to the groundcar she had requisitioned from Headquarters. Biting her lip, feeling her own face wet with sweat, she worked the cargo compartment's latch one-handed, dumped her burden unceremoniously inside and slammed the hatch home.

She walked away some little distance, wobbling, and came to rest on a street-side bench. Even at this distance, she could feel it—the thing in the box, whatever it was—though the headache was bearable, now. She'd had the self-same headache for the six relumma since she'd made her find, and was no closer to solving its riddle.

The Scout leaned back on the bench. "Montet sig'Norba," she told herself loudly, "you're a fool."

Well, and who but a fool walked away from the luxury and soft-life of Liad to explore the dangerous galaxy as a scout? Scouts very rarely lived out the full term of nature's allotted span—even those fortunate enough to never encounter a strange, impulse powered, triple-heavy *some*thing in the back end of nowhere and tempted the fates doubly by taking it aboard.

Montet rested her head against the bench's high back. She'd achieved precious little glory as a scout, glory arising as it did from the discovery of odd or lost or hidden knowledge.

Which surely the *some*thing must carry, whatever its original makers had intended it to incept or avert.

Yet, six relumma after what should have been the greatest find of her career, Montet sig'Norba was still unable to ascertain exactly what the something was.

"It may have been crafted to drive Healers to distraction," she murmured, closing her eyes briefly against the ever-present infelicity in her head.

There was a certain charm to Master Healer Inomi's instruction to drop the box into a black hole and have done, but gods curse it, the thing was an artifact! It had to do something!

Didn't it?

Montet sighed. She had performed the routine tests; and then tests not quite so routine, branching out, with the help of an interested, if slightly demented, lab tech, into the bizarre. The tests stopped short of destruction—the tests, let it be known, had not so much as scratched the smooth black surface of the thing. Neither had they been any use in identifying the substance from which it was constructed. As to what it did, or did not do . . .

Montet had combed, scoured and sieved the Scouts' not-inconsiderable technical archives. She'd plumbed the depths of archeology, scaled the heights of astronomy, and read more history than she would have thought possible, looking for a description, an allusion, a *hint*. All in vain.

Meanwhile, the thing ate through stasis boxes like a mouse through cheese. The headache and disorienting effects were noticeably less when the thing was moved to a new box. Gradually, the effects worsened, until even the demented lab tech—no empath, he—complained of his head aching and his sight jittering. At which time it was only prudent to remove the thing to another box and start the cycle again.

It was this observation of the working of the thing's . . . aura that had led her to investigate its possibilities as a carrier of disease. Her studies were—of course— inconclusive. If it carried disease, it was of a kind unknown to the scouts' medical laboratory and to its library of case histories.

There are, however, other illnesses to which sentient beings may succumb. Which line of reasoning had immediately preceded her trip to Solcintra Healer Hall, stasis box in tow, to request an interview with Master Healer Inomi.

"And much profit you reaped from that adventure," Montet

muttered, opening her eyes and straightening on the bench. Throw it into a sun, indeed!

For an instant, the headache flared, fragmenting her vision into a dazzle of too-bright color. Montet gasped, and that quickly the pain subsided, retreating to its familiar, wearisome ache.

She stood, fishing the car key out of her pocket. Now what? she asked herself. She'd exhausted all possible lines of research. No, check that. She'd exhausted all orderly and reasonable lines of research. There did remain one more place to look.

THE LIBRARY OF LEGEND was the largest of the several libraries maintained by the Liaden Scouts. The largest and the most ambiguous. Montet had never liked the place, even as a student Scout. Her antipathy had not escaped the notice of her teachers, who had found it wise to assign her long and tedious tracings of kernel-tales and seed-stories, so that she might become adequately acquainted with the library's content.

Much as she had disliked those assignments, they achieved the desired goal. By the time she was pronounced ready to attempt her Solo, Montet was an agile and discerning researcher of legend, with an uncanny eye for the single true line buried in a page of obfusion.

After she passed her Solo, she opted for field duty, to the clear disappointment of at least one of her instructors, and forgot the Library of Legends in the freedom of the stars.

However, skills once learned are difficult to unlearn, especially for those who have survived scout training. It took Montet all of three days to find the first hint of what her dubious treasure might be. A twelve-day after, she had the kernel-tale.

Then, it was cross-checking—triangulating, as it were, trying to match allegory to orbit; myth to historical fact. Detail work of the most demanding kind, requiring every nit of a Scout's attention for long hours at a time. Montet did not stint the task—that had never been her way—and the details absorbed her day after day, early to late.

Which would account for her forgetting to move the thing, whatever it was, from its old stasis box into a new one.

✧✧✧

"THIS IS AN ALERT! Situation Class One. Guards and emergency personnel to the main laboratory, caution extreme. Montet sig'Norba to the main laboratory. Repeat. This is an alert . . ."

Montet was already moving down the long aisle of the Legend Library, buckling her utility belt as she ran. The intercom repeated its message and began the third pass. Montet slapped the override button for the lift and jumped inside before the door was fully open.

Gods, the main lab. She'd left *it,* whatever it was, in the lab lockbox, which had become her custom when she and the tech had been doing their earnest best to crack the thing open and learn its inner workings. It should have been . . . safe . . . in the lab.

The lift doors opened and she was running, down a hall full of security and catastrophe uniforms. She wove through the moving bodies of her comrades, not slackening speed, took a sharp right into the lab's hallway, twisted and dodged through an unexpectedly dense knot of people just *standing* there, got clear—and stumbled, hands over her eyes.

"Aiee!"

The headache was a knife, buried to the hilt in her forehead. Her knees hit the floor, the jar snapping her teeth shut on her tongue, but that pain was lost inside the greater agony in her head. She sobbed, fumbling for the simple mind-relaxing exercise that was the first thing taught anyone who aspired to be a scout.

She crouched there for a lifetime, finding the pattern and losing it; and beginning again, with forced, frantic patience. Finally, she found the concentration necessary, ran the sequence from beginning to end, felt the agony recede—sufficiently.

Shaking, she pushed herself to her feet and faced the open door of the lab.

It was then she remembered the stasis box and the madcap young tech's inclination toward explosives.

"Gods, gods, gods . . ." She staggered, straightened and walked, knees rubbery, vision white at the edges—walked down the hall, through the open door.

The main room was trim as always, beakers and culture-plates washed and racked by size; tweezers, blades, droppers and other hand tools of a lab tech's trade hung neatly above each workbench. Montet went down the silent, orderly aisles, past the last workbench, where someone had started a flame on the burner and decanted some liquid into a beaker before discovering that everything was not quite as it should be and slipping out to call Security.

Montet paused to turn the flame down. Her head ached horribly, and her stomach was turning queasy. All praise to the gods of study, who had conspired to make her miss the mid-day meal.

The door to the secondary workroom was closed, and refused to open to her palmprint.

Montet reached into her utility belt, pulled out a flat thin square. The edges were firm enough to grip; the center viscous. Carefully, she pressed the jellified center over the lockplate's sensor, and waited.

For a moment—two—nothing happened, then there was a soft *click* and a space showed between the edge of the door and the frame.

Montet stepped aside, lay the spent jelly on the workbench behind her, got her fingers in the slender space and pushed. The door eased back, silent on well-maintained tracks. When the gap was wide enough, she slipped inside.

The room was dim, the air cool to the point of discomfort. Montet squinted, fighting her own chancy vision and the murkiness around her.

There: a dark blot near the center of the room, which could only be a stasis box. Montet moved forward, through air that seemed to thicken with each step. Automatically, her hand quested along her utility belt, locating the pin-light by touch. She slipped it out of its loop, touched the trigger—and swore.

The stasis box lay on its side in the beam, lid hanging open. Empty.

Montet swallowed another curse. In the silence, someone moaned.

Beam before her, she went toward the sound, and found the charmingly demented lab tech huddled on the floor next to the further wall, his arms folded over his head.

She started toward him, checked and swung the beam wide.

The thing, whatever it was, was barely a dozen steps away, banked by many small boxes of the kind used to contain the explosive trimplix. The detonation of a single container of trimplix could hole a spaceship, and here were twelves of twelves of them, stacked every-which-way against the thing . . .

"Kill it," the tech moaned behind her. "Trigger the trimplix. Make it *stop*."

Carefully, Montet put her light on the floor. Carefully, she went out to the main room, drew a fresh stasis box from stores and carried it back into the dimness. The tech had not moved, except perhaps to draw closer round himself.

It was nerve-wracking work to set the boxes of trimplix, gently, aside, until she could get in close enough to grab the thing and heave it into the box. It hit bottom with a thump, and she slammed the lid down as if it were a live thing and likely to come bounding back out at her.

That done, she leaned over, gagging, then forced herself up and went over to the intercom to sound the all-clear.

PANOPELE SETTLED HER feet in the cool, dewy grass; filled her lungs with sweet midnight air; felt the power coalesce and burn in her belly, waking the twins, Joy and Terror. Again, she drank the sweet, dark air, lungs expanding painfully; then raised her face to the firmament, opened her mouth—and sang.

Amplified by Naratha's Will, the song rose to the star-lanes, questing, questioning, challenging. Transported by the song, the essence of Panopele, Voice of Naratha, rose likewise to the star-lanes, broadening, blossoming, listening.

Attended by four of the elder novices, feet comforted by the cool, dewy grass, strong toes holding tight to the soil of Aelysia, the body of Panopele sang the Cycle down. Two of the attendant novices wept to hear her; two of the novices danced. The body of Panopele breathed and sang; sang and breathed. And sang.

Out among the star-lanes, enormous and a-quiver with every note of the song, Panopele listened, and heard no discord. Expanding even further, she opened what might be called her eyes, looked out along the scintillant fields of life and saw—a blot.

Faint it was, vastly distant from the planet where her body stood and sang, toes comfortably gripping the soil— and unmistakable in its menace. Panopele strained to see—to hear—more clearly, hearing—or imagining she heard—the faintest note of discord; the barest whisper of malice.

Far below and laboring, her body sang on, voice sweeping out in pure waves of passion. The two novices who danced spun like mad things, sweat soaking their robes. The two who wept fell to their knees and struck their heads against the earth.

Panopele strained, stretching toward the edge of the song, the limit of Naratha's Will. The blot shimmered, growing; the malice of its answering song all at once plain.

Far below, the body of Panopele gasped, interrupting the song. The scintillance of the star-lanes paled into a blur; there was a rush of sound, un-song-like, and Panopele was joltingly aware of cold feet, laboring lungs, the drumbeat of her heart. Her throat hurt, and she was thirsty.

A warm cloak was draped across her shoulders, clasped across her throat. Warm hands pressed her down into the wide seat of the ancient wooden Singer's Chair. In her left ear the novice Fanor murmured, "I have water, Voice. Will you drink?"

Drink she would and drink she did, the cool water a joy.

"Blessings on you," she rasped and lay her left hand over his heart in Naratha's full benediction. Fanor was one of the two who wept in the song.

"Voice." He looked away, as he always did, embarrassed by her notice.

"Will you rest here, Voice? Or return to temple?" That was Lietta, who danced, and was doubtless herself in need of rest.

Truth told, rest was what Panopele wanted. She was weary; drained, as the song sometimes drained one; and dismayed in her heart. She wanted to sleep, here and now among the dewy evening. To sleep and awake believing that the blot she had detected was no more than a woman's fallible imagining.

The Voice of Naratha is not allowed the luxury of self-deceit. And the blot had been growing larger.

Weary, Panopele placed her hands on the carven arms of the chair that dwarfed all present but herself and gathered her strength. Her eyes sought the blue star Alyedon: the blot approached from that direction. That knowledge fed her strength and resolve. Slowly she leaned forward and, as the chair creaked with her efforts, pushed herself onto her feet.

"Let us return," she said to those who served her.

Lietta bowed, and picked up the chair. Fanor bent to gather the remaining water jugs; Panopele stopped him with a gesture.

"One approaches," she told him. "You are swiftest. Run ahead, and be ready to offer welcome."

One glance he dared, full into her eyes, then passed the jug he held to Darl and ran away across the starlit grass.

"So." Panopele motioned and Zan stepped forward to offer an arm, her face still wet with tears.

"My willing support, Voice," she said, as ritual demanded, though her own voice was soft and troubled.

"Blessings on you," Panopele replied, and proceeded across the grass in Fanor's wake, leaning heavily upon the arm of her escort.

THERE WAS OF COURSE nothing resembling a spaceport on-world, and the only reason the place had escaped Interdiction, in Montet's opinion, was that no scout had yet penetrated this far into the benighted outback of the galaxy.

That the gentle agrarian planet below her could not possibly contain the technology necessary to unravel the puzzle of the thing sealed and seething in its stasis box, failed to delight her. Even the knowledge that she had deciphered legend with such skill that she had actually raised a planet at the coordinates she had half-intuited did not warm her.

Frowning, omnipresent ache centered over her eyes, Montet brought the scout ship down. Her orbital scans had identified two large clusters of life and industry—cities, perhaps—and a third, smaller, cluster, which nonetheless put forth more energy than either of its larger cousins.

Likely, it was a manufactory of some kind, Montet thought, and home of such technology as the planet might muster. She made it her first target, by no means inclined to believe it her last.

She came to ground in a gold and green field a short distance from her target. She tended her utility belt while the hull cooled, then rolled out into a crisp, clear morning.

The target was just ahead, on the far side of a slight rise. Montet swung into a walk, the grass parting silently before her. She drew a deep lungful of fragrant air, verifying her scan's description of an atmosphere slightly lower in oxygen than Liad's. Checking her stride, she bounced, verifying the scan's assertion of a gravity field somewhat lighter than that generated by the homeworld.

Topping the rise, she looked down at the target, which was not a manufactory at all, but only a large building, and various outbuildings, clustered companionably together. To her right hand, fields were laid out. To her left, the grassland continued until it met a line of silvery trees, brilliant in the brilliant day.

And of the source of the energy reported by her scans, there was no sign whatsoever.

Montet sighed, gustily. Legend.

She went down the hill. Eventually, she came upon a path, which she followed until it abandoned her on the threshold of the larger building.

Here she hesitated, every scout nerve a-tingle, for this *should* be a Forbidden World, socially and technologically unprepared for the knowledge-stress that came riding in on the leather-clad shoulders of a scout. She had no *business* walking up to the front door of the local hospital, library, temple, or who-knew-what, no matter how desperate her difficulty. There was no one here who was the equal— who was the master of the thing in her ship's hold. How could there be? She hovered on the edge of doing damage past counting. Better to return to her ship, quickly; rise to orbit and get about setting the warning beacons.

. . . and yet, the legends, she thought—and then all indecision was swept away, for the plain white wall she faced showed a crack, then a doorway, framing a man. His pale robe was rumpled, wet and stained with grass. His hair was dark and braided below his shoulders; the skin of his face and his hands were brown. His feet, beneath the stained, wet hem, were bare.

He was taller than she, and strongly built. She could not guess his age, beyond placing him in that nebulous region called "adult."

He spoke; his voice was soft, his tone respectful. The language was tantalizingly close to a tongue she knew.

"God's day to you," she said, speaking slowly and plainly in that language. She showed her empty hands at waist level, palm up. "Has the house any comfort for a stranger?"

Surprise showed at the edges of the man's face. His hands rose, tracing a stylized pattern in the air at the height of his heart.

"May Naratha's Song fill your heart," he said, spacing his words as she had hers. It was not quite, Montet heard, the tongue she knew, but 'twould suffice.

"Naratha foretold your coming," the man continued. "The Voice will speak with you." He paused, hands moving through another pattern. "Of comfort, I cannot promise, stranger. I hear a dark chanting upon the air."

Well he might hear just that, Montet thought grimly; especially if he were a Healer-analog. Carefully, she inclined her head to the doorkeeper.

"Gladly will I speak with the Voice of Naratha," she said.

The man turned and perforce she followed him, inside and across a wide, stone-floored hall to another plain white wall. He lay his hand against the wall and once again a door appeared. He stood aside, hands shaping the air.

"The Voice awaits you."

Montet squared her shoulders and walked forward.

The room, like the hall, was brightly lit, the shine of light along the white walls and floor adding to the misery of her headache. Deliberately, she used the scout's mental relaxation drill and felt the headache inch, grudgingly, back. Montet sighed and blinked the room into focus.

"Be welcome into the House of Naratha." The voice was deep, resonant, and achingly melodic, the words spaced so that they were instantly intelligible.

Montet turned, finding the speaker standing near a niche in the left-most wall.

The lady was tall and on a scale to dwarf the sturdy doorkeeper; a woman of abundance, shoulders proud and face serene. Her robe was divided vertically in half—one side white, one side black—each side as wide as Montet entire. Her hair was black, showing gray like stars in the vasty deepness of space. Her face was like a moon, glowing; her eyes were dark and sightful. She raised a hand and sketched a sign before her, the motion given meaning by the weight of her palm against the air.

"I am the Voice of Naratha. Say your name, Seeker."

Instinctively, Montet bowed. One *would* bow, to such a lady as this—and one would not dare lie.

"I am Montet sig'Norba," she said, hearing her own voice thin and reedy in comparison with the other's rich tones.

"Come forward, Montet sig'Norba."

Forward she went, until she stood her own short arm's reach from the Voice. She looked up and met the gaze of far-seeing black eyes.

"Yes," the Voice said after a long pause. "You bear the wounds we have been taught to look for."

Montet blinked. "Wounds?"

"Here," said the Voice and lay her massive palm against Montet's forehead, directly on the spot centered just above her eyes, where the pain had lived for six long relumma.

The Voice's palm was warm and soft. Montet closed her eyes as heat spread up and over her scalp, soothing and—she opened her eyes in consternation.

The headache was gone.

The Voice was a Healer, then. Though the Healers on Liad had not been able to ease her pain.

"You have that which belongs to Naratha," the Voice said, removing her hand. "You may take me to it."

Montet bowed once more. "Lady, that which I carry is . . ." she grappled briefly with the idiom of the language she spoke, hoping it approximated the Voice's nearly enough for sense, and not too nearly for insult.

"What I carry is . . . accursed of God. It vibrates evil, and seeks destruction—even unto its own destruction. It is—I brought it before a . . . priestess of my own kind and its vibrations all but overcame her skill."

The Voice snorted. "A minor priestess, I judge. Still, she did well, if you come to me at her word."

"Lady, her word was to make all haste to fling the monster into a sun."

"No!" The single syllable resonated deep in Montet's chest, informing, for a moment, the very rhythm of her heartbeat.

"No," repeated the Voice, quieter. "To follow such a course would be to grant its every desire. To the despair of all things living."

"What *is* it?" Montet heard herself blurt.

The Voice bowed her head. "It is the Shadow of Naratha. For every great good throws a shadow, which is, in its nature, great evil."

Raising her head, she took a breath and began, softly, to chant. "Of all who fought, it was Naratha who prevailed against the Enemy. Prevailed, and drove the Enemy into the back beyond of space, from whence it has never again ventured. The shadows of Naratha's triumph, as terrible as the Enemy's defeat was glorious, roam the firmament still, destroying, for that is what they do." The Voice paused. The chant vibrated against the pure white walls for a moment, then stopped.

This, Montet thought, was the language of legend—hyperbole. Yet the woman before her did not seem a fanatic, living in a smoky dream of reality. This woman was alive, intelligent—and infinitely sorrowful.

"Voices were trained," the Voice was now calmly factual, "to counteract the vibration of evil. We were chosen to sing, to hold against and—equalize— what slighter folk cannot encompass. We were many, once. Now I am one. Naratha grant that the equation is exact."

Montet stared. She was a Liaden and accustomed to the demands of Balance. But this—

"You will die? But by your own saying it wants just that!"

The Voice smiled. "I will not die, nor will it want destruction when the song is through." She tipped her massive head, hair rippling, black-and-gray, across her proud shoulders.

"Those who travel between the stars see many wonders. I am the last Voice of Naratha. I exact a price, star-stranger."

Balance, clear enough. Montet bowed her head. "Say on."

"You will stand with me while I sing this monster down. You will watch and you will remember. Perhaps you have devices that record sight and sound. If you do, use them. When it is done, bring the news to Lietta, First Novice, she who would have been Voice. Say to her that you are under geas to study in our library. When you have studied, I require you to return to the stars, to discover what has happened—to the rest of us." She paused.

"You will bring what you find to this outpost. You will also initiate your fellow star-travelers into the mysteries of Naratha's Discord." The wonderful voice faltered and Montet bent her head.

"In the event," she said, softly, "that the equation is not— entirely—precise." She straightened. "I accept your Balance."

"So," said the Voice. "Take me now to that which is mine."

THE VOICE STOOD, humming, while Montet dragged the stasis box out, unsealed it and flipped open the lid. At a sign from the other woman, she tipped the box sideways, and the thing, whatever it was, rolled out onto the grass, buzzing angrily.

"I hear you, Discord," the Voice murmured, and raised her hand to sign.

Montet dropped back, triggering the three recorders with a touch to her utility belt.

The Voice began to sing.

A phrase only, though the beauty of it pierced Montet heart and soul.

The phrase ended and the space where it had hung was filled with the familiar malice of the black thing's song.

Serene, the Voice heard the answer out, then sang again, passion flowing forth like flame.

Again, the thing answered, snarling in the space between

Montet's ears. She gasped and looked to the Voice, but her face was as smooth and untroubled as glass.

Once more, the woman raised her voice, and it seemed to Montet that the air was richer, the grassland breeze fresher, than it had been a moment before.

This time, the thing did not allow her to finish, but vibrated in earnest. Montet shrieked at the agony in her joints and fell to her knees, staring up at the Voice, who sang on, weaving around and through the malice; stretching, reshaping, *reprogramming*, Montet thought, just before her vision grayed and she could see no longer.

She could hear, though, even after the pain had flattened her face down in the grass. The song went on, never faltering, never heeding the heat that Montet felt rising from the brittling grass, never straining, despite the taint in the once clean air.

The Voice hit a note, high, true and sweet. Montet's vision cleared. The Voice stood, legs braced, face turned toward the sky, her mighty throat corded with effort. The note continued, impossibly pure, soaring, passionate, irrefutable. There was only that note, that truth—nothing more—in all the galaxy.

Montet took a breath and discovered that her lungs no longer burned. She moved an arm and discovered that she could rise.

The Voice sang on, and the day was brilliant, perfect, beyond perfect, into godlike, and the Voice herself was beauty incarnate, singing, singing, fading, becoming one with the sunlight, the grassland and the breeze.

Abruptly, there was silence, and Montet stood alone in the grass near her ship, hard by an empty stasis box.

Of the Voice of Naratha—of Naratha's Shadow—there was no sign at all.

✧ Heirloom ✧

HE WOKE, PANTING, out of a snare of dreams in which he over and over ran to succor a child, hideously suspended over a precipice, the slender branch clutched in terrified small fingers bending toward break beneath the slight weight—

While he ran—ran at the top of his speed. And arrived, over and over, full seconds after the branch gave way and the tiny body plummeted down . . .

He opened his eyes—not too far—and swallowed as the dim light assaulted him. Lashes drooping, he took careful stock.

The dream—it had somehow become *the dream* of late it seemed—was both frequent and bothersome enough that he'd considered once or twice taking it to the Healers.

On other mornings, those not quite so fraught with physical complaints, his considerations had always led him to reject the notion that the dream was prophetic, for hadn't he been tested by the *dramliz*, several times over, at the order of the Delm-in-Keeping as well as at the order of his mother? And the dream never gave face to child, nor location to tree or cliff . . .

The *dramliz* tests were remarkably similar to the piloting tests—somehow he always managed to fail without knowing exactly what it was expected of him. Of course the wizards claimed they *weren't* expecting anything of him, but neither his mother nor anyone else seemed pleased by the results—not fast enough for pilot, nor possessed of whatever *some*thing the *dramliz* probed for—

Well, and he had long ago understood that neither the clan's ships nor the clan's allies among the Healers or the *dramliz* would provide his sustenance, and he had begun casting about for what he could do to support himself, for he was a young man, holding in full measure all the stubborn pride of his House. He would take not a dex from the clan that could not use him. His quartershares could accumulate in his account until the cantra overran the bank and flowed down the streets of Solcintra.

So he had cast about. He could shoot, of course, but one could scarcely make a living as a tournament shooter. Uncle Daav's happy experiment of giving him a gun and target practice at Tey Dor's had brought him close to the gaming set, who had no qualms about dealing with someone not a pilot, or not able to tell the future through true prophecy . . .

Early last evening, however, he had a moment of prophecy. It came when he overheard his mother speaking with Guayar Himself. It seemed that Guayar knew a certain house which had need of one well-placed, and well-taught, and well-versed in the Code, and able to travel with a group of children, teaching as well as protecting. She'd suggested that she knew of *just* such a person.

Travel with *children*?

He had been on his way out, intending to stop at the parlor only long enough to take graceful leave of his parent and exchange pleasantries with her guest. Rag-mannered though it was, he allowed himself to forgo these duties and instead left immediately by a discreet exit that did not require him to pass the occupied room.

Once outside, he had gone, not to Tey Dor's, which had been his first, and perhaps best, inclination, but to a minor establishment which catered to the aspiring gamester. There he had accepted most of the proffered beverages, which was not his habit.

Now, his head hurt abominably, of course, and his stomach was uneasy, though not quite in revolt. Mixed fortune, there. He supposed he should rise, shower and prepare himself to meet the dubious pleasures of the day. After all, it wasn't as if he had never been drunk before.

In truth, he was rarely drunk, being a young man of fastidious nature. Certainly, he was *never* drunk while gaming, and last night's losses at the piket table were ample illustration of his reasons, thank you.

Sighing, he raised his hands and scrubbed them, none-too-gently, over his face, relishing the friction.

Gods, what a performance! He was entirely disgusted with himself, and not the most for his losses at cards. At least he had retained sense enough not to enter the shooting contest proposed by pin'Weltir!

At least—he thought he had. His memory of the later evening was, he discovered to his chagrin, rather . . . spotty.

His stomach clenched, and he took a deeper breath than he wanted—and another—forcing himself to lie calmly, to wait for the memories to rise . . . There.

He *had* turned pin'Weltir down, and when the man insisted, he had refused even more forcefully—by claiming his cloak and calling for a cab. He remembered that, yes. Too, he remembered entering the cab, and the driver asking for his direction. He remembered saying, "Home," an idiotic reply emblematic of his state, and the driver asking again, doggedly patient, as if she dealt with drunken lordlings every night—which, he thought now, in the discomfort of his bed, she might very well.

After that, he remembered nothing, though he supposed he must have managed to give her the direction of his mother's house—and if his mother had been late at her studies and had observed his return—

He wondered if people died of hangovers, and, if so, how he might manage it.

A spike of red pain shot through his head and he twisted in the bed, gagging, eyes snapping open to behold—

Not the formal bedchamber he occupied in his mother's house, but the badly shaped, sloped ceiling chamber where he had spent many peaceful childhood nights.

Despite the headache, Pat Rin smiled. Drunk into idiocy he may have been, but his heart had known the direction of home.

✧✧✧

SOME WHILE LATER, showered and having taken an analgesic against the headache, he glanced at last night's bedraggled finery, flung helter-skelter on the simple, hand-tied rug. He bit his lip, ashamed of this further untidy evidence of his debauch, then gathered it all up and took it into the 'fresher, where he bundled the lot into the valet to be cleaned and pressed.

Returning to his bedroom, he paused at the old wooden wardrobe, coaxed open the sticky door and was very shortly thereafter dressed in a pair of sturdy work pants and a soft, shapeless shirt.

Closing the wardrobe, he considered himself in the thin mirror: a slender young man, dark of hair and eye, cheekbones high, brows straight, chin pointed, mouth stern. In his old clothes, he thought he looked a laborer, or a dockworker, or a pilot at leave—then he glanced down at his long, well-kept hands and sighed.

Looking back to the mirror, he frowned at the mass of wet hair snarled across his shoulders. The *torentia* was all the kick this season, and Pat Rin yos'Phelium Clan Korval, apprentice at play, naturally wore his hair so, spending as much as an hour a day combing and curling the thick, unruly stuff into the long, artful chaos fashion demanded.

But not today. Today, he turned 'round, snatched a comb up from the low bureau and dragged it ruthlessly through the tangled mass until it hung, sodden and straight. Putting the comb aside, he raised both hands, pulled his hair sharply back, holding the tail in one hand while he rummaged atop the bureau, finally bringing up a simple wooden hair ring, which he snapped into place.

The lad in the mirror presented a more austere face now, without the fall of hair to soften it. Indeed, he might have been said to be quite fox-faced, were it not the general policy in the circles in which he lately moved that Pat Rin yos'Phelium was comely.

Poppycock, of course, and tiring, too. Almost as tiring as Cousin Er Thom insisting upon endless repetitions of tests taken and proved—

No.

He would not think of Cousin Er Thom—of *Korval-pernard'i.*

And he assuredly would not think of tests. In fact, he would go downstairs to tell Luken that he was to house.

"GOOD MORNING, boy-dear!" Luken said, looking up with a smile. The manifest he had been studying lay on the tabletop amidst the genteel ruins of a frugal breakfast, the Tree-and-Dragon— Korval's seal—stamped in the top left corner of the page.

Despite everything, Pat Rin smiled, and bowed, gently, hand over his heart.

"Good morning, Father," he replied, soft in the mode between kin. "I trust I find you well?"

"Well enough, well enough!" His fosterfather waved a ringless hand toward the sideboard. "There's tea, child, and the usual. Have what you will and then sit and tell me your news."

His news? Pat Rin thought bitterly. He turned to the sideboard, taking a deep breath. Luken, alone of all his relatives, could be trusted to honestly care for Pat Rin's news, and to take no joy in his failures.

He poured himself a glass of tea, that being what he thought he might coax his stomach to accommodate, and returned to the table, taking his usual seat across from Luken, there in the windowed alcove. Outside, the sky shone brilliant, the sun fully risen. Odd to find Luken so late over breakfast, dawn-rising creature that he was.

"Are you *quite* well?" Pat Rin asked, around a prick of panic. "I had looked to find you in the warehouse . . ."

Luken chuckled. "Had you arisen an hour earlier, you would have found me precisely in the warehouse," he said. "What you see here is a second cup of tea, to aid me in puzzling out just what it is that Er Thom means me to do with these." He picked up the manifest and rattled it gently before dropping it again to the table.

In addition to his *melant'i* as Korval-in-trust, Er Thom yos'Galan wore a master trader's ring. Interesting goods, therefore, had a way of coming into his hand, and it had long been his habit to send the more interesting and exotic textiles to Luken's attention.

Pat Rin assayed a tiny sip of tea, eyeing the manifest half-heartedly. "Sell them?" he murmured, that being the most common outcome of rugs sent by Er Thom, though two, to Pat Rin's knowledge, were on display in museums, and one covered the white stone floor of the Temple of Valiatra, at the edge of the Festival grounds.

"Not these, I think," Luken said picking up his tea glass. "It seems that the clan is divesting itself of the Southern House and the place is being emptied—including the back attics, which I daresay is where these were found."

Korval was selling the Southern House? Not a heartbeat too soon, in Pat Rin's opinion. He had been to the place once, and had found it dismal. Nor was he alone in his assessment. While most of Korval's houses enjoyed more-or-less steady tenancy, the Southern House most often sat empty, undisturbed by even the housekeeper, who had his own quarters in another building on the property.

"Perhaps Cousin Er Thom wants a catalog made?" Pat Rin offered, taking another cautious sip of tea. Though rugs Luken dismissed as back-attic fare hardly seemed likely candidates for cataloging and preservation.

"He doesn't write. Only that the house is being cleared, and that these might interest me." Luken sipped his tea, and moved a dismissive hand. "But, enough of that. *Your* news, boy-dear—all of it! I haven't seen you this age. Catch me up, do."

It hadn't quite been an age, the two of them having dined together only a twelveday ago, though there was, after all, the news which was no news at all . . .

Pat Rin looked down into his glass, then forced himself to raise his head and meet Luken's gentle gray eyes.

"*Korval-pernard'i* bade me take the test again, yesterday." He felt his face tighten and fought an impulse to look away from Luken's face. "I failed, of course."

"Of course," his fosterfather murmured, entirely without irony, his expression one of grave interest.

"I don't know why," Pat Rin said, after a moment, "I can't be left in peace. How many times must I fail before they will understand that I am *not* a pilot, nor ever will be?" He took a breath, and did glance down, his eye snagging on the manifest, the upside down Tree-and-Dragon, sigil of the clan in which he was second of two freaks, his mother being the first. "If I am asked to take the test again, I will not," he stated, and raised his glass decisively.

"Well," Luken said after a moment. "Certainly it must be tedious to be asked to take the same test repeatedly, especially when it is so distressful for you, boy-dear. But to speak of turning your face aside from the word of *Korval-pernard'i*—that won't do at all. Husbanding the clan's pilots falls squarely within his duty—and determining who might be a pilot, as well. He doesn't send you to the testing chamber only to plague you, child. If you were feeling more the thing, you'd see that."

It was gently said, but Pat Rin felt the rebuke keenly. Yet Luken, as nearly all the rest of his kin, was a pilot. Granted, a mere third class, and there had lately been a time when he would have given all of his most valued possessions, had he only been given in exchange a license admitting that Pat Rin yos'Phelium was a pilot, third class.

He told himself he didn't care; that five failures would teach *him* the lesson Cousin Er Thom refused to learn.

He told himself that.

"Child?" murmured Luken.

Pat Rin looked up and smiled, as best as he was able around the headache.

"I hope I didn't disturb your rest when I came in last night," he said softly.

Luken moved his shoulders. "In fact, I had been late in the showroom, and was just coming up myself when you were dispatched from your cab."

Blast. He didn't remember that. Not at all.

"I'm afraid that I was a trifle disguised, last night," he said, around a jolt of self-revulsion.

"A trifle," Luken allowed. "I guided you to your room, we said our sleepwells and I retired."

None of it. Pat Rin bit his lip.

"I made rather a fool of myself last night," he said. "Not only did I fall into my cups, but then I was idiot enough to play cards—and lost most wonderfully, as you might expect."

"Ah." Luken finished off his tea and put the glass aside. "You also told me last night, as we were negotiating the stairway, that you had come away early because a certain—pin'Weltir, I believe?—had become boorish in his insistence that you shoot against him, then and there. Which is not, perhaps, entirely idiot."

He had already determined that for himself, but a part of him was eased, that Luken thought so, too.

"Some things," he admitted, "I did correctly." He tipped his head, then, and shot a quick glance into Luken's face, where he found the gray eyes attentive

"Do you care, father? The trade I have set myself to learn, that is."

Luken spread his hands. "Why should I care? From all I understand, it's a difficult study you undertake in order to ascend the heights of a profession which is exhilarating and not without its moments of risk." He smiled. "I would expect, of course, that you will rise to become a master, if masters of the game there be."

"Not—by that name," Pat Rin said, thinking of those who had undertaken his education. "But, yes. There are masters."

"And you aspire to stand among them?"

Well of course he did. Who of Korval, present or past, had not sought to stand among the masters of whatever profession or avocation they embraced? Certainly not Luken.

"Yes," he said. "I do."

"It is well, then," his fosterfather judged. "That you will mind your *melant'i* and keep the honor of your House pure, I have no need to ask."

He paused for a moment, reaching absently to his empty glass, and letting his hand fall with a slight sigh. Pat Rin got up, bore the glass to the sideboard, refilled it and brought it back.

"Gently done," Luken murmured, his thoughts clearly somewhere else. "My thanks."

"It is my pleasure to serve you, Father."

"Sweet lad." He had a sip from the refilled glass and looked up.

"I wonder if you've given thought to setting up your own establishment," he said. "It occurs to me that bin'Flora has a townhouse for lease in a location near the High Port."

Most of Solcintra's gambling houses were located at the High-

Port. There were several residential streets just beyond the gate, none of them unsavory, though one or two not as . . . fashionable . . . as they might be.

bin'Flora traded in textile—bolt goods more usually than rugs—and the present master of the house, one Sisilli, and Luken had enjoyed a friendly rivalry for possibly more years than Pat Rin had been alive. Therefore, it was likely that the house in question was on—

"Nasingtale Alley," Luken murmured. "Third house on the right, as you walk out from the High-Port."

Pat Rin sipped tea. "Rents on Nasingtale Alley are certainly above my touch," he said to Luken. "I am yet a student."

"Yet an able student, for that," Luken said. "And the rent may not be . . . quite ruinous."

"Ah." He considered the face across from him thoughtfully. "*Shall* I set up my own establishment, Father?"

Luken sighed. "It's a prying old man, to be sure," he said. "But I will tell you what is in my heart, boy-dear.

"Firstly, and true enough, I worry about you, walking about the port with large amounts of coin on you." He raised a hand. "I know your reputation with the small arms, but it would be best not to employ them."

"I agree," Pat Rin murmured, and Luken inclined his head.

"Too, it makes sense to hold a base near your daily business, and this house bin'Flora offers is certainly that.

"And lastly . . ." His voice faded and he glanced aside.

Pat Rin felt his stomach clench.

"You know your mother and I have no love lost between us," Luken said slowly, "despite that which the Code tells us is due to kin. And you know that, as a youngling, you were moved from your mother's care into mine, by the word of the delm."

The delm. That would have been Daav yos'Phelium, his mother's brother, gone from the clan these years, on a mission of Balance. There had been no love lost between his mother and her brother, either, Pat Rin knew, though as a child he had adored his tall, easy uncle.

"I confess that I was a bit puzzled when you went to live with your mother, after your schooling was done." He raised a hand. "I don't ask your reasons, boy-dear, though I know you had them. Nor will I speak ill of your mother to you. I will say that, drawing on my knowledge of you—and of her—perhaps you might consider if you would be more . . . relaxed in your own small establishment."

That he certainly would be, Pat Rin thought, for his mother was a high stickler and kept stringent Code. He supposed that was inevitable, given her reputation as Liad's foremost scholar of and expert on the Code. She also held rank among Solcintra's leading hosts, and it was for that reason that Pat Rin, returning home from university and fixed upon the trade that he would follow, had taken up residence with his parent, rather than moving back into his comfortable place with Luken.

Kareen yos'Phelium could—and did, for who knew better what was due the heir of a woman of her impeccable lineage and *melant'i?*—launch him into society. Luken cared little for society, though his clientele came largely from the High Houses. And Pat Rin had needed the final polish and the ties to the High which only his mother could give him.

He wondered, here and now, sitting in Luken's sunny alcove, if he would have chosen differently, had he known the cost beforehand. For life with his mother was not easy, or comfortable, though he was surrounded by every luxury. He was required to live to his mother's standard, and to study the Code until he was very nearly an expert himself. He studied other things, as well, so that he would have a store of graceful conversation available; he attended all the fashionable plays; patronized his mother's excellent tailor; wore gems of the first water; and was never seen at a stand.

The one . . . relaxation he allowed himself was target practice every other morning, on the lifetime membership to Tey Dor's Club which Uncle Daav had given to him.

Of course, he saw now—had seen last evening with sudden clarity—that his mother had never believed his assertions that he intended to make his way without recourse to the funds of the Clan. She had heard him, for she was a courteous listener, precisely as the Code instructed—heard him, but did not believe. And he had never quite seen that there would need be an *after* to his plan.

"Pat Rin?" Luken murmured.

He blinked back into now, and inclined his head.

"You understand," he said slowly. "That I attempt to . . . produce a certain, and very specific, affect. Produce, and sustain it."

Luken smiled. "I am not quite an idiot, boy-dear."

"Of course not," he murmured, more than half-caught in his calculations. "So, the question before me now is whether the affect will remain fixed, should I retire to my own establishment."

"I should think," Luken said, "that the key would be not to retire, but to continue as you have been, only from the comfort of a bachelor's dig."

A townhouse on Nasingtale Alley could scarcely be called a "dig"—and Luken, as he so often was, despite one's mother's contention that the rug merchant was no more nor less than a block—Luken was right. Pat Rin had only to carry on as he was. The invitations would continue to arrive—and he might even host a small entertainment or two, himself. The gods knew, he had assisted with enough of his mother's entertainments to know how the thing was done.

"Please consider," Luken said carefully. "You are now well-known among the Houses. Your *melant'i* is your own, no matter that it in some measure reflects your mother's, and your clan's, as it must. But—it would hardly do for you to regularly best your mother's houseguests while you yourself sleep under her roof. Nor would it be best for you, seen among the elders of many a House as a biddable young man always at your mother's call, to have to rigorously make a point . . ."

Pat Rin grimaced at this description of himself, while allowing that, from the outside, it might appear thus.

". . .as I say, if you need to press an honest advantage across a table, it might be best if you do it first among the lesser members of the Houses until Lord Pat Rin is more fully known as himself. If being Lady Kareen's son is not your occupation, my boy, then having your own place will afford you both more flexibility in your evenings and more company in the mornings. I say this as one who was, alas, once young myself."

Seated, Pat Rin bowed the bow of apprentice to master.

"It might do," he said, and glanced to Luken's face. "If bin'Flora's rate is possible."

Luken smiled. "Please, know that there are two partners in every trade. The place would have been rented anytime the last two relumma were the matter simply one of cash flow. Not all would-be renters are High House, my boy. Nor," he said with sudden emphasis, "are all High House equally acceptable. Whatever the Code may teach.

"I will mention your interest to Sisilli," Luken concluded, and drank off the rest of his tea.

"As much as I enjoy your company, child, I am afraid that I must leave you for an appointment."

Pat Rin inclined his head, his gaze snagging on the manifest, lying forgotten on the table. He extended a slender hand and plucked the page up, running an eye trained by Master Merchant Luken bel'Tarda down the list of items.

"Shall I inventory these, while you are gone?" he asked Luken. "That will have to be done, whatever else Cousin Er Thom intends."

"So it will," Luken said, coming to his feet. "If you have the leisure, boy-dear, the work would be appreciated. You'll find the lot of them in the old private showing room. And also, since you will wish to have clear sight if not a clear head, I suggest you make use of some of the tea you will find there. It will have Terran wording on it—*McWhortle's Special Wake-Up Blend*—and it should be taken just as the directions instruct. Shall we plan on dining at Ongit's this evening?"

"I would enjoy that," he said truthfully. "Very much."

"Then that is what we shall do," Luken declared. "Until soon, my son."

"Until soon, Father," Pat Rin responded and rose to bow Luken to the door.

IT APPEARED THAT Luken had been correct in his assessment of the lot of rugs from the Southern House, as well as in his understanding of the utility of McWhortle's Special Wake-Up Blend.

The tea was surprisingly tasty for something avowedly of Terran extraction, and equally efficacious.

The rugs . . . He sighed. Not all of the pilots of Korval—put together!—knew what Luken did of rugs, and some had, alas, displayed an amazing lack of both color sense and fashion awareness. The first rug, indifferently rolled and protected by nothing more than a thin sheet of plastic, was synthetic. He threw it across the flat onto the show-zone, where the mass and size were automatically recorded—the overhead camera recorded detail, but really—there wasn't much to say for it. Machine stamped in a small, boring floral pattern, backed with nothing more than its own fibers, with a density on the low side, it might as well be sent as a donation to the Pilot's Fund used-goods outlet in Low Port.

Pat Rin dutifully entered these deficiencies into his clipboard, slotted the stylus, and touched a key. The clipboard hummed for a moment, printing, and a yellow inventory tag slid out of the side slot. Pat Rin picked up the stitch gun and stapled the tag to the corner of the rug, before rolling it, bagging it in a bel'Tarda-logo light-proof wrapper, and dragging the sorry specimen over to the storage bin which he had marked with Cousin Er Thom's number and the additional legend, "Southern House."

Straightening, feeling somewhat better for the tea and in fact much more clear-eyed—he looked suddenly to the shelf above the bin, where a long-haired white cat with excessively pink ears lounged, very much at her leisure. Likely she'd been there the while; that he hadn't noticed her was a further testament to his excesses of the evening before.

"Niki," Pat Rin murmured, extending a finger, but not quite touching the drowsing animal.

Her eyes slitted, then opened to full emerald glory. Yawning, she extended a pink-toed and frivolously befurred foot to wrap around his fingertip, her claws just pricking the surface of his skin.

Pat Rin smiled and used his free hand to rub the lady softly beneath her delicate chin. Niki's eyes went to slits again and her breathy purr filled the air between them. The claws withdrew from his captive finger and he let the freed member fall to his side, while moving his other hand to her ears. His exertions there were shortly rewarded with an increase in her audible pleasure, and he smiled again.

One's mother did not keep cats, or any other domestic creature, aside the occasional servant. It made for an oddly empty feel about the house, even when it was full with guests.

"Thank you," he whispered, giving her chin a last rub and stepping back. Niki squinted her eyes in a cat-smile, purring unabated.

Pat Rin turned back to his work.

The next rug was intriguingly and thickly wrapped in what must have been a local newspaper. He fussed the sheets off and found the rug rolled backing out, tied at intervals with what might have once been elegant hair-ribbons. He sat on his heels and smiled. This, he would examine last. It had good weight and somehow the smell of a proper rug—and would be his reward for doing a careful inventory of the rest of the obviously unsuitable specimens tumbled about them.

He used a utility blade to slit the plastic sealing the next rug, noting the ragged jute backing, and unrolled it onto the scale with a casual kick before bending to retrieve the clipboard.

The work was—comforting. Despite that Kareen yos'Phelium had declared that she would not have her heir made into a rug salesman—had in fact complained of him coming up with callused hands—Luken had trained him well, and he knew himself to be the master of the task he had set for himself. It could not be said that he completely shared his fosterfather's ecstatic enthusiasm for carpet, or his encyclopedic knowledge of their histories, but he owned to a fondness for the breed, and knew a certain pleasure in being once more among them.

The unrolled carpet was a geometric, hand-loomed in bronzes, browns and dark greens, with pale green fringe along the two short sides. It glistened in the light, inviting him to believe that it was silk. But he had seen the backing and was not taken in.

As counterfeits went, it was rather a good one. The traditional Arkuba pattern had been faithfully reproduced; the measurements precisely those to which all Arkuba carpets adhered, to the very length of the pale fringe and the vegetable-dyed thread. Alas, the luster which would, in the genuine article, be testimony to the silken threads that had gone into its manufacture, was in this case misleading. Rather than silk, the carpet before him had been woven with specially treated cotton thread.

A perfectly serviceable and attractive rug, really, setting aside for the moment those issues surrounding a counterfeit hallmark. Pat Rin merely hoped that the nameless ancestor who had purchased the thing had known it for what it was and had paid accordingly.

He entered his observations, tapped the stylus against the print button, and slid it into its slot while the clipboard hummed its tuneless tune and in the fullness of time extruded an inventory ticket which he stapled to the corner of the rug before bagging and dragging it over to the bin.

Niki was still on the shelf overhead, profoundly asleep. He smiled, but did not disturb her.

The protective plastic over the next carpet had been torn at some time—possibly as recently as the move from the Southern House to Luken's warehouses. Pat Rin slit what was left of the sheet, approving, as he did so, the plentitude of painstakingly tied knots along the carpet's underside, and the foundation of wool.

Once more, a kick sent the rug rolling out—and he sighed aloud. Insects had gotten in through the breached plastic. The wool in spots was eaten down to the backing, leaving the skeleton of a handsome rectilinear design he did not immediately recognize. No, this damage had not occurred in the warehouse, being both too extensive and too old.

Sighing yet again, he reached for the clipboard to record the loss—

"Cousin Luken?" The voice was clear and carrying—and unfortunately familiar.

Pat Rin closed his eyes, there where he rested on one knee beside the ruined rug, and wished fervently that she would overlook this room. There was little chance that she would, of course. His cousin Nova was nothing if not thorough. Unnaturally thorough, one might say.

"Cousin Luken!" she called again, her voice nearer this time.

Pat Rin opened his eyes, picked up the clipboard, fingered the stylus free and entered a description of the damage. The mechanism hummed and in due time a red tag emerged. He reached for the stitch gun—

"Oh, there you are, Cousin!" Nova said from the doorway at his back.

Amidst the sound of approaching light footsteps, Pat Rin stapled the red tag to a corner of the ruined rug.

"Father sent me to help you catalog the rugs from the—" She stopped, aware, so Pat Rin thought, that she had made an error.

Gently, he placed the stitch gun on the floor next to the clipboard, and turned his head slightly so that she could see the side of his face.

"Cousin Pat Rin!" she exclaimed, with a measure of astonishment that he found not particularly flattering.

He inclined his head. "Cousin Nova," he stated, with deliberate coolness. "What a surprise to find you here."

The instant the words left his lips, he wished them back. He had spent the last year and more deliberately honing his wit and his tongue until they were weapons as formidable as the palm pistol he carried in his sleeve. Surely, it was ill-done of him to loose those weapons on a child.

"Is Cousin Luken to house?" she asked stiffly.

He rose carefully to his feet and turned to face her.

Nova's twelfth Name Day had been celebrated only a relumma past, and already she showed warning of the beauty she would become. Her hair was gilt, her eyes amethyst, her carriage erect and unstrained. She had, so he heard, passed the preliminary testing for pilot-candidate, an unsurprising fact which had nonetheless woken a twist of bitterness in him.

Today found her dressed in sturdy shirt and trousers, well-scuffed boots on her feet, passkey clenched in one hand, and a glare on her face for the ill-tempered elder cousin—for which he blamed her not at all.

"Alas, one's fosterfather is away on an appointment," he said, moderating his tone with an effort. "May I be of service, Cousin?"

Her glare eased somewhat as she glanced about her.

"Father sends me to help Cousin Luken sort the carpets from the Southern House," she said tentatively. "However, I find you at that task."

It was not meant to be accusatory, he reminded himself forcefully. She was a child, with a child's grasp of nuance.

Though she had grasped the nuance of his greeting swiftly enough. He had the acquaintance of adults who would have not have taken his point so quickly—if at all.

So— "Cousin Er Thom had not written us to expect your arrival and assistance," he answered Nova, deliberately gentle. "I happened to be at liberty and took the work for my own."

She blinked at him, jewel-colored eyes frankly doubtful.

"You are aware, are you not," Pat Rin said, allowing himself an edge of irony, "that I am Luken's fosterling?"

"Ye-e-s-s," Nova agreed. "But Cousin Kareen—I heard her speaking with my father and she . . ." Here she hesitated, perhaps nonplused to discover herself admitting to listening at doors.

Pat Rin inclined his head. "One's mother was adamant that I not be trained as a rug merchant," he said smoothly. "Alas, by the time she recognized the danger, the damage had long been done."

Nova's straight, pale mouth twitched a little, as if she had suppressed a smile.

"Will you come into Cousin Luken's business?" she asked, which was not an unreasonable question, from a daughter of the trade Line. Still, Pat Rin felt his temper tighten, spoiling the easier air that had been flowing between them.

"I've gone into another trade, thank you," he said shortly, and swept his hand out, showing her the pile of rolled rugs waiting to be inventoried. "For all that, I am competent enough in this one."

He sighed, recalling his mother's plans for him, and shook the memory away.

"If you like, you may assist me," he murmured, and that was no more than the Code taught was due from kin to kin: Elders taught those junior to them, freely sharing what knowledge and skill they had, so that the clan continued, generation to generation, memory and talent intact.

Nova bowed, hastily. "I thank you, Cousin. Indeed, I would be pleased to assist you."

"That is well, then. The sooner we address the task, the sooner it will be done. Attend me, now."

He moved over to the pile and kicked a smallish roll out into the work area. Dropping to knee, he slit the plastic, revealing a plain gauze backing. A push unrolled it onto the scale, and Pat Rin looked up at Nova, standing hesitant where he had left her.

"Please," he said, "honor me with your opinion of this."

Slowly, she came forward, and knelt across from him, frowning down at the riot of woolen flowers that comprised the rug's design. She rubbed her palm across the surface, gingerly.

"Wool," she said, which was no grand deduction, and flipped up the edge near her knee. The gauze backing disconcerted her for a moment, then she returned to the face, using her fingers to press into and about the design.

"Hand-hooked," she said then, and was very likely correct, Pat Rin thought, but as it stood it was no more than a guess. He held up a hand.

"Hooked, certainly," he murmured. "Where do you find the proof for 'handmade?'"

Eagerly, she flipped back the edge, and pointed to the row of tiny, uneven stitches set into the gauze.

"Ah." He inclined his head. "I see that your conclusion is not unreasonable. However, it is wise to bear in mind that carpets are sometimes adjusted—fringe is added, or removed, backings are sewn on—or removed—holes are rewoven. Therefore, despite the fact that someone has clearly sewn the backing on by hand, the rug itself might yet have been made by machine. The preferred proofs are . . ."

He extended a hand and smoothed the wool petal of a particularly extravagant yellow flower, displaying a stitching of darker thread beneath.

. . . "Maker's mark."

Nova bit her lip.

"Or," Pat Rin continued, flipping the little rug entirely over with a practiced twist of his wrists. He put his palm flat on the backing and moved it slowly, as if he were stroking Niki. He motioned Nova to do the same—which she did, gingerly, and then somewhat firmer.

"What do you feel?" he asked.

"Knots," she replied. "So it *is* handmade—I was correct."

"It is handmade," he conceded, "and you were correct." He lifted a finger. "For the wrong reason."

She sighed, but, "I understand," was what she said.

"Good. If you will, of your goodness, hand me the clipboard, I will make that notation and then we may proceed with the rest of the inspection."

She picked up the clipboard in one hand and held it out to him over the rug. He took it, his thumb accidentally nudging the stylus out of its slot, sending it floorward in a glitter of silver—

Nova swept forward, her hand fairly blurring as she scooped the stylus out of the air, reversed it and held it out to him.

He blinked. A *child*, he thought, all of his bitterness rising . . .

Some part of it must have shown on his face. Nova hesitated, hand drooping.

"I was too fast, wasn't I?" she said, sounding curiously humble. "I do beg your pardon, Cousin. Father is trying to teach me better, but I fear I am sometimes forgetful."

"Teach you better?" Pat Rin repeated, and his voice was harsh in his own ears. "I thought speed was all, to those who would be pilots."

"Yes, but one mustn't be too fast," Nova said solemnly. "It won't do to frighten those who are not pilots—or to rush the instruments, when one is at the board."

He closed his eyes. Five times, since his eleventh name-day. Five times, he had tested for pilot and failed. Always, the tests found him too slow. Too slow—and this child, his cousin, must learn not to be *too fast*. He tried to decide if he most wished to laugh or to weep and in the end only opened his eyes again and took the stylus from her hand.

"My thanks," he murmured, and bent his head over the clipboard while he took his time making the initial entry.

"Now," he said when he could trust his voice for more than a few words. He looked over to Nova. "We must assess general condition, wear patterns, repairs, stains—that sort of thing. What say you?"

Seriously, she scrutinized the gauze backing, then turned the rug over, clumsily, to study the face, her hands chastely cupping her knees.

"Hands," Pat Rin murmured. "Use your hands."

He demonstrated, elegant fingers—ringless for this work—petting, gripping, pushing—his palms flowing about the top and bindings.

"Feel the nap. Is there a stiff spot which may be a stain invisible to the eye? Pull on the loops—do they hold or come loose? Smell the carpet—is it musty? Sour? All of these details are important."

She sent him one startled glance out of vivid purple eyes before bending forward, her right hand stroking and seeking. She bent her face closer—and sneezed.

"Dusty," she said.

He inclined his head.

She continued her inspection with that solemness which was characteristic of her, and at last sat back on her heels and looked at him across the rug.

"The threads are good, the stitches are firm. There is no staining visible to eye or to hand. The carpet is dusty, but fresh."

"Very good," he said, and plied the stylus once more.

When the yellow tag appeared, he handed it across to her.

"Use the stitch gun to staple the tag to the near corner."

He helped her wrestle the wrapper on it, and used his chin to point at the waiting carpets.

"Please choose our next subject and unroll it while I put this in its proper place."

She rose, a thing of pure, careless grace, and moved lithely to the pile. Pat Rin gritted his teeth and carried the little rug across to the bin.

Niki was sitting tall on the shelf. She blinked lazy green eyes at him as he stroked her breast.

Somewhat soothed, Pat Rin turned back to the work area, expecting to find the next specimen unrolled and awaiting inspection.

Indeed, a rug had been liberated from the pile, and he felt a momentary pang—she had chosen the one he had wanted to study himself. It displayed a promising underside, thick with knots. He sighed, then wondered about the delay.

Knife at her knee, Nova crouched over the roll, head bent above the single corner she had curled into the light. Her shoulders were rounded in an attitude of misery—or defiance.

"Unroll it!" he said, perhaps a little sharply, but Nova only knelt there.

Gods, what ailed the child? Pat Rin thought, irritably, and moved forward.

"Don't . . ." Nova moaned, "I *know* this rug!"

But that was nothing more than nonsense. Likely the thing had been away rolled in a dusty attic for a dozen dozen Standards . . .

He moved down the cylinder, pulling the ribbon ties rapidly.

"Nova, help me roll this out."

She crouched lower, fingers gripping her corner . . .

Pat Rin delivered a smart kick and the thing unrolled with alacrity, as if the carpet had been yearning for its freedom.

Beside him, cowering now, head even closer to the floor and the corner of carpet she clung to, Nova gasped.

He looked down at the top of her bright head, frowning. Nothing he knew of Nova encouraged him to believe that she was a malingerer. Nor was it possible to imagine Cousin Er Thom or his lady wife, Cousin Anne, tolerating this sort of missish behavior for anything longer than a heartbeat.

"Are you ill?" he asked. "Cousin?"

She shuddered, and raised her head as if it were a very great weight.

"No," she said on a rising note, as though she questioned her answer even as she gave it. "I . . .beg your pardon, Cousin. A passing—a passing stupidity." She rose, slowly and with a quarter of her previous grace. "Pray . . . do not regard it."

He considered her. Carpets woven of certain esoteric materials did sometimes collect ill humors in storage. It was doubtful that this rug, which he had already tentatively classified as a Tantara of some considerable age, woven with vegetable dyed zeesa-wool thread that wore like ship-steel, had collected anything more than a little must, if that.

He glanced from her pale face to the rug. Yes—certainly it was an older Tantara, a geometric in the ivory-and-deep-green combination which had been retired for a dozen dozen Standards, and in an absolutely enviable state of preservation, saving a stain on a wide section of the ivory-colored fringe.

Bending, he ran his hand over the nap near the stain—stiff fibers grazed his palm. Whatever the substance was, it had gotten into the rug, too, which meant that there would be more to repairing the damage than simply replacing the fringe. It was odd that the carpet had been rolled away without being cleaned—and unfortunate, too. Most stains could be eradicated, if treated when fresh. A stain which had set for dozens of years, perhaps—it might be impossible to entirely remove the mar.

"We will need the kit for this," he said briskly, straightening. "I'll fetch it while you do a preliminary inspection."

"Yes," she whispered, and he sent another frown into her pale face.

"Nova," he said, touching her hand. "Are you well?"

"Yes," she whispered again, and turned away to find the clipboard.

Irritated, he strode off to the supplies closet.

The diagnostic kit was hanging in its place on the peg-board wall. Despite this, Pat Rin did not immediately have it down and hurry back to the work area. The stained rug had languished for years without care. A few heartbeats more would do it no harm.

Leaning against the wall, he closed his eyes and took stock. The headache was the merest feeling of tightness behind his eyes, his stomach was empty, but unconcerned. In all, he had managed to come out of last evening's adventures in fairly good order. His present irritability was not, he knew, the result of overindulgence, but rather the presence of one of his pilot kin, innocent herself of any wrong-doing—and a poignant reminder of all that he was not. Nor ever would be.

"Be gentle with the child," he said to himself. "Did Luken show temper with you, thrust upon him unwarned and very likely unwanted?"

But, there. Luken was a gentle soul, and never showed temper, nor ever raised his voice, no matter how far he was provoked. He had other means of exacting Balance.

Pat Rin took another deep breath—and another. Opening his eyes, he could not say that he felt perfectly calm—but it would suffice. He hoped.

One more inhalation, for the luck. He had the kit off the peg and headed back to the workroom, and his assistant, and was brought up short on the threshold.

Nova stood in the center of the rug, shoulders and chin thrust forward in a distinctly truculent attitude, surveying the pattern.

"It is a beautiful rug, indeed," she said nastily, as if speaking to someone who stood next to her rather than one on the other side of the room.

"Indeed, show off the pattern. Tell us that it is an antique Quidian Tantara, unblemished, heirloom of a clan fallen on hard times, a clan of rug dealers who have kept this treasure until the last, until your wonderful trading skills brought its true glory to us! And how *like* you to bring it here as subterfuge, hiding the truth of it, magnifying yourself to the detriment of others, and to the clan. Almost, you got away with it . . ."

What was this? Was she speaking to him, after all? Had she discovered a pedigree card tucked into the end of the rug? In fact, from his view now, it might well be a Quidian, the rarest of . . .

She turned and stared directly at him.

"How many times more will you fail?" she shouted.

Pat Rin froze, caught between astonishment and outrage. How *dare*—

"One failure should certainly have been enough," he said, struggling to keep his tone merely courteous and his face smooth. "That there are more can be laid to your father's account."

"Kin will suffer for your lapses!" Nova snarled, moving forward one slow, threatening step.

"Yes, very likely!" he snapped, all out of patience. "But never fear, *cousin.* The clan will not suffer because of me. I will make my own way."

"You fail and fail again, always blaming others," ranted the girl on the rug, as if he hadn't spoken. "You will die dishonored and your kin will curse your name!"

Now *that,* Pat Rin thought, his anger abruptly gone, was coming rather too strong. It wasn't as if Korval had never produced a rogue. Rather too many, if truth were told—and most especially Line yos'Phelium. Taking up trade as a gamester was the merest bagatelle, set beside the accomplishments of some of the honored ancestors.

He came to the edge of the rug. Nova continued to stand at menace in the center, her attitude too—old, somehow. Too tense. And now that he brought his attention to it, he saw that her face was tight with an adult's deep and hopeless grief—and that her eyes were black, amethyst all but drowned in distended pupils.

Too, she stood in something very close to a fighter's stance . . . and was not *quite* looking at him

Pat Rin frowned. Something decidedly odd was going on. Perhaps she was acting out some part from a *melant'i* play? Though why she should do so, here and now, was beyond his understanding.

He held the diagnostic kit up before those pupil-drowned eyes.

"Come now!" He said, with brisk matter-of-factness. "We'll be at work into the next relumma if we stop every hour to play-act!"

The blind, grief-ridden face turned away from him.

"How many times will you fail?" she whispered—and the voice she spoke in was not *her* voice.

Pat Rin felt a frisson of horror. He cleared his throat.

"Nova?"

"Die dishonored," she mourned and sagged to her knees, palms flat against the carpet. "Cursed and forgotten."

He caught his breath. This was no play-acting. He couldn't, off-hand, think of any swift-striking disease that caused hallucination. There were recreational pharmaceuticals which produced vivid visions, but—

"Cursed," Nova moaned, in the voice of—The Other. And there was no drug that Pat Rin knew of which would produce *that* effect.

Come to that, it was not unknown for Korval to produce Healers, though such talents usually did not manifest until one came halfling. Not that this . . . fit . . . bore any resemblance to his limited experience of Healer talent.

Dramliza?

But those talents, like Healing, usually came with puberty. And, surely, if one were *dramliza* . . .

Crouched on the rug, Nova looked distinctly unwell. Her grief-locked face was pale, the black eyes screwed shut, now; and she was shivering, palms pressed hard against the carpet.

Clearly, whatever the problem was, she needed to be removed from the carpet, and brought away to a place where she might lie down while he called a medic to her—and her father.

Pat Rin put the diagnostic kit on the floor and went forward. When he reached the grieving girl, he knelt and put his hands, gently, on her shoulders.

"Nova."

No reply. Her shoulders were rigid under his fingers. He could see the pulse beating, much too fast, at the base of her slender throat.

Fear spiked Pat Rin—the child was *ill*! He made his decision, braced himself, slipped his arms around her waist and rose, lifting her with—

The quiescent, grieving child exploded into a fury of fists and feet and screams. He was pummeled, kicked, and punched—one fist landing with authority on his cheek.

Pat Rin staggered and went down on a knee. Nova broke free, rolled, and snapped to her feet, the carpet knife held in a blade-fighter's expert grip.

Blindingly fast, she thrust. Pat Rin threw himself flat, saw her boots dance past him and rolled, coming to his feet and spinning, body falling into the crouch his defense teacher had drilled him on, ready to take the charge that did not come.

Nova looked at him—perhaps she did look at him—and tossed the blade away, as if it were a stylus or some other harmless trifle, ignoring it as it bounced away, safely away, across the rug and onto the workroom floor. Niki, brought down from her comfort-spot by the noise, stalked it there, tail rigid, and smacked it smartly with a clawed paw.

Slowly, Pat Rin straightened, forcing himself to stand at his ease.

Something terrible was happening, and he was entirely out of his depth. He should, he thought, call the Healers now. And then he thought that he should—he *must*—get her off of the rug.

Perhaps persuasion would succeed where force had failed. He took a breath and shook the hair that had come loose from the tail out of his face. His cheek hurt and he would make odds that he would have a stunning bruise by evening. No matter.

He cleared his throat.

"Nova?"

No answer. Pat Rin sighed.

"Cousin?"

She raised her head, her eyes were pointed in his direction.

Ah, he thought. Now, how to parley this small advantage into a win?

He shifted, and looked down at the carpet. An old carpet, a treasure— a Quidian Tantara, the pattern as old as weaving itself. How Luken would love this rug.

Alas, he sorely missed Luken and his endless commonsense just now. What would *he* do in this eldritch moment? Cast a spell? Trap the offending spirit in a tea box?

Pat Rin looked up.

"Cousin," he said again, to Nova's black and sightless eyes. "I . . . scarcely know you. If you must treat me this way, at least show respect to our common clan and tell me clearly which *melant'i* you use."

He bowed flawlessly, the bow requesting instruction from kin.

Something changed in her face; he'd at least been seen, if not recognized.

"*Melant'i* games? You wish to play *melant'i games* with *me*? I see."

Chillingly, she swept a perfect bow: head of line to child of another line.

"Lisha yos'Galan Clan Korval," she said in that strange voice, and bowed again, leading with her hand to display the ring it did not bear. "Master Trader. It is in this guise, Del Ben, that I became aware of your perfidy in dealing with bel'Tarda."

Del Ben? The name struck an uneasy memory. There had been a Del Ben yos'Phelium, many years back in the Line. Indeed, Pat Rin recalled, there had been three Del Ben yos'Pheliums—and then no more, which was . . . peculiar . . . of itself. He remembered noticing that, during his studies of the Diaries and of lineage. And he remembered thinking it was odd that a yos'Phelium had died without issue, odder still that the death was not recorded, merely that Del Ben vanished from the log books between one page and the rest . . .

Nova's black eyes flashed. She laughed, not kindly. "Look at you! Hardly sense enough to see to your wounds! Well, bleed your precious yos'Phelium blood out on the damned rug if you will, and live with the mark of it. This—I am old. I am *slow*. I could never have touched the man you wish to be. But you—always, you do just enough to get by, just enough to cause trouble for others, just enough—"

"Bah," she said, interrupting herself with another bow: Cousin instructing cousin.

"This one? Well, cuz, I had thought myself well beyond the time of my life where I must marry at contract. But not only will I wed a bel'Tarda because of you, I will bring them into the clan because of you."

Pat Rin froze—what was *this*?

She swept on, a child chillingly, absolutely convincing in the role of clan elder.

"Ah, yes, smirk. I have seen the contracts. Tomorrow, I will sign them. Do you know that the dea'Gauss and bel'Tarda's man of business met this week? No—you might have, had you checked your weekly agendas, but when have you ever done so? Did you know that, between them, they decided that your life was insufficient to Balance the wrong done bel'Tarda?"

There was a laugh then, edgy and perhaps not quite sane. "Do you know that we are forbidden by Korval to kill you? But no matter, cuz, I am to both carry the bel'Tarda's heir, who will replace the man who suicided as a result of your extortion, and to oversee the rebuilding of their business—likely here on Liad!—since the heir and *his* heir died in the fire. The only proper Balance is to offer our protection, bring them into Korval, and insure that their Line lives on. For you—you nearly destroyed the whole of it! And you?"

Another frightening bow, this one so complex it took even Pat Rin's well-trained eye a moment to decode it: the bow of one who brings news of a death in the House.

Pat Rin, mesmerized, saw the play move on—

"You may see the delm, if you dare, or you may choose a new name—one that lacks Korval, and one that lacks yos'Phelium. You may eat while you are in this house, you may sleep in this house, you may dress from the clothes you already own—but you will bring me your clan rings, your insignia, your pass-keys. Bring them to me now. If you will speak to the delm, I will take you, else . . .

"Hah, and so I thought, " she said, spitting on the rug.

"Remove this rug and bring me the items I named . . . Know that if you leave—if you go beyond the outside door it will not readmit you."

With that the girl-woman kicked at the rug and stormed off of it, turning her back and crumpling into the pose Pat Rin had seen before . . .

"I shall take the rug!" Pat Rin announced with sudden fervor, not certain that she'd heard.

He rolled it quickly, slung it manfully across his back in the carry he had learned so long ago from Luken, and hustled it out into the hall, where he dumped it hurriedly on the back stairs to his loft room, and clicked the mechanical lock forcefully.

He snatched the portable comm from its shelf and rushed back to the door of the display room, where he could see the girl huddled in sobs amid the ribbons that had once bound the cursed rug.

His fingers moved on the comm's keypad and he wondered who they had called. A faint chime came out of the speaker . . . another— and a woman's voice, speaking crisply.

"Solcintra Healer Hall. Service?"

✧✧✧

THE HEALERS—a plump, merry-faced man and a thin, stern woman—arrived. The woman went immediately to Nova where she crouched and wept against the floor. The man tarried by Pat Rin's side.

"Did you move anything?"

"I took the carpet away, as she commanded," he said. "I locked the carpet knife in a drawer."

The Healer inclined his head. "We will wish to see both, later." He glanced about him and used his chin to point at the ceiling camera. "Is that live?"

"Yes," Pat Rin murmured. "Shall I—?"

"We will want a copy of the recording, yes, sir," the Healer said. "If you could have that done while we are examining your kinswoman, it would be most helpful."

"Certainly," Pat Rin said, and the Healer patted his arm, as if they were kin, or old and comfortable comrades, and strolled away across the floor.

Glad of being given a specific task, Pat Rin moved to the control desk, keeping an eye on the huddled group. The Healers blocked his sight of Nova, but, still, he was her nearest kin present and the Code was explicit as to his duties—until her father arrived to take them over.

Behind the control desk, he touched keys, taking the current camera off-line and activating the back-up. He accessed the first's memory, and started the preliminary scan.

Murmurs came from across the room as he worked, but the thin, hopeless sobbing had at last ceased, and Pat Rin drew a deep breath of relief. The Healers were here; surely they would put all to rights—

The sound of rapid footsteps sounded in the hallway, a shadow flickered in the doorway, and Er Thom yos'Galan was in the room, face set and breathing as easily as if he had not all but run down the long hall—and quite possibly all the way from Port. He paused, scanning, discovered the Healers kneeling together on the show room floor, took a step—and checked turning slightly until he spied Pat Rin behind the desk.

His mouth tightened and he came forward. Pat Rin touched the 'pause' key and drew himself straight.

"Where is your cousin?" Er Thom asked, without greeting, in a voice so stringently calm that Pat Rin felt a small shiver of pity for stern and commonsense Cousin Er Thom.

He inclined his head. "The Healers have come. Already, I believe the situation improves."

Er Thom glanced over his shoulder. "Could you not have moved her from the floor?"

"She . . . did not know me," Pat Rin said carefully, and put light fingertips against the cheek Nova had punched. "I had tried to move her, earlier, and she fought like a lyr-cat protecting her litter." He took a breath. "It seemed best not to make a second attempt, with the Healers on the way."

"So." Er Thom drew a careful breath of his own. "What do you?"

"The Healers requested a copy of the tape."

"Tape?"

Pat Rin swept a hand out, encompassing the showroom. "We were making an inventory of the rugs you had sent from the Southern House," he murmured. "The camera was on, of course."

"Of course," *Korval-pernard'i* said politely, and cast one more look at the Healers. Pat Rin could all but see his longing to go to his child's side—and then saw discipline snap into place. A wise man—a man who wished the very best outcome for his wounded child—that man did not interrupt Healers at their work.

Er Thom took a hard breath and stepped 'round the corner of the desk.

"Show me the film," he ordered.

THE FEMALE HEALER had gone, taking Nova, Er Thom, and the copy of the work session recording with her and leaving her partner to examine the carpet knife—which he proclaimed harmless—and the carpet.

"Ah, I see," he murmured, as for the second time that afternoon Pat Rin unrolled the thing on the showroom floor. The Healer stepped onto the carpet, and Pat Rin tensed, half-expecting to see his face twist into that expression of angry pain.

But whatever haunted the rug appeared to have no hold on the Healer. He knelt, carefully, at a corner and put his hands flat on the ivory-and-green pattern. Closing his eyes, he moved his hands over the rug, walking forward on his knees as he did so, as if he wished to stroke every fiber.

Pat Rin, relieved that there would apparently be no second playing of the tragedy, removed himself to the control desk once more, and began to shut down for the day. He would inventory the remaining carpets tomorrow, he told himself. Alone.

There was a small burble of sound and a flash of fly-away fur. Niki landed on silent pink toes by the control board. Pat Rin smiled and held out his hand; the cat rubbed her cheek against his fingers, then sat down, wrapped her tail neatly 'round her toes and squinted her eyes in a cat-smile, as if to assure him that all was well.

Yes, precisely.

He returned to his task, comforted by the routine and her silent presence—

"What were your plans for that rug?"

"Eh?" Pat Rin blinked, and looked up at the sudden Healer. "Truly, sir, it is not my place to have plans for it. I do not hide from you that it is an extremely valuable carpet, even if the stain cannot be removed, and that it belongs to Line yos'Galan."

"Stain?" murmured the Healer, tipping his head to one side. "There is no stain, young sir."

Pat Rin felt the hairs rise along the back of his neck.

"Most assuredly," he said, moving round the desk and marching toward the rug in question, "there *is* a stain."

"Here," he said, arriving. He swept a hand downward, his eyes on the Healer's face. "Only look here and you will see where the fringe has—"

The Healer was watching his face, calmly. Pat Rin looked down.

There was no brown stain marring the wave of ivory fringe. He bent, stroked the supple woolen nap which had scant hours before been stiff with—blood. Del Ben yos'Phelium's blood.

"I believe that the most excellent yos'Galan will not favor this rug, young sir," the Healer murmured. "Perhaps you might take charge of it." He raised his hand as if he had heard Pat Rin's unspoken protest. And perhaps, thought Pat Rin, he had.

"I will speak with your cousin on the matter, for it comes to me that such a rug, gotten at such cost, ought not to be destroyed, no matter the pain it has unwittingly brought to a daughter of the House." The Healer cocked his head. "Keep it by, do."

Pat Rin bowed.

"Very well," the other said, with a sigh. "I leave you now, sir. A pleasure to make your acquaintance."

"Wait—" Pat Rin put out a hand as if he would physically restrain the man.

The Healer paused. "Yes?"

"My cousin Nova—what ailed her? Will she mend? How shall— ?"

"Peace, peace," the Healer laughed. "The masters must have their chance at diagnosis, but it seems to me that your cousin has a very rare talent in the *dramliz* spectrum."

Dramliza. Pat Rin closed his eyes. "What talent?" he asked, 'round the pain in his heart.

"Why, she remembers," the Healer said, as Pat Rin opened his eyes. "That's all." He gave the carpet one more long glance.

"I really must—ah, a moment, of your kindness!" He leaned forward, and before Pat Rin knew what he intended, had cupped the injured cheek in a warm and slightly moist palm.

There was a small tingle—and the pain flowed away, leaving only warmth.

The Healer stepped back, placed his hand over his heart and bowed.

"Peace unto you, Pat Rin yos'Phelium. Long life and fair profit."

"Healer—" Pat Rin began.

But the Healer was gone.

PIN'WELTIR HAD GONE some hours ahead of the rest, pleading another appointment, which seemed odd at that hour of the morning—but who was Pat Rin yos'Phelium to comment upon the arrangements of a mere acquaintance? He did note, privately, that pin'Weltir had not recalled this second appointment until Luken had roundly trounced him at piket, lightening his brash lordship's purse by a considerable number of coins.

Still, and excusing the early departure of a guest not much missed in his absence, Pat Rin counted this first party in his own establishment a success. He was quite sincerely exhausted by his hostly duties, yet exhilarated.

The last, late-staying guest bowed out, and the door locked, Pat Rin moved down the hall to the room he had made his study. There, as he expected, he found his fosterfather, seated in Pat Rin's reading chair, thoughtfully gazing at the ivory-and-green carpet.

Pat Rin hesitated in the doorway. Luken looked up, face roguish in the soft yellow light.

"Well, boy-dear! Well, indeed. A most glorious crush, hosted with grace and style! I daresay you will sleep the day through, now."

"Not quite now," Pat Rin murmured.

Luken smiled. "A bit in the upper key, is it? Never mind it—very shortly Lord Pat Rin will find hosting a party three times merry this to be a mere nothing!"

Pat Rin laughed. "Verily, Lord Pat Rin shall be nothing more nor less than a fidget-about-town. I wonder how you might bear with so slight a fellow."

"Now, there," Luken said, with sudden seriousness, "you touch near to a topic I wished to bring before you. I wonder—have you thought of entering the lists at Tey Dor's?"

Pat Rin blinked, and drifted into the room, across the Tantara, to prop a hip against the desk and looked down into his fosterfather's face.

"I had never thought of competing at Tey Dor's," he said then. "Should I have?"

"You might find that you will wish to do so," Luken said, "as you consider the . . . *affect* you wish to sustain. For I do not think, boy-dear, that you would do very well in a long-term role either as fidget or as mushroom."

"Ah." Pat Rin smiled. "Lord Pat Rin shall be flamboyant, shall he?"

Luken raised a finger. "Lord Pat Rin, if you will permit me, boy-dear, shall be *accomplished*."

"I'll grant that's a happier thought," his son said after a moment. He inclined his head. "Allow me to consider the matter, when my head is done spinning."

"Surely, surely." Luken paused before murmuring. "I wonder if you have heard that young Nova takes lessons at the *dramliz* school now—and has passed the preliminary for third class pilot."

Pat Rin inclined his head. "She was by a three-day gone, with a gift for the house. We drank tea and she caught me up with her news."

"Ah?" Luken said. "And how do you find yourselves aligned, if an old man might ask it."

"We are—comfortable," Pat Rin said after a moment. "She—I do not know how such a thing might be, but—she remembers both sides of the . . . incident, and we have, thereby, an understanding."

There was a small silence. "Good," Luken said, simply, and pushed himself out of the chair. Pat Rin leapt forward to offer him an arm.

"Must you leave?" he asked, and Luken laughed.

"I daresay the two of us might now repair to the Port for a game or six, were I thirty years younger!" He said, patting Pat Rin's hand. "But you must have pity on an old man and allow me to seek my bed."

"Certainly," Pat Rin replied, walking with him toward the hallway. "I will summon a cab."

"Assuredly you will, sir!" Luken turned suddenly, face serious. "Lord Pat Rin will have servants to attend to these small matters for him."

"I daresay he might," Pat Rin retorted, with spirit, "for those who are merely guests. But if Lord Pat Rin should ever fail of attending the father of his heart personally, I shall know him for a worthless dog, no matter his *accomplishments*."

Luken paused, then extended a hand to cup Pat Rin's cheek.

"Sweet lad." He let the hand fall away and smiled, softly. "Call for the cab, then, and be welcome."

Quickly, Pat Rin stepped back into his study and made the call. Turning back, he saw Luken framed in the doorway, his eyes dreaming once more upon the Tantara.

"Father?" he said, abruptly.

Luken looked up, face mild. "Child?"

Pat Rin cleared his throat. "I—do you mind?" he blurted. "The carpet—it is yours; the treasure of your Line. It should—"

Luken held up a hand. "Peace." He glanced down at the ivory-and-green design, smiling slightly as he once again met Pat Rin's eyes.

"I allow it to be a gem, and everything that is graceful. Even, I allow it to be a family heirloom. Who best to have the keeping of such a treasure, than my son?"

Pat Rin's eyes filled. "Father—"

"Nay, I'll brook no argument, willful creature! Hark! Is that the cab?"

It was. Luken fastened his cloak and together they went down the steps to the walk. Pat Rin opened the door and saw his father comfortably disposed. That done, he handed the driver a coin.

"Goodnight, boy-dear," Luken said from the back. "Sweet dreams to you."

"Goodnight, Father," he returned, stepping back from the curb. "Sweet dreaming."

The cab pulled away, accelerating smoothly down the long, dark street.

✧ Sweet Waters ✧

THE TRAP HAD taken a kwevit—a fat one, too.

Slade smiled, well-pleased. Beside him, Verad, his hunting-partner and his oldest friend among the Sanilithe, saving Gineah, grunted in mingled admiration and annoyance.

"The Skylady Herself looks after you, small brother. Three times this day, your spear failed to find its target, yet you return to your tent with a fair hunting of meat."

"The hunters before us this morning were noisy and hurried—making the game scarce and distant even for your arm," said Slade. "My spear flies not quite so far."

Verad waved a broad hand at the sky in a gesture meant to take in the whole of the world, and perhaps the whole of the universe.

"It is the trail we find today, hunter."

Slade nearly smiled—Verad's stern-voiced lesson could have as easily come from one of his merchant uncles, for all that those uncles would scarcely acknowledge Verad human and capable of thought, much less sly humor. The humor was lacking at the moment, so Slade kept his smile behind his teeth, and moved quietly toward the trap and its skewered victim.

"If I am a poor hunter," he asked, "is it wrong to find another way to take meat?"

"The tent must eat," Verad allowed. "Still, small brother, a hunter should keep several blades in his belt, and be equally skilled with all."

Slade knelt on the wiry moss, put his spear down, and carefully removed his kill from the trap.

"One skill at a time," he murmured. "*The tent must eat* speaks with a larger voice than *Slade must hunt with erifu.*"

From the side of his eye, he saw his friend make the sign to ward off ill luck. Slade sighed. *Erifu*—"art," or, as he sometimes thought, "magic"—was the province of women, who held knowledge, history and medicine. Men hunted, herded, and worked metal into the designs betold them by the women.

"If you are a bad hunter and discourteous, too," Verad commented, settling onto a nearby rock. "you will be left to stand by the fire until the coals are cold." He blinked deliberately, one eye after another.

Slade frowned, rubbing the trap with *nesom*, the herb hunters massaged into their skin so the game would not scent them.

"What if I am left unChosen?" he asked, for Gineah had been vague on this point. He situated the trap and set the release, then came to his feet in one fluid motion.

"Those left unChosen must leave the Sanilithe and find another tribe to take them."

Slade turned and stared—but, no, Verad's face was serious. This was no joke.

"So, I must be Chosen." He chewed his lip. "What if I do not come to the fire?"

Now, Verad stared. "Not come to the fire? You must! It is law: All blooded hunters who are without a wife must stand at the fire on the third night after the third purification of the Dark Camp's borders."

Tomorrow night, to be precise, thought Slade. He would be there, around the fire—a son of the grandmother's tent could do no less than obey the law. But . . .

"Sun's going," Verad said.

Slade picked up his kwevit by the long back legs and lashed the dead animal to his belt. He recovered his spear, flipped his braid behind a shoulder with a practiced jerk of his head, and nodded at his friend. "I am ready."

✧✧✧

THE SCATTERED TENTS of the Sanilithe came together for Dark Camp in a valley guarded by three toothy mountain peaks. It was toward the third mountain, which Gineah had taught him was called "Nariachen" or "Raincatcher" that Slade journeyed, slipping out of the grandmother's tent after the camp was asleep. He went lightly, with a hunter's caution, and spear to hand, the cord looped 'round his wrist; the broad ribbon of stars blazing overhead more than bright enough to light his way.

He should not, strictly speaking, be away from night camp at all. Man was prey to some few creatures on this world, several of which preferred to hunt the night. But come away he must, as he had during the last two Dark Camps—and which he might never do again, regardless of tomorrow night's outcome.

To the left, a twisty stand of vegetation formed out of the shadow—what passed for trees. He slipped between the spindly trunks and into the shocking darkness of the glade, where he paused. When he had his night eyes, he went on, angling toward the mountain face—and shortly came to that which was not natural.

It might seem at first glance a shattered boulder, overgrown with such vegetations as were able to take root along its pitted surface.

At next glance, assuming one hailed from a civilized world, it was seen to be a ship, spine-broke and half-buried in the ungiving gray soil.

Slade moved forward. Upon reaching the remains of his ship, he fitted the fingers of both hands into an indentation of the tertiary hatch, braced himself and hauled it back on its track, until there was a gap wide enough to admit him.

Inside was deep darkness, and he went slowly, feeling his way along the broken corridor, his soft-soled boots whispering against the dusty plates. His questing fingers found an indention in the wall, he pressed and a door clicked open.

Carefully, for there was torn and broken metal even inside the one-time supply cabinet, he groped within.

His search gained him several small vials, a single cake-bar of the survival food he'd wrinkled his nose at in pilot training class, and an ironic appreciation of his situation. He had fought the ship to the plains, knowing it unable to survive a planet-fall in any of the world's salty seas.

By the seas, he might have found a mix of food and vitamins better suited to his off-worlder needs—but the scant beaches below the cliff-lined continents were all of shale and broken rock, and he had thought an inland grounding might preserve his ship.

Choices made. Or as Verad might put it, this was the trail he found today.

He unzipped the cake wrap, the burp of preservative gas letting him know it was still edible, and—though the sweetness of it was surprising—ate it as if it were a delicacy as he continued to rummage through the former larder.

One more tiny container came into his hand—the last of the wide-spectrum antibiotics. He tucked it into his pouch with the others, pushed the door shut, and crept onward in the dark.

As he moved, his back brain did the calculations: if he rationed himself to a single dose every three days, he could stretch the vitamins he needed to survive through one more migration cycle.

At last, he gained the piloting chamber, where a single go-light glowed, faint. He inched forward and sat in the chair which, with its webbing and shock absorbers, had doubtless saved his life, and reached out to touch a switch.

The stats computer came up sluggishly, the screen watery and uncertain. Despite this, he felt his heart rise. His ship was alive.

Alive, yet mortally wounded. The distress beacon, its power source undamaged, gave tongue every six Standard hours, hurling ship ID and coords into the heedless chill of space. For two full turns of the Sanilithe seasons—almost three Standard Years—the distress beacon had called.

With no result.

A less stubborn man might by now have given up hope of rescue. He supposed, sitting there at the dim board in the shattered belly of a dead ship, on the eve of being either mated or cast out, that he *ought* to give up. Surely, the choices before him were daunting.

Were he cast out of the Sanilithe and left to his own methods, he might hunt well enough to feed himself. Perhaps. Certainly, he could not expect any other nomadic, hardscrabble tribe to adopt him. It bewildered him yet, that Gineah had taken him in—undergrown, wounded, and without language as he had been.

As to the probability of being Chosen at the fire—he considered that approached negative numbers. Worse, if he were, by some passing madness of the local gods, Chosen, he would forthwith have broken every nonfraternization reg in a very substantial book.

The consequences of which were merely academic, unless he were rescued.

And, surely, he thought, flipping his braid behind a shoulder and leaning toward the board, if he were Chosen, his underfed and nutrient-lacking seed would quicken no child among the Sanilithe.

If he were, against dwindling odds, *rescued*, and left thereby the tent of his wife, she would not suffer. Her sisters would care for her, and share with her the profits of their tents, until all converged upon the wintering Dark Camp again, and she might Chose another hunter to serve her.

And if he were Chosen and remained unrescued—well.

The day's trail did not always yield good things.

He touched a key.

The screen blanked, then swam back into being, displaying the last entry he had made in the log, on the night before the Sanilithe broke apart into its several Light Season bands and roamed far, gathering what foodstuffs could be wrested from the sullen land.

Carefully, he placed his fingers on the pad and began, slow and hesitant over his letters, to type, giving as the date Dark Camp, Third.

Last night, the final purification was done by the eldest and most holy of the grandmothers. Tomorrow night, I am to stand around the fire as a candidate husband, for the choice of any woman with need. If this chance comes to me, I shall seize it, in order to remain in proximity to the ship and to the beacon.

If I am not chosen, I will be forced away from this kin-group. Should that transpire, I will shelter in the ship for the remainder of the Dark Season. Then, if rescue has not found me, I will attempt to reach the sea. If I make that attempt, I will record my plan here.

I have this evening withdrawn the last of the nutrient drops and antibiotics from the emergency locker.

He hesitated, his right hand rising to finger the length of metal in his right ear, which named him a son of Gineah's tent, just as the heavy braid of hair identified him as unmarried. Married hunters, such as Verad, had their hair cut short, and wore the earring of their wife's tent with pride in their left earlobe. Slade sighed, thinking that one might wish for a mating, if only to be rid of the braid.

He put his fingers back on the keys. When he had begun this log, he had filled it with observations of custom and language. There had been less of that, as odd custom became that code by which he lived, and the curiously nuanced language the tongue in which he dreamed. Likewise, he had previously recorded the weakness which came to him when he denied himself the supplements and ate only local food. There was no need to repeat that information for those who . . . might . . . read what he had been writting.

He moved his fingers on the keypad, laboriously spelling out his name:

Tol Ven yo'Endoth Clan Aziel Scout survey pilot.

Then, as an afterthought—though he'd done the transliteration earlier in the report—he added one more typed line:

Slade, second named son of Gineah's tent.

SLADE STOOD, Arb on his right hand, Panilet on his left, before them the man-high blaze of the Choosing Fire. It was difficult to concentrate in the flame-swept darkness, for which he blamed the various brews he had been compelled to swallow during the purifications, as well as the chants and songs of those of the tribe gathered to witness the Choosings.

Briefly, he closed his eyes, seeing the flames still, dancing on the inside of his eyelids. The day had begun at sunrise, with Verad rousing him from Gineah's tent and hustling him, with neither meat nor berries to break his fast, to the far side of the encampment, where the hunters of the Sanilithe gathered, each bachelor under the patronage of a married man. Verad stood as Slade's sponsor, for which he was grateful.

There were prayers to recite, smokes to inhale, and strange beverages to drink. There was no water, nor tea, nor aught to eat. Still, he was not hungry and as the day with its duties progressed he found himself remarkably calm, if slightly lightheaded.

At last the waning sun disappeared behind toothy Nariachen. Slade, bathed and oiled by Verad, shivered in the sudden coolness, his naked skin pebbling.

"Drink," his friend said, offering yet another horn cup. Obedient, Slade drank, feeling the liquid take fire in his blood. He handed the cup back, blinking to clear the tears from his eyes.

Verad grinned. "That will put the heat of the hunt into you!"

An aphrodisiac? Slade wondered, as Verad carried the cup away. It seemed likely—and too late to wonder to what lusty adventures the dose in the cup, meant for a broad shouldered and heavily muscled specimen such as Verad, might incite his shorter and more slender self.

"Now . . ." Verad returned, bearing a strip of soft, pale leather. He showed the length between his hands. "Up with your arms, brother! I will dress you finer than any who will stand beside you." He slipped the skin 'round Slade's hips, wrapping it in an arcane pattern. "I took this one after last year's Choosing, when Gineah had held you back from the fire, saying that next year was soon enough." He worked swiftly, making the leather kilt tight.

"One throw of the spear brought it down, and I asked my wife for the skin, for I had a brother-gift to make." A final flourish and he stepped back, pride plain on his wide face, his grin displaying several broken teeth.

"There, now," he said. "What woman wouldn't Choose you? That's the question!"

It was certainly, thought Slade, slowly lowering his arms, *a* question. He looked down at himself. The kilt was . . . brief, and he suspected, from what seemed a very great distance, that he looked ridiculous.

"Don't be so long-faced," Verad said, leaning forward and slapping him on the belly. "All muscle and lithe as a finoret, too! There will be Choosers brawling to have you!" Another broad grin, then a wave of the hand. "Turn around, small brother. I have one more gift to give you."

Careful on feet gone slightly silly, Slade turned, and felt his braid tugged, loosened. Heavy, his hair unwound across his shoulders— two long seasons of growth.

"Like honey," Verad crooned, and Slade felt a comb slip down the length of his mane. "You will glow in the firelight, like a star. The eyes of the women will be dazzled. Doubt not that you will be Chosen. And when you are . . ." The combing and Verad's crooning whisper resonated weirdly in his head—or perhaps it was that last drink. Slade closed his eyes.

"When you are Chosen," Verad continued, "your wife will lead you to her tent. There, she will reveal a great mystery. A very great mystery." The comb stroked downward, soft and hypnotic. "In the morning, she will cut away all of this honey-colored hair and you will return to us as a man and a husband.

"Your wife will take you to the metal worker, and she will put the hot wire through your ear and twist it into the sign of her tent. Then . . ." The comb whispered down once more . . . stopped. "And then, we will hunt together as full brothers." He snorted, for a moment the work-a-day Verad. "And you will practice with your spear until it is said truly that you never miss a cast."

Yes, very likely. Slade tried to say that, but it was too much trouble. Behind him, he heard Verad laugh, and felt a calloused hand on his shoulder.

"To the Fire, Brother."

Slade opened his eyes, and glanced quickly to each side. Arb yet stood at his right hand. Panilet was gone. Chosen. Despite the heat from the fire, Slade shivered, and closed his eyes once more.

ARB HAD LONG BEEN CHOSEN, and the man who had stood beyond him.

The Fire was a black bed upon which a few red embers kept vigil. Slade frowned at them, wondering laboriously if one of the witnesses beyond the circle would come and tell him to leave; if he would be brought his spear, and his tough hunter's leathers, or if he would be cast forth weaponless and all-but-naked.

His mouth was dry, his head heavy; his blood still warm from that last draught. Altogether, he thought painfully, he was in a dangerous and most discouraged state and ought by rights to simply curl up on the moss by the dying fire and sleep off the sorrows of the day.

In the heart of the fire, an ember exploded in a rush of scarlet ash. Slade jerked—and froze.

Walking swiftly across the trampled and vacant moss came a tall reed of a woman, her dark hair braided with feathers and flowers, her short robe of soft suede, her legs and feet naked.

Forward she came, until he could see her face in what remained of the firelight. Wide, pupil-drowned eyes stared down at him from a bony, long-jawed face. Abruptly, she checked and looked wildly about, but there were no other hunters shivering and lachrymose around the dying fire. He was the last.

As if the realization galvanized her, she jumped forward and grabbed his wrist. Her fingers were cold; her grip strong. Without a word, she turned and marched into the darkness beyond the fire. Slade, perforce, went with her; all but oblivious to exalting songs and catcalls from the standers-by.

The sounds and warmth fell away behind them, and there was dust underfoot, her shape distant in the night, and her hand, unrelenting, to guide him.

She came at last to a small tent in the next-but-last circle. Brusquely, she pushed the flap aside and ducked within, dragging him after, her fingers bruising his wrist.

Inside, he was at last released, as his captor—his wife—turned to lace the flap. Slade looked about, finding the interior of the tent as cluttered as Gineah's had been neat and shipshape. In the center, beneath the air hole, was the fire, banked for the night, bed unrolled beside it.

He felt a hand on his arm and turned to look up into the face of his wife.

In the relative brightness, he saw that she was younger than he had at first supposed—scarcely more than a girl, even by the standards of Sanilithe—her forehead high, and her jaw square. Her lean cheeks had been painted with stripes of white and yellow and red; those on her left cheek were smeared. Her eyes were the color of summer moss—gray-green—and very wide.

Still, she said nothing to him, merely reached with hands that trembled to begin working the knot in his kilt. His manhood leapt, eager, and she gasped, the first sound he had heard from her, snatching her fingers away.

Gods, Slade thought, his mind sharpening slightly within the shrouds of drugs and exhaustion. *She's terrified.*

"Wait," he said softly, catching her hands. She flinched, and looked at his face—at least she did that—and did not pull away. "Wait," he said again. "Let us trade names. I am Slade."

She swallowed, and glanced to one side. "Arika."

"Arika," he repeated, struggling toward gentleness. "It is not necessary—"

She pulled her hands free. "This tent requires a hunter."

"Yes," he said, trying to soothe her with his voice, trying to ignore the increasing demands of his body. "Yes, I will hunt for the tent. But it is not necessary to continue this, now, with both of us tired and frightened."

She stiffened at that, and awkwardly reached for his hands, looking sideways into his face.

"I—there is nothing to fear, inside my tent," she said, haltingly. "Slade. There is no harm here. I am—Tonight, I will teach you a mystery which will, will bond us and make us stronger for the tent."

A set piece, poorly learned, he realized, holding her cold fingers. And all honor to her, that her first thought was to soothe his fears. He smiled, carefully.

An unmarried hunter of the Sanilithe was a naive creature. He learned of the mystery of sex on the night of his Choosing, from the woman who had Chosen to become his wife. It was that same wife who would later decide how many children the tent might rejoice in—and a married hunter was not at all certain quite how those children came to be. Verad spoke of seeds, but in the context of a fruit eaten, perhaps from a tree known only to the *erifu* of women.

Though obviously herself terrified of the upcoming mystery, Arika would be scandalized to find that her new and unshorn husband came to her fully tutored. Still, Slade thought muzzily, he *was* the elder here, and it was his duty to ease her way, as much as it was hers to ease his fear.

"First," Arika said, breathlessly, slipping her hands away. "We must remove these skins . . ." Her fingers were at the knot again, somewhat steadier. Slade left her to it and reached to the laces of her robe. She froze.

"What do you?"

He smiled again, as guileless as he might, in which endeavor he was no doubt assisted by the drugs.

"If we must remove the skins, it will go quicker, if you remove mine and I remove yours." He affected a sudden shyness, dropping his eyes. "Unless there is some reason in *erifu* that I should not . . . ?"

She frowned, as if trying to recall a long-ago and not-very-well attended lesson. Finally, she jerked a shoulder—the Sanilithe negative. "It does not offend *erifu*. You may continue."

Continue he did, taking care with the laces while she fumbled with his kilt. He did not wish to reveal her too soon. Best, if they became naked and equal in the same moment.

He felt the knot at his hip loosen all at once, slipped the last of the lacing free and slid his palms over her shoulders, easing the garment up, just as the kilt fell unceremoniously to the floor. Softly, he smoothed his hands down her back, slipping the robe down and off, to pool about her feet.

She visibly swallowed, her pale eyes moving down his body in quick glances. Obviously, she hadn't the least idea what to do now.

Slade stepped forward, lifting a hand to her hair, stroking it back to reveal an exotic and enticing little ear. He heard her gasp, but she had heart, did Arika. She slid her fingers into his hair, silking it back to reveal his ear. Greatly daring, she ran her finger 'round the edge and he felt his blood flare as he copied the motion, then stroked the line of her jaw. She followed his lead, her fingers moving in a long stroke down the side of his neck.

He cupped her breast, she ran a light hand down his chest; he bent and put his lips around one pert nipple. She gasped, back arching, and it came to him that *erifu* would have required that she also drink the Choosing drugs, to be ready to welcome the new husband in fullness . . .

"Slade," she said huskily, and her hands were in his hair, drawing his face up, her gray-green eyes looking deep into his. "We—should lie down."

A good idea, he thought, *before one or the other of us falls into the fire*.

He stretched out beside her, and she touched him, tentative fingers warm now, and indescribably exciting. He moaned, and pulled her to him, exhaustion burning away into the brilliance of passion.

SLADE OPENED HIS EYES to a tent wholly unfamiliar, a heavy weight pinning his arm to the sleeping mat. Carefully, he turned his head, and discovered his wife, Arika, deeply asleep, her head on his shoulder, hair tangled with last night's passion, lashes sooty smudges on her thin cheeks. In the spill of morning light from the fire hole, her face was achingly young.

Surely, he thought wildly, *surely a child of this age ought to be with her tutor and not roistering about in the darkness, soliciting strange men into the service of her tent?*

He drew a hard breath. The Sanilithe came quickly to adulthood, and quickly to old age. Gineah, revered grandmother that she was, with two daughters and a hunter-son, all grown and mated—Gineah had between fifty and fifty-five Standard Years. On the planet of his birth, she would have just reached the height of her powers, with another thirty to fifty years before her . . .

The planet of his birth, he thought, suddenly bitter; which he had wished with all his heart to escape—and found his wish well-granted.

Carefully, not wanting to awaken the girl-child asleep on his shoulder, he drew a breath, and looked about him.

It was not the largest tent he had seen among the Sanilithe, nor the tidiest, though it might, considering the numerous patches in the skin walls, make some claim to the shabbiest.

Scattered around, in no order he could discern, were baskets, pots, robes, and rugs. Poles lined the walls, and from them hung familiar clusters of dried herbs and medicinal plants.

Gineah had divided her tent into sections—a place which was *erifu* and off-limits to ham-fisted sons of the tent, a place to store foodstuffs and water, a place for that same ham-fisted son to keep his weapons, his skins, and his bedroll. The center was common area, where meals were made and where grandmother and son might dawdle over their warmed beer, talking far into the night.

Well, and Gineah's tent was as distant from him as his mother's house, now that he was married.

He sighed and brought his gaze back to the child's sleeping face. The stripes of paint adorning her cheeks were smeared and faded. The Sanilithe did decorate their faces—certain signs were *erifu*, others were, as far as he understood, nothing more than exuberance. It seemed to him that he had seen stripes like these before—white, yellow, red, in alternation—and suddenly, he remembered.

Mourning stripes. Someone of this tent had died—recently. The stripes were worn only for three days after the deceased had been commended to the fire.

Outside, a woman's voice rose in the welcome-morning song. The girl asleep on his arm stirred, and opened her eyes, face tensing. He smiled, deliberately.

"Good morning, Arika," he said softly.

Her face relaxed, though she did not go so far as to smile. "Good morning, Slade," she returned, seriously, and looked upward to the patch of sullen sky visible through the smoke hole.

"We must rise," she said abruptly, snaking out of their tumbled bed and rolling to her feet. "There is much to do."

Naked, she hesitated, staring about the disordered tent, then darted to one side, where she found a tunic. She pulled it over her head; emerging, she frowned at Slade, still slugabed.

"Rise!" she snapped, and reached for the pair of leather leggings hanging over a cracked storage pot.

Sighing, he rose, found his kilt on the dirt floor by the edge of the fire, picked it up, shook it out, and wrapped it around his loins, feeling even more foolish, now that there was no kindly drug diluting his perceptions. Quickly, he knotted the leather, wishing for shirt and leggings.

"Slade."

He turned. Arika held her hands up, showing him the blade in her right, and the comb, in her left. "I will cut your hair, now, and we will go to the smith. Then we will go to the tent of Grandmother Gineah and bring away those things she allows to be yours." She smiled, very slightly. "The sooner we do these things, the sooner we may eat."

Eat. His stomach, reminded of its fast, set up a complaint, and he moved sprightly indeed and sat on the floor at her feet.

"Be still now," she said, and plied the comb, surprisingly gentle; and then the knife, in long, practiced sweeps.

Slade closed his eyes as the weight of his hair fell away, leaving the back of his neck chill.

"Done."

He lifted his hands to his head, feeling strands barely two fingers long. Gods alone knew what he looked like, but at least he was rid of the braid, which had a penchant for becoming entangled in twigs, and flirting with fires . . .

"Come." Arika was already unlacing the flap. "The smith."

Indeed, the smith. He rolled to his feet and followed his wife out into the new day.

SOME WHILE LATER, earlobe stinging and stomach rumbling, he stood two paces behind his wife, before Gineah's tent.

A shadow moved and the grandmother stepped out, plump and grizzled, her arms encircled with the many bracelets of her station.

Before him, Arika spread her arms wide in the traditional greeting to one of the Wise.

"Grandmother," she murmured, respectfully.

"Daughter," Gineah replied, and moved her eyes, pinning Slade with a bright blue glance. "Hunter."

He bowed, which the Sanilithe did not do. "Grandmother."

She stepped forward, her eyes on Arika. "You could have come to me."

Arika bit her lip, and shook her hair back in what Slade was beginning to understand as a nervous gesture. "I swore to Keneple that the tent would endure," she said, her voice not quite steady.

"And a tent must have a hunter." Gineah sighed. "Child . . ." She stopped.

"Please," she said, after a moment, "allow your hunter to enter my tent and collect those things which have been made ready for him."

"Yes . . ." Arika whispered. She straightened shoulders that had begun to sag and looked to him, chin up.

"Slade, you may find what Grandmother Gineah has left for you and bring it forth."

"Yes," he said in his turn and slipped into the tent that had been his home for two full turns of season.

Inside, all was neat and familiar; it smelled of herbs, and leather; smoke and the scent of Gineah herself. Tears rose to his eyes. Blinking them away, he turned toward the corner which had been his.

There were several bundles there, as well as his spear, his knives, and the unfinished length of braided hide he had been working on as he sat at the fire with Gineah in the evenings.

He knelt and examined the bindings of each pack, in no hurry, wanting to give Gineah as much time as possible to share what wisdom she might with his girl-wife. It came to him that it was Keneple who had died, and who Arika mourned. The name meant nothing to him, but that was not unusual. Well as he knew the names of those with whom his tent traveled in the seasons of gathering, little did he know the names, or the faces, of those who traveled other routes.

Kneeling on the mat among his bundles, his Choosing became real to him: he was now tied to a tent that would follow a different route, come the Light Season, and which held allegiances and debts that he did not understand. The ones he would hunt beside would not be the same men he had come to know—who had come to know and accept him, with all his incomprehensible difficulties—as a brother.

He gasped. This time, the tears escaped to moisten his cheeks. To be taken from everything and everyone he knew—and, yet, what did it matter? He was the alien here, shipwrecked and dead to all he had been. To lose one tent, one old woman, half-a-dozen savage brothers—what was that, against the magnitude of his other losses?

Crouched beside the small pile of his belongings, he wept, then wiped his face with his forearm and forced himself to his feet.

He draped the bundles about himself as Verad had taught him to do, slipped his knives, carefully, into the waist of his kilt and hefted the spear.

Outside, Gineah embraced Arika, and stepped aside. "Take care of my son, who is now your hunter, Daughter."

"Grandmother, I will." Arika swallowed, and Slade saw that her cheeks were also damp. "You are welcome in my tent, always."

Gineah smiled upon them, and raised her hands in blessing above their heads. Then, wordless, she re-entered her tent.

Arika licked her lips, nodded to Slade. He followed her across the camp, to their shabby and disordered home.

KNEELING ON THE DIRT FLOOR next to the fire pit, Slade unrolled his bundles. The first held his hunting leathers and boots, as well as a vest sewn of kwevit hides with the fur attached. He dressed quickly, rolling the kilt and putting it with the vest, then turned his attention to the rest, chewing on a strip of dried meat Arika had given him.

She was at the back of the tent; he could hear her moving things, possibly attempting to impose order upon the clutter, a project of which he heartily approved.

Opening the next bundle, he found the furs and skins of his own bed, and several sealed medicine pots. He smiled, profoundly warmed, for Gineah took care with her potions, which were genuinely soothing of bruises, cuts and strained muscles.

Another bundle gave up his second pair of leggings, three sitting mats, and pots containing dried legumes, jerked meat, and raisins. Too, there was the bag ritually made from the skin of the very first kwevit he'd taken and meant to carry what Verad called "the hunter's touch," which was the only property besides his weapons and his clothes that a hunter could be said to own. The knot was undisturbed, and inside, among the scent-masking potions, feathers, and special stones that he had been given by his brother of the hunt, was his paltry supply of Liaden nutrients. Slade smiled again, and thanked Gineah in his heart.

"Where do those things come from?" Arika's voice was shrill. He spun on his knees and looked up, seeing her face twisted with anger, her eyes blazing green fire.

"Gineah gave them," he said, keeping his voice gentle.

She was not soothed. "Return them! *I* am the mother of this tent—and this tent is not in need!"

Very slowly, hands loose at his sides, Slade rose. Deliberately, he looked about him, at the clutter, at the tatters, at the soot. He looked back to her angry face.

"The tent must eat," he said.

"The tent *will* eat," she snapped. "The hunter will see to it."

"Yes." He moved a hand, showing her the bounty Gineah had sent. "These were given by the grandmother, to the hunter. I have seen that the tent will eat."

She glared, lips parting, then turned and stomped away.

Sighing, Slade looked about him for an uncluttered corner to call his own.

THEY WORKED IN SILENCE, he on his side, she on hers. It was not so large a tent that they were unaware of each other, and had they been in charity, Slade thought ruefully, they might have made a merry time of it. And, really, it was wrong that they continued thus in anger. Unless he did something very stupid on a hunt, they would be partners for—some time. They needed each other's goodwill and willing cooperation—the tent could not function, else.

Sighing, he straightened from tidying away his sleeping roll, and turned.

Across the tent, Arika stood with a pot cradled in her arms, her head bent, hair obscuring her face.

Biting back a curse, Slade crossed to her side, and put a careful hand on her arm.

She gasped, and started, eyes flying to his face, her lashes damp, the remains of the mourning paint running in long, smeary lines down her cheeks.

"Peace," he said, as gently as he knew how. "Gineah meant well. We should not be at odds because of her kindness."

She swallowed, and shook her hair back from her wet cheeks. "I— Tales of Grandmother Gineah's good works are told around story fires wherever the Sanilithe gather. I will be proud to tell my own story, that the grandmother so valued her son she gave his wife-tent a Dark Season's worth of provisions, as a measure of her regard."

"A good story," he said, softly. "And nothing to weep for."

Arika snuffled, and raised a hand to scrub at her cheeks.

"I weep because—" Another gulp, and a wave around at the general chaos. "It was not like this. It was orderly and, and *erifu* and— and the babe was born dead, and Keneple caught the milk fever, and the grandmothers did what there was to do . . ." The tears were flowing again, and she hugged the pot tight to her chest.

"So, she died," she whispered. "It was past time to leave for Dark Camp . . . They helped me with the pyre before they left. I packed the tent in haste and, and—" She bent her head, hair falling forward to shroud her face. "*Erifu* has been broken, and I don't know how . . ."

He slipped an arm around her waist, as she cuddled her pot and wept, offering the comfort of his warmth.

Gently, he asked, "Keneple was your mother?"

Arika sniffled. "My elder sister. Elae—her hunter—fell from a rock ledge at Far Gathering and broke his neck. We—" Her grief overtook her, then, and there were no more words for a time.

Slade stroked her hair, murmuring nonsense phrases, as he had heard Gineah murmur to soothe a sick child.

Gods, he thought, the tragedy unrolling before his mind's eye. *Every one of the tent dead, save herself, within the space of one summer walkabout?* Mother, hunter, and hopeful babe—gone, leaving one grieving girl-child, who had promised her dying sister that she would not allow the tent to lapse . . .

"Arika," he murmured. "Gineah taught me. We can together put things right. Our tent will be *erifu* and the envy of every hunter!"

She looked at him sidewise through her hair. "The grandmother taught you how to order a tent? But that is—"

"Who says no to a grandmother when she requires a thing?" he asked, smoothly.

That argument had weight. Arika straightened. "We do as the grandmother says."

"We do," he said, and smiled at her. "Let us begin in the Windward corner."

SLADE SHIVERED in the light wind and held his end of the braided leather rope loosely by the knot. The other end was tied to the most robust of the shrub-like trees in the thicket with a knot Verad would have frowned upon had he seen it, for it looked to be more *erifu* than the knots men might use. All around, the rocks, bushes and moss glittered silver in the starlight—ice, and treacherous footing for even a skilled hunter.

As had become his habit since his mating, Slade hunted alone. He regretted the loss of Verad's companionship, but the elder hunter had grown even more disapproving of Slade's methods. Hunting alone, he had perfected those methods. It was seldom, now, that their tent was without fresh meat.

Today, Slade thought, might be one of those rare days when he returned empty-handed. If the binkayli failed to swarm, if his throw went awry, if the leather parted, if the branch gave way—if, if, if . . .

One-handed, Slade reached to his belt and worked the knot on the hunter's touch. Though he hunted solitary, he was often enough among other hunters at the end of the day, when casual groups might form to discuss the weather, the hunting, the lie of the land for tomorrow's hunt. Thus, he had added several odd quartz bits, the tail fur of an ontradube, and the sharply broken stub of the same creature's small antler to his collection of magical items, as further camouflage.

Finding the vial of vitamins by touch among the lot was a chore, but he succeeded, and squeezed the drops into his mouth. He grimaced at the taste, and at the state of the container, and dropped it back into the bag.

Checking his hold on the leather, his nose hair bristled. Cold, cold, cold.

From his left came a rolling rumble, as of dozens of hooves hitting the frozen ground. Slade tensed, then forced himself to relax, pushing all thought of failure—all thought—from his mind, just as the binkayli burst out of the silvered thicket, barely six paces from his crouching place, running hard across the open land.

He threw, the lasso arced into the spangled air, spun and fell about the neck of a well-grown binkayli stallion.

Oblivious, the stallion raced on. The rope stretched, the noose tightened. The branch held, held—and broke in a clatter of scattered ice.

Slade swore and leapt. His boots skidded on the icy surface, he twisted, clawing for balance, and fell badly, left leg bent beneath him, head cracking against the ground.

Half-dazed, he saw the rope and the branch speed across the icy ground in the wake of the stallion. The pounding of hooves vibrated through his head, and finally faded away.

IT WAS LATE when he limped back into camp, leaning heavily on his spear. He staggered to his own tent, standing silver and serene 'neath the changeless winter sky, pushed the flap back, ducked inside—and froze.

The air was pungent with some unfamiliar odor, and thick with smoke. Arika sat, cross-legged and naked, before the fire, eyes closed, holding a hunter's gutting knife between her palms. Two women he did not know knelt, fully clothed, facing her.

Slade moved as quietly as he was able, meaning to retire to the corner where he kept his hunter's gear, to warm himself, and rest his injured leg.

One of the strangers looked over her shoulder and leapt up, her eyes wide and angry. She grabbed his arm, none-too-gently, and shoved him toward the flap.

"You are not allowed here!" she hissed. "Go! Do not return until you are summoned!" Another shove, and a third, which sent him stumbling out into the cold, ice-rimed camp.

Slade stood for a moment, gathering his wits; shivering, aching, and angry. Then, leaning hard on his spear, he limped away, toward Gineah's tent.

"REST, TOMORROW and tomorrow," Gineah said, rising from her inspection of the injured leg. "The muscles are angry, and you—you are a very fortunate hunter, young Slade. You might have broken that leg, and then you would have been a dead hunter, alone in the freezing darkness, without a brother of the hunt nearby to aid you."

He smiled up at her. "I was fortunate, I know. I will be more careful, Gineah."

She snorted and motioned him to sit up, as she crossed to the cook fire and the pot hanging there. "At least your head is hard," she said—and then, "You should not hunt alone."

"I must," he said. "My methods frighten Verad, and the others are more timid still."

Gineah ladled soup into bowls and brought them back to the hearth fire, handing one to Slade.

"Eat." She ordered. "And while you eat, tell me what your wife was about, to allow a stranger to send you from her tent."

So he ate, and told her of his strange homecoming, with Arika entranced or uncaring, the smoke, the knife, and the woman who had banished him.

"So." Gineah looked at him straightly across the fire. "Your wife, young Slade, is a Finder."

He blinked, trying to read her face, and, as usual, failing.

"What is a Finder, grandmother?"

"A woman of great *erifu,* who may cast her thought out to find that which is lost. The best Finders improve their tents many times over. Your wife is young, she has some years before she reaches the fullness of her gift. But she is already known as a Finder of great talent. The tent will improve quickly, I think, and you will no longer live on the edges of the Dark Camp."

Surely, Slade thought, *this was* good *news?* In the house of his mother, the birth of a Healer was cause for rejoicing. Yet, Gineah looked more doleful than joyous.

"This troubles you . . ." he said, tentatively.

Gineah sighed. "Finders . . . do not thrive. The heat of their gift consumes them. Not all at once, but over a time. Sometimes, a very long time."

He stared at her, thinking of Arika, young and frail and fierce, and his eyes filled. "Is there no—"

"Cure?" she finished for him. "Child, there is no cure for destiny."

"Then," he asked, blinking the tears away, though the empty feeling in his chest remained. "What should I do?"

"Be the best hunter you are able. Be her friend, as I know you can be, O, wisest and most *erifu* of hunters. If children come to the tent, care for them. And pray that they were not born to be Finders."

Something moved near the flap of the tent, loud to Slade's hunter-trained ears. He came around, began to rise—and fell back as fire shot through his leg.

"Rest!" Gineah hissed at him, and went to unlace the flap.

"Grandmother," he heard Arika's voice, thin and vulnerable. "Is Slade with you?"

"He is. A woman pushed him from your tent while you were Finding, child. What greeting is that for a hunter returned to his tent wounded?"

"Wounded?" He heard her gasp and called out—

"A fall, nothing more. Gineah . . ."

She stepped back, motioning, and Arika entered.

She was wan, and unsteady on her feet, her eyes great and bruised looking.

"A fall?" she repeated, and knelt beside him, touching the leg Gineah had wrapped. "Is it broken?"

"No," he soothed her. "Not broken."

"He must rest," Gineah said. "Tomorrow and tomorrow. Eat from stores. If there is a call upon your gift, you will come to me, rather than turn this hunter out. Am I understood?"

Arika hung her head. "You are understood, grandmother." She

looked up, and Slade saw tears shining in her eyes. "Slade. You should not have been cast out. Next time, I will be certain that those who watch know that your presence will not disturb me."

"Thank you," he said, sincerely, and touched her thin cheek. *The heat of their gift consumes them . . .* he thought, and wanted nothing more than to fold her in his arms and protect her from that fate.

"So," said Gineah, and his wife stood, to attend the grandmother with due respect, and to receive two medicine pots.

"Rub the leg with this, morning, midday, night. If there is swelling, three drops of this, in noginfeil tea. If there is fever, send, and I will come."

"Yes, Grandmother," Arika murmured, and tucked the pots into her pouch. She looked down at him doubtfully.

"Can you walk?"

The leg was considerably stiffer, despite the warmth, but he thought he could walk. "If I can rise," he said.

Gineah held out a plump arm, and Arika offered a thin one. It took the support of both, but gain his feet he did, and stood wobbling, arm around Arika's waist for balance, while Gineah fetched his vest and his spear.

THEY MADE LOVE, their last night in Dark Camp. After, in the soft silence, Arika snuggled against his chest, and he put his arms around her. She had gained weight since they had married, and the tent had improved as well—in some part due to his efforts; in greater part, so he had it, to hers. As the Dark wore on, more came to ask the Finder to locate this or that misplaced item, animal, or—rarely— person. They paid well, those seekers—in fur, in food, in good metal knives and spear tips. He watched her closely, having taken Gineah's words much to heart, but, truly, she seemed more well, not less.

"Slade," Arika murmured. "Tell me about your home."

He stirred, breathing in the perfume of her hair. "My home?" he repeated, lazily.

"Gineah told me that you were not of the Sanilithe," she said, nestling her head onto his shoulder. "She said you were not of the

Trinari, or of the Chinpha. She said that you had fallen out of the starweb, and were no ordinary hunter at all."

Shrewd Gineah, he thought, stroking Arika's hair, *and really—what does it matter now?*

"She said," Arika continued, "that she expected your tribe to come for you, and held you away from the Choosing. But when they did not come after two full rounds of seasons, she sent you forth, for a hunter of the Sanilithe must live by the law of the Sanilithe."

Slade sighed.

"Did you fall out of the starweb?" Arika asked him.

What does it matter? He thought again. For surely Gineah was correct—no one would come for him now.

"My . . . starship . . . was caught in a storm," he murmured, which was true, if not factual. "Yes, I fell out of the starweb."

"And before it fell? Did you live on your starship?"

As much as I was able, he thought, and sighed again.

"Much of the time. I was . . . the hunter . . . who went ahead, to find how the land lay, if danger crouched, or if sweet waters sang . . ."

This she understood, the order of march during the gathering season being: scouts, hunters, gatherers, tents. She also knew that scouts often took harm from their duty. She shifted, pressing her body against him in a long hug, and nestled her cheek more closely against his shoulder.

"Tell me about your mother's tent."

His mother's tent—almost he laughed. Instead, he stroked her hair and stared up into the darkness.

"My mother's tent was . . . full," he said slowly. "We lived in—a permanent camp. It was not necessary to wander in the Warm Days, to spread ourselves thin so that we did not strain the land. It was," he said, even more slowly, feeling his way, "a land of plenty. The camp—it was called 'Solcintra'."

"There must have been many people in your camp, Solcintra," Arika said after he had been silent for a time.

"Yes," he said, "many, many hands of people."

"What else?" she asked, and this time he did laugh.

What else, the child asks.

"Is my question funny?" Arika demanded, between hurt and angry.

"Not at all," he assured her, smoothing her shoulder with his hand. "Not at all. Listen, now, and I will tell you . . ."

And so he told her, of spaceports, and shops, and healers, and traffic, and sometime before the gray uncertain dawn wavered into being, she fell asleep. He held her then, silent, his thoughts still on the city, his kin, the sky he would never see again . . .

ARIKA GAINED WEIGHT as they traveled into the light, until he was forced to believe what he had not thought possible. And one night, as they sat companionably at the fire; he mending a frayed rope, she mending a broken basket, he asked a question.

"I wonder," he said, watching her face out of the sides of his eyes. "Will the tent soon welcome a child?"

Her hands froze, and she raised her head to stare at him across the fire.

"Perhaps," she said haughtily. Arika was always haughty in fear.

He preserved his pretense of oblivious industry. "A child in the tent would be—a joy," he said. "But the hunter should be informed, if he will soon need to hunt for more."

She looked away, throat working. "As to that—it is not certain. The women of my tent . . .do not always . . . birth well."

Her sister, he remembered, whose baby had been born dead—and who had herself died of the birth. He plaited his rope in silence for a few heartbeats, then asked, quietly, "Is it the Finder blood that puts the babes at risk?"

She swallowed. "The grandmothers believe so. They call it a 'gift', but it eats us up, even those it allows to be born."

"It does not have to be," he said, carefully. "My mother, my brother, my sister—all are gifted as you are, with an extra pair of eyes, that see what others cannot." He raised his head and met her stare across the fire.

"You have the blood," she said, with certainty.

"I do. My mother bore three healthy children; my sister and my brother, who have extra eyes; myself, who has but two. So . . ." Here was the dangerous ground, for hunters knew nothing of such matters. "So, Arika, my wife, if the child in your belly is one that we made together, it may be that my . . . blood . . . will lend her strength enough to be born—and to thrive."

"It may be," she said quietly, and sighed, putting her basket aside. "Slade. How do you know these things?"

He opened his eyes wide and made a show of innocence. "Things?"

"That without a hunter, there is no child. How does a hunter put a child in a belly, Slade?"

Well, he had botched it. He sighed, then smiled at her. "Why, when we enjoy each other, and you take me into yourself . . ."

"Enough." She sighed in her turn. "These things are *erifu*."

"Among the Sanilithe, they are *erifu*," he allowed. "In my mother's tent, these things are common knowledge, shared among sisters and brothers."

She closed her eyes. "You make me tremble," she murmured, and looked at him once more. "But I see the fire has not leapt up to consume you, so it must be that the spirits of your grandmothers allow you this knowledge." She bent her head. "The child who—will—come to us is a child of my blood—and yours." She smiled, very slightly. "May your blood make her strong."

ARIKA WANED as the child waxed. Slade held her at night and tried to will his strength into her, for she, his precious, for whom he hunted, did not have his blood to make her strong. Lying awake in the dark, he made plans to dose her from his dwindling supply of supplements; plans which he abandoned as morning overtook him. His Arika was a child of this world, and even as her world was slowly poisoning him, so his needed vitamins might very well poison her.

He did insist that she refrain from gathering, and when she protested, told her that he would gather. Gineah had taught him something of plant lore. This was true enough, though not as she heard it. Gineah had shown him the fruits of her labors in the evenings when they both had returned to the tent, laying out and naming those things she had gathered.

"I will bring everything to you, and you will decide if it is good," he told Arika. "But you will not go out alone, soft on your feet as you are! You put our daughter and yourself in danger, and I do not allow it!"

A grave breach of *erifu,* that, and yet, strangely, she laughed.

"Slade. How will you hunt and gather? Or will you give your spear to me?"

"No, never that," he said, lightly. "A tent mother must not kill."

"A hunter's work fills the day—and a mother's work, too. How will you fit two days into one?"

"Let me try," he said, urgently, and took her hands. "Two days. If I fail to gather, or to hunt, we will—think of something else."

It was perhaps a measure of how weak she was that she allowed him his two days of proof.

HIS SCHEME WORKED WELL: in the morning, he set his traps; his afternoon went to gathering plant stuffs. When his sack was full; he turned toward the camp of the day, collecting game from his traps as he went.

On the morning of the sixth day, he encountered Tania, the grandmother of their group, at the edge of the camp, gather-bag in hand.

"Good morning, Hunter," she said politely.

Slade touched the tip of his spear to the ground in respect. "Good morning, Grandmother."

"I see that the mother of your tent sends you to gather in her name."

This, Slade thought, *could be bad.* He allowed no trace of the thought cross his face. Instead, he replied calmly, "Grandmother, it is so. Her talent gnaws the mother of my tent to bone."

Her eyes softened. "It is a harsh gift," she said slowly. "Do you prepare the gather?"

"No, Grandmother; she prepares what I bring, and shows which I should choose more of, and what is not as needful to the tent."

"So." She stood up, shaking out her bag. "*Erifu* is preserved. Good hunting."

After that, no one questioned him.

And Arika grew ever more fragile.

In the evening, she sorted and prepared what he had gathered, while he performed other needful tasks. After, they would lie in each other's arms and he would stroke her until she fell into uneasy sleep.

So, the short summer proceeded. Slowly, the sky darkened, and the wind carried an edge of ice, warning that the time to turn to Dark Camp approached.

Slade returned to their tent somewhat later than usual, burdened by numerous kwevits and an especially heavy sack of gatherings.

At first, he thought the tent unoccupied, then, he saw the shape huddled, far in the back, where the medicines were kept.

Heart in mouth, he dropped his burdens and rushed forward. Arika was barely conscious, her body soaked with sweat. Carefully, he straightened her, turned her . . .

Her eyes opened, and she knew him. "Slade. The child comes." Her body arched, and she gasped, eyes screwing shut.

THE BABY HAD COME QUICKLY, which had been a blessing. He cleaned her and put her to Arika's breast, turned—and looked up into Tania's hard, old eyes.

"Hunters do not deliver children," she said, coldly.

"This hunter does," he snapped, perhaps unwisely.

"So I see." She stepped forward. "I will examine the mother of your tent, Hunter. She is frail and I am many years your elder in the healing arts."

He took a hard breath. "Grandmother, I know it."

"Good," she said, kneeling at Arika's side. "Walk around the camp, twice. Slowly, as if you search for hunt-sign on hard rock. Then you may return."

Almost, he protested. Almost. He had just reached the entrance when he heard his name and turned back.

"Grandmother?"

"You did well," she said softly. "Now go."

THE CHILD—Kisam, their daughter—clung to her small life by will alone, and in her stubbornness Slade saw generations of Clan Aziel. She nursed, but it seemed her mother's milk nourished her only enough to keep her soul trapped in her body—and in that, too, he saw the effect of his blood.

His blood.

She sucked the supplement from the tip of his finger while he cuddled her and prayed, chaotically, expecting the tiny body at any moment to convulse, and release his child's willful spirit—

"She is stronger," Arika said next day, Kisam tucked in the carry-cloth against her breast. "Slade, does she not seem stronger to you?"

"Yes," he murmured, leaning over to stroke the small head covered already with plentiful dark curls—her mother's blood, there. "Yes, she does."

THEY TRAVELED SLOWLY toward Dark Camp, for Arika's strength was low, and Kisam yet frail, though much improved. And truthfully, the slower pace was not only to accommodate the child and her mother. Slade walked sometimes unsteady, his legs weak, and betimes a high, busy humming in his ears, and flashes of color across his vision. The spells passed shortly, and he did not speak to Arika of the matter. And every other night, as his wife lay in the sleep of exhaustion, he would nurse Kisam from his dwindling supply of vitamins and tried not to think what would happen, when, finally, they were gone.

So they arrived at Dark Camp among the last, and pitched their tent in the fourth tier, considerably higher than last year. There was firewood waiting, and a fire-circle, built properly by women's hands, by those who owed still on Findings past.

Slade saw Arika settled by the fire, and Kisam on the nurse before he turned to stow his weapons—and heard the buzzing begin, growing until it was a black well of sound into which he toppled, head first, and swooning.

❖❖❖

HE OPENED his eyes to Gineah's somber face.

"He wakes," she said, and Arika was there as well, her eyes wide and frightened.

Carefully, he smiled. "Forgive me, Grandmother. A stupid faint . . ."

"Not stupid, perhaps," another voice said, speaking the Sanilithe tongue slowly and with an odd nuance.

Slade froze, looked to Arika, who touched his face with fingers that trembled. "A woman of your mother's tent has come, Slade."

A woman of his—

He pushed himself into a sitting position, despite Arika's protesting hand on his shoulder, and Gineah's frown. For a heartbeat, his vision was distorted by spangles of light; when they melted, he saw her, seated like any ordinary guest by the fire, the baby's basket at her side, a horn cup cradled between her two hands.

She wore leather and a wide Scout-issue belt, hung about with a profusion of objects. Her hair was brown and curly, her face high-boned and subtle.

"Do I find Slade, second named son of Gineah's tent?" she asked, in the native tongue.

"Hunter," he corrected, "for the tent of Arika Finder."

Her eyes flickered. "Of course. No insult was intended to the mother of the tent." She raised her cup, sipped, then looked to him, face bland. "I have come to take you back to the tent of your mother, Hunter. You have been sore missed."

Arika was gripping his shoulder hard enough to bruise. He reached up and put his hand over hers.

"My mother's tent has many hunters, this tent has but one."

The Scout inclined her head. "Yet this tent's hunter is ill, and soon will die."

Which was certainly true, thought Slade. Death or departure equally deprived the tent of its hunter. And the hunter would rather die than depart.

"His mother, his sisters—they may heal him?" Arika's voice was thin, her hand beneath his, chill.

The Scout inclined her head respectfully. "Tent mother, they will."

"And after he is healed," Gineah—shrewd Gineah—murmured, "he will be returned to the tent of his wife."

The Scout considered her. "The grandmother knows better than that, I think," she murmured. "Between the *erifu* of the Sanilithe and the *erifu* of we who are not the Sanilithe, there is a . . . disharmony. We are each correct, in our way, but not in the way of the other."

In her basket, Kisam awoke and began to cry, and Arika rose to go to her. Slade watched them for a moment, then looked back to the Scout.

"It is possible," he said to her bland and subtle eyes, "that the addition of a third *erifu* will balance the disharmony and allow health to bloom."

She raised an eyebrow, but said nothing.

Slade leaned forward. "Take this tent to the sea. I will give you a message for my mother and my sisters." *And for Scout Headquarters*, he thought.

"The sea will not aid you. It—" The Scout frowned, looked to Gineah. "Grandmother, I apologize for the breach of courtesy, but I must speak to Slade in the tongue of his mother's tent."

Gineah moved a hand. "Speak, then."

Yet, having gained her permission, the Scout did not at once speak, and when she did, she spoke the language of home as slowly as if it, too, were uneasy on her tongue.

"I had seen your log, and your determination to gain the sea, were you turned out. Not a bad plan, in truth, Pilot, excepting only that this world lacks those things which your body must have in sufficient quantity to sustain you. I have done the scans and can show you the results. Those who are born to this world, they have adjusted to the lowered levels and function—as you see. You, who were bred upon a world rich in nutrient—you can only sicken here, and die."

So, then. Slade took a breath. "Our daughter will die soon. A few days, now."

Comprehension lit the Scout's bland eyes. "You have been giving the child your supplements."

"What would you?" he said irritably, the words feeling all odd angles in his mouth. He sighed. "If I must go, then, allow them to come. My wife, she is—a Healer of a sort, and frail. Perhaps home will heal her, too."

The Scout paused, head to one side . . .

"Slade." Arika was back at his side, Kisam in her arms. "What does this woman say?"

"She says that the sea will not aid us."

Arika frowned. "The sea? What do the Sanilithe have to do with the sea?"

"I thought that the *erifu* of the sea might bring the child of our tent to health, and myself."

She bent her head, her hair falling forward to shroud their child. "The little bottle," she whispered. "It is almost empty?"

He reached out and stroked the hair back from her face. "You knew?"

"I woke in the night and saw you give—it is a medicine from your mother's tent, isn't it? She shares the *erifu* of your blood."

"Yes," he whispered, stroking her hair. "Arika—come with me to my mother's tent." From the corner of his eye, he saw the Scout start, but she held her tongue. He *knew* the regs forbade just what he proposed. Damn the regs.

Arika raised her head, showing him a face wet with tears. "And then I will die, sooner than my gift would eat me."

He glanced to the Scout, saw her incline her head, very slightly, and lost her face in the wash of tears. He bent forward and gathered his heart into his arms.

"Arika . . ."

"No. Slade." Her arms tightened, then loosened, as she pulled away. "You must take our child, make her strong, so that she may do the work of our tent—and yours." She reached to his face, smoothing away the tears with cold fingers.

"It is the trail, hunter. The only trail that is given."

He stared at her, unable to speak. She rose, and he did—Gineah and the Scout, as well.

Arika held their daughter out; he took the small burden, numbly.

"Commend me to your mother," Arika whispered, then spun and was gone, out of their tent and into the night.

He moved, meaning to go after her—and found Gineah before him. "I will look after her, Slade. Go, now."

In his arms, his daughter whimpered. He looked down at her, and then to the Scout, standing patient and silent by the fire.

"It is time, then. My daughter and I are ready."